# THE
# OTHER SIDE
## OF
# LILLY

LOUISE DANDO-COLLINS

ISBN: 978-0-9944488-8-0 (ebook)
ISBN: 978-0-9944488-7-3 (print)

THE OTHER SIDE OF LILLY
Author: Louise Dando-Collins

Front cover portrait by John Pfeifer

The characters represented in this novel are an amalgam of many people I have known, and do not depict any person, living or deceased, their actions or attitudes.

Louise Dando-Collins

Writing this book,
was like giving birth to Ayers Rock.
I thank my husband Stephen Dando-Collins,
for planting the seed, and for holding
my hand during gestation and delivery.
And with deep gratitude for his poem:
'CRITICAL INTELLECT'

With special tribute to Betty McGhee,
who gave me life.
Mary Polly Milton Leith McGhee,
who gave me shelter.
Williamina (Mina) Baird who gave me love.
Dr Susie Owens who uncovered my demons,
and helped me slay them.
    AND
Robert, Christopher, Julie-Anne, and
Matthew, who brought me joy.

Still thou art blest, compar'd wi' me!
The present only toucheth thee;
But, Och! I backward cast my e'e
On prospects drear!
An' forward, tho' I canna see, I guess an' fear.

ROBERT BURNS
'TO A MOUSE'
1785

# CHAPTER 1

"This is where I'm supposed to talk about sex, isn't it?"

Dr Warner shrugged. "Talk about whatever you like."

A beautiful, smiling version of Nefertiti, the Egyptian queen of 14th century BC, sat behind the desk opposite me. So, this was Doctor Ruth Warner, a forty-something, gentle-looking woman, whose dark brown eyes were unmistakably, undeniably kind. We were sitting in her office at Sydney's Rozelle Mental hospital – a modern yet sparse office filled with intoxicating perfume from a display of pink stargazer lilies sitting on a shelf behind her.

This quiet place was like an oasis in the desert, with a welcoming feel to it for tortured travellers like me. Coming and going through these miserable brown halls filled with sad and demented souls would be a daunting experience, but with this pleasant office as my destination, I told myself I could cope. "Would you like to take off your hat?" she asked in a sympathetic, well-intentioned manner, breaking the silence.

Sitting hunched in a chair across the desk from her, my knees clamped tightly together, my hands clasped, I wore a felt broad-brimmed hat pulled well down over my forehead with its raw scars, and hid behind super-sized sunglasses that went everywhere with me. "I'd rather not, thank you."

"Fine. Let's begin."

"Where do you want me to start?" I asked, taking the initiative in my usual, 'let's get down to business' manner, with more than a touch of belligerence thrown in. My mood was far from happy. Feeling defensive, I

1

prepared to go on the offensive, but if I was expecting a battle I was to be disappointed. And as soon as I realised I would not be faced with a barrage of probing questions, I calmed.

The psychiatrist gave me silent permission to be angry. She allowed, and understood my anger, and my fear. And in so doing, she took the wind out of my sails, to the degree that my aggression seeped away, and I became easier to work with.

I began talking about Vince. I let Warner know exactly what I thought of him. I'd been harbouring my anger about his betrayal. She let me vent it. Then I turned my attention to Mitch. How he'd abused me throughout our failed marriage, and how his new money had helped steal my beloved children from me after the divorce.

"Tell me about your parents."

I flippantly brushed over this, feeling it played no part in my present predicament. Although I did explain to Warner, with some pride, that my mother, Betty, as I called her, had been a famous British musician. Excusing my mother's abandonment of me, I told how she had toured constantly with this and that band while I was growing up, and as a consequence, had been unable to parent me. I explained that my grandmother had raised me, and had brought me to Australia as a fourteen-year-old, along with her own son, who was a year younger than me. Andy was actually my uncle, but Mary Campbell raised us as brother as sister.

When the psychiatrist asked me specifically about my own two children, the question touched the rawest nerve. Suddenly in this 'safe' environment – much like a church confessional – I burst into tears.

The clever Dr Warner had just opened the first door to my psyche. She had shot her arrow straight into my heart. The excruciating pain of losing my children returned. It was as if it had only happened yesterday. All the years of papering over the cracks in my heart were for nothing. My heart bled.

The first appointment was abruptly concluded on the stroke of the hour, just as I was tearfully recounting the story of the last day that Adam and Kate had been with me. The day their father Mitch and his lawyers had taken my babies away from me.

"That will be enough for today. I'd like you to return twice a week for the time being," Warner said in a businesslike tone. "Make an appointment with my secretary. Tuesday's and Thursdays."

In something of a state of shock, I wiped away the tears, looked at the impassive doctor's face, then stood and walked from the office feeling more confused than when I'd entered.

I walked home thinking about my 'consultation.' The doctor had remained dispassionate throughout the entire appointment. I found this seeming lack of compassion puzzling, for I knew very well that I could not have remained unaffected had the positions been reversed. Not that sympathy was what I sought. But a little show of understanding might have let me leave Warner's company feeling slightly better than when I'd entered. I wanted a sign that my situation would improve via these meetings, but the appointment had come to an antiseptic conclusion – without ceremony – after I'd bared my soul, while the doctor had remained totally detached.

Heavy of heart, I trudged along beside Sydney's Rushcutters Bay, to 'walk things out.' The fresh breeze blowing in off the harbour smelled salty and clean. It seemed to awaken and refresh my spirit. It caressed my skin and blew wisps of hair across my cheeks, and I found myself greedily inhaling deep breaths. And I remembered the words of an ancient Chinese proverb: 'A Journey Of A Thousand Miles, Begins With the First Step.'

On this languid trek home, I lapsed back into thoughts of my television days in Brisbane only the year before, and the kindly face of Stephane Grappelli the modern world's genius of the violin flashed into my mind. My task had been to interview him, and, as a fledgling reporter, I was immensely honoured. There would be just the two of us and a sound engineer in the room. My marriage had just crumbled, and the darling maestro had the empathy to feel my pain without me having said a word.

He began to tell me a story, his romantic French accent adding to the magic of the moment. "You know, Leely," he said, his voice kind, his eyes alight with mischief, "some twenty years ago, I broke ze little pinky of my left hand. The one I need so much for my violin notes. I was very unhappy about it! But you know what I did, Leely?" His eyes danced alluringly before me,

3

and I was smitten. "I practised, and I practised, forcing my leetle finger to work, and work very hard! And after a while, I could use it better zan I ever could before!" He smiled a wondrous smile, and sent me love with his twinkling eyes. "So, my dear Leely, I promise you, zat out of sumsink bad, comes sumsink good!"

He leaned in close to me and sang 'Lily of Marlene,' a sweet love song, then played it for me on his Stradivarius. Then he kissed me tenderly on the cheek. I promised myself that I'd use this memory when times got really bad.

# CHAPTER 2

I heard footsteps crunch on gravel, and looked out of the lounge room window to see three strangers. Two were men in business suits, the other was a hefty uniformed female police officer from Queensland Police. Mitch, my husband led the way to my front door.

My involuntary gasp, and the fear now etched on my face brought an abrupt end to the giggles of my children. Kate my four year-old daughter rushed to the window to see who was approaching the house.

"It's Daddy. It's Daddy, Mummy. Adam, come see. Come see. Daddy's here!" She jumped up and down with excitement. Adam, only two years old, ran to see what the fuss was about. Kate moved to open the door of the old house but a volley of loud knocks beat her to it. She hesitated with her hand on the handle, looking up at me anxiously. The angry battering on the door had alarmed her. This was not what she expected when her father came to call.

My heart was pounding. Tears welled up in my eyes as sudden shock swamped my body, draining me of strength. Despite the warnings, despite formal court proceedings, despite the judge's decision, I'd told myself this couldn't happen. Mitch wouldn't really take my children from me! He knew how I loved them. How they loved me. But I'd been in denial for weeks.

I cautiously opened the door, only halfway, and the severe looks on the stranger's faces told me my little family was in danger. Kate didn't run to her father the way she usually did. She stayed close by me, huddling to one side,

5

while Adam clung to my skirt on the other.

The taller of the two men spoke in a formal, monotone voice, without the hint of a smile. "Good morning, Mrs Lightwood. I'm David Lowe from Murdoch Clarke Solicitors, and this is my colleague, Pieter Heckle." His eyes were locked on mine throughout. "We've been accompanied today by Sergeant Vera Webber who'll be overseeing the proceedings to make sure the official court order is carried out. As you know the Family Law Court has granted your husband full custody of his children, and we're here to assist with a smooth transition."

"A smooth transition?" I heard myself whisper.

Too late my arm pushed at the door to shut it, as if to bar them entry, it was met with force from the other side. The policewoman had anticipated my reaction and was on the doorstep in a flash. Far stronger than me, her biceps filling her upper sleeve, she was powerful enough to prevent my quick response and pushed back the door despite my emotional might. With great force, she rammed it back, and I was flung with it against the wall, my children hanging like limpets from me.

Now she warned me of the consequences of non-compliance. "You can't fight this, Mrs Lightwood. The court has given your husband custody of his children. You were given all the documentation and plenty of time to prepare for today."

Suddenly she was inside the house, followed by Mitch, who barged in, and swept my baby Adam up into his arms.

"Mummy...?" Adam whimpered, questioningly, close to tears, sensing that something was very wrong.

Mitch then thrust my baby son into the arms of Sergeant Webber. Her dark uniform with its medals and badges and her holstered automatic pistol terrified him. He wriggled furiously to escape her clutches, and began to sob when he saw the anguish on my face.

"Nooooo!" I screamed. "Don't take my baby!"

Then Kate began to cry. "Mummy... what's happening? I'm frightened. I'm frightened, Mummy." She looked up at her father. "Daddy... don't hurt Mummy..."

"It's alright, darling," I sobbed, holding her close to me, my voice trembling as I fought for breath. "It's alright, darling, it's alright…" I lied, as I tried to comfort her.

Mitch moved swiftly, taking Kate up into his arms, saying, "Have you packed their things in a suitcase?"

I shook my head and felt tears on my cheeks.

"We'll take them as is," growled Mitch to his accomplices.

The policewoman made for the door with my baby in her arms. And Mitch, now carrying a sobbing Kate, wasted no time in following. The two solemn-faced solicitors departed without a word to me.

"The children don't have their favourite toys," I cried out to them, and the words reverberated through my head. 'They don't have their toys… the children don't have their favourite toys… their toys… their toys…'

Then I heard myself scream. "Ahhhhhhhhhh," as if an electric shock had hit me in the pit of my stomach. I doubled up in pain. When I looked up, I could see my innocent children taken further and further away, each staring back at me with terror etched on their face, their arms outstretched to me, as if expecting me to rescue them. But they were being carried off to another life without me.

#

The next thing I knew I was in a hospital bed. Tied by my wrists. The nurses said my weight was down to 35 kilos. I'd stopped eating and drinking. It was a path I'd chosen to take because there was nothing left to live for. My every waking moment had been devoted to caring for my children, but Mitch had taken them from me in the custody battle. His new money had bought him a team of the best lawyers, while I had a 67 year-old legal-aid lawyer who hadn't even read my case.

This was the 1980's, and the law permitted these abhorrent abductions, and I was left with the thought I'd never see my children again because Mitch was leaving Australia to live in Hawaii. So I decided I'd stop living. What was there to live for? I saw nothing of value in life. So I closed all the curtains and closed the door on the world. I withdrew from society, and my life disintegrated as I retreated into a state of misery, hoping I would die. I'd lost my treasures, and nothing would bring them back. There seemed no answer. How could I, without health, strength, or funds, fight a battle of this enormity?

#

It took more than a year of intense therapy for me to feel mentally stable again. Stable enough to want to live. My depression and my suicidal thoughts were brought under control. My inner fire ignited slowly, when my physical and mental health returned, and I dove back into life knowing full-well there were years of struggle ahead. Only now I had a cause – to win back my children.

# CHAPTER 3

"Well, are you coming to Sydney with me, or not?" Vince Parker, as high-flying sales manager at television's Channel Eight in Brisbane, was not one to waste words. He'd previously raised the subject of his promotion at his birthday dinner the week before, and the words had been vying for space in my head ever since. We'd been romantically linked for only just over a year now, so it was a lot to ask of me. "The boss wants me down there ready for work next Monday. So I leave Friday, Lilly," were his words as he poured me a pre-dinner pinot, out on the sun-dappled terrace of our apartment at St. Lucia, Brisbane's University suburb. It was a big promotion for Vince, with big benefits - free air-travel, a huge expense account, and lots of free-bies.

Vince was a fine-looking specimen. Athletic, always at the gym, light brown hair, quite tall, broad-shouldered, and very popular with everyone. What I first fell in love with, were his hands. He kept them manicured and took pride in them. They looked like a teacher's hands.

"Oh please… don't rush me Vince! Just when everything's going so well." He'd thrown a spanner in my works, and this was a big decision for me to make. My fear about leaving Brisbane overwhelmed me, and I was confused. The wound of losing my children was still raw, but I'd applied a proverbial Band-Aid, and thrown myself into work to earn a living, despite feeling the pain of the loss every waking hour, and often in my sleep. It was now three years after that fateful day, I had a successful job in television, and was thriving. Now, suddenly, I was asked to uproot and start again.

"Come on, Lil…"

"I'll only go if you promise to find me a job at the channel in Sydney!" The words spewed out, and I dared not look up at him as he handed me the wine. I loved my job, and was lucky to have it. Not that I was aware of it then, but my personality got me through many a door. I was a people pleaser. A doctor at Brisbane's Mater Hospital had introduced me to the head of the news department at the local television station, and next thing I knew, I was working both sides of the camera, culminating in my own women's interview programme.

"If a job is all it takes," Vince now said, "sure! I'll find a spot for you, Lilly." His confidence, gave me confidence.

"You will?" I was overjoyed. It was the perfect solution - I'd keep my two loves! Both Vince and a job in TV. I felt my heart beating excitedly at the thought. Jumping up I kissed him, almost spilling my wine.

"Of course I will! You're a natural talent. You'll fit right in." There was that magic smile of his again.

This would mean capital city television! But as Vince and I had been together only a relatively short time, there was an element of risk, leaving behind the familiar, leaving friends. But I thought, 'Who doesn't love Sydney?'

Then there was the problem of what to do about mum. When I say, 'mum,' I'm talking about my grandmother. She raised me, insisting I call her 'mum.' So she'd always been 'mum' to me. She'd had a slight stroke shortly after Vince and I teamed up, and had daily care, so when I told her I was moving to Sydney, she insisted she not be left behind. So at eighty-two years of age, she came to Sydney too.

After much searching, I would find a suitable retirement village with nursing care at Palm Beach - a northern beach suburb. Despite her being in the best of care, I would still feel guilty about her being in a retirement facility, and would try to see her as much as I could.

#

"It's been four months, Vince," I called from the doorway of our terrace house in Selwyn Street, Paddington, as he slipped into his new Mercedes sedan to race off to North Sydney for another day at the channel – without me.

"I'm working on it, Lil. Working on it!" he said, without a glance to me as his car door thudded shut to lock him in, and me out.

Nothing had come of his promise to find me a job, and I was bored stiff. Besides, I was saving up for a decent lawyer to try and win visiting rights to my children. Looking down, I saw the home-delivered *Eastern Suburbs Courier* lying on the doorstep in its plastic wrap. My boredom led me to the Positions Vacant column over morning coffee. And when I saw an advertisement for a Personal Assistant to Eva Goldberg, Australia's wealthiest woman who owned The Goldberg Art Gallery nearby, I phoned my dear friend Heidi Ching who had her own art gallery in Brisbane.

"What do you think, Heidi?"

"Absolutely fantastic idea, Lilly. You're made for it." She promised me a reference, if I needed one.

#

With heart pounding inside my chest, I pushed open the great glass entry door, and was met by Eva Goldberg herself. Madam Goldberg, Eva to her friends, looked like something out of a 1940's movie, with a look of sophistication and glamour that would have been at home on a Bette Davis film-set. A striking looking woman with jet black hair, who used bright crimson lipstick to accentuate the beautiful teeth, which, I guessed, were an advertisement for Double Bay's most expensive dentist. As for jewellery, she wore an enormous string of pearls, which looked to me like authentic Paspaley pearls, and a truly dramatic ruby, emerald and diamond ring that took my eye. Her face was heart-shaped, and wore a haughty, contemptuous scowl, till suddenly she smiled, dazzling me, and I liked her immediately.

After looking me up and down in my favourite sand-coloured Trent Nathan business suit, she asked me two questions as we stood in the foyer. The first was, 'How much do you want in wages?'

I had to think quickly. This meant she was canny with money. I quickly sliced a third off my generous television salary, and suggested an amount. It seemed to please her.

Her approving smile was followed by, "Will you sign your name here please?" She moved to the vacant reception desk on which sat a blank piece of paper.

I duly signed.

"I want you to meet Mr Butler, my business manager. He's coming now," she said. A giant of a man lumbered in, and Eva greeted him as if HE were the boss. Like a fan would greet Pavarotti, she looked coquettishly into his eyes, smiling up at the titan saying, "The best applicant so far, Mr Butler."

I held out my hand in greeting, and offered the overweight giant my best smile.

He ignored my outstretched hand, and merely pulled out a handkerchief and blew his nose with a piercing rasp. There was no conversation, merely a condescending 'Hello' before Goliath made some excuse to hurry away again.

I departed the gallery with a feeling of cautious optimism about winning the position, but with an uneasy feeling about having to deal with the unfriendly Butler. I thought that his eyes were too close together and his nose was much too long. His droopy slack jowls made him look unhealthy and forlorn, and his huge body was a mass of bouncing blubber. He'd not looked me in the eye once. I suspected he was the type who made life more difficult than it had to be.

I walked home trying not to be too excited by the prospect of working at the gallery – in case it was denied me. All through the years, I personally had owned nothing of beauty. That was probably one of the reasons I truly appreciated beautiful things. The Goldberg Gallery was the largest privately owned art gallery in Australia, with over eight thousand square metres making up the main gallery. The prestigious Goldberg represented the finest works, by the most renowned artists. And if I got the job, I would get to work with them. Those few minutes in the gallery had stimulated me. My mind was made up, I *wanted* to work there!

I understood there was much that was pretentious about the art world. From my time in television interviewing celebrities, I'd discovered that could also be said of ballet, theatre, the worlds of film and literature. But I was attracted to the art world's glamour and apparent sophistication. I imagined that gallery life would make day-to-day events colourful and vibrant. The vivacious Eva had beguiled me.

Once again, next day, I stood in my pyjamas on the front doorstep and waved another goodbye to Vince, envious because he had reason to wear a suit, and I didn't. I closed the front door as his Merc departed, to face another lonely day. Heavy at heart, I headed for the shower, when the phone rang.

"Hello. Is that Lillian Lightwood?" said a voice I vaguely recognised.

"Yes. This is she," I answered politely, excitement rising in me.

"You may start at The Goldberg Gallery tomorrow, Miss Lightwood," said Eva. "Tomorrow at 9 a.m. Precisely!"

That night, when I told Vince I'd got the job, he seemed pleased, but over dinner and after a few drinks, gave me a hard time about it, asking, "What the hell do you know about art?"

He, who wouldn't know a pizza from a Picasso, I thought to myself. I'd been elated all day, but his comment made me suddenly doubt that I could handle the position. So I tried to convince myself that I was a quick learner with an agile mind, and was willing to do whatever it took to be successful. Maybe have my own gallery one day! Saying I was pleased I'd won the job would be an understatement. My independent streak demanded I pull my weight financially. And I would soon discover that Vince was so busy in his new job - always flying here or there - that I hardly ever saw him, so, Eva's gallery was the answer to my prayers.

#

The very next day, I entered my new workplace - The Goldberg Gallery - for the first time, at precisely 8.58 a.m. to become Eva Goldberg's Personal Assistant. Eva would later tell me that she'd secretly had my handwriting scrutinized and interpreted by her aged husband, Henry Goldberg. Handwriting analysis was a quirky family habit, of which there were many, I was to learn. And through Henry's 'reading,' it was discovered that I was very ambitious, apparently. But, Eva would say, my colourful background in television was 'invaluable for her illustrious Goldberg Gallery.'

The foyer reception area, from which I would operate, consisted of a room twelve by six metres, with a tiny cubical 'the bunker,' at the far end behind my reception desk, with a sliding glass window through which I could talk with gallery assistant Georgie – a beautiful blonde in her early twenties. She was, I soon learned, the dogsbody of the place.

Directly opposite the main front door, were three steps which led down through an open entrance to the magnificent main gallery. To the left of these steps, opposite the curved mahogany reception desk where I was to be stationed, another three steps led up to a small showroom, where more intimate exhibitions were held. At the far end of that room, a long corridor connected with the framing area, the workshops, and a kitchen.

I was soon busy typing correspondence for Eva, as she stood dictating at my shoulder. To my relief, she accepted my suggestions on structure and language. Barry Butler appeared on the scene to talk to her, but never gave me as much as a 'Hello'.

Georgie, my new office chum, warned me about Butler during our first private chat that lunchtime. 'Don't trust him,' were her words, in a posh British accent.

I thought everything was going well, but sadly, that very first afternoon Eva upset me. I had brought a tiny photograph of my two little ones to work, and sat it under the counter of the reception desk so that I could always see them.

Picking up my treasure, she slammed it face down. "No! I cannot have anything personal of yours on my reception desk!"

Despite the fact that no-one but me had been able to see the photograph, my cherubs were consigned to a drawer.

# CHAPTER 4

I would soon learn that Eva was a creature of moods. Extreme moods. And woe-betide anyone who struck the belligerent Eva. One young artist by the name of Nicholas Drake picked the wrong day to come selling his wares, hoping that Eva would give him an exhibition. The 'tyrannical' Eva would hold court this day - sad for Nicholas, but my meeting him would prove to be providential, because he'd one day play an important role in my life.

"Your ten o'clock appointment's arrived, Mrs Goldberg." I said through the intercom, then waited for her reply before I returned the phone to its cradle. I looked over the reception desk to the long black leather sofa opposite, where Nicholas Drake was seated with his precious artwork on his knee, safely tucked inside a huge faux leather folder. He was visibly trembling, so I gave him my best smile, but it didn't register. Both The Goldberg Gallery and its extremely wealthy owner had reputations that reached far beyond Australia, and here he was, a nineteen-year-old art student, brave enough to ask the doyen of the art world for an audience.

I could hear her footsteps coming from inside the main gallery. Could hear her animated conversation with Barry Butler. But only she climbed the three steps up into the reception area where I sat, witness to everything that followed.

The words tumbled from her crimson lips. "So, here I am! Now show me your work!" There was a tone of scorn in her voice as she stood, arms folded, her luminous Paspaley pearls seeming to light up the room. Georgie had estimated the value of the pearls to be at least $300,000, and she should know. Georgie was a classy member of the English aristocracy, out in Australia to learn about Australia's great artists. Guinness was her surname, and when she returned to London in nine months' time, she was to marry Lord Jeremy Fellowes. Royalty!

Young Nicholas Drake jumped to his feet, saying, "Er, where, Mrs Goldberg?"

"Here!" An arm unfolded, and she pointed directly to the floor beneath his feet. The spot on which she would emasculate young artists the likes of Nicholas.

I could feel him squirm at the lack of privacy. His oversized raincoat, and hand-knitted rainbow-coloured scarf were a hindrance, as he unpacked his portfolio to place his work carefully at her feet – small, unframed oils, abstracts every one. His dark eyes darted about furtively as if he were in danger; like a wolf confronting a threat, with a mixture of calculation and defensive mistrust. I could tell he was quaking in his boots at the thought of rejection. But despite his anxiety, his gaunt cheeks concertinaed into a smile as he tried to win her praise, or at least her approval.

As he gave a commentary on each work, his voice quavered. To his horror, Eva used her foot to scatter his treasures for examination. He mumbled, till he became lost for words, while she strutted around the artworks disdainfully, without responding to him, like some Middle Eastern potentate deciding who among their subjects should live or die. Finally, she delivered her verdict. "These paintings are not for us. You need to find your own style. It's all rubbish!"

His eyes widened, his mouth hung open, and his utterance of objection was halted in a flash when Eva shot him a look that said, 'don't dare argue with me.'

Then she delivered a sharp, resounding rebuke. "NO!" Like the crack of a whip. "NO! Not for us!" she spat contemptuously, then abandoned him. Shouting for Barry Butler, she moved on.

Nicholas Drake was left standing, absorbing his sentence from the artistic judge with the despairing eyes of a concentration camp victim. He looked over at me pleadingly.

My heart went out to him, so as soon as I saw the back of Eva, I came quickly over to help him re-pack his portfolio, and soften the impact with kind words. "Well, I like them, Nicholas," I said, reassuring him as I bent to pick one up from the floor, holding it up to admire it, showing my appreciation of his imaginative work. "I would love to have these hanging in my home."

The background of the painting was black, but the colours were striking. Reds, greens, marigold and orange shades, with a dash of apple green. They were vertical abstract shapes; dazzling strokes that took on the shape of swirling costumes. They conjured music, dance and gaiety. Fun!

"I think you should splash them with gold leaf, Nicholas. Be extravagant! The frames should be gold, too," I added, enthusiastically. "Talk to Angelo, one of our framers, he'll be at the Duke of Windsor around the corner for lunch, at midday." I pointed out the direction of the hotel to make it easy for him. "Angelo always wears a red spotted kerchief around his neck. He's Italian." I wanted Nicholas to embrace my enthusiasm, and follow through with my suggestion. "Just mention my name, he'll look after you." I could see the tension leave his face, his deep eyes soften and light up. His utter devastation at Eva's judgement had evaporated, and I was pleased to have helped him. I knew well what rejection was like.

"Thank you. Oh. Thank you…" he stammered. "Er, what is your name?"

"Lillian. But everyone calls me Lilly. Lillian Lightwood." I smiled, able to tell he liked the sound of it. "Oh, and I haven't been here very long, but there is one thing I've learnt from Mrs Goldberg… she says that Australian artists don't make their paintings large enough."

"Oh…"

I nodded, and focussed my eyes on his sad eyes as I tried to make him feel better about the verdict, and 'take in' what I was saying. "Look," I said in an up-beat manner, pointing to the newly hung Brett Whiteley above my desk. Then I swivelled further round to point out the Lloyd Rees behind the long black sofa beside us, an ethereal, dreamy work, with swirling soft tones depicting a seascape. Both were huge.

Our eyes met again.

"Mrs Goldberg says we should make them enormous, like the Europeans do. Imagine this one," I said, holding his painting up to the light, "with a beautiful gold frame. Wow! The wealthy Double Bay ladies would love it! Make this your own individual style, Nicholas, and stick to it."

He was all packed now, like a Bedouin ready to depart on another journey, so as soon as I heard Eva's voice again, I opened the grand foyer door for him, and bade him a warm farewell, adding, "Don't ever give up, Nicholas! You won't make it if you stop!" I lived by that code. I'd never give up the hope of being reunited with Kate and Adam.

# CHAPTER 5

The Goldberg Gallery changed its exhibitions every three weeks. The change-over was a busy time. A time of removing already exhibited work by one artist, and the 'hanging' of another artist's work. A time when the public was invited into the gallery to have a glass of wine, view the new artworks, and hopefully, buy them. I was excited at the thought of my first 'Opening Exhibition,' but sorely disappointed Vince couldn't be there.

"I really wanted Vince to attend tonight, Georgie," I said, covering my typewriter for the night. "I wanted to show off the gallery while it was bustling with people. Vince thinks working here must be boring, and I'd like to prove him wrong!" I gave a wry smile. "Besides, I'd really like you to meet him," I added, now tidying my desk before the public came in. "He's flying off again to Melbourne and won't be back till Sunday. I'm not too happy about this new job of his. He's never home!"

"Oh, I am sorry, darling! I hoped he'd be able to make it, too. I was looking forward to meeting him. Telling him what a lucky chap he is to have you!" She smiled at me. "Does that mean you'll be alone this week?"

"Well, yes..."

"Then let's have a meal together tonight after the Opening. We'll go to *Claude*, it's just round the corner. They have the best chef! It's a BYO, so we'll take a bottle of the French wine Daddy sent me! My treat, it'll cheer you up!"

"Oh, Georgie. Thank you!"

So only two weeks into my new appointment, not only had I made a friend, I was to experience my first gallery 'Opening.' It would be a glamorous evening affair, and give me clear insight into the art world. Georgie had told me what to expect, so I'd dressed with particular flair that day, and sure enough, the event turned out just the way she'd described it would be - a spectacle of colour and design.

In came a steady procession of patrons to create pageantry such as I'd never seen, pushing open the great glass door, allowing in the cold night air to bite in a repetitive icy blast. My position behind reception gave me the best seat in the house to view Sydney society close up, as one by one, two by two, the invited guests entered in a lengthy parade. A feast for my eyes, after the clock struck six. Art patrons, celebrities and media thronged together noisily in Eva's exalted halls.

Despite my years in television, I was mesmerized by the medley of famous faces flitting frivolously past my reception desk at the anticipated joy of the occasion. I'd never seen so many diverse celebrities in the one place, at the one time. They merged into a patchwork of colour and style. Smiling, posturing for each other's benefit, and for the press cameras.

Society women wore expensive clothes that didn't fit, hats that didn't suit. They wore minks, long and short, some old, some new, some fake. Leather suits, chiffons that swirled. Bright taffeta, with handbags to match. The material rustling as they swished it for show, like five-year old girls dressed for a party. Sandals, boots, and strappy little sling backs, outrageously high heels. The day's stormy weather obviously playing no part in wardrobe selection.

There was a scattering of jean-clad males with flowing scarves. Dress suits, bankers' suits, ad men attire - lavish bows at their Adams apple, coloured jackets, open-necked shirts. Many of the guests on their way to, or from, other functions. It made for the most Pickwickian of gatherings. The gallery buzzed.

Georgie covered the phone for me as I went wandering and eavesdropping. Excited chatter, friends catching up. Glasses clinking, drinks spilling. Some I decided, had not the slightest interest in the art. The exhibition was the first showing painted by a high court judge's wife. Paintings of the famous Bungle Bungle Mountains. Although a myriad of glowing, ruddy tints of colour, the unique Bungle Bungles did nothing for me. Their feeling of isolation would not be welcome in my home.

I moved through the crowded gallery dispensing catalogues, observing 'peacocks' strutting priggishly here and there, posers holding glasses, drinking delicately, swigging, swallowing hard, glancing at paintings, each with their own practised stance. Aficionados offering expert critiques of this work, and that. Heads bowed, bobbed, ducked, nodded in agreement, shook in disapproval. Mouths sipped, wagged, and pouted. Spectacles went on, spectacles came off. Closer scrutiny was deemed necessary, so that here and there little ceremonial dances were performed, two steps forward, one step back, before the exchanges of opinion resumed, and artistic thirsts demanded further slaking.

Georgie told me later, that Eva had been running for red stickers all night to stick on the paintings, to depict that they'd been sold. "She's already calculated her profit, Lilly," my goddess friend had said, as she viewed the crowd with me in the doorway to the main gallery. "Thirty-three per cent of half a million is not a bad night's work," she smiled, her lively blue eyes dancing with mischief. "It was the Brett Whiteley, and good old Sir Sidney Nolan that shot the figures up," said Georgie with irony, "not the Bungle Bungles!" Looking at this devine creature we called Georgie, it was easy to imagine her as a supermodel on the world stage, but she'd chosen instead to study art and its history, then gracefully blend into a life of riches when she married her English lord.

Although it was not yet seven, the dedicated drinkers were hovering anxiously around the long, now untidy drinks table with empty glasses in hand, looking decidedly unhappy. The decanters too had been drained. There was an interminable auditory rise from the assembly.

"More wine!" yelled a rowdy patron, his wine glass held high in protest.

I was about to alert Eva, who, when I spotted her, seemed to have her shoe stuck on something like a join in the floor, but I was beaten to it by Barry Butler who ran like a schoolboy excited to tell a tale on a fellow student.

"The girls didn't buy enough wine, Mrs Goldberg." His timing was not good.

Eva snapped angrily, glaring up at him. "What did you say?" came the angry retort, as she re-fitted a shoe on her dainty foot.

Butler was taken aback by her famous look of disdain at the inconvenience of the moment, and it unnerved him. It would seem that Butler, her favourite employee, was not exempt from her temper. He stammered. "The girls... the girl's didn't buy enough wine! We... er, we need more wine, Mrs Goldberg," he repeated, with a hand going to his head uncertainly, like a child in class.

"That's rubbish!" She pushed past him then marched over to the drinks table where she found nothing more than a dribble of orange juice. Six wine casks had been drained. Eva never bought good wine. Her parsimony was legend. "My God, they're greedy! It's not even seven o'clock! Go over to the Duke of Windsor and buy four more casks." Her arm flew in the air in the direction of the exit. Her hand flicked him away for good measure.

"Is four enough, Mrs Goldberg?" he dared question.

"It's more than enough! GO!" Again, the arm in the air, dismissively.

On his return, Eva snatched two of the casks from her delivery boy.

"Put those two in the fridge," she ordered. Then, with patrons parting like the red sea at the sight of her, with one cask under either arm, she marched through the crowded gallery ready to do battle like a heavy-weight wrestler, without the slightest hint of embarrassment. She thumped them down on the drinks table, turned to face the multitude to shout over the cacophony:

"THIS DRINK IS COMPLIMENTARY - NOT COMPULSORY!"

# CHAPTER 6

It didn't take me long to fall in love with Sydney. I loved the bustle, the crowds, the shopping, even the busy traffic. It was my New York. People just got on with their busy lives. Although with the cost of living in Sydney, I imagined it would be difficult for families trying to manage on one wage - parents would have to sacrifice a great deal. But every time I thought of children, I knew I had to re-direct my thoughts. I'd taught myself this most difficult of tasks.

Vince had no children, despite having been married for ten years, and divorced for five. He knew my story of course, but I shared my past with him on very few occasions. That said, one day as we strolled through Centennial Park, I was drawn back to see my children's faces again in my mind's eye.

It was a glorious Sunday afternoon, and I saw hordes of happy families, mostly ethnic people who took advantage of the heavenly park, perhaps because at home they had tiny back yards, and here, amongst the 220 hectares, they could spread out in the vastness of the green, well-kept stretches of lawn. Here, families held long picnics in the sunshine, and had fun.

This day, I saw young and old alike throwing Frisbees, playing soccer, flying kites, laughing, and my mind drifted back to Kate and Adam. Holding Vince's hand, feeling calm in the serenity of the park, I made mention of them, but I was greatly disappointed with the response.

"I know you miss them, Lil. But it'll pass. Come on, cheer up!" His words sounded so flippantly insensitive to me. He just didn't 'get it.'

"Sometimes, I feel as if you're giving me a polite 'performance,' when you listen to my tales about my children," I said sadly.

"That's a bit rough, Lil. I'm sure they were great. It's just that kids and I don't go together."

"So you keep telling me, Vince. Don't worry I don't plan on having any more! Kate and Adam are my life." I well knew that mothers' forever grieve for a lost child, no matter how many more they may have. My heart belonged totally to Kate and Adam, no matter how love touched me in the future.

"Well, you know how it is. Not having any kids myself, you can't expect me to understand what you've been through."

I knew what he'd said was a fact, but I felt there was a lack of compassion behind his words. Yet Vince wasn't exactly uncaring, it's just that he lived for today. I'm sure he thought I should be able to forget my children - the way a person 'gets over' a partner - in time! I knew he'd never understand, so I didn't dwell on thoughts of them in his company. But I would dearly have loved some encouragement about things being different for me in the future.

#

As for my working life, it took me no time at all to work out that Eva Goldberg was the world's biggest gossip. Anyone not in her company at the time would be a victim of her gossiping tongue. I listened to all of it, as did Georgie. Me sitting behind reception, and she in her separate, glass partitioned office, usually with her head down, writing.

Mostly, Georgie was kept busy cleaning and dusting, checking stock, wrapping, and moving paintings around with Butler and the two framing boys Angelo and Freddie. I on the other hand, was forbidden to leave my desk, or the telephone unattended, and spent every day as witness to each colourful event, visiting patron, artist, family member, or client, who wanted to ingratiate himself, or herself, with the famous Eva Goldberg.

Often, patrons would ask the favour of taking a painting or sculpture home, to 'try it out.' When in fact, they were borrowing the piece to impress their guests at a dinner party, or fund-raising event. Eva knew this, but she had her favourites.

It was one such busy day, as I was trying to type the next exhibition's catalogue; a list of the paintings for sale, the price, their title, and perhaps an anecdote from the artist about his work, when Eva indicated, by plonking herself down on the sofa opposite me, that she wished to start one of her stories. These tales would last until she decided she'd something better to do, and on occasion, they were tediously tiring.

Different moods dictated where she sat. This was a time for the big black sofa which stretched from the mighty glass entry doors, along the wall, and stopped at the foot of the small gallery up the three steps. At other times, when the narrative was to be more 'intimate,' she would pull up a three-legged stool and sit very close to me, rubbing her calves. Georgie, usually in the bunker listening in, today was helping Butler with new stock arrivals.

Eva's conversation with me was interrupted by Lloyd Rees struggling to enter the building, his whispy, shoulder-length white hair blowing in the wind. Rees, the world-renowned ninety-two year old Australian artist was soon to fulfil a life-long dream – a trip to Paris after an absence of fifty years, compliments of Qantas, for he'd donated a painting to be hung in a VIP lounge newly completed there. Rees had come to see Eva to organise the details of his forth-coming exhibition at The Goldberg before his much anticipated trip.

I recognised him immediately, and was thrilled to meet the charming, grand old master, so I hurried to his aid as soon as I spotted him. Taking his skeletal arm, I helped him manoeuvre his aged body towards the long black sofa, where the stories and lies were told, and secrets shared. Where family members were inclined to discuss their private business, as if I were an object, or a pet dog that could not repeat their secrets.

As was usually the case with a visiting artist, Rees would sit and talk to Eva in the foyer, because her private office was down the three steps to one side of the grand gallery; restrictive for an aged veteran. She only used her office for private telephone conversations, or paper work. Otherwise, she held court right there in the foyer, so that she could keep an eye on every eventuality. And be seen! The gallery was her stage.

'Hello, DARLING!' was how she began each and every welcome, with emphasis on the word darling, followed by, 'How are YOU today?' Then the smile came out to dazzle, as if Lloyd Rees were the only artist she had, which of course was not the case. She had eighty artists, most of whom were exclusive to her.

She too had risen to assist him on entry, then planted herself down next to him on the sofa to talk, as he was hard of hearing. She kissed his cheek, and snuggled intimately close to the frail old man. This intimacy was a habit I'd noticed. She treated all of her male artists as if they were boyfriends. In a flash she was headlong into conversation about his forth-coming exhibition, like a child excited about Christmas.

"You know, Lloyd," she yelled in his ear, "there's a lot of interest in your work. Your name is world famous now. I've had calls from some of my overseas clients telling me to buy for them, and send the work sight unseen."

"Overseas what, Eva…," he croaked. "Can't hear you!"

She put her mouth closer to his ear, which was devoid of a hearing aid, and I noted that her Chanel No 5 made the old man sneeze. Not once, but five times. Sneezes which rattled his thin bones. She made a face at me. I went to the rescue.

"Can I get you a drink, Mr Rees?" I asked rather loudly, bending close for him to hear, able to leave my post if Eva were present.

"Yes, dear. That would be nice." He answered in a raspy whisper. "An orange juice, if you have it. But put a little water in it, will you?" his voice sounding centuries old. When I returned with the juice, he held out a shaking, bony hand, took hold with an uncontrollable wobble, making me glad I'd used a tall glass, and hadn't filled it.

No sooner had I scurried back to my desk, the phone rang. It was for ME, and I was embarrassed. When Eva saw me merely listen, and not converse, she bellowed at me, wanting to know who it was.

"It's my, er, mother, Mrs Goldberg… she's er, she's been ill." I gave a pitiful look.

"Tell her not to call during working hours! Do you hear?" Her glare was fierce.

"Yes. Mrs Goldberg." I spoke into the phone shaking inside, for to make myself heard by my mother, I had to cut through her familiar tirade.

"Leaving an auld woman alone, after all I've done for you…!"

"I'm sorry, mum," I said, adding, "You know I'm not allowed phone calls at work. Please don't ring here again." I knew that wouldn't stop her, but it sounded good. Clearing my throat, and trying not to be emotional, I put down the phone hoping her abuse hadn't carried into the foyer. And was grateful the scene was interrupted by Barry Butler, who'd descended from the small gallery. The focus would now shift to him.

"Mrs Goldberg, please excuse me," he said, standing with his back to me, between my reception desk and the big black sofa, on which sat two stars of the art world. "The parcel you're waiting for from Italy has arrived, but it doesn't look like the prints you're expecting. Do you want me to open it, anyway?"

Georgie was at his heel and spoke out with her usual enthusiasm. "I'll open it for you, Mrs Goldberg!"

"I decide what is opened, and what is not in my gallery!" Eva shot back, focussing her poisonous glare on Georgie now, and only after a dramatically long pause, did she turn to look at Butler again and command him to carry out the job. "You open it, Mr Butler," and off he went to do her bidding with a savage glance at me. My friendship with Georgie was threatening to his fragile ego. It hadn't taken me long to work out he had an attitude of 'divide and conquer' to maintain his sense of hierarchy.

"Now, listen, Lloyd," Eva tried again, yelling at the old man, "there's great publicity over the Qantas thing. You're a lucky man, Lloyd." She slapped the old man's bony knee, and her eyes danced with mischief then crinkled into a wicked smile. He was now her captive audience. "You know these auctions we have are way out of control, Lloyd. The prices are silly. It just can't go on. It's hysteria. They're ruining the business!"

He did a lot of nodding. As for comprehension, I doubted it.

"Why don't people come and buy from me instead of these auctions? It's much cheaper! I think they just like to be seen at the auction. They like to be on show. They like the performance. It's like a game, a competition, and all their doing is pushing up the prices."

Rees was content to sip away at his juice and listen, with the occasional nod of agreement in response to Eva's conveyer-belt dialogue, but he stared at the floor throughout.

"You, know Lloyd, they just show off. Show ponies, all of them. In America, they even clap at a big sale. They clap for the winner, the one with the most money." She took to clapping, but even that didn't get a response. "Just push, and push up prices. I've got the best paintings Lloyd." Her arm went up like the actress she was, to demonstrate the beautiful artworks on display in the foyer. "They should buy from me, don't you agree, Lloyd?" There was no visible response, and it crossed my mind that he must have read my lips to understand the offering of a drink, but he couldn't read Eva's whilst his eyes were on the floor.

Butler re-entered the scene to stand at the top of the stairs to Eva's left. "Excuse me Mrs Goldberg, I'm sorry to bother you again, but the parcel from Italy, it really doesn't look like the prints you're expecting." Butler's bloated face had become a blotchy bright pink, showing great anxiety.

"What are you talking about," she snapped. "It's from Italy – isn't it?"

"Yes, Mrs Goldberg, but…"

"Then open it. Open it!" she roared at him, then waved him away dismissively with her hand, before turning her head sharply back to Lloyd, her annoyance palpable.

"Very well, Mrs Goldberg," Butler muttered, then diligently headed off to do his mistress's bidding, but with a look of great discomfort. He returned only minutes later, more anxious than I'd ever seen him, almost in tears, acting like a fearful student in the headmaster's office.

"What now?" she growled.

"I'm really sorry to bother you again, Mrs Goldberg…"

His trembling voice told me he was agitated in the extreme. The normally very much in control giant was beside himself with worry over this.

"But this parcel…" He had dragged a square box to the top step, and, playing with his fingers nervously at stomach level, he turned to look at the delivery, then to Eva again, fear etched all over his ugly face. Finally, he stooped to angle the box so that Eva could view it from where she sat. "I'm really worried about this, Mrs Goldberg. It er, really doesn't look right!" He tilted it more acutely so that Eva could see inside.

Exasperated by the continual distraction, Eva heaved herself out from her cushioned cradle to the edge of the sofa, with a look that could kill the devil himself for interrupting her parley. "Just a minute, Lloyd," she panted with a mix of exasperation and effort as she rose. "Can't I get a minute's peace?"

Grumpy in the extreme, now, I thought. Beware!

As soon as her eyes made contact with the box, her jaw dropped. She went deathly pale and let out a monumental shriek. With a look of absolute horror etched on her face, she was out of her seat like a wild cat pouncing on its prey, threw herself at Butler screeching at the top of her voice. "STOP! STOP! Oh, my God, what have you done? That's a 'CHRISTO!'"

Christo, both famous worldwide for wrapping whole buildings, beaches, islands, and cliffs, also produced his famous wrap-art in interesting, yet more practical sizes, suitable as art for the wealthy to display at home. In ignorance, Butler, on Eva's instruction, had opened, and cut to shreds, the beautifully wrapped Christo. Dainty pieces of ribbon lay strewn around the outer box and the carpet. The golden velvet parcel inside lay prized open like a body during autopsy, and the exquisite art was ruined. In a matter of moments Butler had destroyed a work of art worth thousands of dollars. And there was no diagram for re-assembly.

I could only gasp, and seemed glued to my seat awaiting a bomb to go off. But when Georgie came upon the scene again, she saw the look of terror on Butler's face, Eva's rear end pointing skyward, her hands clamped to her cheeks like Edvard Munch's painting, 'The Scream.' While Australia's most famous artist, Lloyd Rees sat shaking, a confused, silent witness, wondering what the fuss was all about. Georgie told me later it looked like a Tom and Jerry cartoon on hold.

I watched on in silence, while Georgie saw the funny side of the whole fiasco and began to laugh, bless her heart. It broke the ice. Lloyd joined in when the penny dropped, his false teeth clattering, and his skeletal frame jerking.

"If you ask me," the legend proffered, "it looks better that way anyway."

This was Eva's cue to join in the merriment, and she laughed until the tears rolled down her cheeks. "Don't worry," she said eventually, wiping her eyes, inwardly loving every minute of the drama which placed her centre stage. "I'll fix it, and they'll never know," she stated with arrogant confidence, as she re-gained her seat after shooing Butler and Georgie away.

But, it would eventuate, that as much as Eva tried to 'fix it', nothing could make it like new. The gallery in Rome that had sent it to The Goldberg Gallery, had to make a whopping insurance claim. When the insurance inspector's came aknocking, Eva denied knowing anything about its destruction.

"Yes, it came here!"

"What did you do with it, Mrs Goldberg?"

"Sent it straight back to sender."

"You didn't open it?"

"NO! Of course we didn't open it."

"Who could have opened it then, Mrs Goldberg?"

"Well I can't speak for the Customs men."

# CHAPTER 7

Vince was pouring himself a gin and tonic as I came in the door of our little terrace house in Paddington.

"The England cricket team's in town" were his words of greeting to me. "The Bakers have invited us to join them for dinner. Come on, it'll do you good." He gave me one of those looks that was hard to argue with, the one that reminded me I had a duty to please. But it was not welcome.

"The Bakers fancy going to Treguardo, so go slip into something bright and we'll join them. It'll cheer you up," he said, sitting down on one of the twin sofas in the lounge-room in front of the fireplace to watch the early news on Channel Eight, without as much as a kiss on the cheek. Treguardo was the local Italian restaurant where food and fun were legend.

"I've just spent the day at Palm Beach with mum," I answered wearily, putting down my handbag. "You know how that drains me, Vince." Her hurtful vitriol was still ringing in my ears. "You should be ashamed, leavin' an old woman in a home! Daughters are supposed to look after their mothers. You're off havin' a good time, and you've left me here to rot," were the last words she'd spoken as I'd said goodbye.

I came around to stand in front of Vince, showing him how absolutely worn out I was, hoping he'd understand. But he'd been distant of late, and I couldn't seem to break his 'absence.' "Please let me off the hook tonight," I pleaded. "The traffic was horrendous. Stop-start all the way there and back in the heat. I'm done for."

"Look, Lilly, you're always saying you never see me. Well I'm here, and I'm making the offer to take you out for dinner. So go make an effort. Take a shower, you'll feel brand new. You always do! Why should I suffer because of that old bitch?" His eyes returned to the television set.

I knew better than argue. I wasn't good at it.

They didn't like each other, Vince and Mary Campbell. My mother was jealous of the time Vince stole when I was free from work. Before he came along, I took her everywhere on my free television celebrity ticket. Wining, dining, VIP invitations to functions, shows, and she bathed in the shadow of the TV celebrity I'd become. As for Vince's dislike of her, that was something I hadn't yet fathomed.

Giving in to him, as usual, I dragged myself to the bathroom and took a shower to go through the ritual of being in attendance. My dark hair was cut relatively short at the time, and I thought that to wash and blow dry it quickly would freshen me up. I was fortunate to be of slim build, and my friend Heidi had once said that clothes looked good on me, no matter what I wore, which was nice. I'd recently bought a new lipstick, and it helped to make my smile sparkle, and thanks to my Scottish heritage, I needed no make-up on my face. But I knew my big blue eyes to be my best feature, so I didn't hold back on mascara or eye shadow to bring attention to them.

It turned out to be a great night. There's something about an accordion, those red checked table-cloths, and a bottle of Chianti that brings out a joyous spirit in everyone. I hadn't felt so good about myself, my knowledge, or my identity, since my TV days. Happy times like these helped ease my pain.

#

I felt a warm glow after the happy evening, and a joyous memory came flooding back as I lay next to Vince, comforted in his naked embrace, despite the fact he'd fallen asleep the minute his head touched the pillow............

My Daddy Bob was laughing happily at Mina and me. He knew our singing would lead to frolic and fun. He joined in as Mina tapped out the chorus of one of her favourites from the Timber Corps in 1942, when she'd felled mighty forest trees for the war effort. She was only tiny, just touching five foot tall. She, and I, a four year old, sang with gusto, as we banged and clanged on pots and pans from the kitchen as our musical instruments. I was never afraid of her. She tried to make me happy. All the time.

*"On Monday we have sausage fried,*
*On Tuesday egg and spam;*
*On Wednesday we have kippers (dyed),*
*On Thursday beans and ham;*
*On Friday we have spam and egg,*
*On Saturday first-grade salmon,*
*But on my life, on Sunday morn,*
*Real egg and glorious gammon."*

# CHAPTER 8

It was one of those days at the gallery when all was quiet. The rain lashed down. Butler was 'out for the day,' which could mean anything from a doctor's appointment, to picking up an artist from the airport. Eva was visiting the Art Gallery of New South Wales lunching with the curator, the ebullient Edward Dribble - a man who went nowhere without an entourage of pretty young women employees. Eva and husband Henry, were making a donation of a Nolan, an oil painting by Sir Sidney Nolan from their personal collection, to be placed on permanent display for the public.

I had slid open the tiny window of connection between Georgie and me, to talk freely as we sat at our desks, although I liked to stand and stretch now and again, because my decrepit chair was so uncomfortable. Age had withered it. Time had impaired it. Loose and missing screws made it close to dangerous. The seat waggled like a yoyo, threatening to collapse. I named it 'Mr Wobbly,' and had mentioned its near death condition to Butler on numerous occasions, but the information landed on deaf ears.

The conversation with Georgie focussed on Eva, and I questioned if she had been successful by nothing more than pure good luck, because she understood nothing about promotion.

"Husband Henry's money, darling!"

"Oh, of course!" I nodded. "And what made her open the gallery in the first place?"

"Oh, that's fascinating, dear girl," Georgie said, putting down her pen ready to convey all. "She does have a UK art degree, so there was always an interest. And of course she was very beautiful when she was young. Artists probably fought to paint her. I've seen photographs of her as a teenager, in Petrocelli's book over there. Absolutely stunning, darling!"

Swivelling involuntarily on 'Wobbles,' I then asked how Eva had met the wealthy Henry Goldberg.

"Well apparently, my dear," she continued, leaning her forearms on her untidy desk, concentrating to be accurate with the facts, "his first wife died, and the woman he married to replace her was unable to cope with his three spoilt children. That's when Eva turned up fresh off the boat from England as a 'ten pound Pom,' looking for a job as housekeeper. She was penniless, and had her own baby son to look after."

"Oh, I see…"

"It would seem, my dear, that Eva turned out to be so capable at managing the children, that wife number two got the boot, and Eva married Henry and all his billions! But you can see for yourself how hard she works. She built this gallery from nothing. It used to be an old brewery, Cooks Brewery, and now it's famous world-wide as The Goldberg Gallery."

The rain outside was thumping down, and we had to raise our voices now and then to be heard, but we felt cosily safe in our glamorous, giant cocoon without supervision.

"But-what-a-complex-character!" I said, my tone depicting my frustration with my perfumed tank of a boss. "She never ceases to amaze me." I was eager to know more about this fascinating woman who controlled my working life. "She's the best manipulator of people I've ever seen – when it suits her. But I don't believe what I see sometimes! She has no concern for her reputation."

"But darling, that IS her reputation!" Georgie stated, then added kindly for my benefit, "She had a dreadful effect on me too, at first. I came to believe she'd much rather have pretty young boys working for her, but Butler would get too jealous!"

"Why?"

"He's gay, darling! Didn't you know?" She raised an eyebrow at me. "I'm sure she's schizophrenic, my sweet - the way she so often leaves the room as one person, and returns as another. And I shall admit that her sharp tongue takes a bit of getting used to - she's as subtle as a bottle of sulphuric acid, my dear!"

Our shared confidences had an illicit edge, but it was a relief for me to know I wasn't exaggerating, or imagining my perceptions.

"It's her lack of breeding that shows, darling." Georgie took advantage of our solitude to groom her gloriously thick, long blonde hair with a silver brush. "Where I come from, breeding is all that matters!"

I didn't agree wholeheartedly. I knew that people could re-invent themselves. I had!

"Tell me about your background, Lilly. You speak so beautifully. Is your family well to do, like mine? We're terrible snobs. I've been taught to be extremely discriminating."

This made me hesitant to tell her the truth. I'd been abandoned by everyone in my life, one way or another. Dumped like an unwanted puppy. But I gave it no thought. I held no bitterness for anyone. No grudges. I just got on with living. Nor did I want to mention at this stage that I had children, so I answered through a cloud. "Just my mum, a widow, and two brothers." I explained that I'd been born in Scotland. Though I neglected to mention that I too, was a ten pound 'Scottish Pom' immigrating to Australia when I was fourteen.

"Most of my family's friends have titles." Georgie smiled at the memory of home, and her sense of pride in her privileged life. "It's back to polo and tea parties for me; shopping in Kensington, skiing on the Alps in February next year, and holidays on the Cote d' Azure."

"What brought you to Australia?"

"Well darling, I'm coming into a large inheritance when I'm twenty five, and Daddy wanted me to prove I deserved it by surviving on my own for three years. So here I am, with only nine months to go to finish my uni degree." She punched the air with a sense of victory. "Whoopee, I'm nearly there. I can soon say goodbye to the crazy Eva Goldberg! But please, don't tell the witch when I'll be off." She gave me a pleading look. "She'd replace me at the drop of a hat."

"No, of course not," I assured her. "But how have you been able to stay sane under the same roof for so long?"

There was a sudden flash of lightning that seemed to penetrate the foyer, followed by a clash of thunder above. The storm was close, and suddenly we felt vulnerable, as if Eva knew what we were up to.

"Spooky!" said Georgie. "Can you keep a secret?"

"Of course! I want to survive this harrowing experience too, you know."

"Well, I've been taking notes," she whispered. "I'm saving all this rich material for a kiss and tell book, entitled, 'The Queen of Arts.' I really want to be a writer!" She became all distant and dreamy, as if harbouring secret hopes for her future. "It's the ultimate dichotomy, Lilly. All her wealth and power, and the manners of a pig! I've seen her grab a foot long cucumber from her shopping bag without washing it, and munch on it right here in reception, like a 16th century baron would a turkey leg. She doesn't care who sees her! She thinks WE'RE the peasants!"

Our clandestine conversation was cut short when the telephone rang and made us jump. Georgie answered on her phone and held her hand over it to talk to me. "There's a woman speaking in some foreign language. Can't understand a word, darling."

My mother, again! I took the call, and with one eye on the door, I listened while she gave me a mouthful about living in the retirement home - how it was God's waiting room, and how all her new friends were dying around her. "Christ Almighty, the bloody auld fogies aroon' here are fallin' doon like nine pins."

# CHAPTER 9

The last to leave this particular evening, all alone in the gallery, I pulled out the tiny drawer from under the reception desk to look again at my little ones before I journeyed home, as I did every evening. And tonight, with no-one around, I brought the photograph up to my lips, kissed it, and said aloud, "Someday I'll see you again. Won't be long!" But again, a lump formed in my throat, because it felt so very improbable without the means to make it happen.

I was just about to lock up and turn on the alarm system, when a group of twelve or more young adults entered the gallery. They were clean, well-dressed, and one might say, intelligent-looking, as if they were young doctors, or visiting university students. They were keen to take a quick look through the gallery. Despite me having had enough gallery for the day, I decided that if they made their visit brief they were welcome.

"Yes, do come in, but I can only allow you ten minutes. The main gallery is down those three steps." I pointed. "Fine Arts, with mostly antique furnishings, is past the lovely botanical garden section. If you walk on through and return immediately, I'd be pleased." Then I fibbed, saying, "Charlie is coming to lock up soon." I didn't want them to think I'd been left alone this particular night, when Butler had hurried home to an emergency with his 'flatmate' Xavier. An emotional emergency, I imagined.

Xavier was much younger than Barry Butler, very handsome, but wildly neurotic. His flirtatious, immature nature was geared to make Butler jealous.

Which wasn't that difficult. And the 'Charlie' I'd named, was a handsome, flirtatious forty year old who had his own framing shop nearby, and was frequently asked in to help our boys with oversized paintings, or, extremely valuable ones. We all loved Charlie. He had a cheeky way with him, and was quite loveable. His was the first name that came to mind.

The smart young group said how very much they appreciated my cooperation, as they streamed in past me and promised to be no more than ten minutes. I kept myself busy, tidying up, readying for the morning as the minutes ticked away. After a while, my watch told me that only five minutes had gone by. So I began to flip through an auction magazine to see what the market was doing, and I noticed three works of Robert Boissevain. He painted in oil, but had a delicate technique creating a filmy, watercolour effect. He was famous for his dog-roses, a delicate flower the socialites loved. He also painted groups of aborigines sitting under shady trees in the Outback. But he was most famous for his nudes, and there was a juicy story attached that Georgie shared with me one day. There was always a story!

'His wife too, was once an artist,' she'd said. 'She used to pose for him in the nude, then stole the handsome brute from his wife, and since that time, has not allowed any other female to pose for him. She hopes, that by the time she's lost her appeal, Robert will have lost his eyesight!'

Looking at my watch, I realised that a full ten minutes had passed and there was no sign of the group. I started to get anxious. I've always had a great imagination, and was worried about destruction for starters, and about handling the group when I found them and needed to chase them from the gallery without back-up.

Before I went to do anything at all, I decided the clever thing to do was lock the main front door, and set the alarm. They couldn't unlock the door to escape with anything valuable unless they knocked me out cold. Nor could anyone else get in without me knowing. Now, we were all locked inside together.

I went to look for them. First, I went down the three little steps, then right, to Eva's private study. Not a sign of anyone. Next, off I went through the massive main gallery. No problem, the lights were still on. Everything looked in place. No empty spaces on the wall. Nothing seemed amiss. The vast space was devoid of people, and intact. My footsteps could be heard as I walked the length of the cavernous room.

Ahead of me lay the tropical garden area that led through to Fine Arts. It had its own entry doors made of French glass. Opaque. Almost black. The space had a separate, additional alarm system. On the other side! The double doors would not open. I couldn't understand it. How could that be? Butler had left me to lock it down from the reception area. He'd left me to set the alarms to everything! Unless someone else knew the code? Who could that be? My mind went blank. Couldn't think clearly, blaming it on fear. I was alone. Totally responsible. What had I done? Had I made a major miscalculation?

Taking hold of the majestic brass door handles, I tugged. No movement. They wouldn't budge. It was solidly built. Bullet proof. I'd have to return to reception and release the alarm from there. Had I locked these people in? I hadn't meant to. Hadn't touched the alarm system for that area, yet. Couldn't hear anything. Not a sound, because of the mighty doors.

There was a gentle light by a crescent moon shining in above the cantilevered glass ceiling inside, creating wonderful shadows. It was a beautiful, ethereal space. Especially by moonlight. Dusk had descended. So I moved closer. I peered through the mighty doors, pressing my face up against the glass. The shadows made beautiful, sensual shapes. But wait! They were moving! How could that be? I couldn't believe what I saw! All those young people were naked. And copulating! Eva Goldberg's garden by the light of the moon had become the Garden of Eden!

Naked bodies were draped all amongst the plants! Naked bodies were making love! Naked bodies were having sex! I sprang back as if I'd done something wrong, and literally shook my head. Blinked my eyes. Looked again. There was no mistake. Nor had they stopped. The scene was one massive orgy. Then FLASH! And FLASH again! The flash of a camera. Someone was taking photographs of the group in coitus. The whole scene was lit up before my eyes like a scene from Decameron, Boccaccio's ground-breaking book of 1353.

What had I done? What would happen now? Oh, my God, don't let Eva or Barry catch me involved in this. What could I do? What would I do that would keep me from trouble? I found myself backing away from the scene. Slowly. Very slowly. Further. Further away. Then I turned, and started to walk back the length of the main gallery on tip-toe, hoping they'd not spotted me snooping on them. Certainly not wanting to be part of it! I didn't want to play their game. I chose my own partners. Mostly unwisely. But they were my choice! Tried to think. Think! Think! Think! By the time I found myself back at the reception desk, my head had cleared.

I know! I'll put on the loud-speaker system and tell them the gallery is about to close. That'll do it. But my voice? I was quivering. Surely my voice would too? I took three deep breaths. My finger hovered on the control button for the microphone. Telling myself to be brave, I did what I always do in an emergency. Took control. Went into my zone. Into command mode. Pretended to myself. The way I always sang to myself when I was a child, to comfort myself, keep myself happy.

"The Goldberg Gallery is closing now." My voice was not hurried, it was calm enough to surprise even me. It sounded very much in control, as if nothing untoward had happened. "All patrons must leave the premises. I repeat. The Goldberg Gallery is closing now. The building is being locked. The security patrol will soon patrol the building. And the alarms will be set. The Goldberg Gallery…"

Hardly had I finished my sentence, before the first couple appeared. Then two, then three… I counted six couples and an extra person, all fully clothed now, though one or two were doing up buttons as they walked past me, and out into the night as if nothing had happened. They thanked me politely as they made their way out while I held open the main front door. It was only when the last female made her exit that I heard a faint snigger.

Quickly locking the door, I was alone again. But I went back to check the scene. The way a housewife checks to see if the stove is turned off before leaving the house, worried that they might have damaged a plant or two. But no, on inspection, all was well. The moon still glowed in the balmy night sky, shining down through the glass ceiling from the Heavens. The stars twinkled at me as if to say 'all is well.' It was still beautiful. But the magic frolicking nudes had disappeared, as if they'd never been.

I dared not share the experience with anyone. Not even Georgie. It was not until weeks later, when Eva and I were un-wrapping a triptych for an erotica exhibition that the puzzle came together. A three-painting work depicting that orgiastic scene in the gallery was dancing before my eyes. I heard myself gasp aloud and put my hand to my mouth.

"What's wrong with you, Lilly?" asked Eva, looking at my shocked reaction to the triptych. "It's only a bit of youthful merrymaking. I thought you were more Bohemian than to be shocked by this bit of fun!" she scolded. "It even looks like my garden out the back. Who's the artist, Lilly?"

I was shaking but I managed to tell what I read on the back - the title of the painting - "The Twelve Nubile Sprites." And then I read the signature name on the front right corner. "De Bauchery."

"It's beeeeautiful! Don't you think?"

#

Beauty and love came to visit me on only two occasions at Mary Campbell's boarding house in Dundee when I was a child. The dour North Sea city was home to Kieller's jams and marmalade, and the famous tinned Dundee Fruit Cake. The city was also full of jute factories back then. All I imagine, gone the way of history now. But many Indian and Pakistani students who were studying the jute industry stayed at the boarding house, and they took a shine to me because they missed their families back home.

One day my favourite students dressed me in a sari made of the most exquisite, sparkling red silk.

"Please, Lilly. May we dress you in this Indian gown. We would like to show our families that we have a beautiful sister here in Dundee, just like our sisters at home," Askari said, his smile glistening against his cinnamon-coloured skin. He held a precious 'Box Brownie' camera in hand.

The three stood grouped in our living-room babbling excitedly. Ahmed held the golden red silk to my waist, and I was to spin round and round to encase my body in its shimmer. The outfit was complete when the last metre was draped over my shoulder to hang down. I felt like a princess as the camera clicked.

And later, when I was ill with Scarlet Fever - a contagious disease, I was placed in intensive care, on my own, desperate for company, and the three friendly students came to visit with a gift. Not permitted inside, they stood huddled together at my hospital window, and began to un-wrap the gift-parcel they were carrying. Each student stripping away a share of the paper, until finally, the most exquisite bride-doll appeared, lying beneath cellophane, in a window-boxed cardboard casket. I was speechless as I looked out from my hospital bed, crouching against the window pane to get closer.

"Look, Lilly," Askari had said, looking at me intently to read my response. "Do you not agree that she is a very beautiful doll?" His words were followed by the usual wobble of his head.

"And look how her eyes can open and shut," said Sundeep. "And what is more, she can talk." He took the doll from the box in which she lay, then with the broadest of grins, tilted it to and fro, until a wailing 'Mama' burst from its cherubic lips.

"And look, she has lovely long hair, like you, Lilly. Do you like her?" Ahmed queried, followed by the familiar wobble, and the great grin.

Surely my wet eyes gave them the answer?

"What will you name her?" They chorused.

"PONKIE." It was my Daddy Bob's nickname for me.

My new love was to be short-lived. On my arrival home from hospital, Mary Campbell declared that the doll was 'too good to play with.' She snatched it from me and thrust it out of reach, high up on top of the old piano in the parlour. There to sit, tantalising me from a distance. Never to be touched, or loved by me.

# CHAPTER 10

The gallery filled my days. My week-ends flashed by between visits to mum and my domestic duties at home. And, if I were lucky, Vince would fill my nights, although I was seeing less of him, not more. And my heart of course still ached for my babies. Making the meagre wage I was at the gallery, it was hard to save for legal representation, but save I did.

I was soon to meet Sir Sidney Nolan. He'd put Australia on the artistic map with his series of iconic figures from Australia's pioneering days. He painted flat figures in scenes that told vivid and colourful stories of the times, often depicted in a comical way, and was getting top prices.

"This work is all rubbish, Lilly," Eva Goldberg cursed, as she tugged to free a painting from its protective shield when it arrived as we worked together in the foyer.

I was her confidante, because Barry Butler and Georgie were busy in Fine Arts at the far end of the cavernous building. She was in one of her Machiavellian moods, and Nolan's work was about to cop a thrashing. His latest oils had just been delivered, together with a diverse array of his paintings, some stretching back to his first youthful sketches in the 1930's. Eva had scored a coup - a Nolan retrospective.

"I'm sure it will sell, Mrs Goldberg," I said, enthusiastically.

"Pah! His work's been rubbish since his first wife died thirty years ago!" she said, holding up one of the offending art pieces, making her face of disgust.

I'd come to realise that Eva's entire coterie of artists were subjected to her malicious tongue behind their backs. She told endlessly of their broken marriages, homosexual proclivities, their suicides, drug-taking, and broken love affairs. Eva loved every juicy morsel, and thrived on her inside knowledge of society's art icons.

"He's very pure and proper now, but you know," she continued, eager to add a punchline to her story, "he lived with his male lover for years before he married his latest wife!" She placed the painting up against the wall.

I made no comment. It saddened me to hear the way she spoke about these art world heroes.

"And you know what, Lilly, Sidney's son-in-law was a famous politician, but he didn't get voted into parliament the last time, and he felt so sorry for himself that he jumped out of a twenty storey window." She bent her head back to indicate the height. "And you know what, the window he jumped out of was Sidney's!" Back went the head again, this time in maniacal laughter. "It was a huge scandal." Eva's panther eyes screwed up tightly to divulge the next juicy portion. "His daughter was left all alone with no money, so she paints like Sidney, and uses the family name, 'Nolan,' on her paintings, giving her huge prices." She tugged at a two metre by two metre painting of an Aussie bushranger, while I held tight to the container it came in.

"Is that legal, Mrs Goldberg?"

"Well, she does it!" Up went the padded shoulders in an accentuated shrug. "And she sells a lot, and makes lots of money!" She paused to catch her breath before continuing on. "Sidney, and Mary his wife, live the celebrity life now, Lilly. They go on expeditions to Kenya, China, and New Guinea." She nodded to accentuate her point, and her eyebrows rose as if to ask if I understood his celebrity. "He's even painted pictures of the royal family, so now his paintings hang in the palace, with Michelangelo and Leonardo da Vinci!" Those brows arched even further, mockingly, then added, "Just look at this rubbish, Lilly!"

#

The day of Nolan's expected arrival had come, and there was an excited buzz in the air. Georgie had seen it all before. Despite loving art, she'd become a trifle cynical about the artisans. Gods with foibles are no longer Gods.

Butler was everywhere that morning, waiting to ingratiate himself with Sir Sidney and Lady Mary. He gaily preened in the foyer antique mirror without shame.

"Help me straighten this Delvagio," he demanded. Not only did he refuse to look at me when he spoke to me, he refused to use the word 'please.' He also refrained from using my name. I jumped up to assist anyway. He was referring to a painting which now hung above the long black sofa. All $95,000 worth.

It seemed an incongruous painting to hang in the glamorous front foyer of this beautiful gallery. It was an ugly painting, with a grimy feel to it. A vigorous, industrial, action-packed work, with a palpable heat emanating from it, depicting weary, dirty workmen feeding a raging furnace in a smelting works. As I regained my position at reception in the dangerous old swivel chair, I thought the painting would be better placed in the office of a foundry. I couldn't help but comment on it.

"Don't you think the legs of the subject in the foreground are too small for his body? It looks as if the artist ran out of canvas."

Butler stepped back to get a better perspective then shot me a look fierce enough to knock me off the chair. "No! They do not! That's exactly the sort of comment I'd expect from an amateur. I suppose you think you know better than Delvaggio?" He gave me a contemptuous look.

I didn't, of course, but I did know better than to argue with Butler. Like a tortoise withdrawing its head into its shell, I lowered my eyes and said nothing. I would be the first to concede I had a lot to learn about art. But in my opinion, art appreciation was no different from wine appreciation, it was simply a matter of individual taste. But in this case, I was absolutely convinced that the subject's legs were much too short for his body. It was plain for anyone to see! It reminded me of Henri Rousseau's work. A Frenchman considered a 'master,' who knew nothing of draughtsmanship, perspective, or the tricks of the Impressionists.

"Here comes Sir Sidney now," cried Butler, "the limousine just pulled up." He slid his thick fingers through the straw-like hair at his temples, and moved to stand at the entrance ready to greet the legend with his practised smile.

Georgie meanwhile, had answered the constantly ringing phone, and called out to Butler that his partner Xavier, was on line one.

"Bugger!" he cursed. "Why did he have to call now! I'll take it in Fine Arts," he said petulantly, "where it's quiet. But make sure somebody calls me before Nolan does his press conference in the main gallery." Then he stormed off to take his call in private.

"Must be important," whispered Georgie, through the partition. "Xavier's the boyfriend I told you about. He and Barry run the Gay Mardi Gras. They've been in trouble with Reverend Light. He's trying to close them down."

She saw my confused look.

"You don't think all the calls he gets here are about The Goldberg business, do you? He and Xavier have their own little gallery, darling, 'Campsite,' in Underwood Street. All the motor-cycle gays in their studs and leather go there." She gave a quick wink.

In walked seventy-four year-old Sir Sidney Nolan looking sickly enough to be a ghost. He was reed thin, stooped, pale, and clad in a loose-fitting grey suit, giving the impression that he'd recently lost a great deal of weight. Behind him trailed his frail wife Mary, shaking like a life-size puppet, her head bobbing up and down as she negotiated her entrance in jerky steps.

"Good morning, Sir Sidney, Lady Mary," I said, as both Georgie and I stood to greet the pair.

Nolan managed a gentle smile, and made a bee-line toward me. "New girl?"

Before I could answer, Lady Mary spoke out, so I merely smiled. She croaked like a raspy kitten, and said she was off to inspect the gallery, so Georgie bolted to help her down the stairs.

As soon as Mary's skeletal arm touched the railing, Eva's voice could be heard from afar. "Hello, Mary. How are YOU, Darling?"

Nolan came toward me, leaned on the reception counter, and gave me a warm, friendly smile. "You've got to be Irish my girl, with that colouring." Again, I was about to respond but was interrupted. This time by Eva herself yelling at the famous man.

"Sidney, DARLING!" She barged onto the scene rising from the gallery like Satan appearing from Hades. She vamped towards the great artist wearing a red 1940's style suit that was to die for. She walked with a confident swagger - legs splayed like a Broadway dancer, and forced herself on Nolan in a shrill welcome, with air kisses and embraces, nearly knocking the delicate man over. "Come darling, sit. We'll talk." And she virtually pulled him down onto the settee beside her, then draped an arm along the back of the sofa, ready to hold court.

Eva used language as a defensive tool for difficult questions, and at other times, times like these, as a seductive device, to charm and manipulate like a temptress. She was an accomplished actress. The gallery was her stage, and she was delivering another flawless theatrical performance for Sir Sidney Nolan.

"I thought we'd never get here, Eva," Nolan confessed. "Bloody long flight from England."

"Ah, but first class, darling. First class! Not sitting with the cattle. I've been travelling too, you know. Guess where?" Eva had taken over the conversation and did not permit Nolan time to answer. "I just came back from Kakadu. Wonderful! You should go, it would inspire you. I saw crocodiles this big." Her arms spread as far as she could stretch them, one slamming right across the front of Nolan's chest.

Watching, and listening with fascination, I kept my head low. I knew not to intrude on Eva's star performance. The gallery door swept open. It was a regular customer who immediately recognised Nolan. Boldly she approached him and asked for his autograph. She took up a gallery catalogue and produced a pen from her Hermes bag, and thrust them both under the Knight of the Realm's nose.

"It'll cost you," he blurted, defiantly, with a mischievous wink to me.

The middle-aged socialite thought he was joking. She tittered, but her hand remained outstretched, complete with pen and paper.

"Fifty thousand," said Nolan with a straight face, but with an Irish glint in his eye.

"I-beg-your-pardon?"

"Fifty thousand dollars for my signature. Why should I give it away for nothing? It's taken me over fifty years to make it valuable," remarked the shrewd old man.

This really tickled Eva and she burst out laughing, while the woman was left standing with egg on her face.

"Hmmph! Well, I never!" she spat indignantly, and scurried from the gallery, spitting chips, mumbling under her breath about how rude they both were, while Eva kept up the laughter like a crazed chimpanzee.

I could tell that Nolan was very pleased with himself. I too, allowed myself a smile, and shared it with him. But the frivolity was brought to a quick end, when a scruffy television producer appeared from the main gallery to interview the celebrity pair.

Eva wiped her wet eyes. "Look what you've done to me Sidney. I can't go on television like this. Tell them to wait for me." She leapt out of her seat and reached out for Nolan's hand and pulled him to his feet, and was off to do her face, leaving Sir Sidney to adjust his suit and straighten his tie.

It was then that he noticed the Delvaggio painting above the sofa. He took a step back to give it the once over, then he glanced around at me and said without preamble, "I don't like that! Looks like he ran out of canvas!"

Butler arrived back just in time to hear it, and to see the aged Nolan flirt with me. In retrospect, I realised that it was that very moment, that created the foundation of a stalagmite of jealousy.

# CHAPTER 11

"Butler's furious! You've been invited to Eva's mansion in Point Piper and he hasn't!" Georgie had raced out of her bunker to tell me the moment I arrived at 9a.m.

"I beg your pardon?"

"Seems Nolan took a fancy to you - the dirty old devil. He asked Eva to bring you along for one of her feasts, darling. You simply have to tell me everything that goes on! I'm green with envy!"

I slumped down on Mr Wobbly, rolling back involuntarily against the wall. Mouth agape. "Well, I never!"

"They're usually glamorous affairs, Lilly. You'll have to frock up."

All I could think about was Butler's reaction to this. "How long do you think he'll make me suffer?" I asked earnestly.

"It may never end," she giggled. "But it'll be worth it! Jean Metcalfe has told me how lavish it all is, even by her standard,"

"Who, Georgie?" I asked, still reeling.

"You know, Metcalfe, the newspaper giant in the U.K. Her family are friends with mine. Seems that Eva is as generous at home, as she is mean at work. You'll have gold crockery and cutlery, and chrystal goblets as tall as your arm is long," she said playfully.

"Oh, my!"

"The mansion is plastered with masters. Caravaggio, Monet, Rubens, Raphael, Dali, Da Vinci, and she has four Picasso's in the front entrance hall!

And of course, she loves Drysdale, simply loves him! 'The best draughtsman Australia's ever had,' says she. Oh, and Lilly," she smiled wickedly, "I do hope you like chicken. Eva's culinary expertise only stretches to her famous paprika chicken. For Henry, you understand, along with his fruit soups, probably strawberry."

Hearing approaching footsteps, Georgie scampered back inside her cubby hole.

#

Vince didn't seem at all disgruntled by my evening out when I rang to tell him. "Don't worry about me. I'll eat at 'Shippies' with the lads. See you at home when I get there. Could end up a late night." He was referring to a well-known sea-faring watering-hole he frequented.

The Goldberg mansion was on Point Piper's peninsula. The cabby knew where. Eva had instructed me to come straight from work to help her in the kitchen. I freshened up as best I could, perfumed, with my favourite Estee Lauder, and felt lucky I'd worn my red silk-jersey shirt dress that day, having been told it suited my dark hair and fair skin.

#

I was taken to the kitchen immediately upon arrival by a most courteous butler. I did not afford myself the indulgence of luxuriating in the grandeur of the man-made masterpiece that met my eyes, but I knew I'd probably never see the likes of it again.

As soon as I entered the kitchen, I met Sheila the charlady, whom I'd learn, was paid $5 an hour to scrub and clean The Goldberg's residence, and came from Tottenham in London, where Eva was born and bred. The irony of life. How different their destinies were, I thought as our eyes met, and she handed me an apron with Picasso's, 'The Lovers' adorning it. Sheila's tired old face said everything. There was sadness, poverty and pain etched in every deep crevice.

Tonight I'd meet some of Eva's favourite artists and socialite friends. Company I could only aspire to, being a new girl in town, and by their standard, penniless to boot.

The Sanderson's who lived next door, were the first to be taken to task. Eva was furious with them, for despite many pleas, they would not sell her the remaining four of the Nolan series they owned. Eva wanted to be named as the beneficiary to the Art gallery of New South Wales when she donated them. Her face, plastered thick with make-up like an oil painting, screwed up dramatically into that of a dried-out tribal elder at the reminder of her defeat when she told me.

"Angus is a retired British army general. His wife is nothing! Just a show-pony who lunches." She talked as she worked. Expensive cheeses were thumped down on the bench. "The Sanderson's have just returned from a three month world cruise aboard the 'Evening Star.'" Then she giggled, adding, "They said the voyage was way too long. Everyone wanted to kill each other at the end!" She laughed at their plight as she neatly assembled two large cheese platters for the table. "Twenty-one days is the maximum Lilly," she told me with some authority, as if it would one day affect me.

She took two sizzling casserole dishes from the commercial wall oven, then putting each down on a tea-towel, went about poking at them like an artist dabs at their painting, much like an afterthought. A 'finishing touch.' Tweaking her handiwork, as if the gentle prodding would make all the difference to taste and texture. She handed me a spoon and told me to try her paprika chicken sauce, though I feared how much paprika was in it. But sample I did, to find it was really tasty, and told her so, and was given the reward of a self-righteous grin.

"The Sanderson's made millions from Kathy's family properties here in Australia," she continued her commentary on the neighbours. "They sold all the family land to a Japanese consortium - $595 million. It's easy to make money that way, Lilly!" She delivered her look of contempt before placing the two casseroles back in the oven.

It did flash through my mind that selling-out was more profitable than a general's pension, and certainly easier than tilling the land.

She reached for an elaborately carved oblong box from a nearby shelf, brought it over to me, opened it to face me, and in an abracadabra moment, behold, I saw Kings Solomon's treasure. A magnificent set of gold cutlery that made me gasp. It was the effect she'd expected, because the smile came out before my gasp did.

"Sidney's been with me a long time, Lilly." Her maternal voice introduced itself. "I had to help him when he was young, you understand." She shrugged. "I made him famous, you know." Then her face took on a scowl, as if she'd held a grudge for years having had to help Sir Sidney Nolan financially, early on in his career. Had she not done so, she added, he would have starved.

"That was good of you, Mrs Goldberg," I said.

"Well, I needed to fill my new gallery, you know, Lilly," she said. "Pah! What could I do? I carried all of my artists!" She kept glancing at me for my reaction, so my empathy was working overtime.

It was praise she was after. It was free, and I was willing to provide it. How well I knew what to be taken for granted was like.

"Davotec! He's another one of mine that's world famous. He's a great story," she said with some pride. "He looks great for seventy six. He's got a new pacemaker, and had his cataracts done."

She took up a tea-towel emblazoned with a reproduction of the Mona Lisa. Then the smile disappeared as quickly as it had come, when she added, "But he's stone deaf, and he refuses to use a hearing aid! He's still painting though, and getting big prices!" She wiped her hands vigorously on Mona Lisa after rinsing out a bowl which had contained copious amounts of crushed garlic.

I listened as I worked. A half a pound of butter was given me to add to the cooked potato to be blended by the Bamix, then a measured jug of hot milk was to be slowly poured into it to make it into a glue called 'Paris Mash' - for Henry. The fluffy cream mash was to be emptied into fancy tureens which were to go into a separate warm oven, with more butter to be placed on top. Did Eva have murder on her mind, adding all that butter?

All during this time she ranted on over the top of the noisy Bamix. It was difficult to concentrate, let alone hear her. The art world's doyen raved on about Davotec as if she fancied him. It wouldn't have surprised me if she'd been quite a gal in her day.

Davotec was in fact a very impressive artist, with a distinctive style established during his pre-war years in Paris, when he'd splashed raw colour with bold over-confidence. During the war, his creative energy had found a new physical outlet with the arrival of the conquering Wehrmacht. In 1940 he'd joined the Resistance. Then, when Yugoslavia, his homeland, had fallen under the jackboot, he'd managed to return home and join the Chetnik partisans. He became notorious for his reckless bravery against the Nazis. Eva took great delight in telling me he'd killed Germans with his bare hands.

She went all girly on me, then warned, "Don't look into his eyes, though, Lilly. They'll frighten you." Was it the danger element that fascinated her I wondered?

She delighted in telling me about the wonders of plastic surgery, and I was to guess who among the guests had had their face re-sculpted. My first thought was, if it's so wonderful, then I shouldn't be able to detect it!

"You'll meet Maria Theresa von Brauchtich. Was married to Count Maximillian from Silesia. She's always crying poor, but her jewellery is crying real, Lilly! She has lots of money to spend on herself. She bought herself a new boyfriend. A young model type. To satisfy her, if you know what I mean. Must be only twenty-five years old. Takes him to Cannes, the Caribbean, New York, but she holds on tight!" She served up a wry smile.

"Now, off you go. Go mingle, and I'll go change. That way." She pointed through a long hallway where the evening lights of the glorious harbour flickered at me through the windows like Disneyland. I was in heaven. I'd promised myself that one day I'd take my children to Disneyland. Yes, they were always in my thoughts - no matter what.

# CHAPTER 12

On entering the sumptuous room decorated in the Palladian style, a modification of classic Roman, with grooved gold pillars, many mirrors and paintings which screamed money at me, I first spotted Henry, Eva's husband, sitting in a grandpa chair wearing his slippers and a droopy old cardigan, while those around him wore evening attire. The guests remained standing, grouped together, talking about the value of the dollar and the stock market. After seventy-six years of commercial hard grind, Henry had amassed hundreds of millions of 'fuck-you' dollars, and he didn't give a damn. He and Eva both had built their own, individual dynasties. His was all about money, hers about art, and self-promotion.

Despite Eva being known throughout the industry as a tyrant, I was coming to believe that she'd played a big part in the lives of her artists and their successes. She'd probably spent years 'mothering' them, for her own benefit, as well as theirs. Selfless, for selfish reasons. Her collection of artists were mostly household names. They'd been with her for years, and, from what she was telling me, she'd always made a point of paying them as soon as an artwork was sold. An ideal way of keeping them under her wing, ensuring she didn't lose them to other galleries after spending time nurturing them.

I recalled one day at the gallery, looking through the long metal filing drawer which held names, addresses, and the telephone numbers of her artists, when I'd noted that the word 'deceased' popped up on every other index card. She'd probably acquired those artists perhaps in their mid-years, seen something in their work that no one else had seen. Nurtured them. Then had out-lived them.

A maid handed me champagne in a Lalique goblet, which I accepted with a smile. Hanging back, I listened to the money talk, when a chap introduced himself. He was, I'd say, just touching forty, very pleasant on the eye, had thick black hair, the way that Greeks and Italians do, with a touch of colour to his skin, but was smoothly shaved, and had a lovely contour to his determined chin. He had bold, confident charisma, and penetrating, naughty dark, dark eyes. Was friendly and easy to talk to. He also appeared to be on his own.

"You're a new face?" he said, greeting me with a warm smile, champagne in hand. "What's someone so young and beautiful doing here amongst a bunch of oldies?"

I smiled at his impudence.

"Tell me. I insist!"

I was speechless.

"Okay. Cat got your tongue? Looks like I'll have to protect you. Stick with me all night and old age will never creep up on you."

I laughed, and found myself liking him. "Thank you, kind sir. If only it were that easy," I smiled, then made an attempt to be as jovial as he. "I'm a relatively new employee at The Goldberg, but it seems that Sir Sidney has taken a fancy to me, and asked that I attend this evening. How good is that?"

"Now, let's see if I can beat that...?" He pretended he was trying to think up something that would trump me. "Ahah, I know, I'm Henry's son! Believe that?" He teased.

"No."

"I'm... Eva's son?" He gave me a cheeky grin, as I shook my head playfully in response. "What shall we drink to... may I ask your name, young and beautiful lady? Mine... is William. I never give more detail than that on the first date."

"I'm Lillian Lightwood," I smiled, looking into his eyes, "and I think we should drink to champagne." I held up my glass boldly, showing no fear of a jousting session, glad I'd found a friend.

"Where would we be without champagne?" He said philosophically. We clinked glasses. "It's fine to clink when there's liquid in the glass, Eva tells me." His voice mellow, but strong and powerful, with no trace of accent from family or heritage. Then, suddenly he was reciting a little poem about champagne to entertain me. "You know what Madam de Pompadour said about champagne?" He looked from the sparkling liquid and into my eyes, to tell me that Madame de Pompadour was the Mistress of Louis XV. Then he affected a French accent, saying, "It is the only wine which does not impair the beauty of the woman, giving brilliance to the eyes, without flushing the face.'"

I couldn't help but be amused. I took another sip. "It really does dance on the tongue, but I find that I can't drink more than two glasses, it goes straight to my head."

He smiled, knowingly. "I think it was Napoleon who said, 'in victory one deserves champagne. In defeat one needs it!'"

"And you have plagurised that platitude just to impress?" I said to my new friend.

"Of course!" He grinned cheekily. It was a cue to allow him to continue his performance:

*"I drink it when I'm happy,*
*I drink it when I'm sad,*
*Sometimes, I drink it when I'm alone,*
*When I have company, I consider it obligatory,*
*I trifle with it when I'm not hungry,*
*I drink it when I am."*

He leaned closer to me, and I could feel his hot sweet breath on my cheek.

*"Otherwise, I never touch it – unless I'm thirsty."*

I laughed at his theatrics, and we continued to warm up our conversation like old pals as I surveyed the guests circulating around us. I was looking in particular for the Sandersons and Maria Theresa's toy boy when a woman in her fifties with a kindly face and a lovely smile entered, and walked straight over to William and I to introduce herself to me.

This was the Jean Metcalfe that Georgie knew well. As she spoke, I could hardly hide my enchantment at her sparkling, young, mischievous eyes. The bold streak of grey hair on the right side, that hung down to complement her face as it formed a gentle wave over the one cheek bone. A most pleasant looking woman, I concluded.

"Oh, you must be Lillian," she held out a hand as she introduced herself and we shook hands, then William and she exchanged gentle hugs, they knew each other well. "Georgie has told me so much about you. I'm a friend of her family in England, and I made contact with her as soon as she arrived in Australia. We've been friends ever since. A dear, dear, girl. We've had many a lovely evening together, and I've had the pleasure of showing her around Sydney."

"Oh hello Jean, please call me Lilly. I've been looking forward to meeting you, too." The more we spoke, the more interesting she became. She was well-read and well-travelled but did not boast despite her wealth. Worldly and knowledgeable would describe her at first meeting, then, after a more intimate conversation, I'd add libertarian.

"Are you learning lots of wonderful new things at The Goldberg, my dear? It's a fascinating world. You know, I once thought, that if we were to put Eva's artists all in a room together, we could never pick which one was responsible for which art."

I nodded in agreement, saying, "It's always a surprise when I meet the artist for the first time. The work doesn't paint a picture of the artist," then I couldn't help but make comment on Jean's amazing sapphire and diamond necklace.

"This set belonged to my great-grandmother Veronique," she said, fingering the amazing gems, which were the same purple/blue that Arthur Boyd used to represent the sky in his paintings of the hot Australian Bush. "My great-grandmother was French, from Parisian aristocracy, but married an Argentinean cattle breeder and lived in Argentina. I was lucky enough to inherit her exquisite jewellery collection. You know Lilly, you must come to the house with Georgie next time, and I'll show you. Rare museum pieces, some of them."

I must have had a grin like a Cheshire Cat because I saw William smile at me.

We three began to discuss art, and Jean said that her favourite artist was Kandinski, the Russian artist credited with painting the first purely abstract works.

William teased her, saying the public had been fooled by his 'wild splodges of colour.' He then offered his opinion. "My favourite, if anyone's asking, is William Dargie. An Aussie! Winner of the Archibald Prize, eight times. A real master!"

Jean just smiled at him good-naturedly. Their different tastes, but closeness, was obvious. I was impressed by William's choice, because Dargie really was a master of portraiture, and I was curious to know how much more he knew about art. But I was content to listen and watch their verbal swordplay, until I was distracted. My eyes were suddenly drawn to a young male model-type, whom I imagined to be the 'partner' of Maria Theresa von Brauchtich, who herself looked every inch the countess.

This young man was quite extraordinary to look at. So absurdly effeminate, but mathematically picture perfect. Angelic, and delicate looking, reminiscent of Botticelli's masterpiece 'The Birth of Venus' painted in 1485, where Venus has emerged from the sea on a shell, which is driven to the shore by flying wind-gods amidst a shower of roses. A show-piece, only to be viewed. I couldn't imagine this pair of 'dolls' having any wild fun together. Not even laughing together - it would stretch the skin!

Ready to discuss this vision with my new friends, William and Jean, in an artistic sense, my attention however, was drawn to Eva who had floated into the room wearing a full-length designer-gown in black sparkling chiffon. Noisily, as was her way, seeking attention, she began to round up the guests like a mother goose rounding up her goslings, to direct them from the loungeroom to the magnificent dining room.

We were instructed to form a line, in couples, like following on behind royalty, with the shuffling Henry in the lead, and Eva holding him erect, as she pulled him along. In the process whispering to me, "It costs me a lot of money to be nice to people," as she passed by.

William held out his arm for me and escorted me in. As we entered the dining room, I was nearly overwhelmed by the opulence. There would never be enough superlatives. The room was floor-to-ceiling mirrors, again with the Renaissance décor, and gold leaf, like Versailles, and I had personally seen nothing to compare with it. The gold cutlery, crockery, extra table-settings for mere decoration, and floral arrangements, seemed to consume the eighteenth century, ten metre long, French antique dining table.

The chairs were magnificent, with bold arms and more gold leaf. There were crystal candelabras full of gold candles that flickered at either end of the table, with a chandelier that hung above, the size of a car. And yes, the drinking goblets were just as my good buddy had predicted, as tall at your arm, from finger-tip to elbow. Enough to take one's breath away.

Eva finally settled Henry in his throne-like chair at the head of the table, as we all waited politely for her to specify where each person should sit. I was placed between Sir Sidney Nolan on my left, and my new friend William, on my right. As I sat surrounded by our reflections, between the dazzling jewellery the women wore, together with the sparkling mirrors, I thought it a trifle intimidating for a girl in a red jersey dress. I'd become very aware of my own presence amongst this monied gathering, though no-one else seemed to notice the decadence, or my feelings. But I was glad to have William to one side.

Everyone was talking at once, and there was a pleasant excitement in the air. Personally, I thought these surroundings would make tripe taste good. Knowing Eva as I did, I suspected she'd ask me if I could tell who the devotee of plastic surgery was. It was easy. Mrs Sanderson had really overdone it! Giving close inspection to the guests as I was, I became aware that there were thirteen people seated at the table. Didn't the Last Supper have thirteen? I hoped it was not an omen.

# CHAPTER 13

I was soon to witness something totally out of place. Jergen Jacobsen, a fifty year-old artist opposite, and one to my right, suddenly bent to the leather bag he'd hung on the back of his chair, pulled out a huge, ugly-looking medical syringe, pulled up his shirt to reveal his naked belly, clenched tight a thick handful of his belly-fat, then plunged in a syringe-full of insulin, and returned the syringe to its case.

No-one seemed to as much as blink, although I did glance over at Jean Metcalfe who raised an eyebrow. Then, as if sharing a secret, she looked down demurely. Although she too thought it the height of ignorance, our own etiquette required we ignore the uncouth offence. I thought it rude in the extreme. What was wrong with the bathroom?

Out came the strawberry soup, served up by two waiters dressed in black suit and tie. Where had they been hiding, I wondered? There was a continual hum of conversation that grew louder as more wine was consumed, with the odd laugh out loud, and the throwing back of a head. Everyone relaxed more by the minute, and as I sat taking in the scene I wondered what Georgie would think of it.

Some sat demurely, arms held in tight, delicately lifting the liquid strawberries by holding the spoon with decorum, fingers loose, dipping it in gently with grace, and gathering the gluey red mash in the gold spoon, from near to far, not making a sound, with mouths formed to make the perfect slurp. Some lapped it noisily like a cat, their tongue and jaw still emitting lapping sounds long after swallowing. Then gasping out loud, followed by a satisfying belch.

It was beginning to turn into a food orgy, with groaning and moaning once more wine took hold, with much filling of glasses of red, or of white, or expensive pink fizz. Till gluttony appeared along with the Paprika Chicken, when Davotec ate like a hungry cannibal. His head so low to the table, I could only see the top of it as he devoured the feast directly opposite me. He binged with voracity, no nibbling or pecking for him, only gobbling and guzzling, with a frantic chewing of French bread, mouth wide open, no hands to conceal the mastication. A burp, then a fart.

As for Nolan, he showed great interest in me, until he discovered that I was not Irish. Apparently he had a thing for Irish girls, or so Eva had informed me.

"SCOTTISH?" he said insolently. He looked at me over the top of his spectacles. "Oh, I thought you were Irish, my girl," his tone dismissive. He turned his back on me and hardly spoke to me after that. But thankfully, William at my other side was friendly. We got on well. He said he was in public relations, so I was able to talk about my television days when I was producer/presenter of my own programme in Brisbane. He was polite enough to seem interested.

I thought later, that I hadn't had a chance to look into Davotec's scary eyes, because suddenly, there was a commotion at the table. Davotec, being deaf, bellowed out a remark above the cacophony in answer to a comment by Eva. The way that some deaf people do, thinking everyone has the same complaint.

He boomed, "Who's a liar?" Everyone stopped to look at him.

"Not a liar, a FIRE!" Eva bellowed back, laughing, explaining that there had been a fire in one of her factories. The joke spread the length of the table, drawing sniggers and laughter from everyone, even old Henry.

Nolan was in the middle of a mouthful of paprika chicken, and, trying to swallow and laugh at the same time, suddenly gagged and choked, and started coughing. His knife and fork dropped, making a clatter, and he began to retch and splutter and gasp for air, grabbing, and pointing at his throat using sign language as if he'd lost the power of speech. Frantically he gesticulated, fear etched all over his face. He splattered and spat. He dribbled and drooled, his throat making hissing, rasping, guttural croaks and groans, with fragments of hot spicy bird shooting from his mouth over the antique table and everything in close proximity. And then he regurgitated till he disgorged what he'd swallowed with an expulsion of ugly vomit.

With eyes popping, and his spectacles tumbling from his nose and onto his gold plate, he pushed himself away from the table, and repeated the many gestures, gagging all the while. Then he staggered to his feet but quickly fell to his knees, knocking down his chair in the process, his hands at his throat. Everyone was alarmed but Davotec. He kept on eating.

Quickly pushing my chair aside and crouching over Nolan to sit him upright, I heaved on his diaphragm again and again. But he kept trying to talk, and indicate his predicament by pointing again and again to his throat. He was trying to say that a piece of bone was lodged there, and despite being able to manage small gasps of air, he was obviously still in danger. His face was turning blue.

William had, with great presence of mind, jumped to his feet and called for an ambulance, then he eased me away from Sidney, and without a second thought, stuck his finger down Sir Sidney Nolan's throat and brought forth a slither of chicken bone, along with blood and saliva, which fell onto the thick Persian carpet.

Eva was screeching and screaming like a mad woman. The young narcissistic Adonis and his countess had fled the room. The scene was much too ugly for their aestheticism.

"No, Sidney. No!" Eva, unable to stand still, was pacing up and down. "You can't die at my dinner table. I'll never live it down! Don't die Sidney. Don't die!" Her guests meanwhile, stood back to give William room to work.

Mary, Sidney's wife, was wailing like a moggy, so while William thudded Sidney's back, and poked down his throat, I tried to comfort Mary as best I could with Eva screeching throughout.

The geriatric artist managed to keep gasping for breath till the medics arrived, and was whisked off to hospital accompanied by Mary and Eva. One medic told us on the way out that had we not taken action, Eva's house guest may not have survived. I began to tremble after the event, which is usually my way. William became aware of it, and went straight to the drinks cabinet to get me a brandy. He returned with a grand brandy balloon and offered it to me.

"Here you are, Lilly," he said, thrusting the crystal at me. "Drink this. Gulp it down. It'll steady your nerves. I'll see you home." He presented me with a generous Napoleon cognac.

I thought better of it, but my shaking hand said that I should.

It would transpire that the ambulance crew had to perform a tracheotomy on Nolan because he kept passing out. Fortunately, the actual paramedic who tended him had no idea who he was, therefore was undaunted by his fame. To him, Nolan was just another elderly patient, and with a steady hand, he cut Sir Sidney Nolan's throat, prising the bloody flesh apart to insert a tube through which his patient could breathe.

Next morning, Goldberg Gallery staff congregated together in reception to read the newspaper reports of the incident. Georgie thought I should receive a medal for my performance, saving Sir Sidney's life. My eyes shot to those of Barry Butler when she said it. His response was scorn. I said nothing. Later, Georgie declared that the least Sir Sidney could do was give me a free painting.

The newspaper headlines declared: 'SIR SIDNEY NOLAN NEAR DEATH."

It was not a good time to be around Eva, because the paprika chicken jokes had already begun to surface in the art community. By mid-afternoon a multitude of people had called, or visited the gallery to quiz Eva about the incident. Centre stage, in the limelight – Eva's favourite spot. Her favourite role – storyteller. Her tongue loosened a little more, and the drama increased with each telling. But her defences were up nonetheless.

"It wasn't my fault!" she yelled, after answering one of the calls, slamming down the telephone in reception as if to break it. "He did it himself, the stupid old man!" Then her look of anger suddenly changed to one of pleasure. "But it will push up the prices!" she grinned.

When Georgie and I shared a glance through the glass partition, I saw her mouth the words, and point her finger at Eva. 'I wish someone would cut HER'S.'

Suddenly, a hatchet was flashing before my eyes. I was back in Dundee as a very young child. I had not yet been to school. My Daddy Bob and Mina had gone to Australia and left me behind in Mary Campbell's boarding house..............

It was freezing cold, I remember. The mud squelched under her boots as she marched with bloodied axe. Squawking chickens thrashed for freedom in feathered hysteria as she grabbed hold of a pair of legs and jerked the plump victim through the open door of the wire cage. Deftly, using her foot to keep the chicken in place on the wooden block, a swipe of the hatchet lopped off its head. She hung the carcass for plucking. And in much the same way, she repeated the barbaric ritual, wiping her blood smattered cheek with her sleeve. In the morning, Mary Campbell would tear at the greasy carcasses, pluck and ravage the feathers in mechanical enmity, and gouge out their innards. My young eyes were never protected from such sights.

So often now I got these flashbacks of my past. It hadn't happened to me in my television days. Was the gallery taking its toll on my health? My mental well-being? My relationship with Vince? I didn't exactly feel loving, let alone sexual, after spending a day at the gallery with Eva. Vince was a high-maintenance man, and I just wasn't there for him. Nor he for me. Between his needs and Eva's demands, I was feeling like a wound-up toy bumping into furniture, unsure of which way to turn, afraid a total melt-down was inevitable.

# CHAPTER 14

Expecting another stressful day at the gallery with the unpredictable Eva Goldberg, I was pleased to find that neither she nor Butler had yet arrived, so all was peaceful. Between dramas caused by Eva's volatile mood swings, Butler's sarcasm, and his manipulative schemes designed to make we girls look bad at every opportunity, the gallery seemed like a battle-field. Georgie and I treasured any time we were alone together.

This was one of those precious times when she spoke about home and family. Her eyes came alight when she told me stories of her fiancé Jeremy Fellowes, and I must admit I felt jealous. My relationship with Vince seemed to be going nowhere, and this conversation made me aware of it.

"Jeremy is such a dear. You know he phones me every single day to tell me how much he misses me. He's flying out again to give me a special birthday weekend in July. I can choose whatever I want to do. Wherever I want to go. I think we'll just go to the Ritz and stay in bed!" she laughed.

She sounded so very much in love with him.

"I can't wait to have his babies."

I suddenly became choked up, but I hid it well. I'd never found the right time to tell Georgie about Kate and Adam. It's not that I didn't trust her with my past, it just seemed to be so ugly in comparison to the life she'd led, and I didn't want to tarnish what we had.

"You know, Lilly, I even love his mother, because he's so good to me!" Her eyes twinkled as she gave me an impish grin.

Then the gallery door opened to let in a freezing wind, but our visitor was the delightful Jean Metcalfe, valued patron of the gallery, and dear friend of Georgie. And, it would transpire, to my great good fortune, that Jean would become a true friend of mine as well. But for now, Jean and I, having shared the evening together at Eva's mansion, could share the colourful story of Nolan first hand, for Georgie's benefit.

Jean mentioned that brother-in-law Keith, the newspaper giant, had just bought *The News on Sunday*, to complement his other British tabloids in the UK, and revealed to us that he was having teething trouble with his new 'baby.'

"I'd like to buy him a little something for his desk," she said, smiling her gracious smile. "Do we have any Shona, or Petrocelli sculptures that would be easy to send?" She glanced around the reception area.

My mind shot to a tiny bronze sculpture that had been sitting on a shelf ever since I'd joined the gallery. It was a piece so small that it could fit into the palm of a hand, and would make a great paperweight. I jumped up, went over to a sliding glass case beside Georgie's bunker, withdrew the sculpture, and proudly held it out to Jean.

"That's just the very thing!" she said. "How clever of you to think of it." She cradled the perfect piece in her hands, and lovingly admired its beauty. A very tactile piece, which she obviously liked. A tiny, nude, new born baby in the foetal position, curled up, and fast asleep.

The precious sculpture meant a great deal to me. I felt connected to it somehow. The baby was beautifully formed, and looked so peaceful. Naturally, it reminded me of my own children. And again in the course of five minutes or so, I'd managed to hide my heart-ache. "It's a work by Donald Friend," I told her. "He knows the human shape so well. He made it in the 'Sixties,' and has only just presented it to sell. Let me wrap it for you." I reclaimed it to wrap while Jean gave me her credit card to pay for it without asking the price, which was four thousand two hundred and fifty dollars. Although, personally, I was sorry to see it go.

While I completed the purchase, the girls caught up with family news. Then suddenly Jean asked us if there was anything wrong with the heating.

"It's so chilly in here. You girls must be cold, sitting here all day?"

"No, darling, there's nothing wrong," Georgie volunteered. "She just won't spend the money! Mean as can be!" Georgie was no longer reticent to hold back her criticism of Eva, despite being in Jean's company.

But my head swivelled around quickly to look at Georgie, showing how alarmed I was. I was big on loyalty. Grumbling at home, or between Georgie and me was one thing, but I would never dare bite the hand that fed me. Jean could see I was ill at ease about Georgie's outburst and was quick to put my mind at rest.

"It's alright, Lilly. I've known Eva for many years." She gave my hand a comforting pat. "She's rather famous for her parsimony." Jean smiled playfully at the thought of Eva's tight hold on her cash. "I remember one time, when Sir Robert and Lady Mary Oliver from Bath in the UK, asked if they could use the grand piano for the opening of their antique silver exhibition. Their daughter was a concert pianist, and would perform to maximise sales, but the old Steinway – the oldest one in Australia - which just sits there, day-in day-out, was touched by nothing more than a feather duster. Miserly old Eva wouldn't part with a cent to have it tuned, and didn't tell the Olivers until it was too late. And, I'll have you know, that the Olivers are first cousins of The Queen. Tell me, did Georgie ever share the Mrs Pembroke story?"

She sat down on the big black sofa to tell the tale, while Georgie stood leaning against the doorway to her burrow, wearing a scarlet sweater she'd knitted herself, with matching red slacks and fancy red brogues, totally unaware of how amazing she looked. "I told you Jean was great fun, didn't I?" she said.

"We lived in the same building at the time," Jean began, while I risked my life back in Mr Wobbly to listen with interest. "Well, I've seen Eva angry. Many a time! But never as bad as that first encounter on 'Mrs Pembroke Day!'"

"This one's a corker," said Georgie, ready now to brave the big black sofa to join with Jean in the telling of the story.

"It was when she was moving into the penthouse on the eighth floor. What she didn't know, was that old Mrs Pembroke, who shared the seventh floor with me at that time, had died two weeks before, but nobody knew for days." Jean removed her gloves and placed them beside her handbag. "Eva was up and down in the lift all day moving in, and got madder as the day went on, because, although the old dear was brought down in a thick medical plastic bag, the most over-powering odour still lingered in the lift."

Georgie made a face.

"I myself had just returned from overseas, and I felt a little guilty when I became aware that she'd died," said Jean, adjusting the loose leather cushion behind her back, "her body left like that for days." Jean went on to explain that Mrs Pembroke did have family who lived close by, but said they were negligent about their visits to her. "She died alone, poor dear!" She looked genuinely sad at the memory.

"Horrid family!" Georgie remarked, flicking back her long blonde locks.

"It was the trouble Eva caused with the body corporate, pardon the pun. She demanded to know why she hadn't been contacted. She was very unhappy in that building right from the start. That's why she bought the great mansion next door. I don't think she ever really unpacked."

\#

No sooner had Jean Metcalfe departed The Goldberg with the gift for brother-in-law Keith, than Eva entered, loaded up with shopping for Henry. Spotting Georgie out of her chair, she shot her a nasty glance of disapproval, but decided against saying anything when Georgie rushed to her aid. She needed attention - she was in one of her moods. Her family had been giving her grief, and sadly her miserable frame of mind seemed to float in when she did, and hang like an invisible mist on every painting.

"My daughter bought a huge diamond," she said to us, as the shopping landed heavily on the reception desk. Demanding an audience was de rigeur, no matter what we were doing. "Henry was furious with her!" she thumped down noisily on the desk with a jewelled fist, making my heart pound. "He said, 'You stupid girl, thieves would cut off your finger for such a diamond!' So, you know what she did?"

"No, Mrs Goldberg," we two said in unison, like conjoined twins.

"She had a replica made!" Up went the hands in the air! Our faces must have been blank. "Don't you see how stupid that was?" Two hands were on the counter now, arms splayed, as she leaned in towards me.

Too afraid to give a wrong answer, we were silent.

"Pah! Henry went crazy! He threw his coffee cup on the floor and broke it. He kept yelling at her, saying, 'You're even MORE stupid now, because now they'll cut off your finger for a bit of glass!'" Again she thumped, and we jumped.

Full alert, Georgie, thought I.

Eva barged behind the reception desk beside me, and got busy rummaging through papers looking for her private telephone book just as the phone rang, while Georgie cleverly took the opportunity to make herself scarce. Eva snatched up the phone to answer it herself, almost bowling me over, without an 'excuse me.' I was forced into a tight space with her, so I pushed my rickety old chair back out of the way to make an exit.

Suddenly she yelled at the top of her voice to Georgie before I could find open space. "GEORGIE! GEORGIE! Pah, where is that silly girl?" And because she was standing right beside me when she screamed, I jumped with fright. Her voice was shrill. Like a fishwife castigating her child for playing in the mud, not telling them once, but over and over, and over again, each mouthful building her anger until she justified it with a hiding. This blind fury sent me back thirty years to hear Mary Campbell's voice from the past............

"Come back here, y' wee bastard," Mary Campbell called out after her youngest boy Andy, as the family walked to the church for the Funeral Service in the bitter cold. "Gi' me a look at y' before y' go runnin' off."

Andy hurried back for inspection while his eight year older brother Ian held a sadistic look of pleasure on his face, ready to enjoy watching the young lad get a wallop.

"Oh, Christ Almighty, what the hell have y' been eatin'?" She grabbed young Andy roughly by the collar, pulled out a handkerchief, spat on it, then wiped round the lad's mouth.

He knew better than protest.

"Now, ah'm warnin' y" she yelled at us. "Dinna pit a foot wrong, or y'll be sorry. An' dinna speak 'till yer spoken t.' The reverend thinks we're a respectable family, so dinna forget it!"

With whisky-driven pride, Mary Campbell marched us to the Victoria Road Presbyterian Church wearing her Russian Astrakhan fur coat and hat, perceiving herself to be the epitome of respectability, with never a thought to the fact that her three children had been fathered by three different men. None of whom had been her husband. Whilst I was the bastard child that no-one wanted! Abandoned firstly, by my American serviceman father. My mother - Mary's daughter - a famous musician. And foster parents, who'd left me to immigrate to Australia, and sent me back to my grandmother Mary, at the boarding house. Where now, at five years of age, I could be usefully put to work on my hands and knees scrubbing the linoleum floors. I was expected to earn my keep.

After the service, we walked in a light, drizzling rain, and Mary was heard to mutter, 'Happy is the bride that the sun shines on, blessed are the dead that the rain falls on.'

Gathered together around the graveside, standing on the rain-soaked St Andrews Church cemetery ground, the relatives and friends whispered amongst themselves. Then the stirring sound of a hymn wafted out over the still air. The coffin containing Hugh Campbell's body was lowered into the ground as the minister said a prayer, and delivered a short sermon.

"All life is a struggle, both without, and within. There are conditions against which man must contend. His very existence is a series of efforts and accomplishments. His measure of humanity depends upon his measure for wrestling successfully with the elements of nature without, and with the enemies of virtue and truth within."

His words were meant to bite. Suicide was a disgrace.

From under a black veiled hat, the deceased man's sister told Mary in no uncertain terms, that she would not attend the wake. She blamed Mary for his suicide.

Two female cousins whispered nearby.

"Was depressed. That's why he did it, Morag."

"Did it to escape her, I'll bet. Heard she's got a fancy man already! And she's let the poor man's bedroom before he's even cold. And how d'you suppose she came by those fancy fur coats of hers? Not from ten shilling's bed and breakfast, I'll be bound! It takes real money to buy furs like them."

"You don't mean…?"

"Aye, I do! A good man was Hugh. He fell, you know. Broke his ankle. Got gangarine. Mary can wring a chicken's neck, slaughter a pig with the best of them, but said the stench of his rotting flesh was enough to turn her stomach."

When it was all over we walked home, shivering, and chilled to the bone. I heard and saw it all. I must have been only five, but it lodged in my memory forever more. When we reached the house, again we were warned.

"Wipe y'r feet thoroughly at the doorstep, d'y' hear, I'll no have ye bring Death into the house!"

# CHAPTER 15

I forced myself to think of happy things in quiet times. Eva would be at the Art Gallery of New South Wales swanning it with Edward Dribble and his entourage, Butler would be in Fine Arts making his personal phone calls, Georgie might be at lunch, or running errands for Eva. A customer might have left after a purchase, and a friendly chat, that would leave me smiling. My emotions seemed to be hovering right on the surface these days, and when I was low, the thought of my missing children haunted me. I felt emotionally vulnerable here at the gallery. High highs, and low lows.

I would reach back in my mind for happy memories with my Daddy Bob and Mina. They had rescued me from the Boarding House - for a while. I often thought of them now, and I hadn't for years………….

Recent snow flurries caused by icy north winds direct from the Arctic Circle had created a frosted jewel-like coating on the city of Dundee, which glistened in the magical twilight of a Sunday evening in January. Even industrial Dundee had its moment of beauty in the snow. I was four years old, and had just had my last Christmas with Mina and Daddy Bob, although I was unaware of it then.

Explosions of laughter resounded crisply in the freezing air. The spirited sounds of children and happy families from two year-old toddlers, to grandparents in their eighties were braving the icy conditions to play in the snow. Rugged up in brightly coloured hats, scarves, mittens and overcoats, the lucky ones wearing fur-lined boots, all adding life to the pristine scene of winter. Cheeks glowed, eyes sparkled, and hearts were glad.

William Wallace Parade had turned into nature's perfect sledge run, and a merry assortment of homemade sleds took squealing children racing down the slippery slope.

My friend, big Frankie McDonald was to take his turn, while I waited impatiently next in line for my turn at the top of the brae, jumping up and down at the thought of the anticipated thrill.

As soon as he took off with a hefty push from his dad, I jumped into my fire-engine red sleigh, custom-made by my Daddy Bob, with the name 'Ponkie,' the nickname he'd given me, emblazoned on either side. Exhilarated by the thought of the ride ahead, I gave an excited wave to Mina and Daddy Bob waiting to 'catch' me at the base. With gloved hands holding tightly to the reins, clad warmly in a blue gabardine pants suit, with a matching bonnet not quite big enough to imprison all of my curls, I squealed with excitement from the expected thrill when I felt the familiar push on the sled from adult hands behind me. The voice said, "Off you go now, lass. Careful, mind!"

I quickly gathered speed down the mighty slope, and with a rumbling from beneath the juddering sleigh as its metal skies licked fast the slippery ice beneath, I felt a similar rumble in my breast from the joy of it. Controlling the mighty carriage like a professional all the way down, the icy air stinging my cheeks as I flew. I pulled hard to one side to negotiate the curve at the bottom, arriving with a smile stretched across my face, only for my steed to topple over on a mound of packed snow at the base of the slide, sending me tumbling out onto the hard ice at Daddy Bob's feet.

I remember that Mina let out an involuntary gasp, and put her hand to her heart before running over to me. The blood drained from Daddy Bob's face. He stooped to reach out to his treasure. I lay motionless on the hard ice. Afraid of what he would find, he blasphemed under his breath, then remembered where he was.

"Oh my, Ponkie, are you all right? Are you all right, lass? You haven't hurt yourself, have you?" He feared the worst when he picked me up, for I lay like a limp rag doll in his arms.

But when he looked into my face, and stroked my cheek, I opened my eyes, and burst into a fit of the giggles. I had been pretending, again.

"You little devil. My, you had me worried for a minute. My word you did!' He hugged me hard.

Mina and I exchanged winks.

"That was the best fun I've ever had!" I heard myself say.

My mind raced again to my own precious, golden-haired children. I hoped they were having fun, wherever they were, and I cried a silent tear.

# CHAPTER 16

"So I have to go on my own, Vince?" I said angrily. I'd just showered, was ready for breakfast, and was hit with the news of an unexpected trip just before I faced another day battling Eva. Vince and I had been invited to meet with the renowned artist John Olsen at a cocktail party at the gallery that evening. Olsen was to give a descriptive talk about his artwork, his style and method, then demonstrate his technique. He'd just returned from Italy, and had some newly inspired paintings of Provence to show off. Vince had promised me he'd come. Not only was I disappointed, I was becoming increasingly tired of our situation. Since we'd come to live in Sydney our lives had changed, and I hardly knew him anymore. "You're always letting me down, Vince. Where will you be this time?"

"Back in Brisbane," he said, packing his best suit. "Sorry, but I have to go to the Gold Coast for the weekend. Life's tough when you're the boss," he said, smugly, putting his shaving gear in his small suitcase along with his gym gear. "Conference. See you Tuesday."

"Tuesday?"

"Sorry, Lil. That's how it is. It'll slow down. I promise. Don't worry about breakfast I'll have something at the airport. Must fly," he added facetiously, giving me a peck on the cheek.

What was the point of complaining? He always seemed to have an excuse. Besides, he had a plane to catch, and I had to get to work by nine. I panicked if I was late. I didn't like to keep people waiting. I was always early. Never late!

It was only a short distance through the winding streets of Paddington. Sydney's New Orleans. Where two, three and four-storey Victorian terrace houses stand row upon row, street after tree-lined street. A century ago – a slum. Today, gentrified, and inner-Sydney's most trendy address, with its mostly beautiful, and expensive terrace houses, and lilac coloured Jacaranda trees, of great majesty and beauty when in flower. The negative side of living there, was cockroaches, cockroaches, cockroaches. Big, black, cockroaches!

Again, as I hurried, I heard the little girl's voice in my head screaming frantically, totally out of control - in fear of not getting to school on time for my very first day.............

"I'll be late! I'll be late! I'll be late…"

"Name?"

The teacher repeated the question in an aggravated tone when I didn't answer.

"Name?"

I couldn't speak.

She thrust her head down into my face, reminding me of a snowy owl from a fairy story. The woman's head movements were jerky, her nose hooked and sharp. Her spectacles round and thick. Her voice, shrill, but clipped and determined. "Come, come, now child," Miss Dracker said, her head wobbling profusely, before pulling in her chin until it disappeared. "You must know your own name, child?" she retorted condescendingly.

The other school children in the classroom let out a roar of laughter. She growled at them. They hushed.

Then she turned again to me who stood alone by her chair for this inquisition. "WELL? Don't you? Don't you know your own name, girl?"

My head bowed in shame, and the tears began.

"Oh, my goodness me! Your name, girl?"

Did she have to speak so loudly at me?

"Lillian," I squeaked in fear.

"IS-THAT-ALL?" She belted out the words which began with a roar, and finished as an indignant question.

The class sniggered aloud, adding to my shame.

"Well, what else, is it? That can't be ALL you've got, surely?"

More sniggers.

She jerked back in her chair, paused a minute, then grabbed my hand, stood, swivelled me around, and marched me to the door as I cried tears that choked me. "Never in all my thirty years of teaching have I encountered such a to-do. Over a name! Bless my soul!"

The words tumbled forth as she dragged me out, and, holding open the door, she told the class in no uncertain terms that they should 'sober up,' and practise writing their names in their jotters until she returned. She had led me outside the classroom in a march, and banged shut the door behind us.

"Now!" She began her interrogation again. "Now," she repeated, with a deep sigh, folding her arms in front of her. "Tell me what this is all about, girl." Suddenly she seemed giant-sized as she peered down at me.

I looked up fearfully into her exasperated face. Mine was stained with tears. All I could offer her was my truth. "I don't know who I am, Miss. I really don't know what my name is. My gran says I have to call her 'mum,' and that I should be named 'Campbell' – like her boys. But my real mother said I should be called after her new husband, Mr Worthington. I don't know where my father is… I don't know who my father is."

My head bowed once more at the disgrace of it. Then my demeanour changed as I remembered. I looked up proudly into the eyes of my inquisitor as I pleaded for empathy, understanding, and a solution to this 'disgraceful' problem. "But I've got a Daddy Bob… and he said I was HIS little girl, and he's a Baird!"

# CHAPTER 17

The Goldberg was all abuzz. An Erotica Exhibition was to be held the following month, and the artists had begun sending in their artworks, each one more shocking than the last.

Eva came bouncing in elated about something, ready to throw her heavy bags of shopping down on the reception desk, her umbrella still damp. I had a pile of letters typed and lying there, so I swept them up quickly, as soon as I heard her at the great glass wall of an entry door. A practice I'd mastered.

With childish glee she started squawking about an article she'd read about Donald Friend, in the *Sydney Morning Herald*. Donald was one of the gallery favourites, and an icon in Australia. He was to play an important role in the forthcoming exhibition. Eva made us stop everything to listen to the article about The Goldberg she was to read aloud. For this performance, Georgie was permitted to come out of her bunker.

"'While there are canvases from a variety of renowned international artists, the main body of work is from Australia's Donald Friend. This major Goldberg Gallery exhibition includes representation from such world greats as Picasso – three blue period pieces – together with the best from Australian artists. David Hockney offers us whimsical treatments of the male organ, making them funny, rather than erotic, more a mockery of the male apparatus.'"

She was enjoying this review. Could obviously see the dollars roll in as a result.

"'Brett Whiteley provides the only truly exciting, erotic work, catching the explicitness and urgency of mood. However, as always, Donald Friend's work will be popular with a certain sector of Sydney society, owing in the main to his controversial experiences in Bali. There, with the wiggle of a little finger, he could find a number of nubile male subjects to meet his needs – artistic and otherwise.'"

Eva looked up at her small audience with the look of a child celebrating its birthday.

"'Reputedly a one-time boyfriend of Errol Flynn, and a flamboyantly handsome Oscar Wilde character in his day, Friend is now afflicted with emphysema and other ailments. His wiggle finger no longer holding the same power, he has settled back in Australia to end his days. In his youth, the lure of his particular Indonesian siren had obviously exerted its spell, for Friend returned time and again to reside on the island of Bali. He built a moat-encircled studio and home, and within its confines seemed to have found himself a haven.'"

Hardly stopping for breath she continued excitedly, as Georgie and I reacted accordingly.

"'Now sixty-nine – Donald Friend, a shortish man with a round, character-lined face, articulate and voluble, looks at the world with passion tempered by caution. A romantic realist whose current days are filled more by memories than inspirations, his lungs shot to pieces with the complaint he chooses to ignore as he chain smokes his way to the cemetery. Friend, the obese and aging gargoyle, is, in this upcoming exhibition, obsessed with the beauteous spirit of youth, its energy, its innocence.'"

"This is wonderful! Absolutely wonderful!" Eva said, looking up to deliver her sparkling smile at me, just as Butler entered the scene from the main gallery. "Mr Butler have you seen this?" she queried.

"Yes. I read it earlier, Mrs Goldberg," he said dismissively, as if to mock this female assembly, and moved off in the direction of the small gallery, mumbling as he went, saying that he needed to talk to the framing boys.

Eva continued. Nothing could dampen her spirits. "'We are presented with Friend's bliss in Bali, with languid houseboys draped in sarongs, or brownly nude. Some sit and play chequers, some leisurely squeezing limes – the best in the world, says Friend, for his mid-morning gin. In his Bali of yesterday, he is lord of the manor, both mentor and employer. A man of importance. A demi-God.'"

Eva boasted that she'd been to his moat-encircled paradise, and said how she loved Bali, and the Balinese. "It's so beeeeautiful there, girls!" Then excitedly read more. "'Some have likened Friend to Gaugin, some to Rasputin. Youth has always been important to him, ever since he lost his own. He grows older, but his canvases remain ever young, giving Friend a Dorian Gray-like quality. He will never draw or paint as in those Bali days. Which makes this exhibition the last of the Bali works all the more attractive to buyers. In an introduction to his exhibition, Friend has written, 'I am an old monkey, clever but not wise, mischievous without malignancy, aggressive or defensive as occasion demands, desirous of respect, contemptuous of familiarity.' Those who know him well, call him, 'The Devil.'"

Eva hopped up and down with unabated excitement, waving the newspaper in the air triumphantly.

Little did she know that Georgie had written the article, under a nom de plume. She'd had it accepted because of her tenuous link to Keith Metcalfe. My dear Georgie was not only a lover of art, but a manipulator of words, and would one day, make a great writer. Eva had no concept that all of her antics, her vulgarities, her 'colour' was being transcribed to paper as we worked. Georgie was forever jotting down the daily scenes in her diary, and we kept that a precious secret between us.

Eva's glee would be short lived. The word was out that a new gallery was to open virtually opposite The Goldberg, and she spotted the enemy's gallery van from the corner of her eye as she danced, suddenly changing her mood from reveller, into that of a tyrant. She rushed to the front door and screamed right through it at the enemy van parked outside her own front door. Her joyous mood had disintegrated before our eyes.

"NO! You will NOT park in front of my gallery!" she screamed, before fleeing outside like a mad woman to shoo the driver away as if he were a stray cat.

Georgie and I shared a look of expected trouble. Would it be another difficult day?

When Eva returned to the foyer, her face was red with anger. Her temper had got the better of her. I often had fears about her blood pressure.

"That Treadmore Gallery will NOT park their van in front of my gallery! Do-you-hear me?" Her foot stamped on her hallowed ground. "As soon as you see him girls, get rid of him. Do-you-hear-me? I want you to inspect the street every hour and let me know! Georgie, I want you should spy on the gallery. Go over and see how big it is, and come back and tell me. NOW, Georgie, NOW!" She pointed outside, then repeatedly jabbed a finger toward the door, urging Georgie to hurry. "See what they're doing to the terrace over there. GO!"

"Yes, Mrs Goldberg." Georgie immediately set off to obey her orders.

Eva stood at the open Goldberg Gallery entrance waiting for a report on her new opposition.

I simply waited to see the outcome.

"It looks as if they're totally gutting the terrace, Mrs Goldberg," Georgie advised on return, several minutes later, "to open it up for one big, blank space. There are workmen everywhere." She looked at Eva and waited for further instruction, but none came.

"Pah!" Eva cursed, turned, and re-entered, followed by Georgie, and the tirade began. "That damned Oliver Treadmore said he would NEVER come back to Sydney! Not ever, because of all the doggy pooh in the streets." Her arms flailed about as she ranted. "Why did he come back, that damned man? The doggy pooh's still here! Maybe I should send him a welcome card, with a big lump of doggy pooh in a box!" She laughed at her own joke.

Georgie moved quickly to take a duster from the cupboard in her office, to find a job and make herself scarce, while Eva moved to the partition between reception and Georgie's bunker, and slid the window shut with a thud. Flopping down heavily on the small, three legged stool, close to me, legs apart, she began rubbing her calves. Was she aware I could tell what colour knickers she was wearing?

Clearly, Eva wanted to talk. Her mood had suddenly changed, from excitement and glee about the newspaper article, to anger about Oliver Treadmore, then drifted on from anger and disappointment, to one of contemplation about life itself. I was expected to be her audience.

"Mr Butler's depressed," she began. A compassionate voice made a debut. "His closest friend died of AIDS. Too many of his friends have died, and he feels it's getting too close to him now. He told me about a big dinner party he had recently for Xavier's birthday, where twenty-seven out of the thirty boys there, had it."

I could only listen. Her sympathy for Butler seemed to be genuine, and a painful grimace accompanied every word. Everyone was saddened by this most heinous disease. It was robbing the art world of its talent.

"First Rock Hudson, then Liberace. And I know Warhol was bi-sexual." She nodded to me, her sole sympathiser.

I knew her well enough by now to expect the daily topic to circumnavigate in her mind as if travelling on a train circuit, right back to her own plight. Sure enough, she went on to confide intimacies about her husband Henry. How, that in her eyes, he'd become no more than a nuisance now that he was old and helpless. She told me how the housekeeper had to scold him for his thoughtless, aggravating, petty domestic habits. Like using the talcum powder in such an extravagant way, that he sprayed the whole bathroom when he used it, causing the angry housekeeper to clean the walls each time. How he dropped his peas on the carpet when he ate, then trampled them in when he stood. How he left the toilet bowl in a filthy manner when he discharged and splattered his volcanic, igneous bowel movements, sprayed his urine on the toilet seat, or the floor, and sometimes wet the bed, and more.

I had come to learn that listening to Eva's woes was an obligatory part of the daily ritual. There was no escape. I learned to nod in all the right places and mirror her face.

"You know, Lilly, my husband was a very powerful, brilliant man." She swivelled precariously on that stool like a teenager. "But look how sick he is now. He's bent up and shrunk!" She made a sour face and hunched her own bent back to imitate Henry's stooped posture. "Henry's afraid to die, Lilly. He cries in his sleep. He really cries like a baby. He keeps me awake all night.

And I must get my sleep, Lilly. What can I do?"

This was all served up with dramatic pauses, hand gestures, and elastic grimaces for effect. She spoke to me like a beloved relative on these occasions. But at any other time she was hard to 'manage,' because her volatile nature was so unpredictable.

I could well do without her cancerous vitriol, day after day. Having to jump to the neurotic woman's constant demands, I was beginning to feel over-loaded. Plus, there was Butler's pettiness to contend with day after day. He was hardly civil to me now. He hated to see Eva and me in intimate conversation. She'd begun to call me her 'angel,' when she was in a good mood, and boy, did Butler hate that! I thanked God for Georgie, every day.

Eva continued feeding me her pain. "I go swimming in our indoor pool every morning, five o'clock. To keep healthy, you understand. After that to the hairdresser, before I come here." Then out of the blue. "Do you have a nice young man Lilly?" she asked provocatively, rubbing those calves. Without giving me a chance to confirm or deny, she said, "Clever girl!" I'd said nothing. I would never share my private life with her.

Never would I tell her I was finding it increasingly difficult to talk to my 'young man,' Vince. He was preoccupied with his new job. He showed no interest in gallery matters, so it was useless having a conversation with him about it. Besides, he was never home, which meant I was unable to share my woes with anyone but Georgie, and dear Jean Metcalfe, when we three had a meal together. I was feeling perpetually tired, and felt more troubled with each passing week. Not that Eva would have cared. Her next comment will stay with me forever.

"You remember that girl you helped the other day, Lilly? The one in the chair?" The vixen showed its face.

Indeed, I did remember. The plight of the teenager had been indelibly imprinted on my mind. The girl had been left a quadriplegic after an automobile accident, and had since withered to skin and bone. I'd helped her enter the gallery when I saw her waiting at the entrance, and with Georgie's assistance, had physically lifted her out of her electric wheel-chair, and sat her frail body down on the big black sofa, until we carried her chariot down to the main gallery, and put on the brake to steady it. I'd been astonished to find she weighed next to nothing.

Then, we physically carried the disabled girl down the three steps by joining our hands together under her, as she tried to remain upright in our arms. Gently, we lowered her into the chair, and strapped her back in, leaving her to operate it, using her one, very limited, yet mobile, twisted hand. All this was done at her request.

"You see," Eva sniggered, wickedly, "it was good that you helped her. She came back to buy that painting she liked! She got plenty of money from her accident! Good girl, Lilly!"

I felt positively ill. And wished Georgie had overheard for her memoir.

# CHAPTER 18

The next morning began badly. I stepped in dog droppings and had no time to return home to change my shoes, and subsequently throughout the morning, I was sure the stink of doggy-do accompanied me everywhere. Already behind schedule, I'd left all manner of jobs undone. Vince didn't know how to use the washing machine, and he'd wanted a particular shirt washed for the following day, so I demonstrated the workings of the machine to him and left him to it.

I felt so uncomfortable in dirty shoes, that I told Georgie I'd race home for lunch, change the shoes, have a quick yogurt, and clean up my morning mess rather than face it at night.

Pulling on the brake, I switched off 'Jeremy Jag's engine, and let out a big sigh. I just sat there for a minute in the driveway of the old house in Selwyn Street, trying to regain my equilibrium. Then I walked toward the door. I unlocked it and pushed it open.

The scene which met my eyes left me breathless. I walked through to the kitchen, and stood at the dining room doorway trying to reconcile the fearsome sight in my logical mind.

Large drips of water were seeping through the kitchen ceiling and were splashing on leftover breakfast things in the sink. One particular drip was playing a tune on a dessert spoon sitting in a corn-flake bowl. The sugar, a large bowl of fruit, the teapot, the tablecloth, the breakfast dishes, the lovely Tasmanian oak table, and the carpet below, were a soaking soggy mess. As was a basket-load of my clean washing sitting on a chair. Looking up, I could see that the whole ceiling looked decidedly unstable.

Then, as if struck by lightning, I bolted up the stairs to the bathroom, having remembered that Vince had used the washing machine before leaving home. I took the stairs two at a time in my high heels. Running through the upper hallway with my feet hardly touching the ground, I found water gushing out to meet me.

The sight which met my eyes in the bathroom took my breath away. Water lay eight centimetres deep, and for a split second, I feared the very floor beneath my feet would give way as I waded through to reach the washing machine - the obvious source. It was as I'd imagined. The rubber tube from sink to washing machine had slipped out, and was aimed at the floor. Water flowed like Niagara Falls. Directly below was my newly painted kitchen.

Frantically I turned off the tap, kicked off my saturated high heels and fled. Back down the stairs; back to the kitchen to grab buckets, pans, towels, anything I could think of to scoop up, and soak up the water.

With only enough breath left for a desperate prayer, I reached the kitchen just in time to have the entire kitchen ceiling come splashing down on top of me with a thunderous crash, and a huge white plastery cloud, followed by the Niagara Falls of water! Then silence. Deafening silence. And a vast gaping hole where my kitchen ceiling had been. I sank onto a chair – stunned. Unable to as much as force a tear. I sat covered from top to toe in a coating of white plaster. My hair had turned white. My beautiful black suit looked ruined, as did my discarded kid shoes.

There was only one thing for it. I shook the wet white plaster from my hair, took off my jacket and skirt, searched among the debris for the electric jug, and made myself a coffee. And sitting there, in my undies amid the chaos, sadly shaking my head, I looked pitifully up to where the kitchen ceiling had once been, and said aloud, "I didn't really need this. What's in store for me next?"

In my despair, I rang Georgie and told her I wouldn't be back to work that day. I sat with my lonely mysery, wallowing in it, and in flashed another ugly scene from another time and place. That too, had passed, I told myself. Life must improve.............

Clutching a raggedy old 'teddy bear' while I ate my porridge, with wee Andy crying pitifully in his playpen, she lifted him and used her apron to wipe the slime from his nose, and jigged him up and down on her hip to quieten him. His tears subsided, and his curly black head burrowed into his mother's pendulous breasts, and his thumb found his mouth.

The black Bakelite wall phone rang. Mary Campbell snatched it from its cradle, answering, "Dundee Guest House… Och, it's you, Sophie. Can y' no come in this morning? This bloody funeral will set me back days! Just when ah was hopin' t' wash some blankets an' get them dry in the windy weather. Oh, an' ah have an'ither joke, for ye'. What's the meanin' of 'indecent'?" she laughed, then continued, "If it's LONG enough, THICK enough, HARD enough, and it's IN far enough - it'd be in, DECENT!" She roared with laughter. "That was telt t' me by a New Zealand bomber pilot last night, when ah booked him in. Great big fella he was too. On his way to Inverness – the special anti-submarine trainin' school. Had Maori blood in him. Bet he had a whopper!"

#

Days later, again I was behind schedule at breakfast time because Vince and I had words. I needed to talk, but each time I'd tried, I was hit with a brick wall.

"This has got to stop, Vince. We're going nowhere," I grabbed a chance to get some attention before he headed out the door for work. Silly, I know. But I had no choice. He was hardly ever home at nights. And if he was, he was fast asleep on the sofa.

"I did warn you about this new job. Don't say I didn't, Lil"

"It's ridiculous the way we're living. We're living separate lives."

"For God's sake. Listen to you. Nag, nag, nag."

"Vince… please…"

"Don't Vince, me… I'm off to work. Don't be like this when I get back, or I'll go right back out again!" Then he left, slamming shut the door leaving me in stunned silence.

Now I had to face another day at the gallery listening to Eva.

Jumping into the car, I reversed down the driveway too fast, and with a great screech of brakes, turned the wheel, pointed Jeremy Jag towards the traffic signals at the corner, and raced to beat the red light. Jeremy Jag had come with me from Brisbane. I loved the old dear, a 1962 Mark 2 Jaguar, complete with whitewall tyres.

Red. Always red when you want them to be green. I slammed on the brakes. The sound of Jeremy's revving engine sent my pulse racing, and I found myself bouncing impatiently in my seat like a five year old to try to motivate the lights into changing. The words, 'I'll be late. I'll be late. I'll be late,' filling my mind, just as they had when I was a child. Then, and only then, did I see the motorcycle cop standing on the pavement opposite, arms folded, watching; and worse, now he motioned me to pull over to the kerb. "Who me?" I said aloud, stabbing a finger to my chest.

"Yes, you," he mouthed, and nodded with a none-too-happy look on his face. His own finger determinedly pointing to a spot along the road.

I groaned. When the lights changed, I put my foot gently on the accelerator and carefully drove to the designated spot. As I pulled up, flushed with indignation, I sat waiting for the policeman who seemed to take forever to walk across the road and come alongside the driver's door. Feverishly I wound the window down and looked up at him like a guilty child who'd broken a window, for that was exactly how I felt.

His speech was emitted in a growl. "Good Morning, miss. That was a snazzy bit of backing you did there."

I was so embarrassed I was dying a little inside, and hoped that none of my neighbours were watching. Why did the policeman have to be standing on my corner of all corners? "I'm sorry, officer," I responded, full of contrition.

Luck was with me. He issued nothing more than a lecture about driving out backwards like a Le Mans racer. I left him standing there, watching me like a hawk. The fact that he didn't take his eyes off me made it all the more embarrassing. I took off with an almighty kangaroo hop like a learner. Glancing back at him in my rear-view mirror, I saw him shake his head as if to say, 'Women Drivers.'

Close to 9am, I parked the car not far from the gallery's main door. The gutters were streaming with rainwater from a recent downpour. I grabbed my brief-case, handbag, and a thick folder containing samples of material for new curtains, and brochures of French Provincial furniture to show Georgie. I'd been collecting them, to perhaps update the furnishings in the terrace. Slamming the car door shut, I went to stride away but was abruptly pulled back with a mighty jerk. The tail of my coat was caught in the closed car door. Most everything fell into the gutter, and scattered, then began to float downstream. I let out a yell and a satisfying expletive.

The whole soggy mess would have to come into the gallery with me to be disposed of. I couldn't leave it all there polluting the street. I turned to see Charlie the framer, just as another shower came down. He came quickly to my aid.

"Oh, am I glad to see you, Charlie!"

"Here, let's rescue the coat, first, shall we?" he said, opening the car door to free me. "And let me have that folder before you drop anything else." He gave me his grandest grin.

"Thank you, Charlie. Thank you."

"Bad start to the day, huh?" There was always a twinkle in his dark, mysterious eyes.

"What can I say?"

Together, we retrieved the soggy paperwork.

"Always happens when you're in a hurry, doesn't it?" he said kindly.

"Always. And frankly, Charlie, I always seem to be in a hurry!" I smiled back at him. "I really will have to slow down. A policeman gave me a stern warning this morning." He raised an eyebrow at me as we scurried inside. "Where have you been, lately, Charlie? I haven't seen you since you came to collect the damaged Margaret Olley frame."

"I've been waiting patiently in the wings for you, Lilly. I figured that you'd find me when you were ready!"

"Charlie!" He was famous for his quick quips. I just enjoyed him.

We shared a laugh.

"Can I make you a coffee? It's only us girls in this morning."

"Sure. Love one!"

We each had a big mug of coffee, and caught up with news, me at my desk, Georgie on the stool, and Charlie on the black sofa. As we sipped, and enjoyed Charlie's company and his happy disposition, he told us a colourful story about his time away recently, at a health farm in the hinterland, in Queensland's rainforest.

"Nudism was part of the action, and I brushed up on my tennis," he said, that cheeky grin appearing again.

We two girls gasped in mock horror.

"Amazing story, really," he smiled.

"Georgie will steal it for one of her books!" I jibed.

"That's okay. Feel free, Georgie."

"So, you played tennis, naked? I hope this isn't going to be too rude, Charlie?" I asked playfully.

"You can make up your own minds," he grinned at us. "My opponent at the tennis game was Olga Svenson, a very well-built Swedish girl. Big. Blonde. And beautiful."

"Well-endowed, you mean?" asked Georgie. "Must get our facts straight, Charlie."

"Yes. That too!" he laughed.

"So?" we asked melodiously.

"Everything was going great. There we were, prancing back and forth, totally naked, like innocent babes, whacking away at the ball. And all the time Olga's boobs were bouncing up and down, and my balls were blowing in the wind."

"CHARLIE!" We chorused.

"Well, that's how it was! But my thoughts were pure. I swear. Completely on the game. We were actually having a serious game."

"AND THEN?" We asked in duet.

"The strangest thing… Olga started to feel cold, and stopped the match to put on the bottom of her track suit, which meant that she was now, only topless."

"YEEEEEES?" We said, like Tweedledee and Tweedledum.

"Well," he grinned. "I began to feel aroused. I couldn't help myself. It was looking at those huge boobs. It was embarrassing, really. I hadn't even noticed them before, but as soon as she put on those pants…!"

I found myself biting my lip to stop from laughing, but Georgie couldn't hold back, she roared out loud, and this only encouraged Charlie to be even cheekier with his tale.

"And once I became aware that I was getting aroused, I began to feel my pride and joy bouncing against my legs. Well, that was the end of it. It just got bigger and bigger, slapping against my legs, until I had a 'Roaring Roger.' I'm not one to be embarrassed. With or without my clothes on, but I blushed like a schoolgirl."

"OH, CHARLIE!"

# CHAPTER 19

"I want a room wi' a water view. I'm stuck here a' the time, so I want the best!" She huffed.

It was just not on. All she need do was walk a few metres, and there was the glorious sea! If ever she became incapacitated, there was a fleet of wheel-chairs at her disposal. She was living out her days in the best that money could buy. This situation at the water's edge was unique by any standard. Sydney's northern beaches had hundreds of small coves, and every one of them delivered a magnificent view of paradise. The peninsula on which the facility stood was to die for. And of course to die in!

There were sailing boats. A ferry close-by. A pedestrian walk. Manicured lawns. Palm trees. Many species of exotic birds. An attentive and caring staff. I almost, almost wished it were me here in the lap of luxury.

Feeling guilty that I couldn't part with any more money, it was a sad journey home. Mary had told me, time and time again, that if it weren't for her 'taking me in,' I'd have been in an orphanage. I was always grateful, and forever reminded to feel grateful. For every morsel of food. For the roof over my head. Little did she know how often I'd wished I'd been placed in an orphanage, to at least be equal to other children. Many's the time the threat of being sent to the Dr Barnardo's Home had sounded like a grand idea!

#

I'd just come back from my lunch break at the bistro along the street from the gallery, where I'd seen two devine little children of around two and four; a boy and a girl who were sitting with their mother at the next table. Although excitedly chatty, they were very well-behaved, sitting up straight in their chairs, their hands below the table. It was obvious they'd had experience in dining-out. Both had lovely blue-eyes, were curly headed, with the most beautiful golden curls. They struck up a conversation with me about their favourite ice-cream. The boy liked raspberry, and the little girl favoured chocolate. They were so sweet that I felt my emotions stir, so I bade them farewell with moist eyes, and hurried to leave.

I was soon cheered up, because when I entered the gallery I found William talking to Georgie in the bunker. He turned to look my way and smiled, then came to welcome me with a kiss on the cheek.

"Great to see you, Lilly." His joyful spirit was very welcome.

"I received a note from Sir Sidney, William. Here, I'll show you." Going behind reception to collect it from my private little drawer, I showed it off proudly.

William took it from me and read the complimentary words I'd always treasure, and which, together with the signature, according to Georgie, were as valuable as any Nolan painting! The note read, 'Who would have known that you had nursing skills to add to your other talents? Your friend, Sir Sid.' William was obviously impressed.

"This is indeed something to treasure, Lilly. Keep it safe!"

We exchanged pleasantries until the phone rang, and I had to get busy. With a friendly wave and a smile, William took his leave through the bullet-proof glass doors.

Answering the phone, I heard my mother's voice, and replaced the receiver quickly, hoping she'd think she had a wrong number. Eva was hovering. I resumed my seat, and was just about to type a letter, when Georgie called out to me in muffled tones, to tease me about William's recurring visits to the gallery.

"That's the third time he's been in this week, Lilly. I think he likes you. It'll be a lunch invitation, next."

#

"I've come all the way by truck from Ballarat," said the rather dishevelled looking woman in her sixties, as she hauled in a six by four metre painting, wrapped haphazardly in cardboard. "I've got five more of these in the truck. Parking's not good around here. Is it?" She let the package slide from her grasp and land on the foyer floor, then turned and went out to fetch the rest of her work, saying, "Mrs Goldberg will love these. Erotic plants," said she, referring to the stylized paintings she had to offer. A variety of trees, plants and flowers of every description, having sex, as animals and humans do.

While Georgie volunteered to give her a hand, running out after her, I took the first of her paintings down to the main gallery, not wanting the entrance area blocked. Eva was holding court with journalists and photographers in the main gallery. They were all around her, shooting footage, taking photographs, and writing copy for the forthcoming, titillating erotica exhibition. The artists Eva had chosen to exhibit had left no pose undone - Karma Sutra diagrams in artistic form.

Eva normally had little time for the art critics, saying they were usually failed artists, with no talent. Now, they were valuable to her. This was national coverage she was getting. The Goldberg Gallery was on the front page. Daily. Even the BBC had sent their Sydney camera crew.

"There's nothing nasty in this," I heard her insist to the waiting throng. "There's nothing pornographic! Lilly? Lilly, come here. Am I right?"

My God, she wanted me to rescue her! Where the devil was Butler when we needed him? I stood close as if to protect her from the crowd of vultures.

Eva moved to a particular painting by Donald Friend, and the crowd followed like a swarm of bees, to be shown a detailed painting of two male nudes copulating on a Bali beach. The penis of one inserted into the anus of the other. Two sets of hairy testicles visable, as were their neat, tightly-pulled-in buttocks, and arched backs, in a gymnastic feat that only Friend could conceive. The rapture on the subject's faces at the time of double ejaculation was unforgettable.

Eva spoke out in favour of the work. "I think this should be shown on the front page of your newspapers! It's a natural act. It gives great pleasure, as you can see by their euphoria. What is wrong with a little joy in the world today? Am I right, Lilly?"

My heart nearly stopped. "Yes, Mrs Goldberg."

"Donald Friend is a master of his craft," she continued. "This is a work of taste by a man of great artistic spirit. He is an honest man, and we should be proud of him!" Her ostentatious gold bracelet jangled as she waved her arms to give dramatic effect to her words. Flashing her pearly whites at the group of startled reporters, she gave an outrageously young female journalist a copy of the latest publication from Donald Friend, a book entitled 'You May Fondle For Pleasure.'

Eva then read an excerpt from a book to the television crews. "'He possesses the bawdiness of a medieval monk, the wit of Moliere, with flashes of Oz humour.'" Eva continued to extol the virtues of the exhibition while the young female reporter flipped through the illustrated tome, glancing at me with shock etched on her sweet face, then handed her copy of the book quickly over to her male counterpart.

"Too hot to handle, love?" he whispered, grinning.

Eva gave her version of a sales pitch, critiquing several of the artworks and the lude sculptures and statues, some life-size, which left nothing to the imagination. Then she moved the crowd on to a two by four metre artwork depicting a nude man lying on his back in a 'personally volcanic moment.' In another, an Indian prince gazed out at the viewer. He lay, reclining on a couch whilst his most masculine possession was being painted blue by an enthusiastic young lady. Eva proclaimed this to be "A beautiful erotic work of great symbolism."

When she finally broke free, she was accosted in the gallery's foyer by the woman from Ballarat, who insisted that Eva not only look at her work, now standing uncovered against the wall, but buy it, and display it!

"This work is rubbish!" Eva declared. "Rubbish, I tell you! NO! It's not for us! Pah!" And she stood her ground eyeballing the grey-haired woman, with the confidence of her reputation, and her money in the bank as back up.

Ballarat babes too, can be fiery, and this one gave as good as she got from Eva. But it did her no good. Eva had her quickly escorted from the gallery by

Butler who'd decided to make an appearance. The despicable Butler was more than willing to tackle an aged female pensioner.

Georgie and I felt for the poor old dear. After all, she'd come all the way from Ballarat, been rejected by Eva, then been turfed out by Butler, who used no civility, no compassion, nor any care when dumping her precious artworks back onto the tray of her truck. Butler re-entered the gallery with a grin, slapping his hands together as if wiping dirt from them. I wouldn't have been surprised if he'd been a bully at school.

#

The up-coming erotica exhibition had stirred another forgotten memory from Dundee............

I heard sniggers coming from the ice-cold scullery at the back of the Dundee Boarding House where extra produce was stored. Five years old, and curious, I stopped to listen as I passed by.

My grandmother was stooping, snooping, one eye peering into a peep-hole in the wall, while Sophie, the daily help, was digging-in to a fifty pound bag of meal with a large wooden scoop to make swill to feed the Campbell chickens.

Sophie was huge; her obese frame filled the doorway. "Huv ye no plugged up that hole yet, Mrs Campbell? Y'll get caught for sure, one day," she panted, out of breath from her condition.

"Och for Christ sake, Soph," Mary returned in a whisper," it's the only pleasure ah get that does'na cost me anythin'. An' the bastard's are none the wiser! They're too busy jerkin'. Come an' have a look." Her eye returned to the peephole.

Sophie shook her head.

Then Mary turned again with a wicked smile on her face, saying, "Y'll never see a piddlin' wee poker like this yin, Soph! Nae wonder the pair man did'na show any interest in me. He'd be affronted t' show that bloody shrivelled up sausage t' any decent lass!"

Only now, all these years later that I'd remembered the scene, did I make sense of what Mary had been up to.

# CHAPTER 20

Eva had informed the police that the media were defaming her in their columns, and had made a formal complaint. The truth was, she was loving every minute of it. All the attention brought out the best, and the worst in her. The precocious child in her was thoroughly enjoying it, while the vixen was already counting the cash. But she was about to get more than even she had banked on.

A dozen policemen walked in through the gallery door. And none looked like potential buyers. The Goldberg Gallery was being raided by the Vice Squad. The inspector in charge made a cursory inspection of the artworks on show, as Georgie and I held our breath. Knowing Eva didn't like anyone restricting her, in any way, we thought this could be all out warfare. We knew she wasn't the type to give up without a battle.

From the top of the stairs, Georgie and I listened, and stole glimpses of the scene. Butler turned cowardly, making a quick retreat to Fine Arts. These detectives were the authorities, not little old ladies from Ballarat. Eva however, was standing her ground as expected. Defiantly she folded her arms and made a formidable foe. She denied out loud that any pornography was involved. "NO!" We heard her yell at the police inspector. "How can you judge? You give out traffic tickets! You know nothing about art. What qualifies you to object?"

Georgie and I ducked our heads back in as if we were afraid of being struck by a flying object. We thought the inspector did well to take it from Eva. But he did have an army with him. I'm sure he thought it amusing that she dared to have a tantrum in front of him. Of course he knew he'd win in the end - he'd come equipped with a court order. Eva was ordered to either cover up particular artworks, or have them confiscated. He'd come to censor, so that the artworks did not offend public morals.

Eva protested. "But they are works by Australia's most famous artists! They hang alongside masterpieces by Picasso. They'll leave the gallery over my dead body!" She fought like a tiger."Look what you've written here." She waved the court order about. "You can't even spell the artists' names!"

"Look, Mrs Goldberg, if you prevent my men from carrying out their duty, I'll have to arrest you," the inspector said gravely.

"NO, NO!" she wailed, throwing her arms about. "I can't go to jail, I have to go home and cook Henry's dinner!" She came dashing up towards reception calling out my name. "Lilly! Lilly! Call Justice Viers. Quickly, Lilly!"

Eva's long-standing friend Justice Alexander Viers was on the scene in minutes – he lived somewhere close by. I was pleased to see him wearing a tailored jacket for the occasion, and not his usual Hawaiian shirt.

Eva ran to him, clung to him as if he were her big brother come to save her. "They want to vandalise my exhibition, Justice Viers. There are no grounds for them to remove anything, saying this is all pornography. That is totally absurd! It is censorship gone mad." She stood looking at the Vice Squad as if they were scum.

"They say I am degenerate, Justice Viers, but this is art! BEAUTIFUL ART!" Letting go of Viers, she flung her arms outwards in a dramatic flourish to illustrate the artworks surrounding her, saying, "The world is a very dark place, Justice Viers, and these works are life-affirming. You must save this exhibition from these regressive, uneducated, soulless men."

With an air of authority reflecting his high office, the judge intervened on Eva's behalf, just in the nick of time. The Vice Squad were unlikely to take much more from Eva.

"Gentlemen, gentlemen, let us not be too hasty here." Viers admonished the policemen as if they were infants, with his chest puffed out. "The paintings are tame by any modern standard. Only a few buttocks and a bit of harmless frolicking. Even D.H. Lawrence's exhibition of sexual fantasies was allowed to go on show in the thirties – a much more conservative era."

Georgie and I watched, fascinated, as Viers managed to first calm the detectives, then sway them to his way of thinking. The mere presence of this eminent citizen pacified the Vice Squad, to the degree that they departed after covering up just two of Brett Whiteley's paintings, with strict instructions that they stay covered.

But this too, was enough to grab the attention of the media again, which incidentally split into two camps. The highly amused, and the highly indignant.

*The Daily Telegraph* front page headline said, 'Granny Defies Police On Dirty Pictures.' While *The Sydney Morning Herald* editorial featured a long admonition of the police, opening with, 'The time is long past, since Michelangelo's David was displayed plus a fig leaf by official decree. Erotic art is as ancient as man. And this exhibition reflects his most bizarre tastes. But more bizarre by far, is the action of the self-appointed art critics on the Sydney Vice Squad.'

The Court Order also required that Eva display a notice outside the gallery door, warning those who found erotic art offensive against entering the gallery.

"I'll write it as small as I can," said Georgie, always obliging.

"NO! Make it big, Georgie," Eva instructed. "Make it BIG! Then all those nosy parkers will come in!"

The intervention of the Vice Squad was a godsend. The curious and the titillated streamed through the gallery door in their thousands for a solid two weeks. The exhibition was a sell-out. In fact, Eva could have sold everything three times over. Everything went, including the two be-draped Brett Whiteleys – they sold on the first day.

"You know," Lilly," Eva said with a glint in her eye on the last day of the exhibition, "it makes me wonder – how can we bring these Vice Squad men back? Another erotica?"

#

ENGLAND. My Daddy Bob and Mina had immigrated to Australia and left me behind with Mary Campbell. The sight of the big black taxi in my mind's eye woke me from my slumber to remember the scenes............

Sophie took my hand as we stood outside the London train station on our arrival from Dundee, after a day-long journey. Her huge frame waddled from side to side as we made our way to the cab rank. We were going to my 'real' mother's house in an outer London suburb.

The engine revved up as the stately iron gates opened automatically to allow the cab entry to the tree-lined driveway. The twin row of elms widened gradually to show the magnificence of the graceful mansion beyond. Sophie's eyes had never seen such grandeur, and the Lord's name slipped from her lips in disbelief. "Y' needna switch off the engine," she yelled at the cabbie, "this'll only tak' a minute." She heaved herself awkwardly along the back seat, inch by inch, panting, pushing me ahead of her, and out onto the gravel at the foot of the wide front steps. The cabbie put my suitcase at my feet.

"See that yer on yer best behaviour now, lass, 'cause that husband o' hers indoors is a right frosty bastard!" Sophie wheezed, gasping for breath to fill her smoke-damaged lungs. She rang the doorbell which was answered instantly by a smartly dressed butler.

"Oh, my!" he exclaimed, looking us up and down, disgust etched on his haughty face, "You should have gone to the servant's entrance. All deliveries are made at the rear of the building!"

"Och, ah'm too auld t' bother wi' that sort o' nonsense. I hope ah dinna miss ma train o'er this fartin' aroon'." Sophie pulled an envelope from her pocket and handed it to the snooty butler. "That'll explain aboot the bairn. Her grandmother canna stand her greetin,' so ah' was telt t' bring her doon here for her mother t' mind." She gave me a mighty shove in the middle of my back, forcing me into the unfamiliar building, and the butler to jump aside as if I were diseased.

"But surely, SURELY," he exclaimed indignantly, "you're not going to just LEAVE her here?"

Sophie was already lumbering her way back to the cab, her swollen ankles hardly able to carry the load. She had a train to catch. Back to Dundee.

#

The gravel crunched noisily beneath Nigel Steele's size twelve boots as he marched towards the 1934 Bentley. His eyes lit up every time he saw his 'Buxom Barbara.' He loved the musty smell of her, and the way pretty heads turned when the rarified vehicle passed by. He kicked one shoe against the other in turn to rid them of any loose gravel, opened the solid front door with gloved hand, pulled himself up and in behind the wheel and closed the door shut. The reassuringly solid thud gave him a renewed feeling of vigour.

He made himself comfortable on the bespoke leather seat. Looking in the rear-vision mirror at his own reflection, he adjusted the rake of his cap, then, eyes front, he turned on the eight-cylinder power plant and listened to Barbara's gentle growl. Taking a deep breath, he released the hand-brake, applied a little pressure to the accelerator, and let his darling slip silently away. He never once glanced toward the back seat, ignoring his lone passenger. Nigel guided the highly-polished Bentley with the caution and reverence of a hearse driver, on a slow, regal sweep of the driveway until he reached the main entrance to the property, where Chalmers the gardener emerged from the gatehouse to open the gates for him with a friendly greeting.

Nigel responded with a royal wave, nosed the big car out onto the road, then drew away down the lane bound for the main thoroughfare, to take his place amongst the early morning London traffic. The 400 mile journey made more pleasant with the BBC radio for company.

Suddenly, just outside Bridgend, his mind vacant, he was startled by a very loud, sharp bang. It came from the passenger compartment in the back, and it frightened the life out of him, causing him to let slip his Cockney accent. "Christ-all-bloody-mighty! I nearly drove off the bleeding road, you stupid little bitch!" His head turned to look at me. He could see my lip quiver, and his tone softened somewhat. "Look at you! Jeeeeesus! Bloody 'ell."

Guiltily, I glanced into the rear-vision mirror. I looked like a ventriloquist's doll. I had a dark sticky black ring all around my mouth from eating a whole packet of licorice given to me by my mother to keep me occupied on the journey. My right hand held a shattered brown paper bag. I'd blown my hot breath with force into the bag, wrapped one tiny fist around

the top to trap in the air, then belted it furiously with my other fist. And...
BANG!

My Daddy Bob had taught me that!

"I 'ope you 'aven't made a bleedin' mess in the seat back there," growled the unhappy driver, chauffeur to my mother's wealthy husband, James Worthington - photographer to the social set. "Don't touch nothin' for Christsake! We'll pull up at the next pub and you can clean up!"

Our long trip came to an end outside the eighteenth century building down at the Dundee docks. My suitcase sat at my feet again as I stood on the doorstep. Nigel rang the rusty bell-pull and waited.

"Hud yer 'orses, hud yer 'orses," came a bark from inside.

The door opened. With a cigarette hanging from the corner of her mouth and a scowl on her face, Mary Campbell stood in the open doorway, hands on hips. "Christ-all-mighty, ah thought ah'd seen the last o' you!"

Nigel Steele held an envelope out to Mary Campbell and she snatched it from his hand. He stepped back and marched away, back to 'Buxom Barbara' for his return journey to London.

"Aw, Christ! That bitch has'na sent 'er back again after one bloody night, surely t' Christ," Mary raged, yanking me back inside the Dundee Boarding House as I cried the first of many more tears.

# CHAPTER 21

Donald Friend had not made an appearance at the gallery during the notorious erotica exhibition, but the distinguished artist did visit a week after it concluded. He'd slipped quietly back into Australia to enter a Sydney hospital for treatment of his emphysema, and had then crept off to one of The Goldberg farms in the Riverina, to gather blackberries, mushrooms, and his thoughts.

When I first saw him I could not believe the human body could survive in such a state. He looked extremely ill when he arrived, shuffling in slowly on Eva's arm. I was amazed he could function at all. Yet despite his appearance, his brain was sabre sharp.

"Even the sheep are neurotic in Australia now, Eva," he told his long-time patron in a wheeze, as they sat together on the black sofa, sharing memories of times past. "This used to be an easy-going sort of place, but not anymore."

"Yes, Donald. You're so right," Eva agreed with him, as she did with everyone, to their face. "So right!"

He looked over at me with a cold, fish-eyed stare, and said, "Ash tray," accustomed as he was to giving orders to the natives in his tropical paradise, Bali, his home for thirty years. Obediently, I took him a silver ashtray and was caught by Butler giving him a gracious smile. He'd come prancing in on the scene wanting to greet the man of the moment.

"Pretty girl," said Friend.

To which Butler responded with his customary contempt of women. "Well, I don't want what SHE'S got!"

They both laughed at my expense.

Friend then had a coughing fit. "Bronchitis," he rasped, stubbing out his cigarette in the ashtray. He wiped his seeping eyes with a grubby-red handkerchief, pulled from his grubby grey pants, then proceeded to light another cigarette. I was glad Butler decided to offer him a coffee, because if I'd done that, it would be something else for the giant to have a snipe about. Donald was HIS friend! Donald declined the offer and Butler departed.

As a devotee of the great man's work, listening to, and watching this mere shadow of a human being, I couldn't help but think what a sad, sad sight he was, clinging to his last days with nothing more than a defiant spirit.

Donald wanted to talk. "I couldn't live in a place with hundreds of neurotic lorry drivers sitting at red lights praying for them to turn green, and looking like mad ants." He sucked hungrily on his cigarette. "As for the white sickly bodies on the beaches, they look like maggots!" He chuckled, and Eva patronizingly joined in.

He was unaware that she was pretending to agree with him on everything, but Georgie and I were. We could read her like a book, seeing sides of her that the artists never did.

"I am unashamedly homesick for my island home on Bali," Friend continued. "Magnificent Bali. My servants are paid $3 a month young lady, and that's too much for some of the buggers."

He directed the conversation toward me, and sure enough, Butler appeared again in time to witness it, darting me a look of disdain. It would have been rude of me to look away, my desk was directly opposite these stars who craved attention, and if I could, I was willing to give it. Butler had other ideas. He stood with his huge frame blocking the artist's eyes from mine, until Donald waved him out of the way. Oh no, I cringed. Now it was obvious to each of us that Donald's conversation was aimed directly at me. Eva had probably heard it all before.

"I would paint in the mornings, scold my helpers after a few gin and tonics as they rained gales of laughter upon me, and then I'd settle down for a siesta before dinner. What could be more civilised?" He coughed, and choked on the smoke again.

I was pleased the phone rang to break the discourse. A journalist was asking if an interview could be set up with the great man. I made the request.

He exploded. "No. I will not be interviewed!" he said, with unexpected volume. "Tell him to go away. Bloody pests! Bloody telephones! In Bali they still have messages that go into sticks, and little men who run for miles with them."

Eva snapped at me. "Tell the reporter no!"

So, I did. That seemed to satisfy Butler; he went off again, blowing Donald Friend a kiss, before giving me a nasty smirk.

"I'm broke, of course," Donald continued on, with a wink over to me. "I spent all my money! I worked it out to the cent that I had enough until I died. But by my calculations, I died last August!"

Eva threw back her head and roared with laughter. I could only manage an embarrassed smile.

"I was the Benevolent Feudal Lord to the youthful brown nudes of my beloved sybaritic island home of Bali," Donald boasted, adding verbal theatricality to his colourful anecdotes. "We part as good friends. But I see nothing to rejoice in being 70. I am disinclined to take tally of aches and pains, irritations, misjudgement and boredoms, which now make up much of my day." He went on to tell Eva that he was depending on this latest exhibition of his. It had to be a success because he'd run out of money.

"It's a great success, Donald!" Eva assured him. "We sold forty-five etchings on the first day. It's a great success." Then she was hit with something quite unexpected.

"The Treadmore Gallery wants my next exhibition, you know, Eva." He winked over at me, and I was sorry my eyes had strayed again to his.

Jane Treadmore, a partner in the new gallery opposite, which caused Eva sleepless nights, had been ingratiating herself with Donald even before his arrival in Sydney. Pampering him in every way, sending gifts, making promises, in the hope of eventually winning him from his thirty-year association with Eva. The shrewd Treadmore proprietress promised she'd take only 15% commission. Half of what Eva charged.

"Donald, I can do no more than sell everything you give me," Eva countered. "What more can I do?" She made no attempt to hide her frustration with him. She'd been at his beck and call for years. As far as she was concerned, loyalty begat loyalty. But to the wily old artist this was just a game. The joke was on the competing women – Eva and Jane Treadmore. Despite his sexual proclivity, he obviously enjoyed women's company, and loved having them fight over him. He began to chuckle to himself, but it only sponsored another coughing bout.

"You need rest, Donald, darling. I'll take you home," Eva suggested.

Wheezing, he nodded. Tanks of oxygen had been installed at his bedside to provide relief at times like these. With great difficulty, panting and gasping, he allowed Eva and I to help him walk to the door. I was greatly saddened and didn't expect to see him again.

#

When Eva returned, with Donald now out of earshot, her false smile had disappeared, and she launched into a tirade over what she saw as the artist's potential betrayal of her three decades of patronage. "Homosexuals!" she exploded, "They live like a king, but they die like a dog! Married men, they live like a dog, and die like a king!"

Eva was really fired up, and directed her venom at her new competitors across the street. "You know what that Jane Treadmore woman did, Lilly? She sent Donald a box of chocolates. What's wrong with her?"

She thumped down so hard on the reception desk it made me blink. As well as I'd come to know the real Eva, the abrupt return of the mad woman still came as a shock to me.

"Chocolates are like poison for a diabetic," she yelled. "What did she do that for? Stupid woman!" And without as much as a breath, added, "You know what else Donald told me? Treadmore sent him knickers! LOOK! LOOK! He gave them to me." She pulled a sexy pair of crutchless knickers from her bosom that Donald had given her, then twirled them on a finger. "LOOK! Knickers with lipstick kisses on them. He's homosexual, he's not interested in her knickers! But she wants his BUSINESS! She wants his work in her gallery! What's wrong with her? Donald's my friend."

And off she pranced to mark up the prices of Donald Friend paintings which she'd ordered be brought up from the basement stockrooms where they'd been sitting for years. Since the notorious Erotica Exhibition, Donald Friend artworks were running out of the gallery on legs of their own. And now that the word was out that he was dying, they were in even greater demand. Collectors knew that the value of his existing works would double overnight once he died. That's how the art world lived – waiting for its champions to die.

# CHAPTER 22

Time does not stand still in the art world. It's always about the next exhibition. After one is unveiled with fanfare, raised glasses, and sometimes raised eyebrows, the next is being hung. It was a busy morning at the gallery after a sell-out exhibition of works of Brett Whiteley, the infamous, young and reckless, drug-taking, but hugely successful Sydney artist.

Butler was in a foul mood to top it off. He'd been in great pain and cold sweats from kidney stones, and we two girls were afraid to look sideways. Georgie wanted no trouble before she left for England. The mere thought of her leaving filled me with dread. Georgie was more than my pal - having her as a colleague helped me through every Goldberg day.

Eva Goldberg's son Michael, was the doctor who attended Butler when he had the attacks, and gave him morphine, and Georgie would sing, "Give him more, give him more, give him more," even when Butler or Eva was around. I daren't tell either one of them that I knew kidney stones were caused by a dysfunctional thyroid. A doctor friend in Brisbane had told me that. Butler was fat and flabby, and most unhealthy looking. It didn't look like anything worked properly, least of all him.

He, Angelo, and the other full-time framer, Freddie, were all down in the main gallery putting up a new exhibition of paintings. It was all quiet upstairs as Georgie and I were very much aware of Butler's mood, and didn't want to be caught talking. It felt as if he were our deputy headmaster. A jealous, nasty one, who was 'in' with the principal.

The Goldberg's next exhibition was very different to the last. With all hands to the wheel, we toiled diligently to make things happen for young Emanuel Manning, an up and coming portrait artist. His work was startlingly good, but every single one of the subjects looked in pain, with tortured features and grimaces. They reminded me of the work of Frances Bacon. I admired Bacon's creativity, but as technically proficient as Manning's work was, I would never put any of his art on my wall. Not that I could afford it. Eva was putting hefty five figure prices on some of his larger pieces.

Action always started with a phone call at the gallery. And here it was again.

"It's Sister Lawrence from The Prince Alfred Hospital," came a voice in my ear. The hospital sister went on to explain her call in a very anguished manner. "Look, I don't know how to say this, but we've 'lost' Donald Friend. You don't have him by any chance, do you?" Friend had suffered a slight stroke several days before, and had been admitted to hospital.

"No, Sister," I replied, relieved that Vince wasn't the subject of the call. "Mr Friend isn't here. He summoned Mrs Goldberg to pick him up from hospital this morning. I believe she's taken him to the house she's rented for him, close by, here in Paddington."

"Oh… mmmmy God!" Sister Lawrence stammered. "He's not supposed to leave yet. He's not a well man. My God, I was giving him oxygen this morning! I could lose my job over this!" She sounded beside herself.

"Mrs Goldberg told me that Mr Friend signed himself out, Sister Lawrence."

"He should really be back in Intensive Care. He really is most unwell. And what about his medicines?"

I thought fast, telling her, "Send them to us. Send a cab, or courier. I'll personally make sure he gets them."

"Oh, dear, but… oh, oh, very well, I will. I'll put them in a cab, it'll be quicker, the cabs are right outside the door. But this is terrible. It's just not good enough at all. He's a very sick man, you know!"

The call was terminated. I swivelled round on Mr Wobbly to pass on the news to Georgie. She saw the funny side and began to giggle, calling Eva 'Mrs

Meddle.' I saw the irony, but was well aware it was a serious situation. Friend was obviously dying.

"I knew she was doing the wrong thing by taking him out of hospital," Georgie declared, slapping down her pen. "She'll get into trouble if she's not careful, Lilly! Just because he didn't want to stay there any longer, the defiant old tosser." I had to agree with Georgie on that one.

Angry at Eva's stupidity, Georgie got out of her chair and her tiny nook to stand at her door and talk to me, arms folded, one foot crossed over the other, leaning on the door frame. "She's been running after him non-stop, Lilly. She's done his grocery shopping, and she bought him new pyjamas and slippers yesterday!" she said incredulously. "She's done his banking, and you know as well as I do, that she's providing a car-shuttle service for him. It's all done to prevent a mutiny! Eva doesn't want to lose him to the Treadmore, darling."

"I know, Georgie. But it's worrying. Eva told me she's having trouble sleeping. She'll make herself ill if she's not careful. Only this morning I heard her on the telephone taking his order for her chicken soup. To be made just the way he likes it – with barley, and big chunks of chicken pieces, if you please! Doesn't he have any family?"

"Of course he does. He has a sister right here in Sydney! But he's not going to bother her and strain the relationship while Eva's silly enough to run after him."

"Does his sister know how sick he is?"

"I suppose she does. But what can anyone do if he checks himself out of hospital, darling? Eva's fawning over him wouldn't be half as sickening, if she weren't so obviously self-sacrificing for selfish reasons - to keep his paintings in her gallery."

Later that morning, when Eva returned from her mercy mission, and I reported the phone call from Sister Lawrence, she went into convulsions of laughter. Sister Lawrence's dilemma really seemed to strike a funny bone, and despite my being accustomed to Eva over-reacting to just about everything, I'd never seen her so out of control. This situation had really stressed her out. She was hysterical.

Her laughter turned to tears, and she flopped down on the sofa like a dropped puppet, and lay sprawled there, sobbing like a child. I could only let the hysteria run its course, although I was glad Georgie was with me, in case our manic boss had a fit. I stood close-by, keeping an eye on Eva, whilst hoping Butler didn't think I'd caused this scene. Eventually he came lumbering up the stairs with a frown on his ugly face, so I scampered back to my desk.

But Eva wasn't finished with me. "I've wet myself, Lilly. I've damned well wet myself!" She wiped away the tears from her bloodshot eyes and tried to compose herself. Australia's richest matriarch was admitting to us all, that she was sitting in wet knickers.

Georgie said later I should have handed her the crutchless ones with lipstick kisses on them from Jane Treadmore.

#

Donald Friend's unmarried sister, Helen Friend, had been contacted by the Prince Alfred Hospital. They had a duty of care for their patients. They'd want to follow up on Friend after he'd signed himself out of hospital in such poor condition. Helen made an early visit to the gallery next day, ready to confront Eva, and to demand to know why she'd collaborated with Donald in his 'escape' from hospital.

When I informed the artist's sister - a celebrity in her own right - that Eva was out, she deposited herself on the much used sofa, and demanded a cup of tea. The grey-haired actor's face was well known to me from television dramas. With her large hooked nose, and deep-set cold eyes, she often played snooty, or wicked, middle-aged, wealthy women, who ran a dynasty on a cattle property, or a vineyard, or, like Eva, at her gallery.

When Georgie appeared out of her bolthole to view the illustrious sister, I asked her if she would kindly make Helen some tea. She obliged. Helen had decided to wait for Eva's return, determined to have a confrontation. It didn't take a magician to know she was seething with anger, so I pulled up the stool to be closer to her, to give 'sympatico,' my desk being a barrier between us.

She didn't wait to explode on Eva. She let me have it. "You realise that I made my usual visit to the hospital yesterday, and went straight to Donald's private room expecting to see him lying there under the oxygen tent – but the bed was empty! Well!" She gesticulated theatrically. "I naturally thought the worst. I immediately burst into tears, and went moping around and sobbing my heart out. Then I had to scout around looking for the attending sister, and when I found her, she couldn't give me an explanation. I went home devastated, thinking Donald was dead!"

"It must have been the most awful shock for you, Helen." I sympathised.

"I was still sobbing when I got home! There were only the two of us in the family, you understand. And he was such a sweet boy when he was young. I really admired my big brother when I was little. He was very good looking, and he cared for me. Our parents were a bit bohemian, you understand. They were hardly old enough to have children, they were only children themselves, so Donald and I were very close. 'Till he went overseas."

She began to sob, and pulled out a pretty handkerchief to wipe away the tears. It was then Georgie came up behind me with the tea, so I held on to the cup and saucer for Helen until she was ready, hoping that Butler wouldn't catch me sitting there with them in hand, and think it was my morning tea. And I just knew that Georgie would see the funny side of this, and laugh about it when we were alone again, but I kept my thoughts to myself, and my concentration on Helen.

"Are you still close?" I asked, really trying to calm, and console Helen before Eva returned, for I imagined an all-out brawl between the two feisty women. And all the while, I was wondering why Helen had let Eva usurp her power over Donald in the first place.

"We grew apart when he became famous," she continued. "I became a celebrity too, as you would know." She sniffed, then retrieved the tea. "I've had a stage career. Television too, of course. Our paths took us in different directions. Donald is the only family I have." She sniffed again, now with a wriggle of her whole torso. "I never married you see." She sipped. "Though I do have a female partner." She gave me a direct, cold stare, as if to dare me to pass judgement on her.

I kept my face blank. I was non-plussed by her revelation. Each to their own.

"But, where was I?" She tried to regain her train of thought. "Oh, yes – home I go, broken-hearted, thinking my only flesh and blood relative has died, and I was feeling so alone and sorry for myself, crying, blowing my nose, lost in tears, remembering all the good times we'd shared, when I walked into the lounge room without even looking. Well…" She paused for effect, and no doubt to catch her breath. "I don't mind telling you that I got the fright of my life! For there he was, the brother I'd given up for dead! With a gin and tonic in hand. He was sitting happily in dad's old chair in the corner. AND smoking a cigarette!"

"How awful for you!"

"Yes. It was awful! I can assure you it was awful – him sitting in that dark corner! Through my tears, he looked like some ghastly vision - a ghost. My knees went from under me, and I sank to the floor." Setting aside the tea cup and saucer, she blew her nose, and cleaned it thoroughly, over and over, as I waited. "But let me tell you, when I recovered, I gave him the worst tongue lashing he's ever had. I certainly took the smile off his face! Now where's that Goldberg woman?"

#

Helen Friend had repeated her 'ghost' story to others, and it had spread like wildfire. Eva found herself bombarded by Donald's friends and associates who called in, or telephoned, and demanded they be told Helen's story, and the whole Donald Friend saga. How Donald was making Eva's life a misery with so many demands on her time, dictating his needs and wants, demanding Eva run to him at the drop of a hat. She explained to one and all, how Donald was using blackmail, threatening he'd give his business to Jane Treadmore if Eva didn't comply with his every whim.

Eva enthusiastically provided all this information: over and over. Embellishing, polishing as she went. Every time the phone rang. Georgie and I shared furtive glances because we'd come to realise that no matter how much Eva enjoyed the spotlight, centre stage, as soon as the phone hit the receiver, the volcano would erupt.

There it was again - the ringing telephone! I answered, and sure enough, it was Donald himself. I handed it over to Eva, but knew full well it would set her off again.

"That Donald is nothing but trouble! I'm too tired to run after him." Again with arms in the air. "Why does he use me like this. I don't need this interruption to my life. What can I do, Lilly? He phones me all the time. He needs me. Why doesn't Helen do all this running around?" She chattered on like a lunatic chimpanzee. She had answered her own question, but didn't realise it when she'd said, 'I don't need this.'

All she had to do was co-opt Helen into becoming Donald's gopher. But Eva was afraid of losing him. It wasn't all about the money. Donald was a trophy! Like Sir Sidney Nolan, Lloyd Rees, Brett Whiteley, Judy Cassab, Tim Storrier, Arthur Boyd, Margaret Olley, John Olsen and others. An elite family of 'name' artists, the likes of which Australia would never see again. Lose one, she feared, and all her trophy artists might follow Donald Friend out of the gallery door. She wanted the money, but she didn't NEED it!

In fact, one day prior, she'd taken great delight in showing me the palm of her hand, and boasted how there was not a drop of light to be seen between her closed fingers. To her mind, this meant that no money could ever escape through her fingers. And she was very proud of that! Very proud indeed!

# CHAPTER 23

It was my turn to do the early shift. I was to open the gallery at 7.30 for early deliveries. I walked the short distance from the Paddington terrace to The Goldberg, because my car was in for service. It was a lovely morning, and it gave me the opportunity to look in the windows of the antique shops, and antiquarian bookstores in ritzy Queen Street.

All was quiet – except for a ringing telephone inside the gallery. I hurriedly unlocked the front door, dashed in and switched off the alarm system, then pressed the buttons on the switchboard to take it off night switch. As I lifted the handset a second call came through.

"Goldberg Gallery," I responded, "one moment, please." I put it on hold, then flicked down the other switch. "Good morning, Goldberg Gallery."

"Eva… Eva…! Can't move… my left side…" the voice croaked. I suspected immediately who it was… Donald Friend.

"Mr Friend, is that you? It's Lillian Lightwood. Can I help you?"

"Can't get back into bed. Fell," he rasped. "Get Eva. Hurry! Aaaaaah…!" Then the phone went dead, and I felt myself shake, but I had no time to panic; a light was flashing insistently on the switchboard – the other call needed to be answered.

"Sorry to keep you waiting…" I said professionally.

"About time! What kept you? I'm not coming in. My crown fell out! I'm off to the dentist," said the angry voice, and before I could as much as bluster out Donald's dilemma, Eva too, was gone. What to do? Ambulance, police, cab? Silence. I felt as if I were the only person in the world. Donald Friend could be dying, and I might get the blame.

"Having a bad start to the day, mmmm?" said a voice behind me.

I swivelled round with a look of horror and panic on my face.

"Whatever's the matter, Lilly? You look like you've seen the famous ghost of Donald Friend," he quipped. It was Freddie. One of the framers. Tall, brawny, with huge biceps, the quiet, thirty-year-old homosexual, with a shaven head, and a solid square jaw, wearing his usual black T-shirt, had entered the workroom door with his own set of keys.

"Oh, boy! Am I glad to see you, Freddie." I felt instant relief. "Come on. We're locking up again, and going on a mission of mercy." I jumped out of 'Wobbles,' grabbed the key to Donald's house from the keyboard, put the alarm system back on, and hurried Freddie out the back door with me. "You do have your car with you today, don't you, Freddie?"

"Yes, but..."

"I'll explain on the way."

#

After unlocking Donald's front door, I led Freddie down the corridor of the rented accommodation, which was adequate, and in a good state of repair, but not particularly warm and welcoming. It certainly had none of the famous artist's work on the walls. The furniture looked comfortable, but without personal things around, it looked austere. A glance at the kitchen told me there had been no cooking, just a dirty soup bowl and plate or two, probably belonging to Eva. To me it looked like a Geoffrey Smart painting. Everything neat as a pin, but sterile, as if no-one lived there.

We moved through, calling out all the way. "Mr Friend? Mr Friend? Where are you, Mr Friend?" Freddie called out too, to make him feel help was at hand. We found him upstairs as most bedrooms are in terrace houses. There he was, helplessly kneeling on the floor beside his bed in a praying position, groaning with pain.

"Can't get... back... in," he gasped, hardly able to look around at us. His glassy eyes made me doubt he could comprehend what he saw anyway. His stare was vacant, as if no-one was home. But was I mistaken! He would soon come to life. But sadly, he was not a pretty sight.

I felt myself blush with embarrassment for him when I saw he'd soiled his pyjamas, and they were down around his knees, revealing the wrinkled white skin of his droopy, aged buttocks. Blood was dripping from a gash on his forehead, probably caused when he'd fallen out of bed. And, unable to move any further than his bedside phone, the invalid was caught in this disabled, impotent state waiting for help. He'd only been able to remember The Goldberg Gallery phone number.

Rough, tough, heavily tattooed Freddie was marvellous. I was so glad to have him there. He himself was personally nursing his partner who was dying of AIDS, and he was accustomed to the humiliation illness can present. He eased the old man's pyjamas down from his sagging torso, while I went to find clean ones in the chest of drawers. Then between us, we lifted him carefully back into his bed. Friend had become so emaciated as a result of his ailments, he was cadaver-like.

After making him comfortable, I asked which medicines he should be taking, and asked if he wanted me to call his sister.

"I want nothing from you but breakfast! And hurry up about it!"

This was the crotchety old man's response to our kindness. Not with thanks, but with a fevered blasting. His still agile tongue heaped abuse on we two Good Samaritans. Freddie commented to me later. "He's just like someone else we know – they'll turn and bite you like a mongrel dog when you least expect it."

"I'm hungry, Goddam it!" Donald bellowed. "No, I do not want my sister! I want Eva. Where is she? I want food! And what the hell took you so long?" Gratitude was not something for which he was renowned. "Where's Eva?" He wailed, like a lost child.

"She had to go to the dentist, Mr Friend. Besides, I think you really ought to go back to hospital."

"No! I will not go back into that foul-smelling death trap. Do you hear me?"

"But that gash on your head looks bad," Freddie insisted.

"You should be properly taken care of, Mr Friend," I ventured. "You need professional care."

"Then I want Sammy!"

Freddie and I shared a glance of ignorance.

"SAMMY!" he bellowed. "My house-boy. In Bali. Only him. Only him, I tell you!"

"At least let me send for a doctor, Mr Friend." I could tell from his slurred speech and his limp left arm, that he'd more than likely suffered another stroke. And that being the case, the ongoing effects on the artist would be life-changing. Donald was a southpaw. He painted with the left hand.

"No. Leave me alone!" He cried, pedantically. The cantankerous old man had, for more than forty years as an acclaimed artist, been accustomed to getting whatever he wanted. But now, in this situation, he needed proper medical attention. He however, had a different idea. He kept yelling, demanding his former dark-skinned house-boy attend him. And that was his final word on the matter!

While Freddie stayed on and made him breakfast, I returned to the gallery in Freddie's car to open up the gallery, from where I phoned Donald's sister Helen out of courtesy. She said she would take it from there. She'd phone Donald's doctor, who would likely send an ambulance to whisk him back into hospital. I felt relieved. Just as I was putting down the phone, Butler walked in and gave me a tongue-lashing. He thought I'd only just arrived because he'd seen me open up.

Before I could as much as explain, he ploughed into me, like a sergeant-major to a slovenly recruit. "Why weren't you here to open up at 7.30 like you were supposed to?" he railed.

I found myself stammer, just at the size of him, and the scary mood he was in, but I tried to defend myself. "I was!" I countered.

"You just walked in the door two minutes ago!" he yelled down at me.

When I did get a word in to offer my explanation, telling him about our mercy dash to Donald, even that didn't soften his tone.

"You're too big for your boots, you smart arse," he snarled. "You shouldn't have taken on that responsibility. Your job is here, at the gallery. You're the receptionist! Not the manager! That's MY job, and don't you bloody-well forget it." He snatched Freddie's keys from my hand, then the angry colossus turned his back on me.

After this episode I realised there would be nothing I could ever do to win him over.

Sammy was duly contacted by Eva, and the houseboy was flown in from Bali to cook, bathe and care for Donald, just as he'd always done, because Donald had again signed himself out of hospital! Eva paid for Sammy's airfare and other expenses, deducting the cost from Friend's exhibition cheque. The saga of Donald Friend would continue, with Eva both resenting the amount of time he took from her day, and yet revelling in the attention the whole catastrophe brought her. Art world figures and the press constantly rang her for updates on the great man's condition, as if she were his publicity agent.

When Eva first realised that it was his left arm rendered useless by the stroke, his 'painting' arm, she was inconsolable. This would mean an end to Friend's artistic output. But after her initial screaming frenzy she determined on a solution. "We'll just have to teach him to paint with the other hand. That's all."

# CHAPTER 24

Vince and I had shared a pleasant lunch together at Twenty One in Double Bay. Being such a pleasant day we chose to eat outside under an umbrella, in a setting reminiscent of Paris' Champs-Elysee's. There, we watched the pot pourri of folks strolling casually in the warm sunshine catching up with well-to-do friends, and enjoying the best of food in the area's excellent restaurants.

Double Bay, or 'Double Pay,' to the wags, was the most expensive shopping and residential real estate area in Sydney. It was only a five minute drive from The Goldberg in flowing traffic through the winding streets of Paddington, and up the hill past beautiful Rushcutters Bay. Or a delightful walk on a Spring or Autumn day. The shopping precinct was a feast to the eyes, a home of elegance, good taste, sophistication, and gracious living. Neat, tidy and clean tree-lined streets, tantalising shopfronts, with world-class fittings of shining brass and the like. Epicurean delights of every kind from far and wide.

There was a cute little Belgian chocolate shop with glamorous boxes of every size tied with colourful ribbons and bows in its window display, and bonbons so expensive that young people would enter the chocolate wonderland to buy just one heavenly mouthful at a time! A favourite for window-shoppers was the tiny cake shop with unimaginably decadent, yet deliciously dainty French pastries and chocolate cakes. The precinct had the latest and best fashions from around the world. My favourite store was Christophle, which sold silverware and glass. Never would I have my hair done in Double Bay because the hairdressers were more celebrity spotlight seekers than hair-trimmers.

This was Sydney's Rodeo Drive, where Ferraris, Mercedes, Rolls Royces, Bentley's and brightly coloured Porches came out to play. Where the rich, middle-aged women shoppers had a reputation for looking like wrinkled Barbie dolls, clad in Italian knits and leather, with kilos of expensive jewellery. As is so often the case, their money had arrived long after their youthful looks had departed.

With healthy Caesar salads and sipping a light Sauvignon Blanc between our shared snippets of news, we watched the passing parade.

"Are you looking forward to the Christmas break, Vince? How long will you have? I know we've nothing planned, but Sydney is such a great city, there's always plenty to do."

"Sorry, Lil, but I only get three days." His eyes strayed from mine to land on a teenage model-type who had obviously had reconstruction work done on her almost bare breasts, and who was wearing a mini, mini-skirt, and was being led along by a pampered pet poodle. Both wore pink, and a pout.

"Don't worry," I said, vying for attention. "Me too! But surely we can do something special. I haven't been to Taronga Zoo yet. Or inside the Opera House. We could fill those three days to the brink, if we plan it. Movies, dinners, theatre. And art galleries!" I added, tongue in cheek, knowing how boring he thought they were.

"You know it's best not to plan. We'll take it as it comes. There's always some drama or other."

"Can't we even plan a date?"

"Course we can."

"Okay. Then I say we start off on the ferry on Sunday, day before Christmas Eve, and find a nice restaurant for lunch, and book into a hotel on the waterfront."

I got a smile in return, just as I saw William come walking toward us looking particularly dapper. I jumped up to say hello and introduced him to Vince, who took off his shades and stood to shake hands.

"That's a really fancy jacket you're wearing, William," I teased, reaching out to touch his lapel. "You look so suave!" He wore delicate stripes of two-tone caramel and cream, reminding me somewhat of the University jacket that Cambridge undergrads wore with a boater, when they tested their arm on boats on the Thames on sports day. He'd teamed it with a slick bow-tie and a pair of swanky slacks in cream. Very Italian. It seemed to me that our William was about to have some fun!

"I'm off to a wedding." He smiled his great smile at me. "At the Ritz, in Cross Street. It'll be a big do, so my buddy dropped me off."

"Well you look really great," I assured, smiling back at him.

We three shared pleasantries in the sunshine, then William headed off. I explained to Vince how we'd met, saying that William was a close friend of Eva's. Then a thought struck me. I didn't ever remember him buying anything at The Goldberg, so I wondered what his connection with Eva was. She was usually only cringingly fawning over people she could use. He was neither a buyer, nor a painter, that I knew of. I said nothing, and added it to the multitude of unanswered questions in my head.

After lunch, Vince and I walked along the beach of Double Bay where we saw the magnificent homes crowding the slopes of Point Piper and Rose Bay nearby, like the villas on the French Riviera. It was carefree and enjoyable, but as Vince was tripping off to Canberra I drove him to the airport and said a sad goodbye.

Soon I was back in the city, and with car windows down, in the stop-start traffic, the automobile fumes mingled with cooking odours from restaurants and cafes, adding to the palpable stew of thick, hot humid air. The street was ablaze with Christmas colour, and it throbbed with noisy activity. The shops flitted by. People weren't just walking, they were prancing, like ponies; voices were loud, full of seasonal cheer; wagging tongues, happy faces; laughing adults running blindly like children, scampering through the stationery traffic. Groups huddled in restaurant doorways, outside 'gay' bars. Music blasted out from here and there. Everyone seemed to be in teams of two, or packs of six and more, dashing to pubs, theatres and the like. So this was how Sydney lived. I realised I hadn't had time to enjoy it.

Now there was nothing to hurry home for. I was wearing one of my prettiest summer dresses but had nowhere to go, nor anyone to go anywhere with. Amidst all this revelry, a light had suddenly shone on my loneliness. And now with my mind not focussed, I took the wrong lane and was forced to turn into George Street. Then before I knew it, I found myself passing St Mary's Cathedral. It was busy tourist season in Sydney. The streets crowded, crammed with cars behaving badly like dodgem cars.

I'd lost interest in where I was going by this time. I just drove, following a tree-lined road to eventually find myself at Mrs Macquarie's Chair, a landmark on a grass-covered peninsula jutting out into Sydney harbour, named for the wife of colonial governor Lachlan Macquarie, a Scot in a foreign land, just like me. A popular spot with Japanese newlyweds who flocked there to shoot their wedding photographs, using the Opera House and the Coathanger - the Sydney Harbour Bridge - as a dramatic backdrop.

I pulled over, switched off the engine, exited the car with a thud of the door, and went to sit on a park bench, looking out over the harbour. How long I sat there, I'd no idea. But when the day's light was near an end, and the city on either side began to sparkle with lights, I realised that an hour or more must have passed. In the background I could hear the happy bells of the Cathedral making a Christmas peel.

I was suddenly overwhelmed by the heart-wrenching pain of sadness. The faces of my children had come again into my mind. How often I'd tried to block them out at times like these just to survive the pain of their loss. In my mind's eye I saw little Adam, and rosy-cheeked Kate on their last Christmas with me, decorating a scrawny Christmas tree. I remembered their jubilant faces on Christmas morning as they opened their meagre presents.

I gave in to a torrent of tears.

# CHAPTER 25

Butler's voice was heard to bellow throughout the cavernous building. We wondered what was coming when we heard him yell, and march noisily through the main gallery to stop at the foot of the stairs. "Mrs Goldberg, David's out there again asleep on a dirty old mattress. It looks dreadful right outside the garden entrance." His words were meant to make everyone jump into action.

"Oh, pah!" said Eva, her face contorted. "He's not back again, surely? I thought he'd learned his lesson. The dirty old bugger. He smells. I just won't stand for it! Georgie, phone for the City Mission to come and pick him up."

Countless major buildings with cosy alcoves in the inner city had acquired drunks as overnight guests. Big cities all over the world suffer the same problem. And a few of Sydney's derelicts had a predilection for the more salubrious nooks and crannies. They crashed with class at The Goldberg.

A niche by the garden entrance had been adopted by a drunk of the most ravaged proportions. David, he said his name was, in a rare, lucid moment, defiantly used the location as a meeting place for his friends who would drop by to share a convivial gallon of cheap wine with him. No doubt he invited his fellow winos to join him for cocktails at The Goldberg Gallery. This was his loungeroom, and lounge he did. It was also a bedroom for his malnourished bones, and a urinal for his waste.

Butler had frequently tried to get rid of him. And every time he did, he had a fight on his hands. David would let loose with flying fists and a barrage of slurred, yet colourfully original expletives. With a Mission vehicle on the way, Butler went out to stand guard and prepare to wake the vagrant, but David was already awake and making lots of noise. Eva poked her head out of the front door to see what was going on and beckoned us to take a look, then she hid behind Georgie and I while we watched and listened.

David was in a fighting mood. "You fuckin' sausage-breathed bastard!" he raged at Butler as he staggered to his feet. His tattered suit was loud with stains, his beard matted with filth. "Fuck off out of it! Find your own pad!" He was valiantly defending his domain while nearby wealthy neighbours slunk behind their silken drapes.

When finally the Mission worker arrived, it was just in time to see David stumble and fall in the process of throwing a windmill punch at invisible demons, landing face down. With him sprawled defencelessly amongst the rubbish, Butler and the Mission worker were able to pounce on and secure the derelict, then pour him into the Mission van. Finally, he was driven to more suitable accommodation among his homeless brethren.

Eva went on relentlessly about the police doing more to protect her property. "With all the taxes I pay, I should get a 'Privilege' service!"

#

Within a few days David was back in his usual cranny. He was nothing, if not loyal to The Goldberg.

I had just parked my car and was locking it, when I saw the mound of human flesh covered with carpet begin to stir. I had to walk by him to enter the gallery, and was a bit wary. When I heard him mumble to himself in an angry tone, I scooted quickly on past to the main entrance.

The first that Barry Butler was to learn of David's return that morning was when emptying rubbish into bins beside the loading dock, as light drizzle fell. Out of nowhere the displaced drunk came to life and went charging at Butler like a wounded bull, ranting, "You fuckin' poofter bastard! I've killed better than you in the war!"

Whether David was privy to Butler's sexual orientation or not was beside the point; the massive, lubberly Goliath ran for his life back into the protection of the gallery, with David close at heel brandishing not a slingshot, but an empty flagon. Butler just managed to escape inside and lock the rear door behind him before contact. Again, the Mission was called to another loud and ugly scene.

"All this trouble could ruin my business," Eva raged once the vagrant had been evicted yet again. "That dirty old man. Why doesn't he use that Treadmore dump as his urinal, instead of my beautiful gallery?"

Next morning Butler approached the loading dock very gingerly, expecting to be set upon once again. But he needn't have worried. David had indeed returned, but he wasn't going to cause any more trouble for anyone. Butler found the tramp wrapped in an old carpet, stone cold dead. The news saddened both Georgie and me. I knew that he had to be someone's son. Someone's father or brother. I wondered what tragedy could have befallen him to ruin his life by sending him on the path of self-destruction.

Eva, on the other hand just shrugged it off. "You stupid girls! He did it to himself," were her scolding words.

Georgie looked over at me as if to say, 'Doesn't the woman have a heart?'

It was Christmas Eve. And all at the gallery would be going home to comfort and love, whilst this lonely old derelict would keep an appointment at the crematorium. Unknown. Unmourned.

#

"That's a hefty scotch you have there, my girl," said Vince, arriving home at eleven twenty.

"It's Christmas Eve, Vince!" I snapped at him angrily. I'd been sitting in front of the television set watching religious movies all night because there was nothing else on, and was feeling sorry for myself. "I thought at least you would share Christmas with me!" My disappointment in him was pretty obvious. This was not going to be a happy few days. I just couldn't hold it in any longer. "You know how important these times are to me. I hate to be alone with my thoughts at Christmas. You know damned well how I miss my children!"

"Aw, I'm sorry, my love," he swayed toward me. He'd obviously been drinking.

"Don't give me that sorry business!" I snapped, rejecting his words. I'd had enough. I was sick and tired of his indifference to me of late. "If you were caring, and sorry, you wouldn't do it to me, Vince. What's the excuse this time?"

"I need an excuse now, do I?" he said sarcastically.

In silence, I gulped down the last remaining finger of straight whisky and heaved myself out of the chair.

"Look, I'm sorry. Okay?" He shouted at me as he lay a large wrapped gift at the foot of the Christmas tree by the stairs. "In case you're interested, this is your Christmas present."

"But what are you sorry for, Vince?" I yelled. "Coming home at midnight on Christmas Eve? Or for coming home at all?" Then I stormed off to bed, kicking his Christmas gift out of the way as I went.

# CHAPTER 26

Next morning I left early to visit my grandmother. It was Christmas Day, and I was prepared to spend as much time with her as needed. It seemed to be an extra-long drive out to Palm Beach. The traffic was bumper to bumper, so I imagined that everyone was doing what I was doing. Visiting relatives. I also had a scotch-induced headache.

Just as I'd imagined, the car park of the Palm Beach Nursing Home was full. I had to go searching, eventually finding a spot some distance away. It was a beautiful area, and the 'inmates of the prison' as Mary Campbell had described them, were fortunate enough to see the beautiful waters of the Tasman Sea and one of its beaches. It was a very liberal aged care facility where couples were allowed to co-habit, so it was not unusual to see husbands and wives walking together throughout the grounds. But it did come as a surprise to me to see my own grandmother linked arm in arm with a white-haired, unknown gentleman with a walking stick.

Approaching the pair, I was introduced. He said his name was Joseph. We shook hands, then he made himself scarce when he learned who I was. I wished him a Merry Christmas and watched as he moved away. It was obvious that he was special to her, and it made me feel glad she had company. Besides, it meant she wouldn't need me so much. I was feeling the stress of working at the gallery with the volatile Eva, and my home situation of late was a challenge to say the least, and I was always in trouble for not seeing her enough.

I took her arm and guided her over to one of the comfortable outdoor chairs set in pairs under umbrellas so that we could talk and I could give her the gifts I'd brought her.

"Well, what d'y think?" She grinned at me.

I tried to read what she meant.

"Joe's my fancy man! Bit of all right, don't y' think?"

"Er, yes. He, er, looks like a nice man. Is he kind?" I settled her into a wicker chair.

"Och, I'm no' worried about that! The thing is, he's got plenty of loot! That's what matters!"

I was accustomed to her ways, and was glad she was happy. She took the gifts from me one by one and opened them. I'd bought a cashmere wrap for her shoulders, some new slippers, and a dressing gown, and thought I'd done rather well by her. But she scoffed.

"You'll never be able to match what he gives me! He buys me whisky, and pays a driver to take us out to the best restaurant in Palm Beach. And, he makes the driver wait until we've finished, and bring us back here."

"That's fantastic," I said, surprised. "What did he make his money from?"

"He was in real estate! Used to live here in Palm Beach in a big mansion, till his wife died last year, then he moved in here. His family are none too happy about me, I can tell you. But who gives a shite? I'll take it while I can. The bugger might be dead tomorrow!" She threw her head back and laughed.

We spent an hour in the fresh air, and she gave me the background on all who passed by. She seemed to know everything about everyone, and I thought to myself how much like Eva Goldberg she was. They both shared the same trait. Judging people without really knowing them, and finding the worst in them.

The sea breeze had rustled up, and it blew hard enough to drive us inside. I gathered up the gifts, and helped Mary indoors, where happy Christmas tunes were playing through the loud-speakers in public areas. Everyone seemed to be moving toward the dining room to have their special Christmas lunch. There was a joyous spirit emanating from staff and residents alike as they congregated to celebrate Christmas, with an extra-special meal, including wine.

Mary wanted her handbag, so we went to her bedroom suite to fetch it, and give her a chance to go to the bathroom. Whilst I was there, I put the new dressing gown on a hanger and was about to hang it up when I spotted what looked like a package of photographs on the wardrobe floor. Curious, I lifted them to have a close look. They appeared to be photographs of the residents having a Christmas party. There were lots of smiling faces. Happy people. But I hadn't known about this party. I thought they were just about to have it! That was puzzling.

Looking closer, I realised that the surroundings were unfamiliar. The photographs had not been taken at this facility. I was just about to call out to Mary in the bathroom, to ask about them, when I saw what appeared to be a familiar face smiling back at me from two of the shots.

I knew that face! Knew it very well! It was no-one from this aged care home. Turning, ready to ask about it through the bathroom door, my heart pounding, pounding so hard inside my chest I thought it would jump out, I found that I stood speechless. My jaw hung open. I froze, staring at the bathroom door, when it opened.

Mary appeared, looked at me, then at the photographs in my hand, and her pleasant demeanour changed. "You've found them then!" she snapped, obviously displeased at my discovery.

"These look like new photographs! They can't be NEW photographs?" I questioned, still holding them, still rooted to the spot.

"Yes. It's your mother! You weren't supposed to see them," she scolded, making her way past me, as if ready to ignore my questioning.

"What do you mean? This can't be...."

"Yes. It's your bloody mother, alright," she pushed me aside using her elbow. "Sent them to me for Christmas," she said, off-handedly, hurrying towards the corridor door to escape the interrogation, picking up her handbag from the chest of drawers as she went.

"But, they can't be... they can't be NEW photographs of her?" I queried, looking from her to the photos in hand. "You... you told me she was dead!" Incredulous, I followed her as she attempted to make her escape from the inquisition. My voice was shaky - it didn't sound like mine. Confused.

Flustered. The shock made my head feel odd. A dizziness overtook me. The room started to spin. I had to hold myself together. Couldn't make my brain understand. Felt sick. Was choking up.

"Yes! It's her, the bitch!" she spat angrily, her back to me. "That'll teach her to have the good life!" She spun around and snarled at me. "She fucked up her brain with the booze. That'll teach her!" There was a bitter look of resentment on her twisted face, her hand already on the door to make a quick exit, away from me.

Not believing what I was hearing, or what was happening, I looked again at the photographs, more closely, to make sure no mistake had been made. But, yes, it was Betty. My real mother! An older Betty, but still a beautiful Betty! But it couldn't be her? She was dead!

"It can't be Betty… NOW?" I spoke to Mary's back as she hurried through the open doorway. "You told me she was dead! Years ago!" My words fell on deaf ears. She was now well through the door and walking down the corridor. I followed in desperation, evidence in hand. Anxious to find clarity, I raised my voice. "You made a point of it! Like a warning to me! You said she drank herself to death." I didn't care who could hear me.

"Well, she's NOT dead!" she snarled over her shoulder. "But she might as well be! She can't even look after herself! She was in a home before I was!" She turned, and I saw the familiar stare of hatred. A blind had come down. According to her, the confrontation was over. She'd dismissed me, unwilling to be grilled, unwilling to answer to her lies.

I held the puzzle in my hands. It would simply not register in my mind. All through the years I'd held the belief that my real mother was dead – over thirty years of believing she was dead. The Red Cross had found her alone, unconscious – Mary had told me, when I was a child. "But mum…" I pleaded, hearing myself use the word I'd always used. "You're acting as if this is not a big deal!" I was on the move, chasing after her. "Can't you understand how this hurts me? This is the most terrible thing you could ever do to me," I yelled over her shoulder with total disregard to where I was. "Don't you realise what you've done? You've cheated me out of knowing my own mother!" I was visibly shaking. "You LIED to me," I shouted, overwhelmed by this revelation, and confused by her deceit.

"She doesn't deserve to be called a mother!" she shouted back at me. "She never was one! She never looked after you!" Mary turned to look at me and I could see the resentment she'd harboured for years etched on her face. "She gave me nothing for you! She dumped you on me, then went off to have a fancy life. Nothin' but a selfish bitch! She was a drunk!"

There were no words of consolation, no care for my feelings. "How could you do such a thing?" My voice was trembling now, weak, my ragged nerves showing. I spoke now as if pleading. "How could you lie to me all these years? You've been cheating me, keeping the truth from me all this time!"

Then her twisted face came up close to mine. And, as she'd always done when I was in BIG trouble, her forefinger rose to point at me like a voodoo stick, and it stopped me in my tracks. "An' y' can STOP yer screamin' at me. I'M yer mother! Ye've always called me mum, and that's the way it will stay, d'you hear?" Her words became a growl. "She doesn't deserve t' be called a mother." Her face loomed even closer to mine as she made her parting shot. "An' for that matter, neither d'you, y' daft bitch! Ye' should be ashamed o'yerself. Ye' let yer children go!" She bellowed in my face with absolute disgust, then turned and hurried away.

I just stood. Motionless. In shock. Unable to move, till I saw her join forces with Joseph at the end of the corridor. She was ignoring my pain. Jolted into action, I quickly returned to her room, not even needing to use my key - the door had been left open. Going straight to the wardrobe where I'd found the photographs, I reached in to find the envelope they'd been sent in. Grabbing it in the hope the sender's address was on it. Yes, I could see it was there, despite my teary eyes. I put the photographs inside and took it with me. When I slammed shut the antique wardrobe door in anger, it bounced back on its hinges.

Deceived - all through the years. Why had she punished me like this? I could've visited my mother so many times, could at least have made friends with her. I would have loved her, too! I knew I had room in my heart for both of them. I simply could not believe how anyone could be so wantonly cruel.

I fled in pain.

# CHAPTER 27

Eva Goldberg accepted the offer of more space from husband, Henry. Eight thousand square metres – for a second gallery. The vast space was on the first floor of a National Trust-registered building which sat at the very centre of Sydney's heart. This would enable Eva to introduce a dedicated commercial contemporary gallery.

"Now, Lilly," Eva said, greeting me at 9am one morning, before I'd time to take off my jacket, "I want you to run this new gallery of mine. I want you to be solely in charge. Here are the keys," she added, holding out a large bunch of keys of various shapes and sizes. "The code is the birthday of my son, Michael. It's easy to remember. May Day. The first of May, 1950." I quickly wrote it down in my diary camouflaged as a telephone number in case my bag was stolen.

She expected me to find which key fitted which lock among this maze of jangling metal - front door, back door, inside door, the safe, and any other door I happened to need open. Although Eva had surprised me with this latest venture, I always expected the unexpected from her, and tried to see the positive. Oh well, I thought, at least she trusted me to be responsible and reliable.

Accepting the challenge, I waved goodbye to Georgie, and headed out the door to find my own way to the new gallery and open up. Finding no parking, and having to use an all-day parking facility, it was easy to decide on public transport as a cheaper alternative in future. After following Eva's vague instructions, I eventually left Oxford Street very close to the eastern end of Hyde Park, to enter an alleyway beside the Park View Hotel.

Walking through the vaulted archway, which had probably led to a horse and carriage laneway in the early days, I came out the other side to a cloistered set of buildings, and found the ancient landmark I'd been searching for, which in the 1800's had been a huge wool store. Climbing the first flight of steps, I was met with enormous double glass doors to my right, which had 'Goldberg Contemporary Gallery' printed in gold leaf at eye level. Opposite, to my left, there was a sparse architect's office almost devoid of people. I peered inside the gallery door as I unlocked it, to find that the space was already full of sculptures.

The feeling I got from this building as a gallery did not sit comfortably with me. I thought the old saying in business, was 'location, location, location.' The everyday public did not pass by this convoluted labyrinth of out of the way buildings, where old had been outbuilt by new. That, together with Eva's lack of marketing skills, her reluctance to spend money on advertising, told me in no uncertain terms that this business would not last very long as a gallery.

The opening exhibition that would launch The Goldberg Contemporary Gallery would promote two of Australia's finest young sculptors. Eva had told the ever hungry press that the curator of the Musee de Rodin, Pierre Bouliere, was flying out from Paris for the occasion, and was to voice his unhappiness with the Australian government's lack of financial support for the arts.

For the opening, just the week after I'd taken charge of the new gallery, I wore a very smart suit in soft grey wool, with a stark white collar beneath. It was sophisticated, and understated. I'd done all the preparatory work for the opening myself, laying out glasses and a white tablecloth, and had cleaned everything in sight. But it was controversy the media was interested in. And they got it. Bouliere, an aristocrat in his sixties, with beautiful, thick silver hair, smooth tight skin, tanned and pampered looking, delivered his speech with authority, flourish, and a daring amount of pomposity. He too wore a very smart grey business suit, with a black polo neck sweater underneath. He set this off with a floppy, black and white spotted kerchief flouncing wildly out of his top pocket.

"Australia is losing potentially great artists through indifference and lack of appreciation by your government," he declared to the assembled art mafia of Sydney. "The two artists whose work is shown here tonight, are extremely gifted, and have the potential to be gaining an international reputation. In fact, I am pleased to announce here, and now, that your two handsome young men, Monsieur Berger and Monsieur Holland, are hereby invited to exhibit their work in Paris at the Musee de Rodin."

There was a big gasp from Eva to my right. Had she lost her two pretty boys already? Cameras flashed, reporters scribbled amidst enthusiastic applause.

"It is a known fact," Bouliere went on, "that in America, only top artists are important!" He paused for effect, and eyed his audience to gauge their attention. "In England, no artist is important!" Another pause. "In France EVERY artist is important!" Great flourish and self-righteousness with this point, and for effect, another long pause. "But sadly, in Australia, aah… we have to explain what an artist IS!"

There was hearty laughter, stifled laughter, sniggers, smirks, frowns, and nods of agreement from the invited VIP's, as cameramen worked their cameras and journalists surrounded Bouliere.

I could tell from Eva's face she was peeved. It was the injured bulldog look. Bouliere was hogging the limelight.

Eva wasted no time strutting out to centre stage, wearing as much make-up as Barbara Cartland, and as much jewellery as Coco Chanel. "Ladies and Gentlemen," she pushed her way into command position at the lectern. "I know there is a lot of glamour attached to being a gallery director," she flashed THE smile. The queen of the dramatic flourish was now centre stage. "But, the number one service is to the artist! The second duty is to the community you live in." She flashed the dazzle again. "Oh, yes," said she, swivelling around for all the cameras to catch her theatrics, the performance becoming something of a competition now between two players vying for supremacy. "I have to sell - but that is a by-product of a service to the artist and the community."

Her speech continued in a similar vein as she sang her own praises and hogged the limelight, making only a passing mention of the fact that husband Henry's money had made it all possible. She took offence when the media throng moved again toward Bouliere. Their interest had been aroused by his introductory speech, and they wanted more. Masochists and sadists - all seemed prepared to have Australia belittled on the world stage. Controversy sold papers. Before Eva's applause had even died down, they surged around Bouliere like hungry ants discovering a honey pot.

"Do you really think we're ignoring talent in this country?" one reporter asked.

"You think Australians don't appreciate art, Mr Bouliere?" another called.

Before he could answer, he was hit with a barrage of similar provocative questions.

"Do you think we're unsophisticated, Mr Bouliere?"

"Is Australia lacking culture, Monsieur Bouliere?" This question was put to Bouliere by a French TV journalist seeking his response for the French news, hoping his accent would claim attention from the maestro.

"Is Australia uneducated, Monsieur Bouliere?" asked another Frenchman, sounding too eager by half to grab an international headline.

"If so," asked an Aussie, "what can be done about it, Mr Bouliere?"

"Mr Bouliere, do we really HAVE any talent in Australia?"

The media vultures crowded around Eva's guest speaker. When he realised he was in something of a lion's den, and they were looking for blood, the debonair, aristocratic prima donna began to withdraw, no doubt in fear of not being accepted back into Australia again. Diplomatically, he took aside the two young artists, and began to walk the walk with them around the gallery, and talk the talk, as he surveyed their works. Every move, a flourish from France.

Eva's scowling face was in front of me as she demanded justice, "What about my new gallery, Lilly? They don't appreciate the work and money that's gone into it. These two young brats would be nothing without me!" Eva no doubt regretted extending her invitation to Bouliere to launch her new gallery.

# CHAPTER 28

The first morning of my new managerial appointment after the launch, and after turning on lights and switching off a series of alarms, I stood alone in the gallery – Eva's mausoleum. Space. So much space. And silence. Cold, austere silence. The gallery was totally lacking in atmosphere. No wonder Australia's artists would nick-name it 'the Barn."

After taking off my jacket, I went directly to the stereo for something pleasant to play to fill the void. I chose Vivaldi's 'The Four Seasons,' thinking no-one could be offended by it. Then as the music filled the air, I strolled through my new domain, surveying the wares I was expected to sell.

The Contemporary art that I'd seen here, was not really to my taste. I much preferred the 19th century Australian and European masters, whose imagery was so real they took me back in time to when the world was more tranquil. Artists like Conrad Martens, Tom Roberts, Arthur Streeton, and the naughty Norman Lindsay, whose paintings danced with fleshy merriment. These Australians were finally obtaining recognition on the world stage; meanwhile, their European contemporaries, the French Impressionists – Monet, Pissaro, Renoir, Degas, Cezanne and others were already legends. I had noted that all these great Europeans were born within the same decade. They were a club of like-minds, so it wasn't such a coincidence.

I would find that I enjoyed the extra responsibility, and the freedom from Eva's whining, but I dearly missed Georgie. And here, of course, there were no framing boys to give a hand, or the massive Butler to call on for heavy lifting jobs. It was pure hard slog wrapping newly sold, four by four metre paintings in bubble wrap and cardboard, to create a packing case for shipment. This was a physical job, a man's job, and certainly not one to be done in high-heel shoes.

I was in for a surprise one quiet afternoon, as I sat, hoping a potential customer might walk in and I'd have someone to chat to. I'd decided on some lively classical music that was joyful, but didn't demand too much attention, or grate on the nerves by being over-zealous. The gallery suddenly came alive with strings. Violin, cello, viola, guitar, harp and a surprisingly up-beat double bass to keep the beat. It became a happy place, despite its lack of patronage. I was relaxed, and enjoying the sensation of being in such a strange situation - this big barn, trying to be something it was not. It would never be glamorous, despite any artwork. I could only accept it as a new experience.

Suddenly, before my eyes, the most beautiful young woman entered. I caught this ethereal being in my peripheral eye, dancing barefoot to the music. As I turned to watch, she spun and twirled her way around the sculptures. Her delicate frock consisted of layers of silken chiffon the softest shade of sea green. She held out her arms to caress the statues, to embrace the sculptures, touching them gently with her flowing gown - like angel wings - then darted lightly, quickly away, like a butterfly. Then stroking, as if teasing them, flirting, toying playfully, and courting them, as she danced and frolicked. The fluid, soft silk chiffon, encircling, swirling, gliding, curling delicately around the statues, as if they were partners in her ballet.

Afraid to break the magic spell, I didn't move a muscle. I was enchanted. By the girl's grace. Her joy. Her lack of inhibition. The lightness of her footsteps. Her willingness to allow me to spectate. I could not admonish. Or chase her away. It seemed so wonderfully, beautifully surreal. A hallucination? A touch of magic? Round and round she danced with her chiffon wings, flying, gliding at low altitude between her stationary partners. I dare not move. So bright. So brief. So lovely.

And then, she was gone.

The experience had been so delightful that I wanted to share these moments. But what could I say? 'A girl came in and danced around the gallery.' No. I decided to keep it to myself. Never could I do justice to such a beautiful affair, but my mind danced to my children.

As the lonely days passed, I began to think it wasn't safe for any young woman to be in this inner city gallery, or even in the district, on her own. Especially when the street activity nearby verged on the dangerous, certainly sleazy. For this area was only a block or two from the infamous Kings Cross, Sydney's red-light district.

And now, yet another sculpture exhibition had run its course, without success, despite another lavish opening with the same 'rent a crowd' of VIP's who would, as they say, come to the opening of an envelope, just to be seen. Eva had been hoping to encourage appreciation of garden sculpture, with the exhibition filling the whole space. No-one showed any interest in the work because it all looked the same. Nothing had sold. So there the oxidised shapes stood, day after day. Motionless, without the dancing beauty. As if they'd died.

When night was drawing near, the sculptures formed grotesque shadows in the growing gloom, and an ominous atmosphere pervaded the whole gallery. It felt 'haunted,' and made me feel decidedly uneasy. The solitude made it worse. And when it came time to lock up the gallery, it did cross my mind that I could have been raped and pillaged, and left for dead there. The back door and the alarms were at the far end of this ancient warehouse. So, once I'd extinguished the lights, I had to make my exit walking the equivalent of the length of a football pitch, in the dark. I soon bought myself a powerful torch.

#

Sitting at the Contemporary Gallery's long, white reception desk, engrossed in book-work with not a soul in the gallery, and Heydn's Clock Symphony playing soothingly in the background, I felt a presence in front of me. Quickly looking up, I was startled to see a shabbily dressed young man peering down at me, only centimetres from my face. I jerked back in surprise. "Oh! You startled me," I said. And he really had.

"Yo! I'm Nick Vincente." He offered no apology for scaring me.

As he spoke, I couldn't help but notice black sores on his neck and face. "I've come to pick up a box that's been left here. It's an exhibit I entered in the OZ competition."

"What kind of box?" I enquired, pushing my mobile chair back from the desk to escape his foul smelling breath.

"It's about yay-by-yay." He made the shape of a shoe-box with his dirty hands, bringing attention to yet more black sores.

"Can you tell me what's in the box?" I asked prudently, conscious of the fact we were alone.

"The one with the glass dome. It's the remains of my friend, Larry - his ashes."

"Oh!" I gulped, pushing the chair back further to stand up. I knew the box he was referring to. I'd even peaked inside. In fact, I'd felt continually, irresistibly drawn to it. I had dusted it on numerous occasions, wondering why it was so compelling to me. I'd even touched the grey matter within its dome. And now I knew! I was suddenly embarrassed, perhaps ashamed. Had I known what the contents of the box were, I would have treated it with more reverence.

I went to fetch it, and returning, I placed it on the counter. "Anything taken..." I croaked, and cleared my throat. "Anything taken out of the gallery must be signed for." Reaching for the receipt pad, I filled it out, then offered the pen for him to sign. He made a quick scrawl but had not filled it in properly, failing to give the work a title. "What name was the box exhibited under?" I asked, trying to smile pleasantly at the young man who looked more like a damaged scare-crow than a human being.

"Still Life," he replied with a wry smile, then turned on his heel and departed the gallery with his boyfriend under his arm.

# CHAPTER 29

Although I enjoyed the autonomy of the Contemporary Gallery, I'd missed Georgie, and the beautiful artworks I'd grown to love at The Goldberg. Though I need not have fretted. My time at the Contemporary Gallery would soon be up. Eva had, without consultation with me, or warning, put an ad in the newspaper seeking a trainee manager for this gallery, directing all enquiries to me. I was inundated with calls for appointments for an interview. It seemed that I alone was to make the choice of a replacement. This was a first!

Fortunately, it turned out that I could tell a lot about the applicants by listening to their voices over the phone. Feeling that they would have to be mature enough to work here on their own, and not afraid to do so, I decided that they should therefore be of a certain age. Over twenty-five. And I hoped that a few males would apply for the heavy lifting. A bit sexist, but it was sensible.

A handsome, energetic young American by the name of Randy came in, saying that he was from California. I was lucky. He was a bright and friendly twenty-five year old with neat features. Blonde, clean looking and smart, he had a college degree in art, and was willing to do all the hard jobs, and stay for three years. After checking his impeccable references, I employed him. Just like that! Eva couldn't be bothered being involved, and Butler certainly didn't want the extra work. Besides, Randy was very likeable, obliging, and willing to work hard. I was sure I'd made a good choice.

It took me only two weeks to train him, telling him what to expect, and we became friends. I was quite sad to say goodbye to my new American buddy, but I had Georgie to look forward to. Sadly I knew, that everything in life has its price! With The Goldberg - came Eva, and Butler!

#

On the very first morning of my return to The Goldberg Gallery, I found Eva to be in a nasty mood. She was behind my desk screaming down the phone at an interstate art dealer. Not a good welcome, so I slipped into Georgie's bunker to say hello. We mouthed words of greeting, blew air kisses then I moved to hover around reception waiting for Madam to take her leave.

"Where's my money for the painting?" Eva yelled. "You send my money by special delivery, overnight, or I'll call the police!" She thumped the phone down and stomped off without as much as a 'hello' to me. "That bloody man's a crook," was my greeting!

"You're back, I see," said Butler contemptuously, charging off after Eva.

Once they'd gone, my dear friend came rushing to give me a generous hug. "Lilly my love. I'VE missed you, darling! Welcome back. You'll have her all to yourself soon. I booked my flight yesterday!"

"Oh, no Georgie! Don't leave me." She didn't realise how much I truly meant it.

"Sorry, but I'm getting out just in the nick of time to save my sanity. She's been an absolute tyrant since you've been gone, darling. She kept saying, 'I miss my angel.'"

"Oh, no! I hope she didn't say it in front of Butler," I sighed, and grabbed hold of reception, pretending to steady myself. Georgie just smiled. I walked around the desk to get settled. "You must tell me about your plans," I said, looking at my more than pretty friend. "I'm pleased for you, but hell, I wish you weren't leaving. The thought of just one day here without your lovely face to cheer me up is frightening. How long before you leave?"

"Two weeks!"

"Not a good way to start the day," I said, shaking my head while hiding away my handbag in the broom closet. "Does Her Majesty know yet?"

"Hasn't spoken to me since," she sniggered on bolthole re-entry.

As I settled myself on the ever uncomfortable Mr Wobbly, who'd degenerated even further since my 'vacation,' probably from Butler's big fat backside, I noticed a tiny piece of paper amongst some others with what looked like a poem on it. I recognised the handwriting, and read it, and thought how very clever it was! It began:

'CRITICAL INTELLECT'
*The intellectual critic,*
*blight upon talent,*
*literary locust*
*attacking frail blooms and stripping them bare.*
*The intellectual critic,*
*seeking depths where waters run shallow,*
*and ascribing meaning*
*where the only intent was to bleed the soul.*
*The intellectual critic,*
*scathing or skiting*
*at the whim of his liver,*
*his lover,*
*or the prevailing wind.*
*The intellectual critic,*
*powerful by default,*
*leech by profession,*
*descending from Olympus to remind mere mortals*
*that he too,*
*could have waxed as well,*
*Or better – if he so chose.*

I turned to look at my cell-mate through our open glass connection with a grand smile on my face. "Who's been sitting in my chair, and written a very clever poem?"

"Oh, thank you darling." She reached through the sliding glass panel to take the poem from me. "I dedicated it to Aldous Huxley – a great writer. I've been sending the manuscript of my first novella to Aussie publishers, and all I receive back are rejection slips. I'll soon have enough to wallpaper a room!"

"Don't worry," I smiled, trying to comfort my pal. "The UK publishers will snap you up. Talent like yours doesn't stay hidden forever. Just don't give up, because, if you do, you'll…" I couldn't finish my sentence. She finished it for me.

"You'll never reach your goal! Faders fade. Fighters fight on!"

"It's great to be back with you, Georgie."

I tried to go about my work, but it was hard to concentrate. I couldn't settle. Nothing seemed to be in the same spot. Taking a deep breath, I exhaled and tried to relax, taking in the scene around me. I certainly was in the most magnificent gallery, surrounded by beauty and prestige, and was grateful to be here, despite the negatives.

Being ensconced at the Contemporary Gallery for a few months, I'd missed the exhibitions at The Goldberg, and now I felt the need to familiarise myself with the new artworks hanging on the walls. That way, I could speak with authority to customers on behalf of the artists, and their work. With that goal in mind, I asked Georgie to 'hold the fort,' while I took a quick tour.

The Goldberg invitation always portrayed a photograph of the art to be exhibited the following month, and it looked interesting. The upcoming exhibition would show off the works of a new artist, Christina Cray. They were sea scapes. Big, bold and striking. But not an angry sea. Not huge waves. Just horizontal lines melting together mysteriously into a far horizon. The colours, a mix of soft blues, greens, silver sheen, white and cream. Serene. Very easy to live with. And yes, I would gladly put them on my wall.

It hadn't taken long to satisfy my interest, although I could so easily have stayed there admiring the work, but I didn't want to be found absent from my post, so I moved with haste. Returning to reception, I settled down on Mr Wobbly again, just as the phone rang.

"Edward Livingston," said the warmest of voices at the other end. "Juanita Mendez' curator." The wealthy Juanita lived in Western Australia, where her husband was involved in iron ore, but often visited the glorious harbour city of Sydney when a new musical, or theatre production was being launched. She was a great art patron, and had made magnificent contributions to ballet, theatre, and music, and owned theatres, both here and overseas.

I recognised the voice. "Oh hello, Mr Livingston. It's Lilly."

"Ah, Lilly! How are you?" His voice was cheery in recognition. "I didn't receive my invitation for the latest Goldberg exhibition."

"Oh, I'm so sorry. Your invitation must have gone astray. Is it too late to send one out now?"

"Just describe the work to me, Lilly. I like the sound of your voice."

If there was one thing I didn't lack it was enthusiasm! I went into full selling mode. These new works by Christina Cray had genuinely impressed me, and I told him so. I described the work as best as my vocabulary, and my creativity would allow, and was sure I'd done the artist proud, and finished my spiel with, "Mrs Goldberg is very proud of the work, Mr Livingston. Especially the one on the invitation I've described to you, and it hasn't sold yet!" How could he resist?

"Send it to me, Lilly."

"But, Mr Livingston, I haven't told you the price."

"Doesn't matter. Your description sold me. Besides, as you say, she's a young woman with a future, and has a distinctive style. I'll add it to our collection. It's her lucky day! Thanks, Lilly. I'll talk to you again soon."

"Yes, Mr Livingston. Thank you."

Christina Cray, the young artist had asked Eva to put the price on her work because she had no idea what the market would pay. Eva had put it up for sale for $85,000 ignoring the fact she was an unknown artist. 'Sometimes bluff does the job, Lilly!' she'd said, adding, 'It's the flash that bags the cash!'

And I sold it. First morning back!

#

Mesmerized by the click of the keys of Georgie's keyboard as she rattled off a report for Eva's son Michael, who would often drop into the gallery with page after page of typing needs, connected to his numerous cattle-breeding properties, I sat listening, my mind wandering. The busy keys seemed to have a hypnotic beat: Da dada dada dada.....da dada dada da............

I was transported back in time to a little cottage of my childhood. I could hear a drum, tambourine, a wooden spoon rapping rhythmically on pots and pans. The mood was fun. There was gaiety and laughter. I was marching, in circles, following Mina around Daddy Bob's chair. Our little family of three was singing:

*They have no tanks or rifles,*
*They have no stripes or drill,*
*They have no ships or aeroplanes,*
*But England needs them still.*
*They're fighting hard with axe and saw,*
*They're Britain's Women's Timber Corps.*

# CHAPTER 30

Plans were in place to visit Birmingham in England, as I was soon due to have my annual holiday. My real mother was institutionalised there. Meanwhile, I'd written to the superintendent of 'Broadlands,' the care facility she lived in, and had received a letter back. It was explained to me in the letter, that the writer, one of the nurses, had put pen to paper on behalf of Betty, or Elizabeth, as they called her. My mother had merely signed it.

My feelings on receiving that note were mixed. Sadness - combined with self-pity at having my real mother kept hidden from me all those years. I'd been denied the chance to get to know her. And I was shocked to learn, that unable to care for herself, she'd been in this institution for thirty years. The letter had contained little detail, just a cursory overall description of her circumstances - the fact that she had her own bedroom, was able to wander in the garden, and that she loved her food. I felt the only way I'd get satisfactory answers to my multitude of questions, was if I were to make a personal visit to see her in England. Not that I expected much more from a letter, but it left me feeling numb.

There was nothing to stop me from phoning to speak with my mother directly –nothing, except fear. The mere thought of it made me uneasy. What would I say? What would she say? If she were affected mentally, what would she be able to say to me, a total stranger? The truth of the matter was - I was afraid of rejection - a second time. She had rejected me once, I couldn't face it again. Especially now, whilst my emotions were in turmoil. Nor did I want to put her in an uncomfortable position of perhaps having to defend herself, or her choices. Face to face would be so much more forgiving, and friendly. That way, she could see I wasn't looking for any sort of confrontation. Or had any expectations of her. I just wanted to show her my love. I had it in heaps! That primitive urge that's in us all. The word 'MOTHER' is all it takes!

Meanwhile, I refused to visit the Palm Beach Aged Care facility. Following my last visit there, I'd made it clear in no uncertain terms that Mary Campbell was not to call me again at The Goldberg. I'd used blackmail, saying that I would tell her boyfriend what she'd done to me. The phone calls had ceased. My visits had ceased. But there were now four holes in my heart! I'd lost my two children, the mother I never knew, and now my grandmother was lost to me.

#

I was not in any mood for Eva after receiving the mail from Birmingham, but take it, I did, when she pulled that damned stool up close, after slamming shut Georgie's peep hole. This action was merely a symbolic, defiant gesture of exclusion, because Georgie's little nook also had a door, which remained constantly open.

"Lilly." She settled herself, rubbing her calves. Story time! This was going to be a long one, I could tell. "Henry wants me to sell the gallery!"

Wow! This was a new phenomenon. Later, when I had time to think about it, it made sense. Eva was no chicken, but her age was hard to gauge. Her fire, her energy, the way she carried out her duties with gusto, her glamorous clothes, and the money she spent on maintaining her appearance, all made it hard to guess precisely how old she was.

As Shakespeare has Domitius Enobarbus say of Cleopatra in 'Antony and Cleopatra' - 'Age cannot wither her, nor custom stale her infinite variety.' Those famous words came quickly to mind as I looked at her beguiling face, and I could think of no-one else, ever, who deserved them more than Eva.

Georgie had once said she thought Eva to be at least seventy. I thought that was pretty close, but I guessed she could very well be much older.

Whatever the case, I wondered how long Eva could keep up with the demands on her time, either from family, or from business? Added to this, were the extremely stressful times, when artists like Donald Friend caused her such angst, ran her off her feet, and gave her sleepless nights.

It amused me often, as I observed her with fascination, when she would screw up that once beautiful, still lovely, pampered face, saying, 'See, I'm not stupid, yet!' The potential onset of dementia really worried her. She was genuinely concerned about 'losing it.' She hated the thought of losing control.

Wanting to confide in me this particular day, and needing a 'private session' with me while she sat on her little stool, she began by telling me how badly Henry wanted to turn The Goldberg Gallery into condominiums. That thought horrified even me! Was nothing sacred to him but money? Apparently, he'd been badgering her at home about it constantly. It was her worst nightmare, depriving her of the gallery, her 'queendom.'

Intimate, private matters like this were about to be spewed forth for my consumption.

"He wants me to look after him now that he's old and sick! But it's my life, Lilly! I love my gallery! Where was he when I needed him, when the children were young? He was too busy chasing girls and money. Pah! I'll never give up the gallery!"

Undeniably, I felt genuine sympathy for her. There was nothing worse than having something you truly loved taken from you. "It would be awful for you, Mrs Goldberg."

Eva's face suddenly took on a girlish smugness, as she told me how she'd been awarded the Order of Australia for her contribution to the art world. Then her eyes became evil slits. "You know, Lilly. No matter how much money Henry's made, he'll never get one of those! HUH!" she squawked. "Clever girl, aren't I?" she scoffed, chuckling at her own achievement.

Meanwhile I was worried she'd fall off that damned stool!

"You know, Lilly, I have a leopard-skin coat. A real one. I got the hem fixed last year, made shorter. But the last time I wore it to the theatre, Henry wore his slippers. What can I do?" She shrugged, and her ugly, down at mouth face made an appearance. "I told you he was afraid to die?" She said it as a question, and I nodded. "He cries in his sleep. He cries all the time, Lilly."

Her seemingly endless conversation came in bursts, while I was expected to down tools and pay full attention. Each tale unrelated to the matter which had gone before, an uneven stream of unconnected short stories about whatever took her fancy, and all the while, I tried to remain focussed and interested. She truly was fascinating. Georgie shared this fascination with me, and I knew that any time Georgie was present, in her little cage, then she too would be listening through the always open door, and taking notes for her journal.

"You know, Lilly, Henry sold a huge building in the city last week. One hundred and ninety-six million dollars. Now he can't sleep worrying about what to do with his money!" Those padded shoulders sagged, and I got the full, 'pity me' treatment. "When he went to have his first heart operation, six years ago, he sold a big goldmine he thought was no good. He didn't want the children to worry about something that wasn't working. You understand?" Her silken legs were getting the full massage workout. She hadn't moved from the stool, and I was trapped in position, but somehow, I felt a kind of privilege.

"Yes, Mrs Goldberg, I do understand," I said sympathetically. And I did! My heart ached for her. Like anyone, she had emotional issues that caused her problems, and I'd bet she couldn't share them with her children. Rich or poor, children are not interested in their parents' dilemas; they have their own. It occurred to me that she considered me inconsequential, being outside her family, and therefore 'safe' to open up to. So on she went.

"But you know what, Lilly, the other day, this gold mine made a strike! Billions!" Up went the arms in the air, and I was ready to catch her, if she unbalanced – physically. "Now it's worth more money than any goldmine in Australia, EVER, and Henry is crying like a baby again! He sold too soon. PAH! Silly old bugger!"

Then without warning, she sprang to her feet and dashed past me, toward the Salvatore landscape recently hung behind reception. Her mercurial mind had flashed onto a new subject that was important to her in that instant.

"Look, Lilly! That stupid man, Umberto Salvatore. Look!" She pointed toward a four-metre-long landscape which was said to be the high, pyramid-shaped cliff behind Buderim in Queensland, but to my eye it looked much more like the rugged Cairngorm Mountain range in Scotland. Rough, ragged rocks, where the wild wind blows the heather flat, and the deer roam free. "He's used house paint and no primer. It's a new painting, Lilly, and look it's all cracking!" Eva fingered the expensive artwork, flaking off paint as she went. "Do you think we'll sell it, Lilly?" There was not as much as a glance at me. "You think someone will pay $125,000?"

"I... really don't know, Mrs Goldberg."

Then like lightening, the subject was changed again. She sat back down close to me at my desk, and, tapping the desktop with a pencil lying there, commanded, "I want you to phone Robertini. Now, Lilly! Get him to deliver a sculpture, my son Michael wants one."

I did as I was bidden.

Once the mistress of The Goldberg had completed her brief telephone conversation with the talented, handsome, young sculptor, I noticed that her demeanour had changed. The weight of gloom had departed her shoulders. She'd brightened up, and in a more agreeable mood, she pulled the stool even closer, and was ready to continue. And I was beguiled anew by her charm.

Reflecting on this episode that night at home, I wondered whether Eva had really begun to like me a little. Or, as she did with so many artists and customers, only wanted me to think she did! I wondered if anyone knew the real Eva? I doubted whether even she did - she was so accustomed to role-playing!

"Did I ever tell you the story about Eduardo Mullier, Lilly?" She smiled, rocking on the stool.

Giving a little shake of the head, I waited. Bewitched. Charmed even, by her glamorous smile and her seeming trust in me.

"It's a funny story." She screwed tight her eyes, mischievously. "Well now, Eduardo leased a studio from my husband in an old building in the city. When Eduardo was ninety-six, the lease ran out, so he came back to my husband for another lease. He wanted five and five."

I received a tremendously capricious grin.

"You mean....?"

"Yes." She threw her head back and laughed. "He wanted another five year lease, plus the option for five more years, after that – at ninety-six years of age!"

"At ninety six?" I queried, hoping Georgie wasn't missing this gem.

"Yes." Eva was in stitches, convinced I had the full appreciation of the story. "Even Henry laughed at him! Henry really wanted to use the building himself, you know, but he's been friends with Eduardo for such a long time, nearly fifty years, so he gave him what he wanted. Five years, with an option for another five, thinking probably, that in one year, maybe two, Eduardo would die! But, Eduardo is now one hundred and three, and he's still painting!" Back went her head to laugh again, and I became aware there was not one dark filling in her perfected teeth.

"You know, Lilly, these artists live a long time. I think it's the easy life. What about Lloyd? He's ninety two, you know. And Cavelli, he's ninety six. They still paint." She raised her eyebrows and nodded, as if to agree with herself. "They're still good."

I waited, at her mercy.

"Another funny story for you, Lilly... Sali Herman married at eighty-five to a forty-five year old nurse, thinking she would look after him in his old age." She sniggered. "But the wife died straight away! Cancer! Now Sali is ninety-seven, and all alone."

Her glee at his plight gave me shivers.

With flashing mental agility, as if a buzzer had gone off in her head to terminate one train of thought and switch on another, she jumped up again. The joy had suddenly vanished from her face and was replaced with a scowl. "I want you to write a letter to the Chinese Consulate, and thank them for the invitation to dinner." She was on the move now, gathering her bits and pieces ready for a quick get-a-way, throwing everything, including her broken umbrella, into a plastic bag - she, whose husband owned a handbag factory, and a separate umbrella factory.

I presumed she'd been referring to the Chinese Consul General. Eva had exhibited the first works to be allowed out of the People's Republic of China since the Cultural Revolution.

As she departed, she turned to deliver a final directive at me. Nodding toward several people viewing artworks in the main gallery, she instructed, "See that you don't let those customers out without them buying something!"

And she was gone.

Georgie came out of her bunker with a grin stretched from ear to ear. "I heard every word, Lilly darling. Delightful!"

#

Only twenty minutes later, Eva returned in tears. It was genuinely a sad sight. Having a grandmother cry before your eyes is not an easy thing to witness. I wanted to run to her and comfort her, but she was not the type to accept my affection. Certainly not the type I could cuddle or hug.

It seemed that in her rush to get home, she'd parked her car over someone's driveway when she stopped to buy Henry's dinner from her favourite Woollahra delicatessen. There was very little parking in the Queen Street shopping area. Through her heart-breaking sobs, I managed to pick up the latest tragedy.

"The man who owns the house in Queen Street where I parked, was waiting for me when I came back to my car. Yes, I was across his driveway, but he knows me, Lilly. But still, he was so angry with me. He screamed and screamed at me." The tears were big, dripping tears. She did nothing by halves! "He was screaming at me all the time I was putting my groceries in the car, yelling swear words at me in the street, in front of everybody!"

"I'm sorry, Mrs Goldberg."

Her head went to one side in agony, like Bernini's tortured depiction of St Theresa, when an angel of the Lord has pierced her heart with a golden flaming arrow filling her with pain. "They all know me, Lilly. Everybody knows me there! The butcher, the cake shop, the delicatessen, the flower shop, all the fancy little shops. I spend lots of money with them. Every day! All of the shops." More heaving sobs. "My money pays their rent." Her tissue was saturated. "Everybody could hear him! They could see him yelling at me. I should sue him!"

Trying to comfort her as best I could, I led her to her study to call her lawyer. As I escorted her down the three steps, I noticed that Georgie too, was on her feet and concerned.

"He called me 'an old tart,'" Sniff, snuffle sniff. "He told me the police were coming. He said I was 'a selfish old bitch,'" she sobbed. "He said I think I can do whatever I like because I have money. He said I think it can fix everything!" She fumbled in her plastic bag for a tissue.

"I was so upset that I drove away with the door open, and I banged two more parked cars on the roadside! Now everybody is upset with me. He screamed at me all the time I was trying to get away. Everybody saw him, and everybody heard him swear at me." She had reached her office now, and was behind her desk with a hand on the telephone.

I told her how sorry I was, but reminded her that it's an offence to block a driveway. "What if someone was ill, Mrs Goldberg, and had to be driven to hospital in a hurry?"

"You think I can sue for defamation, Lilly?" The words had fallen on deaf ears.

#

As was so often the case now, Vince did not come home until one in the morning. I heard him come to bed, and heard his snores the moment his head touched the pillow.

Next morning when I was in the shower, he tapped on the glass, signalling he was off to work. "Got to rush, Lilly. Got a breakfast meeting! See you later." And he was gone.

Stepping from the shower, I towelled myself down thinking about Vince and our deteriorating relationship. My situation at home had become as intolerable as that at the gallery. I felt like a coiled spring. My enthusiasm was wilting, and I'd lost my sense of humour. We'd not properly cleared the air since the last altercation. I knew there was a very real problem to be ironed out.

Our sex life had become virtually non-existent, and that bothered me. Sexual intercourse had kept me feeling close to Vince. It was an intimacy I treasured. A constant rejuvenation of our union. A cementing of a bond. Although I didn't show it, without that conjugal love I'd become insecure, suspicious, and jealous of his life – a life from which I felt excluded. Instead of telling Vince how I felt, I'd bottled it up. I'd begun to ask myself if Vince had someone else. I couldn't prove anything, and he certainly wasn't volunteering anything, but I'd put money on it.

Were we to just keep on going? Saying nothing? Maintaining the status quo? If he'd found someone else, why wasn't he willing to tell me? And why was he still with me? There must be something I wasn't doing right. As was so often the case, I blamed myself.

Dressed, I headed for the door, fondly touching the photograph of my two little ones which sat on top of the TV set, as I did every time I left the house. In my heart, I knew that the situation with Vince must soon come to a head, but I didn't have the courage to be the one to bring about the inevitable showdown.

# CHAPTER 31

I made a discovery that shook me to my foundation. A mutual friend told me that within a month of his departure from Brisbane, a female TV station employee, Sue Chesterman had followed Vince to Sydney town. As coincidence would have it, an aunt had died and left her a three storey terrace-house just around the corner from our place, in one of Paddington's prime locations, plus a bankroll that could buy her three more.

Not only had Sue moved in on my partner, she'd moved into a key presenter's spot at the network. This was the position Vince had promised me, when I made the move to Sydney. A promise he hadn't kept. A position I would have relished, at a capital city television station. He'd told me the spot had already been allocated. And so it had – to Sue Chesterman. His sexy 'bit on the side.'

Sadly, that same day, I was to say farewell to Georgie. I drove her to the airport with my rage reigned in, valiantly trying to maintain control after my mortifying discovery. I was determined not to let Georgie see how devastated I was. She was heading off to a happy home life, I couldn't unsettle her.

"I'm going to miss you terribly," I admitted, driving my friend along Kingsford Smith Drive, so sad to see her leave and return to England.

We both had tears in our eyes as we hugged outside the Customs and Immigration gate at Sydney's International air terminal. "You've been a true friend, Georgie. I've come to rely on you for your humour and sanity in that stressful place."

"I feel exactly the same. If it hadn't been for you, I'd never have lasted so long." She hugged me again. "I'll thank you in my book 'The Queen of Arts,' Lilly, darling. Remember, I've kept notes. All the crazy things she did. All the nasty ones, too. But I'll rave about The Goldberg Gallery, so you'll have lots of new friends when they visit from England. You can play tourist guide, and have fun with them."

We were each trying to keep the other's spirits up.

"Think of all the good times you'll have when you get home, Georgie. You'll have parties galore." I looked lovingly into the eyes of this beautiful English rose, to let her know how fond of her I was. "I feel as if you've been paroled from jail, and I'm still doing my time. I got life in solitary confinement – with hard labour."

I was not a happy girl at all, at the prospect of having to face Eva each day, without the comforting friendship of Georgie, to share the bad times, but I kept a stiff upper lip as I said goodbye. I did not divulge my problem with Vince. "It's summer in England, of course," I added, as joyfully as I could. "London will be at its best. Hyde Park will be stunning. I wish I were coming with you."

"Well you have the address, and we have a big house in the city, and others in the countryside. No hotels or any of that naff nonsense for you! Oh, I nearly forgot. This is Jean Metcalfe's telephone number. I just want to make sure you have it. She likes you, Lilly, and she'll make a good friend if you need one."

My darling Georgie kissed me on both cheeks, then with tears streaming from her eyes, turned away from me, and walked quickly toward the large automatic doors that were swallowing departing passengers.

"Thank you, Georgie." I called out. "I'll keep it safe." I slipped the note into my jacket pocket. And then my gallery buddy had gone, leaving me staring at the doorway that was forbidden to me.

#

Heading home to Paddington in the flowing evening traffic, I felt very much alone. My whole life seemed to be in tatters. Georgie was the only person I trusted, and the one who'd been there for me. Now that I'd put two and two together about Vince, and Sue, he appeared to me to be nothing more than yet another person who'd betrayed me.

Sad thoughts flooded my mind… Betty my mother had betrayed me, by giving me to Mary Campbell. Mary had betrayed me, by giving me to Bob and Mina. They had betrayed me by leaving me behind when they'd emigrated to Australia. Mary had betrayed me anew, by treating me as a servant, rather than a member of the family. And Mitch my ex-husband had betrayed me, and very nearly destroyed me. I felt at that moment as if I'd been born to be deceived! With that sort of life, I'd been slow to trust Vince. And now he'd gone and betrayed that trust.

Feeling more than a little sorry for myself, I shed a quiet tear on the way home. 'Home.' I thought about that word. Sydney didn't feel like home any more. Thoughts about London had reawakened something in me. Memories forgotten, 'till now. As I drove, I could see a kaleidoscope of colours…………

Beautiful gowns of satin and silk. Aromas of sensual perfumes. Joyful chatter. Laughter. I could feel the bustle of excitement. Pretty girls with flowers in their hair. My real mother was young and beautiful then. I remember, I sat, as a tiny tot, in the middle of a huge bed surrounded by ladies' ball gowns. Extravagant stage costumes. A dressing table covered with theatre makeup, creams, lotions, perfumes, potions. My mother, my talented, musical genius mother, took off her shimmering silk dressing gown, and stood naked in front of me before donning underwear and a magnificent, floor length evening dress. She was the most beautiful thing I'd ever seen. Was I on loan to her? I didn't understand.

She was touring with the Ivy Bensen Big Band as lead trumpet and vocalist. The band had made its name entertaining wartime troops all around Britain. I remembered someone, a man, carrying me on his shoulders, amongst a lot of men in uniform. White, brown, blue uniforms. Pretty girls were dancing in pretty dresses. I was watching my mother playing a trumpet solo, and singing. A beautiful, mournful melody. 'Someone to watch over me…'

American culture had arrived in Britain. I'd seen posters advertising the band while growing up in the Dundee Boarding House. Mary had kept a scrapbook and memorabilia: 'Sexy saxophones, classy clarinets, trill trombones, trident trumpets, frisky French horns, a percussion section second to none,' said the poster, 'chimes, bells, triangles, guitars, zingy xylophone's, castanets, tambourines, grand pianos, double-bass, played by accomplished, dazzling blondes, brunettes, and redheads with cherry lips, and shapely curves – everything from Latin to Boogy. Lead trumpet: 'Betty Campbell - Scotland's Harry James.'

#

In that sad frame of mind, the empty terrace seemed to me a reflection of my empty life. I was hurting, and needed to talk about it. If only I'd been able to talk to Vince it may not have reached the 'edge of the cliff' stage. But what would he have done? He was so wound up in his own world he didn't have time for me. Now, after this painful discovery, my anger was at explosive level.

The more intense my frustration had become since joining Eva at the gallery, the greater my feelings of impotence. Impotence which made me feel I'd lost control of my life, and without control, I felt trapped - without hope. The greater the feeling of hopelessness - the greater my growing rage.

I'd decided on my journey from the airport, that I could not, and further, would not, continue to live this way any longer. But first, I had to talk to Vince, and get things out in the open. What would be keeping him out tonight, I wondered. His programme people? His sales people? Visiting VIP's? Or Sue Chesterman? Another knife in my back!

#

Discarding my jacket as soon as I entered the terrace, I poured myself a stiff scotch, and drank it down in one gulp. Pouring another, I angrily flung off my shoes. I let my listless body drop heavily onto the sofa, like a dumped rag doll.

With the life drained out of me, the alcohol quickly took hold. I felt numb and heavy. My mind drifted to the events at the gallery. The images became ugly and twisted. Eva's panther eyes flashed menacingly before me. Her florid red lips, angry, contorted, cursing, spitting fury. Hunched like a cat about to spring. Eva bared her teeth and snarled at me.

This threatening image which loomed up in front of me seemed real enough to make me shudder. I could never remember a time when Eva wasn't talking incessantly, like a stuck record. Or screaming about something that annoyed her. "I want you to phone…! I want you to write a letter, NOW! Lilly where is…? Lilly, what did you do with…? I didn't sleep last night, Lilly. Donald Friend upset me. I vomited up so strong I think I burned my throat. I was so upset. That Donald is a bully. He asked Henry for a tip on the share-market. Henry said the share-market is going to crash. I'll tell you something, Lilly, now listen… I'm a good girl, aren't I? I'm not stupid, yet!"

Her shrill words rang in my ears. They spewed out with conveyor-belt consistency. They reverberated in my head like deafening, clanging bells from which there was no escape. Sounds from the past were re-occurring, memories long forgotten, remembered. Nasty visions, reappeared. Distant, yet familiar. They were echoes from another time, another place. It was Mary Campbell's laughter! Her shrill voice. Always at me. Chastising me. Telling me I was a bastard bitch, that owned nothing. Deserved nothing. Would always be a nothing! I owed her! Could do nothing right! Faster. Faster. Faster. Work harder. Harder. Harder.

I felt rising panic. A panic that had plagued me since childhood. Eva Goldberg had taken Mary Campbell's place. Had become the new, unrelenting, invincible threat to my sanity. She'd become the domineering figure that forced me to react like a frightened child. The past had become the present. A past that held me captive. I felt closed in. Imprisoned. The old torments were re-lived through the menacing Eva Goldberg.

There seemed no escape.

# CHAPTER 32

"How could you, Vince?" I pounced on the man who'd deceived me as soon as he came in the door. I'd fought the overriding temptation to confront him whilst I was so angry, but my fury got the better of me, and I couldn't hold it in. "I've put up with a lot from you, Vince, but I can't forgive this! How could you do this to me?"

He stood toe-to-toe with me, hands on his hips. "How could I do what?" he bit back, defensively.

"You arranged a job for Sue Chesterman. You've done nothing but lie to me all the time we've been here!"

He knew by the tone of my voice, and my deliberate stance, that this scene had all the hallmarks of a bitter confrontation. He walked away, taking off his jacket.

I knew from experience he'd never admit it. But this time, I wanted him to know what I thought of him. "Don't turn your back on me! Tell me the truth, Vince!" I shouted in an unprecedented fit of temper. "I turned on the TV and there she was! In MY job! Why her, and not me? Did you bring her down from Brisbane with all sorts of promises too?"

"Oh, come on, Lilly – it's only a segment on the Breakfast Show." He slapped his briefcase down on the polished dining table in uncustomary pique.

"What was wrong with ME doing it?" I was flushed with rage. "Why did you have to give it to HER, of all people? What did she have to do for it,

Vince? Did you screw her? Is that it? And it's been going on for ages, behind my back."

"Lilly. Calm down! Calm down!"

"What d'you mean, 'calm down'? Why should I calm down? You betrayed me. You gave HER a job in preference to ME! With all of my TV experience. And you've kept it from me, all this time. I turned on the television, and there she was. Here, in Sydney! I rang her. I spoke to her. And how very smug she was! She told me you'd given her the job within a month of our coming to Sydney! Why?"

"They wanted somebody – fresh. Young!"

That did it! My response to that outburst was to be expected. I was deeply hurt. "Why didn't you tell me, Vince?" My boiling anger was verging on tears. My voice quavering. I'd lost control. "You could have warned me. Why did you wait for me to find out? You made me look a fool. You humiliated me. Damn you!"

"Aw, Christ, Lilly..."

"Don't mess with me, Vince. You know how desperate I was to get back into television. I've been lost without it. The damned gallery's like a sponge – it's soaked up any identity I may have had."

"For Christ's sake Lilly. Stop it! You're behaving like a pedantic child." He moved towards the drinks table, lifted the scotch bottle and held it up at eye level, then made a face of disgust, at how little there was left in it. He turned to me with a glower, then poured himself a drink, emptying the bottle, saying, "Well thanks for leaving me a thimble full."

"You bastard, Vince! How could you betray me like this?" I yelled at him again, ignoring his cheap shot. "You've lied to me all this time. You brought me here for nothing. Why?" I grabbed my prized copy of 'Castles of Scotland' from the coffee table and flung it in his direction.

He sidestepped quickly and it narrowly missed him, flying past and crashing into the wall. He glared at me. "I'm fucked if I'm taking this shit from any woman!"

He downed the contents of the glass then strode across the room. He pushed me out of the way. Grabbed up his briefcase and jacket again, and headed for the front door.

"Where are you going?" I demanded, following at his heel. "Why, Vince? Why did you let me move in here with you in the first place, if it was Sue you wanted? What's wrong with you, anyway? Isn't one woman enough?" I screamed, out of control.

He couldn't look me in the eye. Nor did he want to. His guilt was etched all over his face, and his intentions were to get out of there as fast as he possibly could. Coldly, he glared at me. But did not answer.

"You've let me live a lie the whole time we've been in Sydney. Did you only bring me here to wash your shirts?" My words were wasted. He slammed shut the terrace front door so forcefully, that the whole building shook. Ignoring my pleas, ignoring my need for an explanation, Vince walked out on me, leaving me alone again. My rage had finally erupted. And like a volcano, I still had much to vent. Storming around the lounge-room, I kicked furniture, and shouted, with tears spewing through the anger. I knew I couldn't prove he was having an affair with Sue without a confession – but it was pretty damned obvious. It all added up. I felt like a redundant fool.

No wonder the bastard didn't want me working at his damned television station!

I cried aloud, dragging an unopened Scotch bottle from the drinks cabinet. I opened it defiantly, and screamed, 'BASTARD!' Slamming shut the cabinet with an almighty whack, adding a kick from my foot to thump it closed.

By midnight, I'd consumed a disgusting amount of twenty-five year old malt whisky. I sat alone. My only companions, the whisky bottle and the television set. I gazed dazedly through tear-filled eyes, and a drink induced haze at flickering images on the screen, and thought how ironic it was, to ever have thought television my friend. It was instead, the very cause of my agony! I looked at the whisky bottle with shame. Another whisky bottle, at another time appeared before my eyes, and then I saw a dragonfly on Mary Campbell's neck. It was at the Aberfeldy Boarding House in Brisbane. She had screamed hysterically, and I, a fourteen year old at the time, had had to slap her to bring her to her senses.

"Oh, no!" I was repeating her behaviour. Drinking to ease the pain. I was shocked at myself. But my tears were not only because of Vince. My tears were for my children. I always cried for them when things were bad. I couldn't handle thoughts of them, right now. That was for another day. When I was strong.

I slid from the sofa, down onto the carpet. With my legs parted and outstretched, I sat with the bottle of scotch between, a tissue box on one side, and a pile of tear-soaked, discarded tissues on the other.

I drank and sobbed. Sobbed and drank. I blew my nose. I sniffed. I cursed. I shouted. And when enough alcohol had taken hold, I began to cry like a lost child sobbing for its mother. Loud, pitiful sobs. Aching, heart-breaking sobs. My breath became laboured. I gasped for air in between the heaving sobs. I swallowed thickly. Sucking in air. Coughing.

"Why?" I cried aloud. "Why does it have to be me?"

The silence didn't answer me, so I shouted at it. "Do you hear me? Does anybody hear me?" I screamed. Then I began to rock backwards and forwards, hugging myself, as a child would, to comfort itself. "When will all the pain end? When?" I moaned. "Let me die! I want to die! I want to die!"

Images flickered at me from the television screen. Robert Redford held his gun pointed at a big fat rat. Then the camera closed in on Brubaker's handsome face. At that precise moment in time, I, Lillian Lightwood, even hated Robert Redford! So much so, that I grabbed a shoe and threw it at the innocent cowboy. The shoe bounced off Robert Redford's forehead.

I swallowed another mouthful of scotch. My head was giddy, my eyes swollen. I was angry at the whole world. Angry at Vince, angry at myself for being such an idiot. Naïve. Stupid! What had I done to deserve all this heartache? Would I never find anyone who wouldn't use me? Deceive me?

Mary Campbell's words rang in my ears. "God'll punish y' for leavin' an auld wifie in a home. You mark my words. Girls are supposed to look after their auld folk. Ye'll never be happy in Sydney at my expense! I hope y'll be miserable as sin! Shrivel up, and grow auld. Wissent, auld and lonely!"

If I'd looked in the mirror I'd have seen that Mary Campbell had been granted her wish.

I spent the evening alone with my anger, falling asleep on the living room floor. Only to wake next morning to face the heartache again, with the added pain of a crushing hangover. Dreading the day ahead at the gallery, feeling like death, with a blinding headache, and expecting to throw up at any moment, I was determined to soldier on until I could think clearly enough to make a decision about my future.

Dragging myself upstairs to shower and dress, I passed the bedroom with its king size bed. The bed in which Vince and I had so often made love. It had not been slept in. Vince had not come home.

# CHAPTER 33

With Georgie gone, I'd hoped that Barry Butler might be kinder to me, but no. I'd become Eva's 'angel,' prepared to go the extra mile for The Goldberg, and Butler was jealous of our relationship. Jealous that Eva could be intimate with me about her personal problems.

The telephone rang. An old friend of mine from Brisbane was on the line - Stella Stevens. The kind of girlfriend that can get you into trouble, so you enjoy them only in small doses. But very much in need of company, I was eager to talk to someone, anyone, about my situation, so I listened to what she had to say.

"I'm in Sydney!" said she.

"You're not?"

"On my way to Melbourne. I'm going to be the new reporter for, 'Sun Up.' Dean Saunders and I came up with a new programme idea. We have some filming to do here, and meet with the 'higher-ups' before we head off. So, while I'm waiting for Dean, I'll shop, shop, shop!"

"How fabulous. Can I see you, Stella?"

"Sure can! I have a few nights staying at the Cosmo in Double Bay, and the channel is picking up the tab! Come have a meal with me tonight!"

"Around 6.30? You're just what the doctor ordered, Stella."

"Fantastic! Room 107!"

When I returned the phone to its cradle I had a smile on my face.

#

I knew the Cosmopolitan Hotel well. It was the meeting place for Sydney's who's who. The hotel where Sydney's glitziest glitterati congregated, just to see who could see them. The rich loved to be noticed 'being rich.' It was the expensive 'in' place where tip-conscious waitresses never gave change.

Walking past the ground floor restaurant area to the lifts, I stepped into a mirrored box, pressed the button for the first floor, and half a minute later the doors slid silently open. I walked the corridor to the door labelled 107 and knocked. Moments later the door opened, and I stepped into the embracing arms of Stella Stevens.

Wearing nothing but a white bath towel, Stella greeted me looking like a diminutive young Tahitian maiden. She was a tanned, healthy, and beautiful thirty-year-old. We hugged with great affection. A joy to be around, Stella was hungry for life. She seemed to live more intensely than other people. Was open to a wider array of experiences than most, as if the colours on her palette were a little brighter, the highlights and the shadows on her canvas more contrasted. People appeared beautiful to her. The world was a place to enjoy.

"Lilly! My God it's good to see you." She smiled from ear to ear as she held open wide the door. "Come in. Come in." Her excitement was contagious. She was young, fresh, and full of vitality - just what television needed, I thought, peevishly, feeling miserably redundant.

"Look what we have," she said, sprinting like a ballerina over to a bottle of champagne on ice. She held up a dripping, icy vintage Bollinger like a magician with-drawing a white rabbit from a hat. It had already been opened. She poured a glass for me. "Come on, catch up. I've had a glass already and I feel wonderful!" She held out a sizzling flute and stood right in front of me until I'd had a generous mouthful. And I will admit that I thoroughly enjoyed the light frothy bubbles that danced playfully on my tongue.

"That should brighten me up!" I looked around the room for a place to sit down, only to find that every surface was covered with Stella's new purchases.

She saw me looking. "Just a few things," she giggled.

The only place to sit was the bed – and even then I had to gently push aside a bright, buttercup yellow sundress with blue cornflowers scattered over it. "You must've spent a fortune!"

"Yeeeeees!" she answered gleefully. "Dean told me to buy six new outfits for the show. Have a look at these, Lilly." She held up a profusion of different coloured jackets, in different styles, which could all be worn with a black skirt.

"Very smart! You have great taste, Stella, and the news about the show is great."

"We've been trying to get the programme idea up for ages, but Sam Hutchins was procrastinating. So I took him in hand – in the make-up room – if you know what I mean?" She giggled. "Voila!"

Then as I watched in disbelief, as she untied the towel, and began dancing stark naked around the room, just like someone who'd won the lottery. As light as a prima ballerina. Like a nymphet in a fairy tale; holding out her towel on either side, then in a final sweeping, fluid motion, she drifted over to me, descending on me as I sat entranced. She encircled me in her arms, entwining me in the wings of the towel, then bent to sweetly touch my lips with a kiss.

I found myself hovering between embarrassment and amusement.

She smiled down at me lovingly, with her full breasts, and pert, upturned nipples close to touching my face. She remained close to me like this without either of us speaking a word for a moment or two. Then, beginning with only a hint of movement, her hips began to sway, rotate, and swivel, like a sensual belly-dancer. Suddenly, as if caught by a gust of wind, she swirled away out of reach across the room, then returned to glide down to lie on the bed next to me, with total absence of shyness. Her long black hair fanned out behind her like satin sheen.

"You are a little minx, Stella."

She reached out to touch my hand. "Can't I tempt you, Lilly?" Then with perfect grace, she raised her arm and gently swept a long finger across my lips. Her eyes were as pleading as her words. "Won't you love me, Lilly?" she said, her voice full of raw emotion. "I want you so much. I've loved you for so long. Please love me?"

A surge of mixed feelings overwhelmed me for just a moment. I was not quite sure what they were. My heart was aching for love. My desperate longings had momentarily transformed innocent loving feelings for Stella, into sensual thoughts. Stella's naked seduction, her invitation to make love was suddenly enticing. But I held back. A voice in my head said 'no.' The voice of modesty. The voice of restraint. The voice of reason. No matter how much I needed to be touched, caressed, loved – the voice said 'no.' It told me I valued our friendship so very much that I could never do anything to jeopardise it. Quivering inside, I fought to remain in control, telling myself that my feelings for Stella were not sexual – they were sisterly.

With a trembling hand I reached out to take up Stella's hand. I held it in my own, looking at its delicate form, then I lifted it to my lips and kissed it. My heart ached for just such a love as Stella's worshipping adoration. "No, Stella. It would be wrong for me. This is not what I need right now." My eyes were moist as I looked into Stella's pleading, beautiful face. "I... I... can't."

My protests were interrupted by a kiss. A kiss so tender, so loving, that for that magic moment, I floated away and forgot the world. Forgot whose lips were on mine. Forgot about Vince. Forgot about heartache. I felt limp, weak, and wonderful.

"I love you, Lilly." Her words broke into my dream.

"Yes, I know. I know, Stella," I responded tenderly, filled with conflicting emotions. Gently I pushed my friend away, giving nothing more than a warm smile, to the younger girl who seemed to have always worshipped me. I realised that I was the stronger of the two, and must show that strength.

"But no," I said kindly, but firmly. I hugged her, and we rocked gently together, entwined in each other's arms giving comfort, one to another. "If you only knew how much I need this hug, Stella. If you only knew." Then, looking lovingly into her face I kissed her tenderly on the forehead, then pulled away and stood up.

After fetching a white bathrobe, I held it out, then wrapped my dainty friend in it. I tied the belt around her slender waist, saying, "Now where's that champagne? I need a fresh one."

"Yes. I'll fetch it."

She came bounding back, two filled glasses in her hands. "Still friends?"

"Still friends!" I smiled, clinking my glass against hers.

#

We sat in the hotel suite for an hour drinking Stella's endless supply of champagne. We exchanged stories about our time apart, shared gossip and news about mutual friends. There was much giggling and laughter, with loud gasps of disbelief as a variety of juicy stories and news surfaced.

"How about some food, Lilly? What would you like?"

"Who's paying?"

"Sam Hutchins, of course."

"Well, in that case, I'll have salmon, caviar and crackers."

"And you know what I'd like, Lilly? Some chocolate and strawberries!"

"What a feast!"

Stella lifted the phone to ring room-service, with another giggle.

An hour later, satiated with food and wine, the pace had slowed. We sat together on the plush, lavender-velvet sofa, and only now that I'd relaxed my guard, did I begin confiding in Stella. And bit by tragic bit, I unravelled my troubled mind to disclose my pain.

"I'm so lonely, Stella. I miss you so much. I miss everybody at the Channel. I miss everything. We used to have such fun, didn't we? And I haven't been able to replace it with anything here in Sydney."

Stella sat patiently and listened, though sad at heart to hear of my unhappiness. She could see that I needed to 'get it out into the open, and off my chest.'

"I miss, well, being someone, I suppose. I have no identity here. I'm such a small fish in a very big goldfish pond. I just can't seem to fit in anywhere. I'm a misfit. Who wants a has-been TV star?" I gulped down another mouthful of Bollinger as if it would quench the pain. "I feel such a failure Stella. So far nothing I've done has been successful. My marriage. My children have been stolen from me. They live in another country now, and I have very little money and little chance of winning them back. Now Vince has deceived me! Wasting my time, using me as nothing but a housekeeper. As for the gallery, it's making me crazy. I'm lost, Stella. I don't mind admitting it. I'm absolutely lost!"

"Nonsense! You're just depressed because of Vince. You'll always be successful, no matter what you do for a living. It's your private life that causes you pain." She reached out and pushed back a strand of hair that hung over my eye. "Why don't you come to Melbourne with me? Sam will do anything for me - if I'm 'nice' to him! Easy!"

"Oh, no! I have bad memories of Melbourne. Remember Al Badcock? The mafia man I got tangled up with. I'd never step foot on his territory. Not after the conversation he had at our dinner table with a couple of his hoods. They KILL people!"

"Well your situation won't get any better. Either with Vince, or the gallery. Get out! Don't hang around. Get out. Do it now!"

"But I so badly wanted this to work. Maybe have a gallery of my own, one day. I love the paintings." I bleated despondently.

"Oh, Lilly!" she scolded. "They're only pictures on a wall!" Her lovely dark eyes twinkled wickedly at me. "Beautiful pictures they might be, but it's your life you're talking about! And I want you to be happy with it. You only have the one! It should be FUN!"

"Do I have to admit defeat? I lost everything I had in Brisbane. Status, friends, a future. What a fool I was to follow Vince."

"Never mind, Lilly. I love you. You can count on me. We'll think of something."

It finally dawned on me that my dear Stella was the only one of us making any sense. It was time for me to leave, but I promised that over the weekend, only a day away, I would make a decision, and stick to it.

"You promise?"

"I promise. Thank you for listening." I gathered together my jacket and handbag. "Our talk made me see the light. I'm glad you called. But I want to have a clear head when I make my decision; and make it I will. I owe it to myself!"

"Good for you. You know I've always loved you, and always will." She followed me to the door of 107, where we hugged a great bear hug, then I departed.

# CHAPTER 34

It was a long, lonely weekend spent cleaning the terrace while my mind flooded with thoughts. When the memories went too far into the past and I started to feel sorry for myself, I forced myself to focus on the here and now. Pragmatism was what I needed now. Though practical by nature, feelings ruled me, making it a constant struggle. But I'd admitted to myself that my relationship with Vince had nowhere to go. I needed to trust.

Firstly, I needed my job, so my energies would go into keeping it. I must have no distractions to be able to cope with the enemy, namely Butler, and Eva, in her own way. I'd need cheaper accommodation, although I'd hate to move further away because I loved Paddington and Woollahra. Vince would have to sell the terrace, give me my half, then move into Sue Chesterman's mansion! I had it all worked out for a fresh start.

The first objective would be to visit my mother in England and get my relationship with her settled, one way or another. When I returned, I'd go into battle for visiting rights to my children. Done! I'd knuckle down. Take action! All decisions would be mine. Alone I would tackle the future, come what may.

#

Monday. Business as usual, I thought. But I was now doing Georgie's work as well as my own. Telephones were ringing. Clients were visiting asking for catalogues. Paintings were being delivered. Art works were being returned to the artist, or sent to auction. The flower display at reception was past its best. Charlie came in wanting to talk, but I'd no time for him. The framing boys came looking for a delivery that hadn't arrived. Eva was busying herself everywhere but near me, thank God, but Butler, the big hulk, had been hovering in the reception area all morning taking up space. What was that look he was giving me? Whatever it was, he kept glancing over at me with a supercilious grin on his face while gossiping to a buyer. Treachery with a grin?

Then it happened. In walked William. I smiled and welcomed him, but he approached me at reception without his normal cheery response.

"Lilly." He spoke my name without his usual charisma lighting up the room. "I need to talk to you in private," he said, leaning over the reception desk.

"In private?"

"Yes," he said, in a serious tone, his face blank. He took out his wallet after what seemed like an eternity of silence, and held it right in front of me without taking his eyes from mine. I stared at it, but it took me a moment to realise that it was a police warrant card. It read, 'Detective Superintendent William Donaldson. New South Wales Police.

My eyes went directly to his. "Police? You're a policeman, William? A detective? A Detective Superintendent of police? But William, I had no idea that you…"

"I need you to come down to the station with me, Lilly."

He was strangely very serious, and it frightened me.

"You want me to er… come to the station?" I found myself glancing at Butler, and back again. "The station… now? What for, William?"

"It's in connection to a painting." Even his normally dancing tone was flat.

"A painting? You mean, the Christo?"

"No," he frowned. "I don't know anything about a Christo. I'll discuss it at the station. Bring your things. Your coat, handbag." he said, his eyes still on me.

Coming mechanically to my feet, I looked at Butler again. That look on his face was a smirk! A smirk! Oh, hell! What had he done to me now?

Whatever it was, it was serious. I stood rooted to the spot, while William moved to hold the main gallery door open.

"Lilly?" he called, looking over at me.

When the penny dropped that I had to move now, right NOW, I turned and reached inside the cupboard for my jacket and handbag. Then I followed William out to his car in a confused trance. I was scared. And I didn't know why I should be.

We drove in silence in William's unmarked police car. The Paddington police station was only two streets away. We were there in an instant, and as we approached, young policemen in uniform ran out from inside and jumped into a police car. At least we'd get a parking spot, I thought.

But we didn't stop there. That was odd? A little bemused, I looked around at William as he turned the corner into Oxford Street, away from the station. Suddenly it began to rain. Heavy rain. Blinding rain. Like a tropical storm. The windscreen wipers were frantically trying to keep up with the downpour. It was loud. Traffic seemed to move even faster.

"Why didn't we stop there, William?"

"We're going to headquarters in the city."

I was stunned. Absolutely stunned!

We travelled all the way down busy Oxford Street till we came to the junction of College and Liverpool streets without a word passing between us. This was the very corner on which Henry Goldberg owned a chunk of real estate - a huge, multi-story hotel. A famous landmark. We had to turn past it to park the car in College Lane. How ironic.

William and I hadn't spoken in the thunderous downpour, because I frankly, could think of nothing to say. This too, was a first. Or was it?

# CHAPTER 35

A sign, 'Sydney Police Headquarters,' loomed in front of my eyes, triggering a memory from puberty.............

"Unmoglich," he said in German, meaning 'impossible' in English, attempting as he often did to teach me his language, when I increasingly found myself alone with him. But when I tried to repeat his words in my lilting Scottish accent, it only had the effect of making him laugh. Fighting his mirth, not wishing to offend, he pulled himself together, sat up, and rested one elbow on his bed. Suddenly his smile faded. He looked into my eyes and was still for a moment. His face took on a wistful look, a look I'd only ever seen in movies.

Hans looked at me as if he were absorbing me. There was great longing in his eyes. He reached out and gently stroked my long hair, and I did not resist his touch. He brushed it back away from my face with tender movements, and his hand skimmed my cheek. I quivered. Again, he stopped to admire me, and his eyes became moist. I sat perfectly still as his hand glided down, past my slim young neck, onto my shoulder. Slowly down, brushing gently over the bulge of my breast. Down to the curve of my narrow waist; over the sleek mound of my firm young hip. Down, to the light rayon of the skirt which covered my thighs.

And I did not resist.

Studying me now, with deliberate questioning in his eyes, he stopped, and gazed endearingly at me, sending love. And at that moment I was so entranced by him, I would have let him kill me, if he'd so chosen.

His eyes begged permission.

Trance-like, consumed by his gentle touch, and the mysterious trust I had in him, I sat submissively, enshrined in the blessed worship of him.

No words were spoken.

I sat waiting, watching him, as if looking at spring flowers through a light mist. I did not fully comprehend, or as much as give thought to where this delicate situation was heading. I just wanted him to continue - to appreciate me.

I longed for his touch. I longed for him to stroke my hair. Caress me. Hold me. I wanted and needed him. My impoverished soul was crying out for him to give me love.

His fingers found the edge of my dress, and with his eyes fixed on mine, he watched for my response. I felt as if I were encased in a romantic, fantasy dream sequence, as, slowly, he slid the soft fabric of my skirt upwards. In, and under. His long masculine fingers gliding their way along my firm young flesh. Up. Up and into my panties, and ever so gently, so very, very gently, into my moist vagina.

I did not protest. I had crossed the barrier from friendship to intimacy. And soon, from virgin to woman.

Sometime later, on a balmy summer's evening in the back garden of the Aberfeldy Boarding House in Brisbane, when we again found ourselves blissfully alone, we began to make love. His kisses seemed to make me float on air, and I gave myself to him willingly. His movements were bold and firm as he thrust one more time to shatter my innocence. His penis went all the way into my vagina.

There we lay. Silent and still, coupled together.

At last, I felt sure I'd found someone to love me. I'd entered a wonderland. A magical, heavenly wonderland. Hans taught me how to make love, passionately and tenderly. And to accept it. He was my first true love, and I was to love him for a long time.

But a young girl in love behaves differently, and Mary Campbell did not like this new, happy girl at all. She was afraid she'd lost control of her underling. And she took to the bottle to give herself the courage for an attack.

Drunk, she barged into my bedroom late one night, leaving the door ajar for all to hear. "Yer aye wi' that bloody German," she began, working herself up into a frenzy. "Ye' never help me in the hoose anymore. Yer nothin' but a slut! An ungrateful, dirty little slut. Jus' like yer mother. Yer no good. Yer no use t' me now! Pack yer things and get oot! Ah dinna want y,' yer nothin' but a dirty little bitch." She thumped the end of my bed with a clenched fist. But for some reason now, I was not so afraid of her.

At fifteen years of age, I was thrown out into the night, in a strange land, with no money and no job. There was only one place to go - Brisbane's Girls' Friendly Hostel that catered for girls without parents, or farm girls working in the city. Mary Campbell threw me out, but Hans was permitted to stay, as long as he paid his board and lodgings.

The very next morning, uniformed police arrived at the hostel to question me. One policeman said his name was Detective Norton, the other, a female, was Sergeant Fletcher - the most terrifying of the two.

"We've had a complaint," said Fletcher, after they were shown into a private room by the matron of the Hostel, who shot me darting, angry looks for bringing the police to her doorstep. "We've come to follow it up."

Sitting between the pair on a hard-backed chair in a drab dark room with two unfamiliar, intimidating police officers grilling me about sex, scared me out of my wits.

"Have you, or have you not, had sexual intercourse with a German man by the name of Hans Frederick Meyer at the Aberfeldy Boarding House?" Fletcher asked brusquely.

In fear and trepidation, I found myself unable to speak. My eyes flashed to those of the male police officer as I sought help.

He could plainly see how terrified I was, and took a softer line. "Your mother has laid a complaint, Lillian, and told us everything." By my mother, he meant Mary Campbell. What had she said I'd done? Norton went on to explain. "We just need to hear your side of the story before we take it any further. There's no need to be frightened, but, do you know what sexual intercourse is?"

"Yes," I replied, looking at the floor.

"Carnal knowledge – do you know what that is?" Fletcher spat angrily.

I was silent.

"It means having sex with a minor. That's what your mother has accused Hans Meyer of doing," her authority displayed in her voice to scare me. "And you, Lillian, are a minor."

Silence. Then I heard a torrent of words, like 'sexual intercourse, vagina, penis, ejaculation, semen, cunnilingus,' before I was required to give a definition and explanation of each, to show that I understood their meaning.

"Did Hans Meyer know that you were under sixteen years of age?" Fletcher demanded to know, taking no notes.

I hesitated. What answer did they want? I was determined not to get Hans into trouble. He hadn't done anything wrong as far as I was concerned. "I… I… well, I don't know."

"We'd like you to come down to police headquarters with us," Norton said firmly, but not harshly. "But before we go, Lilly, I don't want you to be afraid. Just let me say that any young man would like a nice girl like you for a girlfriend. Don't waste yourself on just anybody." He'd intended to compliment, but I was so unaccustomed to flattery, his well-intentioned words were wasted.

At police headquarters, I sat, a fifteen-year-old, in a room full of frisky young constables, some not much older than myself, being interrogated about a titillating carnal knowledge charge, as if it were as everyday as a market research interview.

Mary Campbell had chosen her weapon well – humiliation! The memory of that episode in Brisbane would never leave me……….

I jerked back to the here and now. Sydney's gutters were already flooding as William brought his police car to a halt in the downpour. It occurred to me that if the storm didn't stop soon, a lot of low lying Sydney business premises would be flooded.

William reached for an umbrella from the back seat. "You'll get a bit wet, Lilly, but I don't want to take you in through the prisoner's entrance, so if you'll come with me." Courteously, he came around to my side of the car to shield me from the heavy rain.

Stepping out, I too held onto the umbrella. We huddled close. Our hands touched on the handle. As we scampered for the doorway, we must have looked like a couple in love. Close, and caring.

On entering police headquarters, William shook out the umbrella in the doorway without a word. Suddenly, on his territory, this official place, I felt intimidated. I suppose that's what wrongdoers, law-breakers, are meant to feel. The building itself daunted me. The situation and William's silence certainly put me on edge. He'd become a stranger.

Climbing a large staircase we proceeded to the first floor side by side. Now I was in such inner turmoil that I found myself out of breath climbing the stairs. A mature-age police sergeant sat at a high reception desk looking down at me. William signed in, and I was asked to sign something - like a visitor's book - while the sergeant watched on.

The whole area was gloomy. Brown woodwork. Brown-framed photographs lined the beige walls. Brown everything. A young Queen Elizabeth looked austere and sad; the State Premier; former senior police officers; dead heroes.

It occurred to me that the cheerless police sergeant had a job like mine at the gallery. Directing traffic. I'd wanted him to be nice to me, but he'd been so serious, distant, giving nothing away. Certainly not a smile, and it was so dark and unfriendly up here. Menacing. Did killers walk these halls?

When we reached William's office just down the corridor, it too was bleak and soulless. William pulled out a hard chair for me, and I stumbled into it, awkwardly. My heart was racing, while he seemed calm. Sitting across the desk from me, he looked directly into my eyes, while I was speechless, as if waiting for a guillotine to drop.

"Lilly," he began. "I've become involved in this case as a favour to you, and to Eva Goldberg. Personally, I don't want you to have to go through any unnecessary unpleasantness. Okay?" When I nodded, he continued, "You've been accused of stealing a valuable painting." His voice was grave. There was no light in his eyes as they penetrated mine. This was not the familiar face of 'my' William. "A small painting. A portrait. Small enough to go under a winter coat, or jacket. It's extremely valuable."

I sat in shock.

Lifting a folder, he opened it, and read aloud. "A work by Jan Vermeer. An oil. Painted in 1669. It's a personal favourite of Eva Goldberg. It belongs to her, personally."

I found my voice. "And you're accusing me of taking it? Of stealing it? Really, William! Who put that silly idea into your head?"

"I'm sorry to have to speak with you like this, Lilly. You have to take this seriously. This accusation places you in a very delicate situation. You've been accused of stealing something of immense value. It's the sort of offence that carries a prison sentence. You are a suspect."

"But, I don't understand. It's not the kind of thing I would do. EVER! I've been in a position of trust in many, varying jobs, all my life. No-one has ever accused me of a crime. EVER! I'm just not that sort of person. I'd be too afraid of the consequences to do the wrong thing. I have a HUGE conscience. It would never allow me to do anything illegal."

He spoke with authority, but not unkindly. "You're under caution, Lilly. I suggest you get a lawyer."

His sterile office suddenly felt like a gaol cell, and William was talking to me in a manner totally out of character. Our bond seemed to have disintegrated. I found myself in need of speaking out. "You're serious, William? But I just don't believe this." He continued to stare at me. "But you know me, you know I would never…"

His look told me he was very serious, and the situation became very real and frightening to me. This was Sydney Police Headquarters! William seemed to know what he was talking about.

I began asking questions, which was my 'thing,' to get to the root of a problem, to find reason, to satisfy myself, so that I could come to terms with any situation that presented itself, to help me accept the outcome. "Where was it stolen from, William? When was it stolen? How do you know it's been stolen? Did Eva go looking for it, and not find it? Did Butler find that it was missing? Did anybody look amongst the hundreds of paintings in storage? Which gallery was it taken from? There's storage in both galleries, you know. The database at The Goldberg is immense! There are paintings underneath The Goldberg that Eva doesn't know are there, I bet. Especially if Butler was the record keeper. And probably a lot more are missing!"

William gave me a questioning look, and continued to look across at me. Motionless. Hardly blinking. It was disconcerting, discomforting. This was not the William I knew.

"I think I'm allowed one phone call before you whisk me off to jail."

That made him smile, just a little. "It doesn't work like that, Lilly"

That at least was an improvement. He used my name in a friendly way! "Well, how does it work, William?"

"You've been cautioned, Lilly. My officers will be investigating the complaint, but you have not been charged with a crime, to this point. But I wouldn't be surprised if this cost you your job."

"Like a dishonourable discharge?"

Again. The hint of a smile. "I want you to be aware, that you are suspected of taking property out of the Contemporary Gallery." He seemed to give me that information as a favour. "Whilst you were managing the premises for Eva Goldberg. I must insist you get a lawyer. It really is a very serious offence."

Pushing his chair back he came to his feet, and took up his car keys. "I'll take you back to the gallery, now."

Why take me back to the gallery? I'd have to face my accusers! I certainly couldn't work in such a situation! All trust, on either side, had gone! What lay ahead for me, I'd no idea. So much for me taking control of my life, and making all my own decisions!

#

Sure enough, a letter of dismissal was waiting for me on my keyboard, written in Eva's minute, 'constipated' handwriting. It read: 'Due to changes at The Goldberg Gallery, your services are no longer required. A cheque for four weeks' pay in lieu of notice, according to our agreement, is attached. Officially, today is your last day, but we ask for security purposes that you leave the premises immediately.'

I slumped down on Mr Wobbly, just in time for Butler to catch me with a disconsolate look on my face. Damn him!

"Well, what are you waiting for?" he barked venomously, as he stood staring at me across the reception desk, arms folded, using his size to intimidate, a look of menace on his ugly face. With the light shining in the doorway behind him, he'd become a black silhouette figure, looming over me. Not budging. Clearly, he wanted me out. GONE! In a hurry! The voice in my head told me that HE was my accuser. Why didn't he do it when Georgie was here, I asked myself? I could've punched him on his big rubbery nose. But instead, I gave him a look of disdain. Looking around the reception area, and in my private drawer, making sure I'd left nothing personal behind, I went in search of Eva to have a word. I found her in her study. Standing directly in front of her desk with my belongings in hand, I looked down at her. "Mrs Goldberg," I began, in a serious, but as controlled a tone as I could muster. "I just want you to know how much I've appreciated the chance to work here at The Goldberg Gallery. I have been wrongly accused. You will no doubt find the 'Vermeer.' I want to make it very clear to you, that I did NOT take it out of either gallery! Thank you for my wages."

She had not looked up once, simply pretended to be reading her mail. I could do nothing but leave in disgrace. Turning, I walked out of her office to see Butler hovering at the top of the stairs watching my every move, and waiting for me to make my exit. Permanently!

"Satisfied?" he said.

"Are you?" said I.

I departed quickly, before tears gave me away.

# CHAPTER 36

I needed to keep busy. I'd start to pack my things ready to move on to cheaper premises. Vince could pick up his belongings later. And he could make the mortgage payments. He wouldn't get a penny from me! I was going to need every one of them for a lawyer. Who could I call? The only lawyer I knew was Eva's friend, Justice Viers. Conflict of interest indeed!

My brain scoured its memory bank, and came up with Georgie, Stella and Heidi for advice. Full stop. Anyone else who came to mind was connected to Vince. This dilemma was the last thing I wanted to share with him! Then I remembered Georgie had given me Jean Metcalf's telephone number. Maybe she'd know of someone, and I trusted her enough not to pre-judge.

I went upstairs to fetch Georgie's hand-written note from my jacket, and the doorbell rang as I descended the stairs, so I hurriedly thrust it in my pocket. The bell jangled a second time. More urgently, as if the person thought I hadn't heard the first time. Running downstairs now, two at a time, I called out, "Coming. Here I am. Coming!"

When I opened the front door, I came face to face with a group of policemen.

The one in front of the gang pushed the door wide open, and held out a search warrant. "May we come in ma'am?" But before I could answer, he'd stepped aside to allow his team of invaders to barge past me, and into my home like angry soldiers looking for Bin Laden. Before I could even blink, he thrust the warrant into my face saying, "This warrant allows us to inspect the property, and your possessions."

"What, all of you?" My eyes left his to follow the army of men and one woman, who'd stormed into my home.

"Yes ma'am! I'm Detective Sergeant Brian Dobbs," he said, as he too pushed his way in, past me, following on behind his team. Three of these ugly Neanderthals went directly upstairs as if the terrace was on fire. I presumed that they wanted to ransack the place looking for the painting. The lone policewoman plonked herself down on a dining room chair and remained there throughout, watching me like a hawk.

"Can I ask that you're careful, officers? All my worldly possessions are here. Everything I hold dear is here, and I can't afford to pay for any damage. I'll co-operate with all your requests."

They were in, and rummaging through cupboards, making one hell of a clatter when I realised I was still holding open the front door. I closed it, and ran to fetch my most precious possession from the television set. No, not the Logie. The photograph of my children! I clenched it to my breast as I stood watching the henchmen disrupt my home. The policewoman's eyes burrowing into mine as if she were ready to pounce on me.

The leading detective saw me salvage the photograph from what I imagined would be destruction. He stopped what he was doing - pulling out cushions from the sofas - to stare at me. Walking slowly over toward me, he pulled it from my grasp suspiciously. I held back an inward protest, knowing it would do me no good.

But I pleaded for its salvation. "Please, don't break it. It's a photograph of my children. They're not with me anymore."

He looked at the photograph in its silver frame, turned it over, then moved to the lounge room table to dismantle it.

"You'll scratch the table. Please, let me put down a tea towel, or something," I pleaded.

He breathed in deeply, and exhaled, loudly. "Let me do my job, ma'am."

"Then let me keep my treasure intact. Please, officer." I said with quivering lip, close to tears.

"You do it!" He thrust it back at me.

Carefully, I put it face down on the sofa, undid the back, and laid out all the separate pieces for him to see. He nodded then moved on. I was left to put the pieces together again. A tear fell on the glass. I clasped it to my chest once more.

"Bathroom checked," shouted someone after a few minutes, from upstairs.

"Small study done. Nothing there."

"Come give me a hand in here, then Paul," said another, "this cupboard's full of junk. I want it all out. Everything has to come out."

From downstairs I could hear the ravaging of my home. Papers being scattered. God knows what falling on the floor. Footsteps in my hallway. Dirty shoes on the bedroom carpet and the bathroom tiles. Wardrobe doors opening and closing without care. Drawers being slid out and thrown on the floor. Cops talking amongst themselves as if I wasn't there, discussing my belongings.

"Everything off the bed!" I heard one shout. "Move it. Pull it out from the wall. See if it's been tampered with underneath. See if it's been opened up and sealed again. Look inside shoes for keys to bank deposit boxes. I'll check her handbags. Empty every drawer."

The phone rang. It made me jump. It took a second or two to register what I must do with it. In a state of shock, I lifted up the receiver still clutching my photograph in one hand.

"Hello." My voice was flat and I didn't sound like myself.

"Hello, Lilly... is that you?" said the voice.

"Yes." I answered without recognising the caller.

"It's me, Stella."

"Stella? My Stella?"

"Yes, of course it's me! What's wrong? You sound awful. What is it?"

"Oh, Stella..." I began to sob. "The police are here. They're ransacking the place."

"Why?"

"I've been accused of..." I found it too difficult to say the words. "I've been accused of taking a painting out of the gallery."

She said it for me. "You mean someone is accusing you of stealing? Oh, my God! I'll be right over!"

"No! No, Stella. Please, no. Don't come. I'm too humiliated. What are you still doing here, anyway? You are still here? In Sydney?"

"Yes. Still here!"

Her Sydney stay had been extended because Dean was unable to fly down to Melbourne as a result of an ear infection. He was driving down. Stella had been on her own all weekend and couldn't take any more of it, despite a sexual encounter with a conference-attending young geneticist she'd picked up at the hotel bar.

I looked at my watch - it was only 2.30. Early afternoon. I really didn't want to be alone this evening. I had the rest of my life to clean up the terrace. My 'packing' had been started for me. I decided that as soon as these bullies had gone, I would check to see how much damage had been done, then I'd go visit Stella. Perhaps I'd stay at the hotel with her for the night, and face the onslaught in the morning.

"All clear up here, Sarge."

"Nothing downstairs, Sarge."

"The car been done?"

"Yep"

"Nothing?"

"Nope."

"Then we're off?"

"Yep."

The detective sergeant let his team go first. The policewoman had not spoken a word throughout the whole invasion. Still clutching my precious photograph as Dobbs passed by me, he leaned in close. "Not too much mess, love. The chief said to go easy on you."

"That would be William?"

"Yes, ma'am. That would be Detective Superintendent William Donaldson, ma'am," he said with a smirk and a heap of sarcasm.

He departed, following on behind his grey-suited mercenaries in single file as they headed to their cars.

Feeling as if I'd just been raped by a pack of hoods, I made myself some tea and ate a biscuit from the cookie jar, realising I'd not had lunch. Taking up my knock-off Hermes handbag, which had been emptied on the kitchen bench, I replaced the contents, put in the photograph - it was coming with me - took up the car keys then went into 'the zone,' pretending that the mess wasn't as bad as it was, grabbed a jacket, and headed out to the Cosmo to have a meal with Stella. After all, I'd already made up my mind that my life with Vince was over. So, I was 'free.'

#

She welcomed me with open arms, and a concerned look on her face. Pulling me inside her suite she closed the door. I held on tight when she hugged me. I wouldn't let her go. My head fell onto her shoulder and I began to sob.

"Please don't cry," Stella implored. "You'll make me cry. You poor darling! Tell me everything. And don't even ask whether I believe you or not. I would never believe you would EVER do anything so wrong! I'm your friend. Always will be. Come on in, sit down." Then she smiled and looked at me with devilment. "I have more champagne! And I expect caviar, salmon, and a delicious duck pate to be delivered any minute. We'll munch before we go downstairs to dinner. Hey, what's that you've got there?"

"It's a photograph of my children. I was afraid they'd destroy it."

"Give it to me, Lilly. We'll put it on this little table where you can see it. My God, they're beautiful." And she was right. They looked like blessed cherubs. This was my Rubens portrait.

Stella broke away from me and took the photograph with her as I followed on. She studied it for a long time, with a loving, empathetic smile on her beautiful face. After she had placed it exactly where we could see it from the sofa, she poured me a Bollinger.

"Thank you, dear friend," I said gratefully.

"Lilly, I love you. There's no need to thank me. Whatever happens, please remember you can always live with me. Okay?" She hiccupped demurely.

Again, I found myself pouring out my troubles as Stella poured out the bubbles. Butler really got a thrashing. I'd known in recent weeks that my time at the gallery was near an end, because jealousy such as Butler's can never be fought.

We ate and drank, and the night went on and on, until finally I decided it was time to head home. After our last get-together I didn't want a repeat performance from Stella and strain our relationship. She was a dear friend. I needed friends.

"Give me a hug before you go, Lilly," she pleaded. "I love you, so much. Remember that, always."

"I won't forget, Stella. I won't forget." Our final hug nearly made us both topple over. Outside, the cold wind made me bristle. I pulled the lapels of my jacket together to protect my chest as I traversed the Double Bay streets with my precious photograph in my big handbag. I felt decidedly light headed as I walked down Bay Street, toward where my car was parked close to the Double Bay Yacht Club.

Sliding in behind the wheel of Jeremy Jag, I turned the engine over then headed home. I began to think of my lost children; my desperate unhappiness; of Mary Campbell and Eva Goldberg – their tormenting faces flashing before me, their screeching voices resounding in my ears. I was heading home to an empty bed. The bed in which Vince had once loved me.

Along New South Head Road, and only one block from home, came the devastating event that was to change my life.

# CHAPTER 37

Was that a police siren I heard? Lights were flashing. People were calling out to me. I heard the word 'accident.' The words, 'lot of blood,' 'hospital,' 'hurry,' 'blood sample.' Such a flurry. Anxiety. People fussing. Being tender. Caring. Loving. Kind.

Uniformed men were pulling me out of the car. They looked like medics. But I only got flashes of everything. My body, which didn't seem as if it belonged to me, was being put on a stretcher. Full-length - horizontal - I was bumping roughly over the ground, moving fast, 'till the legs of the gurney disappeared underneath as it was pushed into an ambulance. There was a tube running from my arm connected to something, and blood was splashed on my favourite cream jacket.

Lots of instructions were shouted from one to another. Couldn't help them. My body wasn't working. I heard a door slam. Inside the ambulance, a medic was leaning over me, holding a thick bandage over one side of my face. He told me I was losing the precious red blood that kept me alive. He was trying to stop that from happening. His voice was kind.

"We'll be there soon, love. They're waiting for you in emergency. You're lucky it wasn't peak-hour, the traffic can get congested."

The siren started again. I wished they would turn it off because it was so loud and scary, and we were moving very fast, I was worried about the speed. Suddenly the engine stopped. Couldn't see much, but I was on the move again. On that hard trolley thing again. They pushed the gurney through the door of 'Emergency.' I got a glimpse of the sign as I passed underneath it. Next thing I remember, someone was speaking directly to me.

"Tell me who I can call, dear," said the pretty lady in a white coat. "You've been in a car accident. I need a name. A relative."

When I answered weakly, her voice echoed mine.

"Vince Parker? Channel Eight?"

Then nothing.

#

With eyes closed, I lay in a private ward, heavily bandaged, with only part of my face visible. There was a new, friendly, Irish voice, way in the distance.

"Hello, dearie," she said, lyrically. "I'm Sister Delaney. I just want you to know that Dr Farrel has worked on you. That's a good thing. You're lucky! He's good at his job."

"What happened?" I croaked dryly.

"You were in a car accident. Your car was run off the road, according to the police, dearie. But who's that man that's coming in to see you? Not your husband I hope? Irritable bugger, isn't he? Enough to stress you out. Said he was in Adelaide. Didn't want to come. Said he had an important job. Had appointments."

The friendly lady with the Irish voice seemed to float above me, and was peering down into my face, speaking directly to me as if she knew me, and as if my life depended on comprehending what she was saying.

"I told him how serious your condition was, but all he could think about was the inconvenience."

Apart from this 'motherly' voice, my sense of awareness was limited to clean, antiseptic smells. And I felt cold. This nice lady in white seemed to be adjusting my skirt, because I didn't seem able to do it. No. It was a blanket. I was in the cot-like bed! She was tucking me in the way I tucked in my children, at night, with love and kindness.

"Just want you to know, dearie, that we all try and save lives here. Any way we can. That's all." She reached over the cot and pulled up the blanket closer to my chin, then gently caressed my cheek with her soft, plump fingers.

My lips moved in response to her kindness, but I didn't have the strength to speak.

"When the chips are down, people show their true colours, if you know what I mean. I've seen it all, dearie. Sad thing about these terrible accidents, nobody thinks it'll happen to them. My husband tells me it's the 'Fighter Pilot Syndrome.' They must've been crazy, those young boys in the war. They thought they were invincible. Such a waste of young lives! Anyway… you'll be okay! Don't go worrying, you'll be fine. My shift ends now, so I'll say goodnight. I'll see you tomorrow, dearie."

#

Voices. I tried to use my energy to bring them close, and focused on the faces at the end of the hospital bed. It was all a bit of a blur, although one face did seem familiar. But why wasn't my body working properly?

"I'm Doctor Farrell the registrar, Mr Parker," said an unsmiling, weary-looking doctor of around thirty. He produced a folder from under his arm. Why was he talking to Vince?

They stood face-to-face at the end of the bed. Vince seemed agitated, way too worked up to sit down. He was jangling his keys in his pocket. He did that when he was anxious, or angry. I couldn't tell which, but he sounded uptight. Everything was a haze. The doctor produced a diagram of the human face and held it out for Vince to view.

"We did the best we could under the circumstances," the doctor said in a serious tone. "But you can see what a mess Miss Lightwood is in."

Vince looked at the diagram but could not comprehend. "I don't understand," he mumbled. "Surely there must be some mistake?" He seemed unable to accept that beneath all the bandages I now looked like the mutilated creature depicted in the diagram.

Pulling a ballpoint pen from his top pocket, Dr Farrell began pointing to various aspects of the diagrammatic face, describing the facial damage I'd sustained in the accident the night before, when I'd gone through Jeremy Jag's windscreen. In all my mental turmoil I'd failed to clip on my seatbelt, and I'd hurtled forward over the steering wheel like a guided missile.

Then the doctor outlined the necessary reconstruction – as if talking about a car repair. Vince went pale. He hadn't been prepared for this. The diagram illustrated each one of the 105 stitches which held my face together.

"Jesus! That's not Lilly's face, surely, doc? Can't be that bad!" It was way more than a whisper. His eyes flashed to those of Dr Farrell.

The registrar nodded, without the slightest display of emotion.

"What about scarring? Will she be scarred for life?"

"You'll have to talk to the reconstructive surgeons about that!"

"Plastic surgery?"

"Yes. John Davenport is our Chief Reconstructive Surgeon. You should talk to him. You can keep that diagram."

Vince stood holding the sketch, gaping at the red lines which represented the ugly stitches crossing the dozen, jagged slashes which the windscreen glass had gouged from my face.

"Make an appointment to see him," said Farrell. "He'll fill you in on what needs to be done. Now, if you'll excuse me, I have other patients." The overworked doctor departed.

I watched as Vince looked down at the badly disfigured face on the diagram in disbelief. The face of a damaged stranger looked back at him. He moved closer to my hospital bed and looked down at me with horror in his eyes. I sensed that he could not imagine what I looked like under the bandages, could feel him thinking, that after this, I certainly wasn't going to be the same vivacious woman he'd brought to Sydney.

He reached out and touched my arm, but I gave no response. I'm sure he thought I was drugged and going in and out of consciousness, because I couldn't keep my right eye focussed for long, and my left eye was bandaged over. I'd bet he was glad – he wouldn't have known what to say. Grateful that no words were necessary, sickened, angry, and no doubt feeling guilty, he screwed the diagram into a ball, and turning, threw it into a wastepaper bin as he strode toward the door. On the way out, he was met with a group of interns doing the rounds with a senior doctor. As they congregated in the doorway, I heard Vince ask this doctor, their teacher, if he was Dr John Davenport, the plastic surgeon. He answered in the affirmative.

John Davenport was in his forties. Tall, dark, with fine, intelligent features, and of slender, but sporty build. I would learn later, he was a former Rhodes Scholar, and Oxford rugby blue. A fleet of foot winger.

"I was just coming to find you, doc. I'm Vince Parker, a friend of Lillian Lightwood." They both glanced my way. Vince shook the surgeon's hand. "Can I have a word while you're here? I have a plane to catch."

"Er, well, yes. Mr Parker. But the title is actually Mr Davenport. I'm chief surgeon." His voice was deep and reassuringly calm. "How can I help you?" They both stepped further inside my room while the nurses remained hovering in the doorway, waiting, listening to everything. Every spoken word from Davenport would be precious new learning.

"I'd like some details, please, about Lilly."

"Details?"

"I want to know how long it'll be before she's up and about again and back to normal." There was a series of looks in my direction and back again to each other as they discussed my fate.

"Well now, Mr Parker, she'll be up and about again within a week or two, I expect. But she'll be in considerable pain for quite some time. As for 'back to normal,' well, I'm sorry…" Davenport shook his head. He paused, giving Vince time to absorb his message. "Plastic surgery can do wonders these days. We can probably make her ALMOST as good as new! But it's going to take a long, long time. A series of operations at six monthly intervals. And naturally, we won't be able to commence those for at least eighteen months."

"Eighteen months? You're joking!"

"Perhaps two years. Depending on how rapidly she heals."

"Two years? You don't mean to say she's got to walk around like that for two years before you start working on her?" The tone of disgust in his voice told me everything.

"I'm afraid so."

"Why is that, doc?"

"We can't hurry nature, Mr Parker. We wouldn't contemplate touching her until the scar tissue has healed and settled. We need to know exactly what we have to work on. And she'll require counselling, I'd imagine. It's not easy for anyone." He spoke with a calm and kind maturity.

"But, two years? My God! I'd no idea."

"We'll make an appointment for her to come back and see us at six monthly intervals to check on her progress. You never know, we might be able to start work on her after eighteen months. Only time will tell."

#

"Lillian… Lilly, wake up. There's a good girl." The nurse took hold of my right hand. "Would you like something to eat, dear? We have some breakfast for you. Maybe a cup of tea, mmmm? Come on now, wake up, dearie. You should eat something now. Look, here's a nice cup of tea!"

The words broke through. I stirred, and in a split second, was jolted back to reality, aching all over, my face throbbing with pain. Trying to open my eyes, I found that I could only see out of my right eye, because of all the bandages and padding I could feel on the left side of my face. And in that instant of consciousness, I was forced to face a horrid truth – the whole catastrophe was real! The accident had really happened. My body jerked in fright and I gripped the nurse's hand tightly.

"I didn't hurt anyone else, did I?"

"No, dear. Only yourself!"

"You're sure?"

"Yes, dear, I'm sure." She patted my arm to calm me. "Now, I want you to have some breakfast. I'll help you. Come on now. I want you to sit up a bit. Look, here's a straw for you to drink your tea through. That'll help. Come on now. That's a girl."

#

Enormous bouquets of flowers arrived at the hospital, along with telegrams and phone messages all wishing me well. I noticed the photograph of my children sat undamaged by my bedside. How wonderful. Desperately embarrassed by the state I now found myself in, I wanted to keep the full extent of my injuries private, and requested no visitors be allowed to see me. But Stella Stevens came straight to the hospital and ignored the 'No Visitors' sign on the private ward door and barged straight in.

"Oh, Stella, no! You shouldn't have come. Oh, Stella…"

She sat at my bedside clinging tightly to my hand, sobbing. "But you can't stay here by yourself, Lilly. Please come to Melbourne. I'll look after you there."

"No Stella. I have to work through this thing by myself. It's happened for a reason."

When she'd gone, and I was alone again, I gave in to my secret feelings of despair and cried softly to myself.

#

A week after the accident, with emotions in turmoil and a body wracked with pain, I received a note from Vince: 'I'm sorry to do this to you while you're down, Lilly. I realise this is not a good time for you. But I suppose there is no good time to tell a woman you're leaving her.'

Sitting up in bed, resting on a mountain of pillows with my head and face swathed in gauze, with one eye peeking through the bandages, my body bruised and hurting, I tightened my grip around the letter, dropped my head and closed my eyes as if I'd been hit by a bullet. Not at the shock of his leaving me, as much as thinking how foolish I'd been not to realise what kind of person was inside that handsome exterior of his.

Collecting my thoughts when the wave of shock subsided, I found the courage to read the remainder of Vince's cruel missive: 'I've accepted a job offer from Channel Four in London. It's an opportunity too good to miss. And yes, Sue is coming with me. As for the terrace house, stay on as long as you like. I'll keep up the mortgage payments until you're back on your feet, then we'll talk about selling it. Sorry it has to be this way. I hope all goes well for you. Goodbye, Vince.'

I could not fully comprehend the mix of feelings I had at that moment, for amid my despair, there was an underlying sense that I'd received my just desserts. It was as if my life had been building for years toward a disaster like this. As if somehow I deserved this fate; and more, sensed it was coming. I'd always expected to be punished, and it had come in the loss of my children.

The real sunshine in my life. Now this!

And here I lay, in a hospital bed, with every muscle, every bone, every inch of me in pain, alone, and disfigured. And to add to the misery, Vince didn't love me anymore. Maybe he never had. This surely was rock bottom.

# CHAPTER 38

Although I appreciated the kindness and attention given me by the nurses, which made me feel 'safe' somehow, the hospital days seemed like a hazy, repetitive dream. Until Mr John Davenport my surgeon came into my life, to add some sunshine to my pain-filled days.

I first noticed his piercing green eyes. Then the pleasant, but slightly distracted look to his clean-shaven, sculpted face as he walked toward me. The next thing I noticed was the warm, mellow tone to his voice.

"Good morning, Lilly. How are we getting on?" He stood bedside, smiling down.

Friendly, I thought. But in a bed-side manner way. Then I noticed that his hand was nicely warm as it reached out to touch my cold hand. He took a pen-light from his breast pocket, leaned over me and shone it in my 'good' right eye. Then he felt my pulse.

"That's all very satisfactory. Are you feeling any better?" he asked, inspecting the bandages. Those on my head, and those binding my broken ribs. He frowned a little. "Does that feel too tight?" he asked, referring to the bandages around my torso.

"A little," I croaked, and coughed a dry cough.

"Want a drink? Here, let me help you." He reached for the water jug and poured me a glass. Then sitting on the bed beside me, he raised my head slightly with one hand to support me, and helped me take a sip. "I'm John Davenport. Head of the Reconstructive Surgery Unit."

I cleared my throat. "The nurses told me to expect a visit from you, doctor."

Although he continued talking to me in a friendly manner, there was a serious edge to his tone. He spoke without emotion, and I knew this to be a standard practice of doctors – if they show no emotion, they get none in return. An insulated way of handling the traumas which meet them every day.

"Let me explain what we have to do," Davenport began, "but I must warn you, Lilly, it's going to be a long, long haul, and you must help us by keeping well, by looking after yourself." His gaze was direct. Again, that air of maturity and calm about him which commanded respect, without any effort on his part. "Plastic surgery is just a clever way of patching up scars. It's nothing to be afraid of. You'll probably need three or four operations after the scar-tissue settles, but we won't be in a position to even start on that for at least eighteen months."

I could feel a lump in my throat when I thought of the ordeal ahead. I nodded.

Davenport sensed my discomfort and added a touch of optimism to his spiel. "It's not the end of the world, you know. But it will take time." He offered one of his comforting smiles and gently touched my hand. "In three days we'll remove some of the bulk of the bandages and make them neater, and more comfortable for you. In about a week you can go home. Be sure to eat well. Get plenty of rest. No alcohol, and keep the scars out of the sun."

I nodded.

"You're going to be all right, you know." He patted my arm again reassuringly. "But it's going to take a long, long time. There's no way to hurry nature. She'll be doing all the hard work." Then he paused as if to measure my alertness for his next important statement. "You won't be exactly as good as you were, but you'll be almost as good as new." He gave my hand the slightest squeeze, smiled a warm smile, then left.

Long after he'd gone, I remembered his kind eyes, but his serious, no-holds-barred manner reinforced the gravity of my situation. I began to feel sorry for myself as I thought of the years of recovery that lay ahead, and was close to tears when I heard the chirpy voice of a uniformed nurse.

"You were lucky to get him, dear," said the plump and jovial 'angel' as she pulled back the bed-clothes to check the bandages around my ribs. "Mr Davenport is the best surgeon we have, dear. Handsome devil he is too, don't you think?"

"They certainly didn't waste any time operating," I remarked.

"Someone had to sew you up, dear. They couldn't leave you with your face gaping open and one eye hanging out, now could they? Roll over, there's a good girl."

#

Returning to the hospital on my first day-visit since my discharge, after spending a lonely week at home, I lay shivering and shaking as deft hands removed tiny black stitches from my forehead. A tear unwittingly trickled down as the nurse worked on it.

A young intern moved in closer toward me and stood bending over me, breathing heavily only inches from my face, examining my wounds as if I were nothing more than a specimen in some laboratory. "Trouble is love, everybody thinks it'll never happen to them! But, never mind, you'll look like Liz Taylor again in no time," he joked, and moved on.

While the nurse worked assiduously on my face, I kept repeating to myself over and over again the words: 'It's only a face; it's only a face,' telling myself how inconsequential both me and my face were, in the overall scheme of things. Tense and frightened all the same, I grabbed hold of the sister's arm, making the proceedings difficult. "Oh, please," I pleaded, "don't make it any worse."

"It's all right, dear," she said in a soothing voice. "You're still in shock. I'll be careful - I promise. Don't worry. Soon be over."

I relaxed a little. Told by the kindly nurse to sit up after a while, I felt sickly, and swayed dizzily as I came to an upright position.

"Take it easy now," said the nurse, holding me steady, "while we remove some more of these bandages to make it a bit more comfortable."

The bandages were becoming smaller and smaller with each visit, exposing more and more of the damage, which meant that increasingly, the ugly scarlet scarring was becoming more visible to me, and the world, as more of my face was revealed.

"There, that's it for today," said the nurse, standing back surveying her handiwork. "Would you like to take a look in a mirror?"

I shook my head vehemently.

"There's no hurry." With each return visit to the hospital, the conscientious, kind nurses had administered doses of optimism and encouragement. But there was always a note of caution. "Just don't expect too much too soon, now!"

Returning home in a cab, wearing a broad-brimmed hat and hiding behind large sunglasses, I determined I'd try to remain cheerful, and constantly remind myself of all the things I was still able to do. I could still walk, talk, hear, and see, after all. I had my mind, my imagination. My life could still be full and happy. But my optimistic, positive thoughts had a hollow edge to them.

Fighting to ignore the waves of negativity, I would do what I had so often done in the past to keep my spirits up – in the Dundee and Brisbane Boarding Houses with Mary Campbell, in Brisbane's Girls' Friendly Hostel, in the poky little cottage with my husband Mitch, in the early days, and at the gallery with Eva Goldberg. I'd pretend to myself that things weren't as bad as they were.

I jumped from the cab and hurried indoors. Quickly, I closed the door behind me. Now I was safe, and out of sight, hiding my bandages from neighbours and passers-by. I just stood for a while, my back to the door, listening to the silence of the lonely house, catching my breath.

My strength depleted, knowing there was absolutely nothing to hurry for, I thought that rest in bed would be my best option for now. Passing the bathroom, I paused in the doorway. The mirror hung invitingly on the wall like a devilish temptation. For how long, I don't know, I stood frozen on the threshold. One invisible arm seemed to be trying to drag me in, while another held me back. I knew that the new, smaller bandages would now reveal more of the scarring. A voice in my head was saying, 'If you can't look at yourself now, how will you be when all the bandages come off?'

I spoke out loud. "I can do it. I can do it!" Taking a deep breath I stepped onto the white tiled floor of the bathroom. Then stiff, like a robot, I turned slowly to my right and faced the mirror, like an accused felon facing the jury to hear its verdict. It took courage, but I'd always prided myself on my courage.

A little daylight reached into the bathroom via the closed cream shutters. But there was more than enough light to see my face. I gasped aloud at the sight. It was horrific! I swayed with shock, then burst into tears.

Yet the worst was still to come.

#

With each return visit to St Vincent's Hospital the well-trained staff would try to reassure me; tell me how lucky I was not to be blinded by the accident. I still had my vision. My injuries could have been much worse. But the nurses knew that the sharp jutting glass of the windscreen had shaved off my left eyebrow and eyelashes, slashing right through the eye-lid. It had gouged numerous deep gashes into the surrounding skin, mincing the area around the eye. My previously unblemished Scottish skin was gnarled and distorted. Mangled lumps had sprouted. There were deep, warped grooves lining my upper face, and a mound of swollen flesh the size of a duck-egg had appeared above my left eye. With scars and stitch marks all along my forehead from eyebrows to hairline – I looked like Frankenstein. The doctors had not thought about appearances when they sewed me up. They had merely pulled together the ravaged skin simply to close the gaping wounds. Giving me back my 'looks' was to be someone else's job, a long time down the track in the future.

"A miracle you didn't lose the sight in your left eye," was repeated often.

It was indeed a miracle. I knew that. I should be grateful, but it was difficult to be grateful when facing such a hideous reflection in the mirror.

# CHAPTER 39

A massive bouquet of fresh flowers arrived on my doorstep, accompanied by a large basket of fruit, together with a hand-written note of well-wishes, and an article written by a Brazilian surgeon which began: 'Scars Can Be Prevented. I myself have witnessed dozens of individuals make spectacular recoveries without scarring. 'Vitamin E' gives hope. A miracle oil.'

I read the article with interest. Any hope was welcome in my present mental and physical state. The note went on to endorse the work of a Dr Wong, a master in the technique of acupuncture. The note assured me that I would benefit greatly from his 'magic.' And how the healing process would take half the time if I used his services.

And how like Jean it was to give me hope.

#

The days passed for me in agonising slow-motion. I allowed no-one to visit. And many was the time I took the phone off the hook to hide my depression from the world. Just the same, one telephone call took a huge weight off my mind. It seemed to me, in retrospect, the beginning of a turn-around in the events in my life.

"William Donaldson, Lilly."

"Oh, hello… Superintendent!" I felt a little betrayed by William.

"Don't be like that, Lilly. I'm phoning to be nice to you." I could feel him smile at me at the other end of the phone line.

"To be NICE to me? You didn't even tell me you were a policeman! You said you were in public relations!"

"I don't go around telling everyone I meet what I do for a living. I'd never learn anything. People wouldn't talk freely in front of me. Say you understand. Please!"

He sounded sincere, and he sounded sweet. I needed sweet. So I was sweet back. "I understand, William. I do. Really I do. So, you have something to tell me? Might as well get it over with, I couldn't feel any worse than I do now."

"I bet I'll make you smile!"

"I bet you won't!"

"Okay. How's this…? They found the painting!"

"WHAT?"

"They found the painting Lilly!" he repeated. "Hasn't Eva phoned you to say sorry?"

"NO! And I don't believe she will!"

"Well, anyway, it's true! All charges have been dropped, but you need an apology! You've got to clear your good name Lilly, you carry that with you wherever you go! I'll see if I have any influence on Eva to give you a written apology."

"You're joking?"

"No, Lilly. I never joke about my work. This is too serious an offence. It was only the accident that kept you out of jail you know."

"My lucky day!"

"Come on now. I'll take you out to dinner as soon as you're better?"

"You'll what?"

"Well I know that Vince is gone! Overseas. Took her with him. He was a cheat. I saw him at Hyde Park Hotel with her one day. Not long after the night I dropped you off home - after The Goldberg dinner. I check up on everybody. I was sure you didn't take the painting."

"Thanks William, but your believing in me wouldn't have been enough to keep me out of jail, would it?"

"No. But I was thinking about you! Wondering what I could do to help, so I made another visit to the Contemporary Gallery. My tenth visit!" He must have heard me gasp out loud. "And, Eva's closed the Contemporary, by the way. Nobody could've made a go of it! It was too far out of the way. Didn't even have passing trade!"

A sneaky smile found its way to my face, not that I was one to say, 'I told you so.' But I thought it! I could have saved Eva a heap of money!

"Randy's getting a transfer, too," said William. "He's going to work at The Goldberg in future. That'll-be-interesting!" he added, cheekily. We both knew what he meant! How long would it take Butler to get jealous of Randy, we wondered? "Anyway," said William, "when I heard that Randy had just been ordered to start packing up paintings, I called in yet again to the Contemporary, to check all the stock before it left the building. I asked Randy to open up the safe again. And guess what?"

"What?"

"There it was! In between two enormous abstracts, ready for a trip to The Goldberg, as if it had never been missing!"

I heard myself give out another shocked gasp.

"I had a feeling that if the word got back to Butler that I was forever snooping around there, he would 'FIND' it! Butler's excuse, was that Eva must have loaned it to one of her favourite clients, and had forgotten about it."

"And she forgot about them giving it back, too?"

"Seems like it!" he answered playfully. "Anyway, you're off the hook! That's the main thing. I'm sorry I had to go through that rigmarole of officialdom with you. Really I am, Lilly. Please, get better soon. I'm rooting for you. Put this behind you, and fight to get fit and well. There are people out here that love and believe in you."

"Oh…William. Thank you. Thank you." Feeling myself choke up, I quickly put down the phone to sob my heart out. I didn't care if I stretched my stitches. I needed to cry.

When I'd cried enough, I rang Jean Metcalfe. There was a favour I wanted to ask of her. I knew she'd help. I only asked favours from people if I trusted them. And I trusted Jean.

Two days later, *The Sydney Morning Herald* ran a half page article on page three. In the picturesque setting of the foyer of The Goldberg Gallery, Eva - smiling radiantly, and looking particularly elegant in a cream Channel suit, and her Paspaley pearls - was holding up the valuable 'lost' *Vermeer*. My reception desk resplendent, with a magnificent display of lime-green orchids to one side. The article began:

'EVA GOLDBERG FINDS HER TREASURE.

Eva Goldberg, the doyen of Sydney's art world, has had her famous painting returned to her from one of her art patrons who had borrowed it for a charitable event. It had originally been thought the painting had been stolen. Sydney's Children's Hospital is to receive a $50,000 donation from the event.'

To me, those words were every bit as good as an apology! Eva couldn't come right out and say 'sorry,' it would be an admission of false accusation, and I could have sued her. I decided I would cut out the article, frame it, and hang it in the kitchen where I could see it every day!

I rang Jean to thank her for arranging the piece which did the job of clearing my name. I felt as if I'd won something! I was only after an apology, but was thrilled that the Children's Hospital would benefit as well.

# CHAPTER 40

"Come on in, Lilly," John Davenport called out from inside his office.

I entered nervously. This was an auspicious day. The day the final bandages were to be removed – the bandages which covered the worst damage around my left eye. The area where the scars were deep, and an intricate web of stitches held my eye in place.

"Please lie down, Lilly. It'll be much more comfortable for you."

After kicking off my shoes, and climbing up on the surgical bed, I lay quietly while Davenport washed his hands. I could smell the sweet aroma of antiseptic as it permeated the whole surgery. Clasping one hand inside the other, holding so tightly that I had to change hands to free the blood flow, I waited for the unveiling.

Drying his hands on a paper towel then discarding it, Davenport walked the few steps to the surgery bed. He stood towering over me. "Now, let's see what we have here," he said cheerily, before proceeding to gently unwrap the bandages.

I closed my eyes.

Once the bandages were unwound he set about carefully removing the wads of padding beneath. He turned to take up a pair of tweezers from a tray, with which he would lift off the last patch that was stubbornly sticking to the wound beneath. "Just one last piece," he remarked. With an expressionless face, he executed the task.

There was a sting of pain as the last piece of cotton gauze came away. Then there was a sudden feeling of coldness on the newly uncovered skin. Then in contrast, I felt the surgeon's warm breath on that delicate area as he loomed over me to examine each and every scar.

"That's coming along very nicely. Now for these last stitches." In one hand he held stainless steel tweezers; in the other, a pair of slim medical sheers. With great care and patience, he began the painstaking process of removing the last miniscule stitches. Fifty in all remained.

I felt myself blink involuntarily the whole time, for I anticipated the tug of each stitch after the snip of his sheers, but his technique was the very best, and the stitches were released in rows, after each snip, at crucial points. Like knitting unravelling.

Trying not to look into Davenport's handsome face while he worked, but fascinated by his concentration, I managed a peek every now and again.

The methodical mechanic's fingers glided over the risen scar tissue, while his eyes focussed intently on the job at hand. He inspected the scars closely, prodding at the skin from time to time, examining how the wounds were healing. All the while he displayed not a flicker of emotion. "Close your eyes, please. Now open. Close. Again. Okay." Then finally he spoke. "There. All done. You can sit up now."

Taking my time, fearing the dizziness and nausea again, I sat for a moment, then very carefully put on my shoes, and moved carefully to the chair opposite his desk.

Meanwhile, Davenport went again to the sink to wash his hands. When they were dry, he sat behind his desk and spoke in a very sombre, but not unfriendly tone. "I want you to understand, Lilly – and I cannot stress this enough – that the scarring is at its worst just now. And you must be prepared for the worst when you see it. And you must keep reminding yourself, that it IS at its worst! The only recompense is that we've done a fine job up to this point. Okay?"

"Yes. Thank you, doctor. I'm very grateful," I woozily responded, suffering a little nervous shock after he'd worked on my damaged face.

"I want to see you every six months. Make an appointment with Julie at the desk on your way out for the first check-up in six months' time."

Suddenly it hit me. Six months was a long time to be on my own with this grotesque face! A long time between visits to the reassuring Davenport, or to the friendly hospital nurses, whose jovial company and banter was always comforting.

"You will remember Lilly, that this is just the beginning of your recovery," he kindly said. "All we could do at this early stage was patch up the damage. The clever re-construction work will come later. You must keep reminding yourself that it won't always be like this. In time, it will be better. I can promise you that!"

There were those words again. The words that everyone kept saying to me – 'in time.'

Fear overwhelmed me. I lost control for a moment, and a tear trickled down my cheek. I quickly wiped it away, hoping that Davenport hadn't noticed.

"It's alright, Lilly," he said sympathetically. "You've suffered a great trauma. You're only behaving as any woman would in your situation."

I could hold it in no longer. Tears began to flow. "I need help," I sobbed. "I really do. I can't stand to look at myself - I'm so depressed. I simply can't stop crying. I need professional, psychological help. There's no-one at home to talk to, and I need to talk to someone about this." I was fighting so hard to control the tears.

"Yes, of course," he responded, promptly scribbling down a telephone number and a name. "We can only help with the physical healing. This is the person you need." He handed the note to me across the desk after I'd taken up my handbag. "This is Dr Ruth Warner's number." He gave me a gentle smile. "She's a psychiatrist, and an old friend. If anyone can help with the emotional healing process, she can. But, there is one thing," he added, looking deeply into my eyes. "She is in private practice, but she works out of the Mental Health Division, here, at the hospital. Can you cope with that? Can you cope with coming to the Mental Health Hospital for your appointments?"

"Yes. I think so."

"Now, before you go, let me warn you once more." He spoke sternly now.

"Your injury is not a pretty sight. But I promise you – IN TIME – it will be better. Call in and see me after you visit Dr Warner, and let me know how you're getting on."

#

Nothing. Absolutely nothing, could have prepared me for what looked back at me from the bathroom mirror. The swollen, red, raw, angry wounds around my misshapen eye looked like some fearsome, ghoulish mask.

This was not the face I knew. This was not the face I'd pampered over the years, the face I needed to earn my living, to communicate with people; to flirt, to tease, entice, joke, to respond lovingly to my children. This reflection could simply not be true. This monstrosity surely, was not Lillian Lightwood? It was grotesque; so very, very ugly. I was deformed. Destroyed! My face was the face of a war victim. And in a way, I was.

#

The lonely hours melted into each other. Days became weeks. On any given day I had no idea of the date, and nor did I care. I was dispirited and broken-hearted. And angry. Very, very angry. Angry at my circumstances. Angry at myself. Angry at life.

I would pace the floor in restless moments, walking around the small terrace house, ending sometimes in front of the bathroom mirror looking for some sign of improvement, hoping that when I looked again at my disfigurement, I would find it had all been a bad dream. But each time I faced it, it would look right back at me. Sometimes more angrily than before – depending on my tears. There was no escaping this distorted face. It was mine, and it would not go away.

I looked at my favourite photograph of myself which sat on the television set, next to the Logie and the photograph of my children. I touched its frame and shook my head in utter disbelief. How could this possibly have happened to me? Why, oh why?" I said aloud as I looked into the smiling eyes of times past. I wondered sadly if I would ever regain any semblance of my previous appearance. My face, after all, had been my ticket through life.

I must be strong. I must force myself to be positive, not negative. I wouldn't want my children to see me like this. I would see them again one day. I would make myself better for them!

# CHAPTER 41

My first appointment at the Mental Health Hospital, with its dark long corridors, and drugged, shuffling patients meandering its halls, was a frightening experience. I rebelled inwardly, and trembled outwardly. But the clever Dr Ruth Warner opened up my psyche, despite my discomfort and despair. Memories flashed back to mind as if they'd happened only yesterday. All the years of papering over the cracks in my heart were for nothing. My heart bled.

The first appointment had abruptly concluded on the stroke of the hour, just as I was tearfully recounting the story of the day Mitch and his lawyers, had taken my babies away.

"That will be enough for today," she'd said. "I'd like you to return twice a week for the time being. Make an appointment. Tuesday's and Thursdays."

In something of a state of shock, I wiped away the tears, stood and walked from the office feeling more confused than when I'd entered. I walked home thinking about my 'consultation.' The doctor had remained dispassionate throughout the entire appointment. Not that sympathy was what I sought, but a little show of understanding might have let me leave Warner's company feeling slightly better than when I'd entered. I wanted a sign that my situation would improve, but the appointment had come to an antiseptic conclusion – without ceremony – after I'd spent a full hour baring my soul, while the doctor had remained totally detached.

Heavy of heart, I trudged along beside Rushcutters Bay, to 'walk things out.' The fresh breeze blowing in off the harbour refreshed my spirit. It caressed my skin, and blew wisps of hair across my cheeks, and I found myself greedily inhaling deep breaths of that glorious fresh air to invigorate me. And it was then I remembered the words of the ancient Chinese proverb: 'A Journey Of A Thousand Miles, Begins With the First Step.'

#

The empty terrace was silent and still. I wanted it to remain that way. I had much thinking to do. My visit with Warner an hour before had stirred my memories, and my emotions. It had also increased my despair and further confused me.

After making a cup of tea, I sat quietly at my dining-room table, wondering how on earth a one-sided conversation, such as the one I'd just had, could possibly help me. Let alone heal me. My mind danced from recollection to recollection. Warner's questions – my answers – truthful as I possibly could give. Then I suddenly remembered John Davenport. I'd forgotten to call in and see him as promised and made a mental note to do it at the next visit. Although I didn't think I'd have much to report.

Dragging my mind back to the here and now, I flipped through the mail I'd collected on the way in. One envelope stood out from the rest. It bore a golden crest of the famous Guinness family in Britain. I opened it and read lovely words from Georgie:

*'Always thinking of you, and sending you love. Let me know how you're progressing. We're all looking forward to a visit from you as soon as you're better. If there's anything at all I can do, you know I will.*

*Love Always. Your Georgie.' And lots of kisses.*

#

True to my impatient nature, I expected a quick fix. But that was not in Warner's character, or, on her agenda. I would have to do this the hard way. As a direct result of my visits, I'd begun to feel worse, rather than better. I wallowed in deep depression, and after every appointment with Warner, I left feeling wrung-out and upset. The probing questions kept touching emotional wounds. Wounds so deeply buried I thought they were gone forever. And it was enough at times to make me think I didn't need, or want this extra misery. This self-torture two days a week pervaded every waking thought, of every day, and into the night. After each session, it crossed my mind that I shouldn't make further appointments. But somehow I kept returning for more of this punishment and its consequent grief.

Warner's probing took a turn after a few weeks, when the appointments were scaled down to one a week. Out of the blue, her questions focussed on Mary Campbell. "Why do you say 'mum' when you refer to Mary Campbell? She is not your mother. Betty is!" Warner's tone was scolding. "Where is your real mother, now?"

"In a home in England."

"You mean she's institutionalised? What for?"

"She tried to commit suicide, but was found by a social worker just in time. She was rushed to hospital, and although her life was saved, her brain was damaged in an attempt to gas herself."

"Go on…"

"Well, apparently she can't look after herself. I'm led to believe that the suicide attempt, plus a lifetime of drinking, has affected her short-term memory."

"When did you last see her?"

"Over thirty years ago,"

"That long! Why is that?"

"My, er, grandmother never discussed her. I was too afraid to ask. All the time I was with my grandmother, I was expected to forget my mother, and call my grandmother 'mum.' I had to act as if my real mother didn't exist, except very early on in my life, when I was told to write to her, and beg for money for my keep. In fact, I knew nothing about her life at all, until very recently. It was only by accident that I found recent photographs of her…"

Looking down at my lap, I noticed that I'd begun to shred a paper tissue to pieces. Then I looked up again at Warner. "My, er, grandmother, at some point in my growing years, had led me to believe that my mother was dead."

"You mean your grandmother lied to you about your own mother?"

"Yes," I sobbed, unable to withhold the tears.

"Where is your grandmother now?"

"She's in a retirement village in Palm Beach."

"Is she happy there?"

"...Er, no."

"You seem uneasy about this. Why?"

I felt my head drop again. I stared down at the remnants of the tissue in my hand, and toyed nervously with it as I spoke. "She was angry that I put her there. Angry I deserted her. Scottish girls traditionally, are not meant to leave the home while elderly remain. Or so she told me. She told me she hoped I'd be as miserable as sin."

"Tell me more about Mina."

I sighed a deep sigh. These interrogations were so exhausting. "Well, she and her husband Bob looked after me until I reached school age, because the Social Services said I wasn't being taken care of properly. My, er, grandmother had her own two sons, and a boarding house to run." I looked up at Dr Warner to see if she understood the predicament my grandmother had been placed in, because of me. Her face was blank. "Bob and Mina loved me. They really took care of me. Had fun with me, as if I were their own child. They wanted to keep me, but they had to give me up when they immigrated to Australia. I was returned to my grandmother."

"That's enough for today," said the expressionless doctor. "I'll see you next Tuesday."

With the abruptness of a guillotine blade dropping, the appointment was terminated. I was always taken aback by the apparent callousness of these terminations. It was as if a meter had expired. It didn't seem to matter to Warner what was being discussed at the time. It simply ended - till next time. More often than not I went out the door wiping tear-stained cheeks.

This clock-watching unsettled me. Frequently, I felt as if I were just about to reach a crucial point of discovery – just about to unlock a treasure chest that would miraculously hold the answer to all my problems – when Warner would bring the session to a sharp conclusion. The pain of a remembered trauma often functioned as a setback. I felt torn apart by the very therapy intended to help me. In my eyes, this inquisition, this post mortem on my life, was doing more harm than good. It seemed to me that the cure was worse than the disease.

# CHAPTER 42

On the next visit to Dr Warner, I amazed myself by being willing to divulge information about Mary Campbell. Although difficult for me, once begun, with the doctor's skilled questioning, I went on to explain how I'd endeavoured to please my grandmother throughout the years, while feeling I never could. "I did try. I did everything I could to please her. I did everything she wanted of me, and more. It ruled my thoughts, my actions."

"Was she ever pleased with you?"

"I can never remember her once saying, 'thank you,' if that's what you mean. Or 'good girl,' or, 'well done.' It was useless trying to win favour. I could never please." My rising guilt fought for supremacy over my need to speak out about Mary Campbell, and I fell silent.

"And…" Warner encouraged.

"Never once did she show me she wanted me around - that she cared for me. She expected me to perform like a robot, with no feelings." Again, I was astonished by my admissions. I looked at Warner, examining her intelligent face for a sign of disbelief, for I myself found it incredulous that I was critical of my grandmother.

Warner was accepting.

"I lived and worked like a robot - a non-person - only worthy of having around if I was useful. The only company I kept was with myself. My inner person was all I had to bolster my own spirits. I think I sang a lot to keep myself company." Glancing over again at Warner for a reaction, embarrassed by my disclosure, I found she sat expressionless, as before. "I was dutiful, disciplined, and very responsible." I paused.

"And submissive – to the point of being controlled?"

"Well, yes… the word 'no' just wasn't in my vocabulary. I'd never refuse to do anything. But that was the way I wanted it. An insurance. The price my grandmother expected I pay. The price I expected to pay – was willing to pay - for having a roof over my head. I suppose I stopped being a child the day I went to live with her." A still silence followed this statement as I took in my own words. "The only trouble I got into, was if Ian or Andy invented some. I was continually accused, forever condemned, and always browbeaten. I lived with an irrepressible fear, and an urge to hide myself away."

Warner allowed me to deliver the information at my own pace. She nodded and waited for the next outburst.

"She grudged everything she gave me. She let me know that the food I ate was money out of her pocket. The tatty clothes I wore were Red Cross. It was a family joke. The boys' clothes were brand new. They were family, they were worthy. But it built up a fierce independence in me. I've always tried not to 'need' anyone. I think needing someone is a weakness. And yet I'm in conflict when I make that statement, because I don't feel complete unless there's someone for me to be servile to."

"Go on."

"I remember mum… er, my grandmother, even grudged the free rations given out by the government – orange juice, cod liver oil, malt for vitamin B, and things like that – as if she thought they were wasted on me."

"But she needed you to work for her?"

"Yes. I wouldn't have been much use if I'd been sick, I suppose."

"She showed you no affection?"

"NO!" I paused over this. "I never could understand it. I kept looking for crumbs of affection, but it was useless trying to win favour. And when someone is your mother – you're supposed to love her, honour her, aren't you?"

"Not when she doesn't earn your love, or give you reason to honour her."

I sat tearing my tissue. "Maybe I didn't think much of her," I mumbled.

"On the contrary, you love her."

I looked up questioningly, bewildered by my conflicting thoughts, and Warner found the need to clarify.

"Even though someone nearly destroys your life, you can still feel love for them." The good doctor waited patiently for a response, but not as much as a whisper escaped my lips while I thought about this. "Did she ever touch you kindly? A friendly hug?"

A lump formed in my throat. All I could do was shake my bowed head.

"How did you cope with this treatment?"

"I… pretended." This embarrassed me. I felt myself begin to sob, quietly. "I pretended that I belonged, that I was part of the family. Pretended she was pleased with me. Pretended she didn't resent me. I kidded myself that I mattered to her – that she liked me when I worked hard. I… pretended she thought I was useful, needed, and that she was grateful. I pretended she thought I was important… that she liked me, and that she… she…"

"Loved you?"

I could offer no more than a nod. I cried the tears from my childhood that I'd denied myself all through the years.

"You distorted reality. You denied the hatred Mary harboured for you. You could not admit to yourself that Mary Campbell resented you, did not love you, or even like you." Ruth Warner gave me time to absorb her well-chosen words. "But let me make this clear, you were not to blame for Mary's resentment of you. You were not to blame for her anger."

She had obviously noted the uncertain look on my face as I listened. My face always gave me away, but these were words that had needed to be said for a long time.

"She taught you not to belief in yourself. But fortunately you didn't succumb totally to her, because you had a core of strength within you, that made your life different from hers. Even though you carried with you all the traumas from the past, that made you afraid of what you were." Warner's eyes were soft and sympathetic as she spoke, unveiling the truths I found so hard to face. "You've survived the prison of your childhood, and made so much of yourself, despite those awful years. You're lucky to still be sane."

I had some difficulty believing her words, though I knew deep down they were true. The truth within me had been fighting for freedom for years. Now it had a champion who would help it see the light of day.

"It seems to me," the astute doctor continued, when she thought I was responsive enough to absorb more, "that during times of even your greatest sadness, you never blamed your grandmother."

"NO!" I blurted, then quietened. "No! I've never done that. I always blamed myself for my predicament, I never blamed her."

# CHAPTER 43

I likened these visits to Dr Warner, the probing examination, the discoveries, the unfolding facts, the enlightenment, to the unveiling of my damaged face, when, bit by bloodied bit, with each visit to the hospital, the nurses had uncovered more horrific, more serious scarring. In many ways, it seemed to me, this psychiatric analysis had the same effect – the revealing of deeper and deeper wounds with each visit.

Months into the therapy now, and only in Warner's company, I discarded first the hat, then, with great reluctance, the sunglasses. It was the internal scarring I was focussed on now. With a hint of inner warmth showing through her normally steely façade, Warner began a new session.

"Was there no-one who recognised your talents and abilities? Was there no-one who appreciated your intelligence? You are intelligent, you know. You are talented!"

I looked up, surprised by Warner's growing friendliness. Warner, who'd been, until this point in the doctor/patient relationship, clinically, coolly professional, seemingly impervious to my tears, was showing herself to be affable, human, and more – even an ally.

"Pardon?"

"Was there no-one who appreciated you?"

"I don't know what you mean?"

"Well, didn't you have any friends when you were growing up?"

"No."

"Why not?"

"Well, frankly, I had no time. I was lucky if I got to school! I was on duty all the time. I was needed in the boarding house. I even missed exams. Never went on excursions. I would run home from school to help do the vegetables for the boarders' dinner, and serve it up. Weekends were for cleaning. Silver, brass, windows. Making beds. Hoovering. I was a good cook too, for my age, I suppose. Then when Ian joined the Royal Marines, I had to spit and polish his boots." I tried to read her expression, but could not.

"Go on," she urged.

"Nobody liked me at school anyway. Certainly not the teachers – I never did my homework. I was forever getting the leather strap, and I would miss weeks on end of school when my grandmother went on holiday. I was left in charge of the boarding house, with daily help coming in."

"How old were you, then?"

"Oh, I must have been all of twelve. I got so behind at school I was embarrassed. I thought I was such a dunce."

"You put yourself down. You didn't think much of yourself. It's an uncomfortable feeling – one which you projected to others. You said to yourself, 'They don't like me.' And Mary Campbell perpetuated your bad feelings about yourself – consciously, and sub-consciously. That was Mary's way of keeping control over you. She kept you dependent on her, so she could use you for her own benefit."

I nodded. "She reminded me constantly I was unwanted. That I'd been forced on her. I was always made to feel inferior to her, and the boys. Not a day went by that Andy wouldn't remind me I was a bastard child. Filthy, because of it! They all let me know that I was worthless – mostly because I was illegitimate, but also because I was an outsider."

Suddenly, as if I'd gone too far, my indoctrinated loyalty, and my natural pity for my grandmother surfaced. I came to Mary's defence. "But you must realise, that my grandmother had a very difficult childhood." I wanted to make it clear, that as far as I was concerned, none of these things were Mary's fault. "She was raised by her grandmother too – in the Highlands of Scotland, where there was no electricity, no running water. She had to walk miles to school in the bleak winter snow. I know all about her hardships," I said, as I fidgeted with a tissue in my lap.

"I bet you do!" Warner's comment had a facetious edge to it.

I looked up, and into her eyes.

"I bet it was ingrained into you!"

"I suppose it was to make me feel grateful for what I had. At least I had a bed of my own. Mary told me she had to sleep at the foot of her gran's bed – like a dog. She'd been made to feel she was in her grandmother's way, too! She always said that girls were only good for getting married."

"Did she, indeed?"

I sat in stunned silence at my own disclosure, unable to believe I was denouncing the woman who'd taken me in, fed and clothed me.

"Girls should marry a wealthy man, or go on the stage. Was that it?" asked Warner.

I recognised the phrase as Mary Campbell's own words. "How did you know that?"

"That's the way primitives think. That is, uneducated people."

"Is that why she pushed Betty onto the stage?"

"And whose idea was it that you pursue it, too?"

"Television, you mean? Well, er, I thought at the time it was my idea. But my grandmother made me think it was the only way to be successful. The spotlight; prominence meant success to her."

"Who said we have to be in a position of prominence to be considered successful?"

"But the glamour, the praise and adulation. Doesn't prominence equal success?"

The doctor answered me by asking another stirring question, then watched as I sorted out the pieces of the puzzle in my mind. "Do you need all that? Do you really need praise and attention?"

I saw for the first time that it had been for Mary Campbell, not myself, that I'd sought the limelight. It had been another way of trying to please my grandmother. I recalled how she loved to boast to neighbours and friends about Betty's success. And how I myself, had been urged to supply volumes of snapshots taken with celebrities for her endless boasting.

"You've already told me that your mother, Betty, became an alcoholic, trying to keep up with the men in her circle on drinking bouts. Everybody knows that stage work engenders the need to seek adoration from others. When the supply of adoration runs low – the drinking gets worse. It's self-destructive."

#

Filled with doubt and self-denial, I was tormented by these latest revelations. My emotions were constantly in turmoil. Although I now felt I was making some sort of progress, each visit to Warner continued to leave me frayed at the seams.

As confused as I was, I realised that the Mary Campbell still within me, was trying to discredit all the doctor was saying. It was as if a vulture sat on one shoulder, and truth and reality were on the other.

Memories long forgotten flashed through my mind, day and night. I fought the demons in my head, trying to reverse opinions that I'd held all my life. With much time to ruminate and ponder, I fluctuated between contemplation and gloom. Day after troubled day.

# CHAPTER 44

Summoning my courage, I accepted an invitation to join Jean Metcalfe at a friend's apartment in Kirribilli, for a bridge club dinner.

I had combed my hair across my damaged forehead, and hid my eyes behind dark glasses all evening. Jean's coterie all knew about my accident, and gushed friendliness and concern through one course after another. But I felt smothered by the unwanted attention, and as soon as I could, I escaped outside onto the balcony for a breath of fresh air.

Standing alone, I leaned over the balcony, listening to the interminable hum of the traffic on Sydney's Coathanger Bridge nearby, watching a continuous stream of vehicles pour like molten gold into any available crevice. Taking off my sunglasses, trying to accustom my tear-filled eyes to the evening's light, I soon became mesmerised by an air of hallucination conjured in the magical night. The twinkling lights, the stars, the majesty of dazzling Sydney Harbour.

The sound of laughter reached me from indoors. I couldn't help but think that the world of laughter belonged only to happy yesterdays. I was in no mood for socialising, and thought it unfair of me to dampen anyone else's spirits, and deeply regretted having attended.

I looked up to the multitude of flickering stars above, then lowered my eyes to the fleet of busy ferries gliding across the water. A brightly illuminated ocean liner docked across the harbour at Circular Quay, looked like a fair ground. It reminded me of the *Fair Sky*, the ocean liner which had brought me to Australia as an immigrant. Here, I'd met up again with Daddy Bob and Mina. They had sponsored the immigration of Andy, Mary and I, and we went to live with them.

Naively, I'd imagined, and hoped, that they'd be my salvation, that I'd have happy times again. But no! Mary Campbell was jealous of the bond Mina and I still shared, and caused so many arguments with both Bob and Mina, that we moved out of their home within a week. Again I was trapped as Mary's slave, only now, at the other side of the world, in a new boarding house, 'The Aberfeldy,' which she soon bought in Brisbane.

But my joyful memories of the voyage would never leave me. I'd felt free. Absolutely free, for the first time. There were no duties for me on board ship. I remember staying as far away from my grandmother as I could. Hiding at every opportunity.............

Mary Campbell and I shared a cabin with an English woman and her daughter Muriel, who was the same age as myself, and I'd taken an immediate liking to the pretty teenager. Andy had to share with three male strangers across the passageway, and Mary was furious about that. I will always remember Muriel's smile, her energy, her enthusiasm. She was my first real friend.

The first morning on board, I'd hurried out of the cabin, and I walked the entire length and breadth of the ship on an exploratory mission. It was like a fantastic dream come true. The sound of the ship cutting through the ocean waves, the blue, wondrous sky in the windy Bay of Biscay. I felt fresh colour in my cheeks, as I sucked in lung-fulls of salty fresh air. I marvelled at the infinite expanse, the shoreless horizon. The distance from the everyday.

A posh English voice broke through my thoughts as I revelled at this new marvel in my life. I looked up to see Muriel.

"What do you say to a swim, Lilly? Do come!" she said. "Look, I already have my costume." She held up her towel and bathing costume. "Do come! The pool is terribly deep, and when the ship rocks, it makes super-duper waves!"

"I'm sorry, I haven't had breakfast yet."

"Oh, that's easily fixed. They serve breakfast in the main dining room till eleven, and there's a breakfast bar for late-comers. "Come with me for a swim, and I'll take you to breakfast afterwards. Alright?" She held out her hand to shake on it. "Let's go fetch your swimsuit."

Mary Campbell was still in bed when we two girls sneaked into the cabin. Muriel stifled a giggle. Mary stirred, turned over in her bed, and let out a closed-eyed groan. I shot Muriel a look of horror. We didn't move. We waited in the darkened cabin in tentative silence till I thought it safe again. Then I moved to pull my suitcase from under Mary's bunk.

Lifting the lid carefully, I felt inside for my red, nylon-bubble swim suit. As it felt different from anything else in the case, it was easy to detect. Out it slid, and I stealthily returned the suitcase to its resting place. Then, grabbing a towel marked 'Sitmar Line,' hanging beside the sink, Muriel and I slipped back out and into the passageway. With the cabin door closed behind us, I let out an audible sigh of relief. We shared a victorious grin.

"Follow me," said Muriel. "We'll go to the upstairs bathroom on 'A' deck to change. It's much nicer up there." She led the way, smiling, and saying hello to other passengers with whom she'd already made friends. "I found 'A' deck purely by accident whilst I was exploring." With twinkling eyes, she looked back over her shoulder at me. "You have to take a special little stairway to find it, but I know where!"

Pushing open the white, gold embossed door marked 'First Class Bathroom,' Muriel proudly presented me with her discovery. A spacious, oval room, fully mirrored from ceiling to floor with marble fittings and gold taps, it was a splendidly decadent private spa room. And one it seemed, no-one else knew about because the ship was now all one class, and all the other passengers used the main pool on 'B' deck.

"Isn't this fun?" she beamed. "Come on in, it's all ours, Lilly. And look, we can lock it and change in absolute privacy."

She led me in then locked the door. Walking further inside to the centre of the oval room, still holding on to her towel and costume, she held out her arms and did a fanciful pirouette, her brightly coloured red and yellow top, and blue skirt creating a kaleidoscope of flashing colours reflecting in the multitude of bevelled wall mirrors. She twirled until she was dizzy, then flopped down in mock exhaustion on a padded leather settee to catch her breath. I watched wide-eyed.

Then, with a sudden resurgence of energy, Muriel jumped to her feet, threw down her things, and commenced to undress while babbling on about the ship and all the fun things there were to do on board. "Come on, into your costume," Muriel said, hurrying me along, and chatting non-stop. "I'm on my way to Darwin with my mother. You know where that is, don't you? It's the northern-most part of Australia, in the Northern Territory. It'll take half a day to fly there from Fremantle when we land. But we're stopping off at Alice Springs to break the journey – we'll see Ayers Rock. That'll be exciting. Simply everyone must see Ayers Rock!"

Embarrassed by my childish old swimsuit, I was in no hurry whatsoever to change, having already decided I could use my towel to hide my costume from view, until I slid into the water of the ship's pool. Sitting on the settee, I removed my plastic Marks and Spencer sandals, hoping for a moment to undress when Muriel wasn't watching.

"Mummy's a nurse, you know. Oh, I suppose I should say nursing sister." She pulled her light cotton top over her head, ruffling her blonde locks in the process, talking incessantly, giving me little chance to answer. Unfastening her brassiere, she let it slip to the floor, unashamedly revealing a grown woman's voluptuous breasts. I could not help myself, I stood hypnotised. She went on to remove her panties, then stood totally naked admiring her own image reflected ten-fold by the mirrored walls.

She caught sight of the startled look on my face. "What? What is it? What's so intriguing?" she asked. Then she laughed. "Oh, these!" And her petite hands went to touch her magnificently-formed breasts. "They're big aren't they?" she smiled proudly at me, and cupped her bosom in her hands. She looked to the mirror again to inspect her image from another angle. "Don't worry, I'm sure yours will be as big soon. Have they been sore, yet?"

I nodded silently.

Muriel's attention was on her reflection. "I love mine. It feels so good when I run my hand over the nipples like this. And look what happens." Totally unselfconsciously, she stroked her palms over her nipples. The areola immediately shrivelled, changed colour slightly, and the nipples protruded into a hard state of arousal. She closed her eyes with the sheer pleasure of the sensation. "My mother taught me to love my body, Lilly. Don't you love yours?"

I didn't answer. Embarrassed by the sight of Muriel's self-love, I pretended not to notice. Turning my back, I proceeded to undress. Stripping to the waist, I took off my knickers, reached for my costume, and was about to put it on under my skirt, when I felt Muriel gently touch my hand to halt me.

"Don't be afraid, Lilly. I won't hurt you. I just want to show you that your own body can be your best friend. Look."

And with that, she gently pulled me, blushing, around to look at myself in the mirror, and moved in close to me. She put her right arm around my tiny waist and held my left hand in hers like a dancing instructor teaching a pupil. Our skin touched as we stood close.

"Look," she said, kindly, "you're beautiful, too!" Sensing my bashfulness, Muriel reached out to touch my chin and gently raised my face to make me confront my reflection. "Please look at yourself, Lilly. Please." She gave me her most persuasive smile. "Why, your breasts are every bit as big as mine. Look! They've just been hidden under your clothes, that's all." She looked at me in a sweet, reassuring way, and witnessed my expression slowly change as I allowed myself to look, and be convinced.

"Oh…!"

"See!" She giggled good-naturedly, leaning over to kiss my cheek. "Now, are you going to take your skirt off, or am I?" Muriel's fingers were already on the button of my skirt, and the flimsy piece of material fell around my feet. "Look at yourself Lilly, and see what I see. You're beautiful. Really, really beautiful! And you must tell yourself that. And, if you want me to, I'll teach you how to love yourself."

She gave my hand a squeeze, and for just a moment she rested her head on my shoulder, and the two most perfect young bathing belles stood together, naked, holding hands in front of the myriad of mirrors – in First Class………

The sound of the cruise liner's horn at Circular Quay jerked me back to today's reality, and I looked down in the darkness from my Kirribilli eyrie to see the ship's twin funnels billowing grey smoke. It was leaving for another destination, while I stayed behind. I sighed. I too, had to leave something behind - the two beautiful young maidens of my memory.

Around to my right, a Ferris Wheel at Luna Park rotated lazily. On the still night air, I could hear the squeals of delighted patrons. And slowly, I became aware of the tall shadows of concrete monoliths in the darkness all around me, looming like black devils. Blocks of glass and brick, which, I felt sure in my depressed mood, were filled with frustrated lonely people, living lives of unrewarding ritualistic domesticity.

In this melancholy state, my personal struggle suddenly seemed futile. Negativity and sadness overwhelmed me; it all seemed too difficult to go on. How easy it would be to end all the suffering. All it would take was the courage to heave my body over this feeble rail to the ground beckoning fourteen floors below. I began to feel myself leaning forward over the railing. I heard a voice in my head assure me it would be easy. All I had to do was lean; lean forward – forward – and over. All so, so easy.

My mind duelled the demon.

I fought the voice, and won. For the time being. My hands gripped tightly to the rail. But I could not fight the tears. When I'd cried till I could cry no more, I wiped my eyes just as Jean called out from the lounge-room's sliding glass doors.

"Lilly? Are you alright? Please come inside and join us." She put a comforting arm around my shoulder, making me realize that she and her friends were well-meaning. They couldn't possibly comprehend what I was going through.

# CHAPTER 45

Awake and asleep, a continual battle was being fought in my head. Perceived truths warred against newly uncovered facts. Freshly discovered self-worth was thrown into the fray against years of destructive brain-washing at the hands of my grandmother.

"I've been having terrible trouble sleeping," I told Warner on my latest visit. "I'm continually fighting monsters in my head. Sometimes I think I'll go quite mad!"

She let me talk.

"I can't find any peace. There's an Armageddon going on in my head!"

"Tell me about it." The clever doctor spoke in her practised monotone.

I found it very difficult to explain. For now, in disclosing what was troubling me, I was in fact making admissions of my grandmother's abuse. Mary Campbell had become the Accused, and I was now the Prosecution, after years of being on the Defence. Every damning admission was in conflict with my loyalty to my grandmother, and it tore me apart.

But in order to find the truth that would ultimately save me, I was forced to give evidence against Mary. "I could never understand her lack of compassion. She would laugh after she cut a chicken's head off. It would run about the back yard without a head until it dropped. She enjoyed the torture!" I could feel the look of horror that was now etched on my face. "It was a maniacal laugh. She… she drowned kittens. She would put an entire litter in a sack, drop a brick on top of them and drown them in a tub of water." I looked over at the doctor, half expecting a scolding for making too much of this.

But she encouraged me to talk. "Go on."

"It was the lack of feeling that upset me. And the pleasure she got out of it. I couldn't understand it." I could feel my eyes pleading for help to understand Mary Campbell's cruelty.

Warner remained impassive, but her silence gave me the courage and permission to continue speaking freely. "At times like those, I would have to run and hide. To find some peace. To think my own thoughts. To find safety in my own mind. I felt no safety or trust with Mary Campbell."

"Give me an example - an occasion when you didn't feel emotionally safe with her."

"On one of my birthdays she handed me a piece of chocolate. It had a human tooth in it!" Did I see Dr Warner raise an eyebrow at this? Perhaps not. "And, on my first Christmas with her, when I was five, she gave me a huge gift – wrapped in a box so large I thought it might be a bicycle. But as I unwrapped it, I found she had systematically placed box, inside box, until it came down to one the size of a shoe box. Inside, I found my own dirty gym pants wrapped around a huge carrot!"

There was no visual response from Warner. She remained receptive, but impassive.

"But it was her laughter that worried me. The sheer enjoyment she derived from my pain! She laughed like the mad woman in 'Jane Eyre.' I was only five years old, for heaven's sake! I could find no relief from her vindictiveness; was totally bewildered by this treatment. I just couldn't understand it. Still can't. I don't think I did anything... wrong! Am I making too much of this?"

Now Warner felt the need to explain. "It was depraved behaviour. The tooth represented a clitoris. The carrot is obvious, even to you, I'm sure. It was certainly no way to treat an innocent child."

There was a prolonged silence. I didn't know where to go from there. This clinical psychology was all very confusing to me. It was not until Warner became more explicit, and offered further explanation for Mary's puzzling behaviour, that I would come to realise that in psychiatric terms, Mary

Campbell was depraved, cruel and malicious. Not as bad as some, but definitely twisted. No maniac, but no saint either. Just twisted enough to manipulate a young personality.

"It's understandable that you were perplexed by it." said Warner. "You'd never experienced anything like it before you went to live with Mary Campbell. That's why you repressed it."

#

Another tortuous week of coming face-to-face with past agonies. The pain was excruciating. More so than the events themselves at the time. Now I realised that I'd denied Mary's bad treatment of me. Had never stood up to her. Had given in without a fight all through the years, till now – in my mid-thirties.

As memories and thoughts came to the surface, I would quickly jot them down to use as ammunition against the holocaust in my head. I would arrive at Warner's office armed, with renewed gusto to fight, to help solve my problems, and shed light on years of darkness.

I was tenacious in my resolve, so desperately did I want a breakthrough. The time had come for me to rid myself of my demons and my confusion once and for all. And so off I'd go to my appointments, week after week, ready to purge myself, facing renewed pain, in the tender care of the accomplished psychiatrist, Dr Ruth Warner.

# CHAPTER 46

"I had another dream last night!" I volunteered.

"Tell me."

"I saw Mina. Her back was to me, and she was leaving me behind – but she did look back at me, sadly, as if she regretted having to leave me."

"And?"

"She had something stuck on her stocking!"

"What was it?"

"Oh, I don't know," I answered flippantly, not thinking it was important. "The stocking looked a bit wrinkled. It seemed to hang loosely on her calf. Maybe it was just that they were too big for her - she was only just five foot tall. They didn't make stockings as well in those days," I suggested, simply to give Warner an answer.

"It was a penis," the psychiatrist declared.

"A WHAT?"

"A penis," the doctor repeated. "It was a penis on the stocking."

"Oh, my goodness," I said with embarrassment.

Warner was cool and nonchalant, but she went on to explain to me in a caring manner. "Your subconscious is telling you, that Mina left, taking Bob – the penis - away with her."

I sat with my mouth open. I didn't know what to say. I dared not say a thing.

"In other words, your 'Daddy Bob' was the spice of your life. Mina was the bread and butter."

"Oh… alright."

After Warner's explanation, my dream seemed to make sense to me, and I was willing to accept it. Who was I to argue? "I also dreamed about Vegemite, and a four-letter word."

"What does Vegemite mean to you?"

"Nourishment! Vegemite means nourishment," I announced victoriously.

"And the four-letter word?" The hint of a smile? I saw it! I did, I really saw it!

"It was LOVE! Spelled out in front of my eyes in huge letters. L-O-V-E. Huge letters - like the famous Hollywood sign!"

"Can you see what's coming through?" Warner asked encouragingly. "You were telling yourself that your grandmother fed you, but did not give you love."

I shook my head in amazement. This was a genuine revelation. The message from my dream was quite transparent. Never before had I been given such a clear-cut explanation of what my subconscious was trying to say. More than that, I was amazed that it was my own mind telling me these things! "My goodness me, I'm so clever when I'm asleep. I wish I had such clarity of mind when I was awake."

"You will have, eventually. Go home, think about what your dreams are trying to tell you. Your subconscious mind is allowing you to see the answers." Warner said these words with pleasure in her voice, like a teacher to a pupil making great progress with their studies. She knew that I'd turned a corner in my rehabilitation.

The session was over for another day. I gathered my bits and pieces, the quickly scribbled thoughts and puzzling questions that occurred to me day and night. I'd made a habit of bringing these notes to my sessions for analysis and discussion, trying relentlessly, each appointment, to fit them all in. The sessions gave me plenty to deliberate on. In the intervening days I kept delving, digging, filtering, and sifting, desperate to find answers, desperate to assemble the puzzle. But now, although I'd no idea where this was all heading, I was beginning to feel as if some kind of reward was within reach - there was light at the end of the tunnel!

I headed out into the corridor with a feeling of triumph. It had been a long time since I'd felt anything but dispirited, but now I was beginning to feel I'd come a long way. My self-denial had ceased. My answers were truthful and concise, now that I was able to admit I'd been protecting my grandmother all my life.

My head was down. Pre-occupied with my thoughts, I headed for the exit when I heard someone call out my name.

"Hello there, Lilly."

It was a voice I recognised. I looked up and around.

John Davenport was fast approaching from further along the corridor, his white coat flapping at his sides as he strode toward me. He smiled warmly at me. "How are things?"

"Oh, hello Mr Davenport," I replied, remembering he was a 'Mister,' being a surgeon, and quickly reaching to make sure my sunglasses were in place. My vain action surprised me. He was my doctor, after all!

"You're looking well. How are you getting along with Ruth?"

"I'm doing fine," I answered, while reaching to smooth out my fringe to hide my damaged forehead. Again, why was I concerned? "I want to thank you for suggesting Dr Warner. I'm beginning to feel as if we're getting somewhere. It's very painful, and I'm having to fight lots of demons and self-pity, but I really do feel as if we're progressing."

"Well, there's no need to feel you're doing it all by yourself, you know. We're as close as the phone. I'll congratulate Ruth when I see her. She's certainly made you sound more cheerful."

I smiled, repeated my gratitude, and made a quick exit. I felt him watch me go with my head held high, as I negotiated the corridor with some fight in me. She'd made a great difference, and I was forever amazed at her wisdom. I remembered her words:

'Why do you think we psychiatrists enter the profession? More often than not, the interest is generated from a personal need to find answers to our own problems. We're human too!'

#

A Christmas jingle was playing on the radio. Children were singing. Suddenly the cherubic faces of my children danced provocatively in my mind's eye. I could smell the warm, clean smell of their freshly bathed bodies, the plump and healthy feel of their chubby arms and legs. I heard the giggles, those wonderful belly-laughs when I tickled them. How easily they smiled for me. How they chuckled and chortled together, eyes alight with innocent mischief. I could physically feel their tight hugs, hugs which threatened to choke me with love. The needy snuggles when comfort was required, the nuzzles, the cosseting, the cradling, the rocking in my arms when they were weary. I remembered how I'd comforted them when they were sick, how a gentle voice, a simple soft tune, and a stroke of their forehead would close their eyes, soothe their distress, and help them sleep. Loving memories that no amount of injustice could erase.

My waiting arms were empty now. There were no words of sympathy or under-standing that could possibly ease the pain of their loss. Dr Warner knew it, too! For all my progress with my past traumas, all the self-realisation in the world was not going to bring my babies back. All Warner could offer me was a vague hope that one day, perhaps when the children were older, I could be re-united with them. For the time being, I had to console myself with that.

# CHAPTER 47

Christmas was only weeks away. I arrived sullen and withdrawn for my latest appointment. As soon as the doctor had barely said 'Hello,' the floodgates opened.

"Sometimes I get so depressed by all of this, I'd rather be dead!" I snapped out the words angrily. "I feel so stupid crying like a child all the time! But I'm sick of looking like 'The Elephant Man.'" I was angry and frustrated by the seemingly endless journey, but I felt secure enough to display it in her company. There were still many tears to be freed. Tears for the young emotionally damaged Lilly. Tears for the mature, physically damaged Lilly. "One Christmas she splashed boiling water over me," I blurted out, but quickly came to Mary's defence. "It was probably an accident, but I would gladly have let her do it again, for a cuddle!"

"Tell me about it."

"It was breakfast time, and I was crouching down at the stove, keeping an eye on the toast under the grill, and she was pouring boiling water from the kettle into the teapot, right above me. It went all over me."

"What did she do then?"

"I was told to get out of the way." I looked down at my lap and watched myself tear another tissue to shreds. "I was alright in a few days or so. But it was that damned bride doll that really upset me! I wanted to cuddle it so badly," I sobbed, "but she wouldn't let me touch it. She put it up on the piano and said it was 'too good to play with.'" I went on to explain in gasping breaths, how the Indian students had given me the gift of the most beautiful bride doll. I held my breath, trying desperately to control the tears but this memory was tearing me apart.

"Tell me, what does that make you feel, now?"

"DAMN!" I cursed loudly, totally out of character. "It's so STUPID crying over a silly bride doll! How can a grown woman cry over a doll?"

This memory was achingly painful. Yet, at the same time, I felt overwhelmingly ashamed, that I, a grown woman was so emotional, NOW, almost thirty years later, over a doll! I fought and fought so courageously to hold back the emotion this memory evoked. But beautiful 'Ponkie' - as I'd named her - was still dancing before my eyes. Such a comforting beauty - so far out of reach - physically, and emotionally. I felt, at that moment, the pain in my heart was enough to make me die! Till suddenly, words seemed to come directly from heaven.

"It's very understandable. That doll was all you had to call your own!" Warner said these words with such compassion, that they struck me like a tidal wave, washing away my pain. They were unexpected words. Necessary words. Healing words. And they were just what I needed. Her sympathetic understanding would be a lasting comfort. She'd soothed the pain. The doctor had given me permission to be angry at the injustice in my life. She must have seen the relief sweep over me because she went on to explain.

"There's much you'll come to understand." It was time to lend me a helping hand. "When your grandmother said, 'You have nothing to complain about,' when she said, 'You owe me', and, 'You should think yourself lucky, and be grateful for small mercies,' she was in fact, creating a distortion. You didn't have the things you needed for 'growing up.' She stole your confidence. She didn't allow you any freedom to be a person in your own right. She controlled you. Both mind and body."

I sat and listened to Warner's wise words in the calm after the storm.

"In order to grow, children must feel 'free' to grow." She gave me time to absorb this. "But it wasn't as if Mary had no good qualities. She was a hard worker, independent, and she loved her children – in her own way. But YOU were not considered to be one of them. You were considered an extra burden."

Now I felt that the doctor was making excuses for her, because my new-found resentment of Mary was still at its height. "But she laughed at me! At my body! At my breasts!" I spat the words out angrily.

"Were they nice breasts?"

"YES!" I petulantly conceded. At that precise moment, the childhood memory of sweet aromas - a busy hotel room, beautiful, laughing young women with flowers in their hair, readying themselves for a glamorous event; the sounds of swishing taffeta; the sights of coloured silks, shimmering satins, music, gaiety in an unfamiliar place. And I was there to witness this wonder as I sat on the huge bed surrounded with bright cushions. I remembered Betty's breasts as she undressed and donned a beautiful stage gown. It was a psychologically vulnerable moment for a toddler, one who knew nothing of her mother, or one who'd not been witness before to such glamour.

"They were nice breasts – like Betty's?"

"YES! Yes, they were nice!" I acknowledged. "Yes, they were just like Betty's breasts." Here at last was validation that my body hadn't been ugly – as Mary Campbell had led me to believe. The clever doctor had validated my worth. Deep inside me, I'd known myself to be valuable and worthy. Here at last someone was giving me permission to feel proud of myself and my body. Up to the surface flooded more memories. I now realised that Mary Campbell had so denigrated me that I felt too ugly to be loved! But how did Dr Warner know to compare me with Betty? I'd never mentioned that memory to her.

"All those years," Warner remarked, "Mary's own self-hatred and jealousy were inflicted on you. You were her convenient and defenceless victim. Someone she could take out her bitterness and frustrations on, without fear of retribution. It's so much easier to be wicked within a family situation, hiding from the law! As for the men in your life, you've been courting the father you never had. You've chosen men who weren't there for you, or who would ultimately desert you!"

"I have?"

"Because you never knew your father, and your mother handed you physically and emotionally over to your grandmother, you felt abandoned. And who wouldn't? As a result, you had absolutely no self-esteem. No feeling of self-worth. You allowed yourself to be the victim in your relationships. Like a magnet, you attracted poor treatment. It was as if you had a flashing sign on your head saying, 'Walk all over me.'"

It all made sense.

"You held yourself in such low regard that you tolerated the bad treatment from your husband. You didn't walk into the relationship believing he'd be violent. When it started, you thought that things would change. That HE would change. But the battering became so bad, that you began to think no man would ever love you, so you let him walk all over you."

"Was I really that stupid?" I said, sadly.

"Did you ever put your foot down and say, 'I want'?"

"No. I never did claim my rightful place. Ever!"

The memories were all there to validate what was being said. But worse than remembering the painful past, was the knowledge that I'd permitted all this to take place over the years. I'd built my own prison walls by being submissive, out of what I thought was a need. A masochistic need. I let Ruth Warner continue to enlighten me.

"You allowed your husband to keep you a prisoner, away from people. Away from life. The children only served to inflate his ego. He saw them only as a narcissistic extension of himself. They were only possessions! He couldn't relate to them in a close, affectionate way. They were just for 'show.' To prove he was a man."

I bowed my head.

"You repressed your anger. You played the martyr, provoking his temper. His anger made you feel secure, because his bad treatment of you was perpetuating a childhood pattern! You were again dependent, looking for crumbs of affection. A classic structure had developed. Can you see it?"

"Yes. He was cruel, like Mary Campbell. And distant. And I was desperately lonely. I began to do anything for attention. I needed some sort of response from him. I was willing to accept anything."

"But he would only retreat further?" Warner understood exactly. "He viewed your actions as criticism and complaint. And I imagine, he withheld sex to punish you."

"YES!" He controlled that, too," I was stunned by her insight. "Nor was he involved with the family. He was never home. And the less he came home, the more angry I became, and probably made him suffer because of it."

"He withheld love, which caused you to become more insecure."

"How do you know all this?"

Warner merely smiled. "You felt captive by the limitations he placed upon you. Isolated by his indifference toward you. A cycle of abuse began. But, I'd imagine, there were periods when he'd beg forgiveness."

"YES! He did! He promised he'd change. Often! He'd beg me to forgive him."

"And you wanted to believe the unbelievable. That things would get better. You'd become stuck. Dependent. Because of a learned helplessness. You'd mistaken the few periods of civilised behaviour for what you hoped might become the norm, hoping things would improve."

"Yes. And I was sure it was all MY fault. That I caused his anger!"

"And therefore deserved the beatings. People who resort to bashing, usually do it because they don't have the vocabulary to explain their pain. I imagine you were the more intelligent - despite his reputation in the community, and his high-flying job."

I nodded silently. Then after a moment I made a confession. "The saddest thing of all, is that I thought I'd won those fights - because he'd had to resort to bashing me. I saw the agony in his eyes when he realised for himself that he was the weak one. He'd never admit it, but he knew, deep down."

# CHAPTER 48

Jean Metcalfe called with an offer of lunch at her apartment. I hesitated, but she was persuasive, and had shown me such kindness throughout my recuperation that I succumbed. With sparkling Sydney Harbour to feast our eyes on, we headed out to the balcony. Kicking off her shoes, Jean put her feet up on the sun-lounge. "You know, you never did tell me, Lilly... how did that husband of yours suddenly come into such wealth?"

I felt my heart skip a beat. My head jerked around to look at her. It was a story I'd never disclosed. I felt ill at ease about it. Although I knew in my heart I'd not been the cause of my marriage break-up, I was the one burdened by guilt, like a sexually abused child blaming themselves for their predicament. I'm sure Jean noticed my hesitation, but I wanted nothing to tarnish the image she had of me. She was very important to me now, and I deserved a good friend, besides, honesty mattered to me.

"No-one has asked me that before, Jean. Not even Dr Warner," I said with trepidation. "It's an ugly tale, and I don't want you to think badly of me."

"Lilly! I could never do that! You know I understand your background. You must trust me not to judge you."

"I just want you to know, that what happened to me all those years ago, would never happen to me today. I'm very much in control now, and can say 'NO' without fear of contradiction or retribution."

Smiling kindly she said, "If it's too painful, let's not talk about it. But the memory is obviously still tender, so if you want to use me as a sounding board, please do."

Taking a deep breath, I retrieved another wretched memory from deep inside my soul. I had to trust that the outcome of my revelations would not destroy our relationship.

"I was so very young and afraid then," I began. "Belittled and humiliated by my grandmother who invalidated my very existence, to the extent I had no mind of my own – she de-humanised me!"

"Yes… I'm sorry, Lilly…"

"Do you know, Jean, she made me feel so humble, that I once said, 'Excuse me' to a chicken in the Dundee hen-run!"

We both giggled.

Resuming the portrait of my marriage, I explained, "Mitch my ex-husband was an American…"

I went on to tell how his family had migrated to Australia from Utah when Mitch was a boy. His religious upbringing had driven, and shaped him. He was a workaholic, who just kept on running to please his boss, and sadly, how he was never home, despite my yearning for him, as young people do.

"His mother despised me, blaming me for stealing him. Besides, I was not one of their flock." I told Jean how Mitch worked for a dynamic, wealthy American named Archie Simms, a prominent member of the same church. "Archie owned 'Gobble 'n Go,' the fast-food chicken chain, here in Australia."

"Oh those! There's a Gobble 'n Go on nearly every street corner."

"My Mitch was one of Archie's lieutenants. He'd started out stacking boxes in the warehouse, and worked his way up through the ranks." I explained how the wealthy Archie manipulated Mitch, knowing he would do whatever was asked of him, and how easily Archie had made Mitch his humble servant, using his ambition and greed to enslave him. Then, I found myself divulge another suppressed memory. I told Jean about the night all the employees were gathered together to celebrate Christmas at a function in a grand hotel, and how a call had come through to Mitch to say an alarm had gone off in one of the stores.

"It was Mitch who must attend to it, as he did on every occasion. Often, he'd be asleep, tucked up in bed with me, and have to jump out of bed and race off. Many's the time he'd come back frozen to the bone, and the alarm would go again, and off he'd go again. That night at the Christmas party when Mitch went dashing off, Archie Simms said he'd see that I got home safely."

Jean darted a look over at me. "How old was this American boss?"

"He was sixty, and I was twenty-two"

"I think I know what's coming! Go on, Lilly."

"It's not only what you might think, Jean, it's even uglier than the obvious!" Again, I hesitated. "Archie came very close to raping me that night," I revealed, "in his swanky car, parked outside my front door. Fortunately, he became so excited that he ejaculated before he could penetrate, and thankfully, I was able to open the passenger door and run inside my house to escape him."

Jean was horrified. "What did you tell Mitch?"

"Nothing! How could I? I was sure he'd blame me!"

"You poor thing! Simms would have been such an important, almost 'father' figure to you. His actions were like a priest's betrayal of a parishioner's trust! Despicable!"

I went on to explain how persistent Archie had been. How he'd kept on finding excuses to send Mitch away on business trips. And as soon as Mitch was safely out of the way, Archie would come to the house. How I would hide, cowering behind the closed door with my two little ones scared out of my wits. "I'd always been afraid of Mitch because of his explosive temper, and now I had his boss to contend with, too."

"Was there no-one to turn to?"

"No. And I was in such inner turmoil that I ended up asking the family doctor to arrange for me to see a psychologist. I was dangerously afraid. I felt trapped, with no way out." I pointed out to Jean how dependent we were on Archie Simms for just about everything - Mitch's good job. Our home – we paid very little rent in a house he owned. How he gave us free food from time to time, and of course our car was a company car. And I explained how my Mitch idolised Archie because of what he could do for him.

I told Jean how we struggled financially with two little ones and me a stay-at-home mother, and how we were so totally dependent on Mitch's job. "I was afraid that if I spoke up about Archie I could possibly cause us to lose it all. I literally quaked in my boots at the predicament I was in. It would never have crossed Mitch's mind that his boss was pursuing me behind his back." I explained how Mitch thought his boss was a god. How the wealthy Archie, and the job meant everything to him. Certainly more than I did! Or the family - his own children, for that matter. Mitch just lived for the job, the money, and the rewards. "His ego needed massive stroking, and he got it by being Archie's lackey."

I told Jean how I'd confessed my predicament to my psychologist, unaware that the psychologist was a close friend of Archie's family – and a deacon of their church. How he immediately contacted Archie to warn him that I'd spoken out about his behaviour.

"My goodness me! That was a terrible breach of confidence. Just terrible!"

"It gets uglier." I sighed.

# CHAPTER 49

The stirring up of these memories was painful, but I continued.

"Archie, being the smart business tycoon that he was, turned the tables on me!"

Jean's hat nearly fell off at the speed her head spun around. "No? What did he do?"

"Archie went into action very swiftly, knowing how much trouble he'd be in if this was all made public. He was a highly respected married man with a wife and five children. His family were staunch church-goers, and his reputation was that of a paragon of the community. His business was built on it. Certainly all the advertising and promotion was. 'Honest Archie Simms' was the keynote."

Jean was shaking her head, partly in disgust, partly in disbelief.

"His counter-punch changed my life irrevocably," I went on. "Cunningly, he took the naïve young Mitch aside, and told him that I had been pursuing him. And of course Mitch believed him!"

I explained how Mitch's mother had poisoned Mitch's mind, until he was ready to believe the very worst of me. Ruth Warner had explained the psychology of it to me, when my bewilderment raised its head at the prominent role his mother had played in our lives.

"Dr Warner suggested that Mitch had a 'mother fixation.' He'd not yet severed the cord from her. He was still 'in love' with his mother, like a child is, and not with me, his wife. He was truly afraid of her. She ruled him mentally, and emotionally."

"It sounds to me, Lilly dear, as if your marriage was like Princess Di's. There were three people in it, and you were the extra one!"

"How true."

I revealed, with some discomfort, the fact that every decision made in our marriage, was made by his mother. How she used her money to rule the roost, because we hadn't the funds to set up a home. "Mitch wanted nice things, and she wanted him to have them, but we couldn't afford to buy furniture, carpets or the like, so she bought them - for Mitch! This made her feel entitled to run our marriage, too! And I let it happen. I didn't stand up for my rights as a wife. As for clever old Archie, he'd never admit his harassment of me, and I had no proof of what he'd been up to."

"The weasel!" said Jean, slapping her hand on her thigh. "These types never lose. They have no conscience. My husband Richard told me about characters like these. He said they were psychopaths. Only concerned with their own power and pleasure."

I revealed how all of this, just happened to be at the time Archie's company was signing up for a take-over, by an American multinational. Shares were being dished out, and Archie suggested to Mitch, that if he dumped me, he would get a slice of the cake, instead of just being an employee. Archie's company was to be split into four shares. Archie would retain one. His son would get another. His long-time business partner would be given one, and that left one for Mitch - if he got rid of me! It would mean that as a result of the takeover, Mitch would receive a bunch of cash, and shares in the multinational. He went from poverty to riches overnight.

"Archie's price was divorce from me. And Mitch was prepared to pay it."

"Oh, Lilly. My dear girl, why would Simms do that?"

"To control Mitch! To make him his puppet."

I reminded Jean that Mitch would have done anything for Archie, and Archie used him. "Archie knew that money was Mitch's god, and Archie was the high priest of riches. But Archie couldn't possibly go forward into the real big-time, with me hanging around as a permanent reminder of what he'd been up to?"

Jean's look was one of horror.

"While I was on the scene, Archie was at risk of Mitch finding out the truth. When Archie made Mitch the proposition - of the money or me - Mitch chose the money! He's working in Hawaii now, at the corporation's head office." Tears began to well in my eyes as my mind flashed again to my children.

"My dear girl, you've been through so much. So much." Jean sighed, and handed me a tissue. "And then, I suppose, he could buy the best divorce lawyers?"

"He could, and he did! The result nearly killed me."

I took my time as the memories flooded back. The rage at the injustice had subsided, but the humiliation would never leave me. I'd held it under control. I'd simply 'managed' it. Making the story as concise as possible, I explained the elaborate double-cross that I hadn't expected. Telling, how my trusted psychologist had conspired with Mitch's lawyer, to ensure I was excluded completely from any monies that Mitch made from the business, despite the fact that I was Mitch's wife.

"As my divorce settlement, Archie Simms signed over our tired old house in Brisbane's West End to me, complete with mortgage. Archie was willing to give it away in order to keep Mitch as his slave and workhorse. Ironically I had to sell it within a year, because I couldn't pay that mortgage."

"And he walked away a wealthy man?"

"Yes. He did. And the children got not a penny from it."

It was not a good feeling explaining this deceit, but I went on to tell how both my psychologist and lawyer encouraged me to accept the settlement. The psychologist in particular had frightened me, saying that if I didn't accept the old house as a settlement, the case might drag through the court for years. Meanwhile Adam, Kate and I would be homeless.

"Of course, I knew nothing at the time about the secret deal that gave Mitch a quarter share of 'Gobble 'n Go.' I only learned about that later."

"But, didn't Mitch want to provide for the children?"

"That was his masterstroke! He and his lawyers obviously had that all worked out in advance! Mitch came to the house one day with two of his lawyers and a policewoman, and... and... he physically, just took my children away from me." A tear dripped down to my breast as I remembered that tortuous day.

"You mean, Mitch obtained custody of Adam and Kate? Oh, my dear! There are no words of comfort I can give you, that would ever make up for the pain of losing your little ones. Except to say how sorry I am. You had such an army against you."

"Yes. I did!" I said, in tears now. "My free 'legal aid' was no match for Mitch's expensive lawyers. My over-worked sixty-seven-year-old legal-aid lawyer, arrived at the court and admitted to me that he hadn't even read my file!" I explained how Mitch's team was able to prove in court that Mitch would be a much more capable parent than me – mainly because my psychologist testified that I was clinically depressed, had no job, and would be a drain on the mental health-care, and financial system. Meanwhile, Mitch's prospects were about to go through the roof! "The court of course had no idea of the self-indulgent, fast and furious life Mitch lived, or the fact he rarely ever saw his children!"

Jean looked over at me tenderly now, her own eyes filled with tears. "I'm speechless, Lilly," she said, clearing her throat and reaching for a tissue. She wiped her eyes.

"I did try to make contact with my children, but Mitch wouldn't take my calls, and he wouldn't let me see them."

I told Jean how I'd sunk into a deep, suicidal depression, and how it took more than a year to feel well and emotionally strong again. But by that time, Archie had cleverly sent Mitch off to Hawaii to work in head office, taking the children with him.

"But once the house was sold, and I had money in my pocket, I used some of it to go to Hawaii, to seek him out, and find my children."

Jean looked over at me with surprise. "You went after them?"

# CHAPTER 50

A 28 degree day and a whisper of the approaching afternoon Trade Wind met me at Honolulu airport when I walked the tarmac. I'd taken very little luggage, mostly jeans and T-shirts, but I'd bought a white sun hat at Sydney airport to save time on arrival. I went straight to the Avis desk to arrange a rental car, and reminded myself that I must drive on the right-hand-side to get to my destination, the Royal Hawaiian on Kalakaua Avenue at Waikiki.

The friendly hotel receptionist supplied me with a local map, and I went straight to my room to study it after having a quick bite to eat at the Sunworshippers Restaurant off the main lobby. Having a good memory, I memorised the names of the main thoroughfares, and counted the traffic lights, and the seventeen blocks from the hotel to Kamehameha Highway, past the Honolulu Zoo and on to 6th Avenue.

Bold and determined, yet dressed demurely, in a neat and pretty, pink dress, I approached a modern, glass-faced building with its own car park, and the company sign 'Dole Foods International' above the front entrance. The 'Meet and Greet,' grand old American citizen, who earned the extra dollar or two in his dotage, as is the way in the States, pointed to the elevators when I asked where I would find Mr Mitch Lightwood. He said to go to the 8th floor reception area. My heart started to pound the minute I stepped into the elevator, because all the things I'd practised saying to Mitch when I came face to face with him, had vanished from my mind.

When I reached my destination, I faced a chronically obese native

Hawaiian man sitting waiting at the 8<sup>th</sup> floor reception desk. The enormous cheeks of his buttocks flowed over his chair half way to the floor. His direct stare was far from convivial, and I imagined, that just one of his huge hands could have pinned me high against the wall until all the life was squeezed out of me. The mere thought of it took my breath away.

"I've come to see Mr Mitch Lightwood." I said naively, sounding very childlike.

"You have, have you?" His voice was as deep as the Grand Canyon. And here was I, afraid of men of any size!

"Yes. Please."

"Appointment?"

"Er, no, but..,"

"No buts, ma'am. No appointment. No see!"

"But I've come all the way from Australia!" I felt the tears well up in my eyes immediately, because he just stared back at me as if no-one was home. Unmoving. Not a flinch. Just a huge dollop of fat on a chair with a dome-shaped head. A man with no neck. Just roll after roll of blubber. Huge, ugly and cumbersome. At the time I thought even a Walrus at 3,000 pounds more attractive.

I swivelled around to see office after office, all around me, all glass, with people working behind desks. I heard telephones ringing insistently through open doors. Workers laughing silently down the phone line behind closed doors. People talking animatedly to one another without a word reaching my ears, like a silent movie. An empty conference room with a grand round table.

Then I noticed a sign on the wall with the names of staffers on it, and a slide they used to reveal the words 'in' or 'out' to let people know if the workers were in the building, or out. I could read it from afar. I was on the correct floor! The sign showed that Mr Lightwood was definitely in the building. I turned to look again at the Hawaiian man who was keeping me at bay, and I boldly stated, "He's in the building. He's here, the sign says so!" I pointed to the sign. "Which way do I go...?"

"Ma'am. I told you. No appointment. No access!" He spoke gruffly now, and looked daggers at me.

Emitting an involuntary screech that rose from the pit of my stomach, I stood in the centre of the 8th floor reception area with strangers all around me, and let it rip. "MITCH... it's me... LILLY. I want to talk to you! I want to talk to you about the children!" The staff in their glass partitioned offices were obviously startled. Some sat gaping at me. Some got to their feet, long before the Hawaiian could prize himself out of his chair.

"Mitch. I know you're here!" I yelled as loudly as I could, giving no thought to protocol or disruption of the peace. My passion had overwhelmed me. I thought only of my own desperation, my motherly, but now neurotic need to see my children. I'd become obsessed with seeing them again. Nothing else mattered, so I yelled and yelled. "Will you at least come and TALK to me about the children? PLEASE MITCH...!" I screamed again and again, bent double from the velocity of my voice.

Then suddenly the monumental frame of the Hawaiian was obliterating everything from my eye-line. I could see nothing but him. His look was intimidating to say the least, as if he were ready to scoop me up and throw me through a window to the street below. But before he could reach out to me, Mitch appeared from behind him, and stood staring at me from only a foot away. He spat his response at me, with the fearsome Hawaiian towering alongside him as back-up.

"What the HELL are you doing here?" Only he could yell at me in that tone of voice. I could tell he wanted to kill me on the spot he was so angry.

"I... want to talk to you... about seeing the children," I half spoke, half cried, pleading with his piercing blue eyes as I quivered inside.

"Call security," he yelled at the Hawaiian, mad as hell, then, turning back to me wearing a mask of pure hate, furious at my audacity, he hissed at me in a slow and menacing manner, "You... will... NOT... see the children! You're wasting your time, do you HEAR me? You can get the hell out of here, and don't come back!" He turned on his heel and left me standing like a mad fool.

I spotted the ugly Hawaiian put his phone back on the receiver - he'd called security, and I realised that he'd give them a description of me. What to do? Where to run? I headed for the elevator, and thumped the button frantically. As I waited, I heard myself urging it to hurry... hurry... hurry!

The giant Hawaiian had loped over to me in a waddling motion, and placed himself between me and my escape route, 'Michelin' arms outstretched across the lift door-way. Stairs! Where are the stairs? The stairs… "There!" I heard myself say when I spotted the sign down at the end of the hall. But just as I was about to make a dash for it, there was a 'ping' from the elevator.

The obese Hawaiian side-stepped with astonishing agility, the lift opened, and I came face to face with two burly, heavily-armed security men who pounced on me before I could as much as take a step. They swooped out at me, guns on hips, and were on top of me before I could blink. And one either side, each grabbed an elbow, and scooped me back inside the lift without a word, while the Hawaiian controlled the button.

Protesting loudly, tears flowing, legs dangling, I was swallowed up and disappeared from the scene. In a flash, I was on the ground floor, then literally carried out of the building by my arms, and thrust bodily out into the street.

#

Undeterred, I bought two baseball caps and two more sun hats, in my effort to disguise myself, and I requested a different hire-car each day from Avis. I was prepared to wait, and wait, day after day, to watch Mitch leave his work premises to find out where he lived. So I parked across from the exit of the underground car park used by the staff. It was not until day five that he deemed it safe to use his own car to travel home; and with both the setting sun and my hire-car in exactly the right spot, I recognised him driving himself out in a flashy American Mustang convertible.

I followed him all the way to his home on Diamond Head Road at Diamond Head. The rocky volcanic outcrop known as the Headland, where, in 1895 there had been a battle to restore the Queen of Hawaii after being deposed in a military coup. In a superlative area overlooking the water's edge, he stopped outside a set of mighty, ornate iron gates and fed in a security pass, then drove on through to where I presumed his salubrious home must be.

The operating gates were way too slick for me to follow on. It appeared that Mitch lived in a high-security gated community, a fortress called the Citadel, and I was left outside those fancy gates in my tiny hire-car, feeling gutted. I realised that I'd get nowhere near my children. I was stymied.

#

"What did you do next?" Jean urged, as I breathed in deeply to calm myself. Letting out a huge sigh, I continued on.

"Well, now I knew where he lived! So, using dark glasses, my disguising baseball caps, and a variety of rental cars, I waited daily to see him perhaps take the children to prep school."

Jean's mouth hung open.

"Each and every day I sat waiting close to the entrance of the Citadel in the hope that I would catch a glimpse of my children. I'd seen many glamorous women driving big cars with children in them coming out through the electric gates, most probably on their way to school. But I couldn't be sure if MY children were among them, despite knowing that my babies wouldn't have changed too much in a year or so. But I knew I'd recognise them if they were with Mitch."

Again, Jean's eyes flashed to mine. At this point, I didn't know if she thought I was brave, or stupid. In retrospect, I knew I'd been both, but at the time I was absolutely desperate, and would go to any length to talk to them and hold them.

"One morning as I watched, I recognised Mitch's car coming out through the gates, and found that sure enough, my children were with him. I'd been right, they hadn't changed at all, so I followed his car, my heart pounding, and with tears streaming down my cheeks."

I told Jean that we hadn't travelled far along Diamond Head Road, when he entered the grounds of the elite Headland Montessori School for 0-6year-olds. I sat and waited until his car exited the grounds without the children inside, then I headed straight for the principal's office, thinking I'd found the solution. At least I could see them, touch them, talk to them. But Mitch had already warned the school to be on the look-out for me, and I was quickly escorted from these premises, too!

"Oh, my. What a drama!"

"Despite all my pleading, I couldn't even get close to them. No explanation would satisfy the principal. He said a visit from me would 'upset' the children. Mitch had beaten me again, Jean! What I didn't know, was, all the time I'd been watching Mitch, he'd had a private detective watching me! And he was so much better at it than I was!"

# CHAPTER 51

Dispirited, I returned to my Honolulu hotel suite at the 'Pink Palace,' my mind clouded by emptiness. The only picture I could see in my head was that brief glimpse of my children's faces as they were driven to school. Kate in the front with Mitch, and Adam in a carriage seat in the back. I was completely unable to conjure a clear future in my head. I'd blanked out on enterprise. Where would I go from here? My prize was out of reach. I wasn't going to get anywhere near my children, and certainly couldn't live in this expensive manner indefinitely, especially when it was going nowhere.

I lay on the bed in the hotel room alone and sobbing, thinking that my world had come to an end. But it was far from the end. Fate had more trouble waiting for me!

A loud rap on the door startled me. I sat up from my prone position, looked at the door and shouted at it. "Yes. Who is it?"

"H.P.D," bellowed back a gruff, deep voice.

"WHO?"

"The Honolulu Police Department. Open the door, Ma'am!"

I flushed with fear and dashed to the door, not giving a thought to it perhaps being a false claim. I could've been gang-raped or murdered, because I didn't have the sense to ask the voice to verify, by asking to show me a badge.

I unlocked the bedroom door, and before I could take a breath, four uniformed, heavily armed policemen pushed me back inside, threw me on the bed face down, pulled my hands behind my back and handcuffed me. I couldn't even scream I was so terrified. They don't do anything by halves in America!

"Is your name Lillian Lightwood?" A matter of hand-cuffs first - questions later!

"Yes," I squeaked, as a burly cop jerked me back up off the bed to stand upright, while the three other cops checked out the bathroom and the wardrobes.

"Sorry Ma'am. But you have to come down to the station."

"But... why? What have I done?"

"Looks like you've been behaving badly, Ma'am." He grinned. Then he tugged at me with his strong hand on my slim arm, and pulled me out through the open bedroom door, and into full view of every passer-by in the corridor, the lobby, and out through the hotel's main entrance, where a wedding party had gathered to take photographs, and a camera flashed my way. He led me forcefully all the way to the footpath, where two police cars sat parked awaiting my arrival.

I felt a hand on my hair as the policeman opened a police vehicle's back-seat door, and he pushed down forcefully on the crown of my head to make me bend, and I was thrust inside, still handcuffed, and fell clumsily onto the seat. Another policeman entered the car from the other side, and sat in the back seat next to me. To ensure I wouldn't make a run for it, I supposed.

We arrived at the Honolulu Police Station at 801 South Beretania Street, after a journey of twenty minutes in traffic. A busy place, filled with all types of people. Some obviously drug-takers, talking to themselves, or yelling incoherently. I seemed to do a lot of waiting amongst the ugly throng - in handcuffs. I waited, while a disengaged policewoman filled in a form, as I dictated my answers to her questions. I waited to be interrogated. I waited at the mercy of a foreign country's law officers. And after having my fingerprints taken, and enduring a 'mug-shot,' I spent a frightful night in the Honolulu City Jail with drunks and prostitutes.

I was terrified, and almost hysterical with anger. At the time, I couldn't understand what crime I'd committed. The children were my own flesh and blood. I'd created them. I felt entitled to see them again. But that neurotic need had become something of an obsession. And it had got me into deep, deep trouble. I joined in with the crying, and the moaning, and the screaming that went on, all through the night.

Next morning, after a sleepless night and many tears, and without as much as a shower, I was taken to a small court-house. Armed guards were everywhere. There was a frightening feeling of helplessness. Row after row of chairs were filled with people who had, like me, broken some law or other. This was a criminal court. Mitch had filed a complaint with the local police, and it was now a police matter. I saw him at the back of the court with two smart-looking 'suits.' Obviously his lawyers.

Again, I waited. And waited. Till suddenly from afar, a distant place, I recognised my name. A clerk of the court had called out a number. "Docket number 337-4425 Lightwood, Lillian. Harassment, Trespass, and Causing a public nuisance."

I stood in shame, my heart racing as I faced the judge. Judge K.W. Ching. An elderly, white-haired man with obvious Japanese blood, and a very droopy, sad face.

The Assistant City Attorney, Everett Bradley, a forty something, athletic-looking man I'd describe as a surfy type, read out an order from the Family Court of Australia, declaring, "Mitchell James Lightwood is hereby granted sole custody of his two children, Adam James Lightwood, two years of age, and Katherine Elizabeth Lightwood, four years of age." He gave me a quick glance as if to say, 'You got no hope, baby!' Then added a smirk to twist the knife.

Judge Ching spoke out. "Ms Lightwood. You have heard the charges. What say you?"

It was obvious who he was talking to, because he was looking right at me over the top of his half-rimmed spectacles, so I spoke out. "I beg your pardon, Your Honour. I only came here to see my children. I have no wish to cause trouble, but my ex-husband won't let me see them…"

"It seems to me, Ms Lightwood, that this case is not about MISTER Lightwood! It's about your behaviour. You may resume your seat." He looked to, and spoke to, the Assistant City Attorney as I sat. "I believe you have a witness to bring forward who will attest to these charges, Mr Bradley?"

"Yes, Your Honour. Call Mr Frank Sly." He swivelled around to look in Mitch's direction.

Glued to my seat, too scared to look around, I listened to footsteps approaching the front of the courtroom, and as they came alongside I was surprised by a face I recognised. I'd seen this man walk to, and enter his car at the Montessori School. A bald man in his late fifties. Suntanned and weathered-looking. He strode confidently to an elevated box alongside the judge, carrying a small briefcase, as if he'd done so many times before.

"Will you state your name, and your occupation?" said the ACA.

"Yes, sir. My name is Francis V. for Vivien, Sly, and I am, and have been, a private investigator licensed by the State of Hawaii for the past thirty years. I have photographs of the accused stalking my client, Mr Mitchell Lightwood."

I heard myself let out an involuntary yelp and received a cautionary look from the judge for my outburst.

Sly unzipped his leather satchel, and handed photographs to the ACA who presented them, one at a time to the judge. "I photographed my client's ex-wife over a period of eight days," said Sly.

"Is the subject of the photographs in this court?" asked the ACA.

"Yes, sir." He pointed at me. "That's her!"

I jumped to my feet. "But I was only trying to see my children."

"Ms Lightwood, will you kindly resume your seat and refrain from making outbursts in my court," bellowed Judge Ching.

"Yes, Your Honour" I whimpered guiltily, sinking back onto my chair.

The ACA asked Sly, "You were aware that Ms Lightwood had been denied access to her children by the Australian authorities, yet still pursued them to this country?"

"I was. My client was fearful for his children and himself."

"For what reason?"

"What I saw, was a vengeful ex-wife."

"But…!" I exclaimed

"There can be no interruption, Ms Lightwood," said the judge with over-ruling authority. "These photographs are proof enough for me that you've been making a nuisance of yourself here in Hawaii, and I must warn you that this behaviour will not be tolerated. You must respect the law, Ms Lightwood. We must ALL respect the law!"

He could see that I was already in tears, and it discomforted him. "However," he said, clearing his throat, "Ahem, owing to your… em… youth, and my respect for motherhood, I will grant leniency at this time. There will be no conviction recorded. But I must warn you, Ms Lightwood, that if you were to come before me again, you are likely to be convicted, incarcerated, and then deported. In which case, you would not be permitted to re-enter the United States at any future time. Do you understand?"

"Yes, sir," I wept.

My case was the perfect David and Goliath tale. Mitch's money had bought not only expensive lawyers, but incriminating evidence from Sly. He had photographs of me outside Mitch's office, outside his home, and at the children's school in all my various poor disguises. So Mitch's lawyer was able to claim that I'd been making unwarranted, unwanted, repeat visits, after following Mitch to his own country. He painted me as the villain, as a mad woman. And as a criminal, saying Mitch was in fear of bodily harm. He claimed I might be seeking vengeance, either against him, or the children, or both. His new life could not be free from fear while I was around! The judge decreed I was a stalker.

#

Jean was horrified when I explained everything. "You? A stalker?"

"That's exactly what I was, Jean! It took the Honolulu judge to bring me to my senses."

I told her how I'd been ordered to get on the next flight out of the country, or I'd never be able to enter the United States again! I was on foreign soil, and America looks after its own. I felt dirty, cheap, and guilty, and all because I wanted to see my beloved children again, to tell them I loved them. They'd been torn away from me before I could even explain. I left Hawaii in shame, beaten, and broken-hearted, but determined to fight on, to win joint custody, somehow, someway, someday.

"Oh, Lilly, dear, it seems that you were born to be deceived. You've been deceived all throughout your life!" She coughed a tiny cough to clear her throat, and paused to collect herself. "But believe me my dear, *I* would never hurt you, in any way. Please, please, believe that." Rising from her comfortable chair, she kissed me tenderly on the forehead as she passed and went back into the apartment.

Left alone for a little while, I just sat looking out at beautiful Sydney Harbour and thanked my lucky stars I'd survived my past. And, come what may, I determined, I would always be a survivor. I wiped away my tears.

Jean returned with a small bottle of champagne and two glasses on a tray to cheer us up. She sat back down, made herself comfortable, and put her hat back on. With her voice sounding cheery again, my friend raised her glass. "To better times."

"To better times," I echoed.

"You know, Lilly, I really do wish I'd known you then. I might have been able to help. I have the very best lawyers in New York. The head of the law firm was a great friend of my husband, and I just happen to have a rather luxurious home on the waterfront at Diamond Head in Hawaii. It was Richard's favourite residence. You could have lived there to fight for the children!"

"That would have been superb, Jean."

After a little while she suggested something most unexpected. "Have you given any thought to what you might do when you're well again? I mean, after the operations, because I have a proposition for you. I was thinking that you could sell your terrace, and move in here."

My mouth dropped open.

"I have these three spare suites here, with no-one using them. You could take your pick." Now she glanced over at me invitingly. "As you already know, my dear, I spend my time between New York and London with my business interests, and there's the odd cruise or two. I'm away for more than half the year, and it seems such a waste, the apartments sitting here unused. Besides, sometimes I worry about my precious art left here, all alone. What do you say, Lilly?"

"Jean….!"

Like a bulldozer she barged on, determined to help me create a new, brighter future.

"It could be a business partnership, if you like. I'll draw up a legal agreement, whereby you will be my 'caretaker/house-sitter' when I'm not here, keeping check on the cleaners, that sort of thing, and be my 'companion and friend,' when I am!"

All I could do was repeat, "Jean!" She'd taken my breath away. She'd obviously given this some serious thought.

"Promise me you'll think about it, Lilly?"

"Jean, to be fair to you, it's way too early for me to be thinking about anything in the future. I'm still digging into the past to find out who I am!"

She wouldn't give up the fight. "Well the time will come you know, when you'll have to leave the past behind and move on, and I imagine, you've given it little or no thought. Have you?" Again, she gave me a quizzical look.

"Er, no, not really, except that I won't be going back into television looking like a monster!"

"Ahah! But you won't always look like a 'monster,' as you put it." Taking a sip of champagne, she continued. "If all I do today is cheer you up over lunch, and sneak in a tiny seed of hope for the future, then I'll feel that I've accomplished quite a lot." Down went the flute on the table, and a satisfied look swept over her cheeky face.

"A seed?"

"Well, you obviously love art! What about your own gallery?"

"My own gallery? Could that be possible?"

"Well now, if you were to sell your terrace it would be your start-up money. You told me you'd receive half the funds if it were sold. And, if you were to take up my offer of free accommodation – well, you could start buying art."

"My head is spinning, Jean. Absolutely spinning." It was an incredible idea.

"Good. I'm glad you're spinning. Anything is better than being alone and crying!"

"I still have work to do on myself, Jean. I'm still having nightmares. I'm still fighting demons. I don't want to burden you with any of my torments."

"But you will consider it?" She took up her champagne flute and emptied it. "Promise me that! It would be a new beginning, a great chance to get back on your feet and make up for all the losses."

"You'll make me cry again with your generosity." I reached out to touch her arm.

"Ahah! There are no tears in this house, either!" She lay her hand on mine.

# CHAPTER 52

That night as I fell asleep I thought I would sleep the 'sleep of the saved,' as Churchill once said. But no. My sleep was filled with terrifying dreams. I couldn't wait to tell Ruth Warner about them.

"I saw eyes coming at me. Huge, menacing eyes. And teeth. Snarling teeth. He was attacking me, and all I could see were snarling teeth, and mad, crazed eyes. I was petrified."

Warner sat back in her chair, watching me as she listened, reading my expression as much as listening to my words. "You said, 'he.' Does the face remind you of anyone?"

I shook my head.

Warner knew I was hedging. If my answer was not forthcoming immediately, she knew I was holding something back. She sensed that I didn't want to betray whoever it was I recognised. "Well, let's take it slowly. Who was it that played an important role in your childhood that scared you? Who was it that had big eyes, and scary teeth?" Her tone was gentle and calm. "Who used to frighten you?"

My guilt melted a little. "Ian." I hung my head.

"How did he frighten you? Was he much bigger than you?"

"Yes, and strong. Very strong! And rough. And loud, and frightening. He would run at me. Pounce on me. Attack me. Sometimes with weapons. He had a sharp knife. He would grab me and hold me around the head and pretend to cut my throat. He would snarl and shout. And make... killing

264

noises. He'd thump me, and throw me. Jump on me." I glanced up at Warner quickly, then my head bent low to recall the pictures in my head.

"Did you fight back?"

"If I could escape, I would run to the bed behind the screen, lean back on it and use my legs and feet to keep him at bay, kicking at him."

"And Mary Campbell always took Ian's side?"

"Yes! She'd scream, 'You'll hurt 'im. Ye' should'na kick fellas. Stop it afore y' injure 'im.'" She was judge and jury. Her boys could do no wrong."

"You told me that Mary Campbell had been raised in a male dominated world."

"Yes."

"And she too had been made to feel inferior."

I nodded.

"Let me clarify one or two things," Warner said. Her carefully controlled, professional demeanor had eased to a comfortable stage in recent weeks, and my response was reciprocal. She proceeded slowly down the path of explanation. "Your grandmother sees a penis as a symbol of power. She perceives it to have both gender, and anatomical power. She passed this twisted bias on to Betty. And then, on to you. She let you grow with the conviction that you were ugly. Inferior. And she wanted to keep it that way. Feeding you those negative thoughts so that she could continue to control and dominate you, and in that way, maintain her power over you."

I sat calmly taking it all in.

"You were blind to Mary's imperfections, because of your total dependence on her. You couldn't afford to hate her, so you began to turn your anger against yourself. You came to believe that whatever happened, be it Mary's anger, or your own unhappiness, it was all YOUR fault! You grew with an unrealistic guilt, blaming yourself for everything that went wrong - whatever it was!"

"I did!" Suddenly I felt as if a great load had been lifted from my shoulders.

"Mary was very much aware that you were growing into a beautiful woman, with an alluring body which was a threat to her. A reminder that she was getting older, as you were beginning to blossom."

"That sounds right. She would mock and humiliate me at every opportunity."

"If you hadn't known the love of your Daddy Bob and Mina, you wouldn't have been able to show pure, unconditional love to your children! You would have thought the treatment from your grandmother was normal behaviour. It wouldn't have seemed so unjust, had you known nothing else." Warner gave me time to absorb this.

These revelations were sweet nourishment for my troubled soul. These were the truths I'd been seeking all my life.

"You had something precious with Daddy Bob and Mina and you lost it. You've been wracked by inner conflict ever since."

Warner's words received a silent nod in agreement, for it was all now very plain for me to see.

"Tell me, why didn't you make friends with Bob and Mina again after you married?"

"I did go to see them, but they had a replacement."

"A replacement?"

"A girl from England was living there. They didn't need me."

"I see. Again you told yourself you were unwanted."

I looked away.

"Now you tell me the horrible things Mary Campbell did to you, but I see no anger? Your loyalty to her is extraordinary! You've been protecting her all your life. Don't you think it's bizarre that you sacrificed your life for hers? You realise that she treated Betty the same way?"

"Yes."

"You've been lucky. You may not see that now, but Betty lost her life. Mary Campbell destroyed it! You realise Mary Campbell doesn't like girls? She thinks they're 'dirty.' She would have been far more accepting of you if you'd had a penis. That's why you've had a conflict with your sexuality. She's made you feel that being a girl was inferior, that sexually and otherwise, boys had all the fun." Even while I was absorbing this, she threw a question at me. "Tell me, how did Mary get on with her great-grandchildren?"

"Well, she loved Adam! But, she was always critical of Kate. I found myself having to protect Kate from her constant criticism."

"So, she favoured the boy?"

"Oh, my God! She did! She was only interested in Adam. Yet Kate is the most beautiful of children. I could never understand Mary's indifference to her... her lack of feeling for her." This was another light bulb moment.

Warner moved on to open yet another door for me. "Mary's also been jealous of you all through the years."

My head was spinning. "Jealous? Of me?"

"Yes. Jealous."

"But, jealous of what?"

"Think about it."

"The only thing I had all those years, that she didn't – was my youth!"

The doctor gave me a knowing look, as if I'd hit upon a secret. "You realise that you were also on your way to becoming an alcoholic? Just like Betty. You know the car accident was no accident? You were drunk. And yet I see no anger."

"You mean... she did that, too?"

The doctor nodded. She had picked the exact 'psychologically right' moment for this.

"Damn her!" I cursed. "Damn her! How could she try to destroy me like that?" I began to cry as anger overwhelmed me, and I kicked the chair beside me like a child in a temper tantrum. Then, embarrassed, I looked away and cried quiet tears. Mary Campbell's power over me was exorcised at that moment. I rejected her power with an explosion of hatred. "How am I going to get all the anger out?"

"You are already, aren't you? And you will continue to, over time," said Warner reassuringly. "Why don't you write to Mina and thank her," she suggested.

"Write to her?" The tears had subsided, and I had composed myself. An air of calm had descended.

"Yes, drop her a line, re-establish contact," she prompted.

I stood and walked across the room to the window, there to reflect, to catch my breath before heading home. An unaccustomed feeling of relief had flooded over me. Looking out the window over the hospital grounds, I could see before me, in the sunshine, bent and beaten, shuffling mental patients, dazedly traversing a broad expanse of well-tended lawn. Others sat under the trees, some hunched in clusters, some alone. As I watched them, my heart went out to these sad, half-dead creatures, who'd been scarred by fate, or demented by life's stresses.

Dr Warner's voice broke through my thoughts, offering me an apology. "I'm sorry you have to come here to the hospital for your appointments, but it really suits my schedule." She had crossed the floor to join me at the window bay, where, together, we stood in silence for another moment, looking out at the tragic figures.

"They're probably more at peace than I am!" I said with a sigh.

# CHAPTER 53

My week was spent in sleepless torment following my latest consultation, and then one morning I woke after an untroubled, unbroken night's sleep. It was as if the storm had passed. In retrospect, I would wish there had been an easier way. I likened it to recovering from a bout of malaria. I survived, but was weakened, completely drained of energy. But with that frailty, came a calm. Soon, I would find a new, serene place within myself.

On the next visit, I sat in Dr Warner's office in quiet control. There were no tears. No shredding of paper handkerchiefs. There were no scribbled notes for reference. No anxiety. No trembling nerves. I, Lillian Lightwood remained very calm, and very much in control of my emotions and my words, with singular clarity of thought. "Those words I used last week as I was leaving," I began.

"Remind me."

"When I looked out of the window, and I saw all those poor wretches in the hospital grounds. I said then, that I thought they were probably less troubled than I was." My eyes were locked on those of Dr Warner. "Well, I've been thinking. THAT'S what's been wrong with me all these years! When I woke up this morning, it was with the realisation that my grandmother made me believe there was a really bad person inside me!"

She let me talk.

"By bad," I continued assertively, "I mean wicked. EVIL! And I've believed her. All this time!" I continued looking directly into Warner's eyes as I spoke. "But I'm good! I'm loving! And I care about people. I AM NOT EVIL!"

"Well now," she said, a smile stretching across her sublime face, showing how absolutely delighted she was with my revelation. "You have been doing some homework, haven't you?"

"I've been searching for answers all my life. I've been angry, puzzled, and sick!"

THERE – IT WAS OUT!

I finally saw Mary Campbell as the enemy – at last. I'd crossed to the other side.

Ruth Warner thought it time to comment. "You've been in conflict all these years, because Bob and Mina allowed you to escape Mary Campbell for a while, during the critical formative years of your childhood."

I listened with a mature acceptance of Warner's words. These facts would help me break with the past and remodel my future. Because of this new insight, and recognition of the truth, my attitudes would change to help transform my life.

"You know, Lilly, the pre-school years are so important to the emotional stability of a child. The years between one and five have a great significance on one's future well-being. You escaped Mary Campbell during that time. The Bairds introduced you to love and kindness. Then you lost it again when you returned to her. Had you stayed there with Mary all the time - like Andy had to - you would have thought Mary's depraved behaviour normal, and would not have been in conflict. But you would have been a totally repressed personality. As you can now see, a lot of damage was done to you, and you've had a tremendous fight on your hands to kill this dragon that tried to destroy you."

I nodded.

"So," Warner went on, "that's what you've been fighting – you've been fighting for your own freedom of identity – fighting not to be a slave to someone else's personality. It took the car accident for you to face Mary Campbell head on. Only by ridding yourself of her, could you become well, and strong."

"Yes, I see all that now."

"Are you aware of the thread that's been running through your life?"

"You mean the thread of loss?"

"Yes. All throughout your life it's been one loss after another. And the greatest loss, was the loss of your beautiful children. The one thread you thought was guaranteed for life. The thread you thought was truly yours. That precious, golden thread was lost to you."

"Yes. I'm fully aware of the loss that's run throughout my life. I want to put a stop to it. I'm READY to put a stop to it! I'm strong enough to fight back now. And I'm not afraid!"

Doctor Warner knew she was about to lose a patient. I could now go forward with confidence, and the capacity to negotiate life with a new maturity. The metaphorical yoke around my neck was dislodged. I was free. Free to be myself, at last. Unlike poor Betty my mother, I had a second chance. I had cashed in my 'victim card.'

# CHAPTER 54

A small flat package bearing a Queensland postmark arrived in my mailbox. The sender's name and address were inscribed in a small, neat female hand: 'Mina and Bob Baird.' Only a week earlier I'd had the courage to write to them. Now here was their reply. I hurried inside.

Moving quickly through the terrace to the dining room, I drew out a straight-backed chair and took a seat at the table. In the sunlight streaming in through a tiny French window, I tore the envelope open. I removed a six-page letter written in Mina's compact handwriting, along with four black and white photographs which made me gasp.

Tenderly, I held the photographs, the way one would handle an heirloom. A four-year-old beamed out at me. The little girl I used to be. A happy little girl. A beautiful little girl, dressed in four different dancing outfits which I now remembered, posing impishly, and looking for all the world, a sweet, innocent, and well-adjusted, uninhibited child.

Laying the pictures out on the table in front of me, I reached for the letter. I could hardly read the words for the tears in my eyes. Now, I felt Mina beside me, could hear her voice as she wrote of the 'wee Ponkie' that she and Bob had loved, and lost. Her love shone from every page. It was like finding buried treasure. My initial excitement was replaced by a warm, spiritual glow, a joyously rewarding feeling of love.

'Dear Lilly,

What a strange feeling to read your words after all this time, but you are no stranger to us. You think you owe us thanks. Well, we owe you the same, as Bob and I had an awful lot of fun and happiness with you, and for that we are grateful we had you, even for those few short years. So thank you!

'We were very sorry to hear you had that accident and I am positive that after you have had the necessary operation you will, as they say, be as good as new. I have seen this sort of operation performed on a girl who used to work with me, and it was wonderful.

'Now, as for when we left Dundee to come to Australia, we very much wanted to bring you with us, and we begged your grandmother to let you come but she said no. She said your mother was coming to Dundee in a fortnight's time, but it seems this did not happen. But she did come later and took you to England, and you were with her and her husband at the time. You were with them for a month, then shunted back to the Campbell woman as it didn't work out for you in England. I wrote to Betty when I got to know this and asked her to send you out to us, but it wasn't to be.

'You won't remember how you came to us. Well, just after the war, everyone had to register for employment, and, as I was in The Land Army - the Forestry side, this included me, so when my interview came, I told them I wanted an outside job. Well, the woman behind the desk asked me if I would like to look after children a few hours a day, so that was the start. I went to see 'Campbell'- that's the only name she deserves from me, anyway, I agreed to take it on. It seemed easy just to take two babies out for a walk a few hours a day. That's you, and Andy. So that is what I did for about two weeks. Then Campbell asked if I would like to keep you at my house overnight as well, so I took you home, and Bob was delighted with you.

'So, now you were with us for what was supposed to be three months, until Betty's band contract ran out. Well, Betty's contract must have been renewed because you were with us for nearly five years. I was glad when the three months were up and no Betty came to take you away.

'If Betty had had any other job than the band, then things may have been different for you, but there again it comes back to Campbell. She liked the glamour she got through her kids and pushed them into it at too early an age. Betty told me she slept in an air-raid shelter in London at fourteen years of age, while she was in the band touring. Campbell had told everyone Betty was seventeen. It was too young for a girl to be away from home, especially with a war on. Betty liked to show you off to the girls in the band whenever they came to Dundee. I took you to see the band perform when they came to the Palace Theatre. Betty was doing her big solo act on stage, and what did little Lilly do? Call out 'Betty', with a big 'B-E-T-T-Y!' not once, but three times, until I stuck a sweety in your mouth and nearly choked you. Bob, he just laughed and laughed.

'I'm sending you some photos which I always intended you to have. I wouldn't trust Campbell with them as I'm sure you would not have got them.

'Do let me know when you expect to have the operation as I am anxious to hear how it all goes for you. Not much longer and it shall be all over, and you will look back and wonder why you worried so.

'Thank you again for your letter, it was lovely. All happiness to you. Bob sends his love also.

Love Mina.

#

Next day I took my treasure to Ruth Warner. Just the way a five year old would take a prized new possession to show a teacher. This written testimony was the confirmation I'd needed to complete the puzzle. It proved to me that my past was not a figment of my imagination, for there had been days when I doubted my memories. But not anymore. There had been days when I'd wondered if I was crazy. But not anymore. Mina had provided the proof. I wasn't crazy, and I wasn't evil.

Warner took up her spectacles from the desk in front of her, then held out her hand to take my little package. Removing the letter from the envelope, she checked the postmark and the date, as if suspecting its authenticity.

A sudden fear swept over me. Did she find this swift and loving response from Mina too good to be true? "Isn't it marvellous that she wrote back so quickly?" I said with delight. Sitting on the edge of my chair, I watched the doctor's face for reactions. Her silence worried me. For a moment, I saw her as yet another of the powerful parental figures who had manipulated my life and my emotions. Her hesitation said a lot. After all, she was losing a customer.

Warner lay the letter aside after reading it. Briefly she gazed sightlessly out the window as if giving the matter some consideration. As if making a decision. Then she turned to me and broke into a smile. "Lilly, this is wonderful. This really is a breakthrough. I'm so happy for you."

#

I took my treasured bounty of childhood photographs home to put them proudly on display. And I looked at them time and again over the ensuing days, as if I'd just discovered myself. As if by looking at them, I could absorb them, take them into myself, make them part of me. Reclaim my childhood. Reclaim my identity.

"I WAS lovely," I told myself, "I was – I really was." It was as if the declaration made it so. And I was right. An angelic, innocent child smiled lovingly back at me from the photographs, provoking forgotten memories of laughter and happiness.

What a fulfilling, heart-warming feeling this rediscovery was. I felt alive, at peace, and spiritually happy for the very first time in my life. I could see for myself the innocent child I'd been, devoid of any evil, dressed in a Spanish costume with a tamborine, as a little Dutch girl, a ballerina, and in a red satin Christmas outfit with white trim, and a matching beret with a pom-pom – looking for all the world like sweet little Shirley Temple.

# CHAPTER 55

"You heal very quickly." Surgeon John Davenport said, perched close on a mobile stool, one leg either side of me, as he scrutinised my face in his consulting room. "This is fantastic progress for just six months."

"I've been rubbing in Vitamin 'E' oil, and having regular acupuncture, from Dr Wong, in Parramatta," I proudly confessed. "It's magic."

"Well, I'm not going to comment on that. What about Dr Ruth's magic?" His eyes twinkled as he gave me a mischievous smile. "I hear you two have worked well together. I'm sure that's made a difference."

"I can't deny that," I agreed. "My outlook is certainly a lot more optimistic than it was six months ago."

"Well, young lady," he said, cheerily, as he slid the stool over to the corner sink, and stood to wash his hands. "You're ready for your first operation. The scar tissue has surfaced well."

I was staggered. "Already?"

"Whenever you're ready. Do you feel up to it?"

I took a deep breath and was a trifle cheeky. "Do you?"

He grinned.

"Let's get it over and done with then, shall we?"

"Good girl, the sooner we get started, the sooner you'll look like new again."

\#

A stark hospital room. In one day, operated on the next. Just as soon as I'd begun to imagine I saw a glimmer of normality amongst the lumps and bumps, I'd found myself under the knife. It was back to horrid black stitches, black eyes, swelling, pain, and hiding in embarrassment. I'd so hoped I'd see the end of being a patient. But here I was, propped up in a hospital bed with my face bandaged once more. The accident and its aftermath were revisited, the trauma renewed. Depression was my first visitor.

Davenport's face came looming down in front of me as I opened my eyes to his footsteps, and a warm hand, on my hand.

"What, no smile for me?"

I closed my eyes tightly, and turned away.

"Now then, we're not feeling sorry for ourselves are we? Remember what I told you? It'll take time. Don't get depressed and undo all the good you and Dr Ruth have achieved. Remember, this is only temporary. It's not as bad as the accident. You'll see what I mean when we take off the bandages. Okay?"

"Okay."

"Now, we've done a really good job, and I want to see you in two weeks' time. Get plenty of rest. See you in a fortnight." He smiled, patted me on the arm, then was gone.

I did feel sad. Would this torture never end? But, remembering Davenport's words, this would not be as frightening as the last time. It would look much better – much sooner.

#

I was back home in my Paddington terrace, glad to be on my own. I wanted very much to hide. Not to see anyone, or be seen. But I'd promised to visit Ruth Warner for a post-operative consultation, and a week after coming home I ventured to her office, bandages and all.

Warner seemed pleased to see me. "So, how are you coping? It's very easy to get discouraged and depressed in a vacuum, you know."

I opened up, as I always had with her, and explained that some days I felt as if I were back at square one. "Just seeing that mask in the mirror sends my confidence reeling."

"And will that mask be there forever?" she said, sitting in her usual position opposite.

"It had better not be! I want to start living again."

"Any woman would feel the same way. But look at you – you're impatient to get on with life. When you first came to me all the fight had been knocked out of you. You're a different woman now."

"I am, aren't I," I acknowledged, smiling.

#

Two more operations followed over another fourteen month period, and each one temporarily set me back emotionally. Each one meant a return to bandages, stitches, bruises and pain. Fresh scars, red, raw and ugly, and months of waiting for the healing process to take place.

Jean Metcalfe was the only person I permitted to visit, and never when the scarring was at its worst. Thinking that I must be bored, she encouraged my interest in art, and provided me with glorious up-to-date magazines, books, and catalogues on the subject, and coaxed me to sign up for a home study course covering the Old Masters, the Impressionists, and the leading artists of the twentieth century.

Now my empty hours were spent reading about art, its history, styles, and techniques, and about the famous artists themselves. I learned how some artists, like Raphael and Titian, lived like the princes they were, while others, like Van Gogh, died paupers. I wondered if the rich bought paintings by poor artists in order to exorcise their guilt about their own wealth?

I began to think that wealthy collectors, such as the Rothchilds and the Gettys, hoped to buy immortality from the immortality of the past, by surrounding themselves with Old Masters. And I learned how the commercial galleries around the world all have their own style, and have their own styles of doing business.

From the stark white walls of the Pace, in Manhattan, to the traditional ambience of the Hanover Gallery in London's Bond Street, a sixth generation firm, where a painting would be presented to a wealthy client as if it were the Holy Grail. The client was expected to think themselves lucky that such a work was actually being offered to them. The more I read, the more I became fascinated by the psychology of the art trade.

The traditional buyers, the old money, invariably kept a low profile, using often anonymous agents to do their bidding and their buying for them - buying for the love of the artist, a period, or a particular piece. Then there were the yuppy types, the young nouveau riche, who wanted to broadcast their buying habits to the world. When they invested vast sums in art, they were actually buying more than just a picture, they were buying image, and status, were buying into a higher social strata. To them, art would always be a symbol of upward mobility.

As for the poor artist, I came to realize that he, or she, would practically be down on their knees every night saying thank you for being patronised by this name gallery, or that. I was appalled to discover, that there were some galleries in New York which didn't even pay the artist a commission! They retained ALL the proceeds from the sale of their artist's work. The artists supposedly benefitted, by having their work showcased in front of the world's most well-heeled buyers, claiming this often led to private commission.

Feeling almost whole again, all bandages discarded, and with the last of four operations behind me, the scars healing quickly, courtesy of Dr Wong's painless needles, I was beginning to think I might soon be ready to face the world again. But before I did that, I knew I also had to confront my past, or to be precise, another aspect of my past. I flew to Brisbane.

# CHAPTER 56

Protecting their emotional vulnerability by restraining their excitement, they met me at their front door, and bravely endeavoured to keep the conversation flowing throughout my visit.

After the Scottish shortbread and welcoming cup of tea, Bob and Mina took me on a tour of their home, showing me that I'd been with them all this time. For there I was, in photographs all throughout their house, alongside many reminders of their former life in Scotland. But most noticeable of all - in pride of place was an eight-inch statue in discoloured alabaster, of a little girl with wringlets down to her shoulders, holding out her circular skirt, ready to take a bow.

Each had their own comfy chair in front of the television, whilst I sat in-between on the sofa. And each was eager to tell the tale. Mina took the lead.

"Truth was, Campbell had the Welfare people after her. You bairns weren't being cared for properly. The first time I ever clapped eyes on you, you were crying as if to break your heart, sobbing in the corner. As soon as you saw me come toward you, your big blue eyes pleaded with me, and up went your arms to be lifted up," Mina said earnestly.

Bob joined in as we three sat together for the first time in over thirty years. "That house was no place for any child to be in," he said angrily. "It was a terrible place to bring up bairns. But Mary Campbell loved it! She enjoyed the war. It meant money to her. The boarding house was full of people from all corners of the world. Soldiers, sailors, sometimes six to a room. Mostly fighting men just passing through, glad to rest a weary head under a roof."

"And looking for a good time," Mina chimed in.

Bob halted, as if remembering his service during the war, then continued to give Mary's boarding house a serve. "Aye, and every night was party night. There was a stand-up piano in the living room. Just like a corner pub it was. Drinking and carousing into the wee small hours." Bob shook his head. "Any time was party time. No place to bring up kids."

"Aye. It must have been terrible for you, Lilly," said Mina. "If you'd woken up in the middle of the night to see all those wild parties going on, and all those drunk, strange men. And they had brawls and fisticuffs, and the police would have to be called in." She looked over at Bob for agreement. "We heard all about it, didn't we, Bob?"

"A bloody menagerie," Bob declared. "And it didn't stop with the war."

"That's right, Bob. It went on long after the war. Didn't it?"

"Aye," he agreed, then continued to recall his memories. "All those young people had one thing in common - they wanted to forget the war. We all did! I know – I had six years of it myself. In the artillery."

"I remember the stories you told me about your big, twenty-five pound artillery gun on wheels; and I remember marching around the house proudly wearing your medals when we sang the army songs." I watched as Bob choked up with emotion.

"I know one thing for sure," Mina added, "Campbell never turned an American away. No fear! She knew where her bread was buttered. They had the money. And they spent it! Very pleased with herself she was, showing off her silk stockings, chocolates, cigarettes and all."

"For services rendered, if you ask me," Bob chimed in.

"That's enough of that, Bob," Mina reproached him.

"Well, you've heard her say yourself, Mina, 'there's many a man bouncin' anither man's bairn…'"

"Well now, I don't know about that, Bob, but I do know that I was mortified to think that our wee Ponkie would have to go back there. Broke our hearts it did." She looked down, fidgeting with her fingers. "I'll never forget the day the letter came." At this recall Mina was visibly upset, and looked over at Bob for support.

"We never thought our hearts could've been broken when our 'good news' about the immigration came. We took it for granted that we could take you with us to Australia."

"We wrote to your mother," Mina contributed, "asking if she'd let us take you with us. We wanted to adopt you."

"Really?" I said with surprise.

"Well, we'd had you for nearly five years! But Betty said 'no' and Campbell demanded you back, straight away. 'She belongs to the family,' is what she said. It was a terrible blow. It took a long, long time to come to terms with it."

"Not that SHE wanted you!" Bob said, red-faced with rage now. "Just like a dog with a bone, she was! Wouldn't have been so bad if she'd been good to you! She chased us off the property, forbidding us to see you again, and I could see, that to stay in Dundee, with you living just around the corner in that 'brothel,' would've killed Mina. So I put my foot down, and we came here to Australia." Bob took out a handkerchief.

"My, you gave us a lot of pleasure." Mina smiled, trying to lift the mood. "You were such a happy wee bairn. You used to sing and dance, all the time. 'Tip Toe Through The Tulips....'"

Bob rose from his chair and gave a rendition of the old song, complete with gestures.

"You were even prettier than Shirley Temple," said Mina proudly. "And you were bright, and happy. Well behaved, mind. Not spoiled. Oh, no, Bob wouldn't have had that."

I looked over at him and smiled.

"Bob taught you to recite Robbie Burns' poetry..."

"'Wee sleekit, cowrin, tim'rous beastie, Oh, what a panic's in thy breastie...'" he began, and I joined in. Together, my 'Daddy Bob' and I completed the verse of 'To A Mouse,' by the renowned Scottish poet, Robbie Burns who composed it in 1785.

#

The couple stood arm-in-arm at the doorway, until Bob could hide his tears no more. He retreated inside. Mina walked with me to a waiting cab. She wanted to talk.

"You know, Lilly, I've wanted to share an angry feeling I've had for all these years. It's true that Betty said 'no' to our keeping you. And, yes, it's true that Campbell demanded you back. But between you and me, I've never gotten over the fact that Bob didn't put up a fight for you." She looked at me with sorrowful eyes. "I asked him to go to the government, and have it looked into. Fight Campbell for you. Adopt you, legally."

"I didn't know that," I said, standing patiently as she paused at the sad memory. This was not easy for them. I appreciated their seeing me.

"But," she choked on the words, "he never did go to the authorities. He should've told them, or let ME tell them, that you'd be put back into that 'midden' of a place. I knew damned well that Betty wouldn't come for you while she was having all that fun, and there was big money to be made! And Campbell saw you with different eyes when you were five years old. You could run after her - and not the other way around."

I could only nod an understanding of the way she saw things.

"I want you to know, that we never took a penny for your keep. Not one! And when you left us, we had to send for a big lorry to take your toys and clothes with you. Campbell sent them straight to the auction house. All the beautiful toys Bob made for you. A doll's house and all its furniture, your bikes, and sledge. I'm really sorry you didn't get to play with them."

I reached out to touch her hand, and looked at her kindly. I could feel that she'd held a resentment about losing 'her child' all those years ago, but I wanted no blame put on anyone. "Don't blame Bob any longer, now, will you, Mina. Remember, Bob had just come home from the war, and the authorities were the last thing he wanted to deal with. He wanted to give you a good life, and he did, by the looks of things." I smiled down at her. "You have a lovely place here, and I'm okay now. It's time for me to find a new life for myself. Make sure that you enjoy yours. Don't worry about me. I'll phone you from time to time to see how you're getting on. Thank you for being so good to me. It saved my life."

As the cab drove away, she looked a lonely figure standing waving at me, while Bob hid his guilt inside.

#

Travelling to Brisbane airport, I was transported back to Dundee after Daddy Bob and Mina had boarded the MV 'Georgic' at Liverpool, on the morning of April 9th bound for Sydney, Australia. In my mind, I heard my own terrified screams, when I woke in absolute fear and panic, that first morning, after being left behind in Mary Campbell's boarding house.

"I'll be late, I'll be late, I'll be late…!"

Ruth Warner had explained my neurotic panic to me. I was afraid the schoolteacher would be gone by the time I got to school – I'd woken to find that Mina and my Daddy Bob had gone out of my life. That fear of desertion had never left me. Again, I heard my own words to the schoolteacher that first day at Ann Street School in Dundee, when Miss Dracker asked me my name.

"I don't know who I am, Miss. I really don't know what my name is. I don't know who my father is. But, I've got a Daddy Bob, and he says I'm HIS little girl, and he's a Baird!"

The cab came to an intersection. The lights turned red and the cab was forced to pull up and wait. By the time the lights had changed, I'd made another decision. I would call Jean Metcalfe.

# CHAPTER 57

"The terrace house is up for sale, Jean. I've done it! I hope your offer still stands?" I was forced to leave a message on her answering machine because she wasn't at home.

She sounded quite excited when she called back. "Hello, Lilly dear! Well done! Yes, of course the offer still stands! Do tell me what your plans are. It's so exciting. So exciting! I'm thrilled for you."

"Where are you?"

"Vienna. Visiting friends. So, tell me, what's the plan?"

"Plan one. Sell terrace. Plan two, move in with the Picassos." I heard her giggle. "Plan three, find gallery premises."

She asked me what area I had in mind. Did I want to be in the heart of Sydney?

"I'm up for advice, Jean. Any suggestions?"

She said she'd give it some thought.

But then I added an afterthought that made her laugh. "I did think I should stay close to the action. Didn't Onassis say to rub shoulders with the rich and famous? How about I become neighbourly with Eva Goldberg. Gallery wise, I mean!"

She laughed out loud. "You are feeling better, aren't you, Lilly!"

"I'm serious, Jean. If I can rent premises in the same street as The Goldberg, I'd have ready-made trade. Tourists flock to it. And now that the Treadmore is complete - another big drawcard - I can get the run-off from both." I felt myself smile.

"What a clever girl, you are!" Jean said with glee in her voice. "I just happen to know someone with a property a couple of doors away from The Goldberg. Number two, right on the corner. You know the one I mean. It's just been painted ready for sale. It would make a great gallery."

"Oh, Jean, let's not get too excited. My bankroll won't stretch to buying…"

"But mine will!" She giggled like a teenager, then hung up on me.

My friend Jean was about to have the time of her life and so was I.

#

Two months later, the Paddington terrace was sold. The young couple who bought it, loved it, and were not afraid to hold back their excitement in front of me. They made repeat visits. How could I not let them? He was a handsome banker, named Tyson Penny! I smiled when he told me. His pretty young wife was a music teacher who played the harp and sang like an angel, and her name was Angelique. I kid you not! She presented me with a recording of her music, and I found myself playing it repeatedly. It gave the terrace a 'blessed' feel. Tyson was so proud of his young, pregnant wife, and their love was obvious.

They delighted in the sunny kitchen, and the cute little slit of a French-window in the corner of the dining room where the morning sun's rays shone in and made it a happy place. This would be the couple's first child. We had something in common. We were all beginning a new life.

As for letting Vince know what I was up to, I wrote him a letter to inform him the terrace was up for sale, and said his things would be put in storage.

He phoned me when he received my letter, saying that he'd go along with whatever I wanted. Saying I could keep any of his furniture if I needed it. I gave it all to the young couple. All, except an unusually long table that had been made in Tasmania by master craftsmen. It was round at one end, and flat at the other, which was intriguing to me. I eventually discovered it had been commissioned for Prince Alfred, Duke of Edinburgh, second son of Queen Victoria, to be fitted as his dining-table on the Royal Train when he made a visit. The claw feet had stamped it as important, and I called in an antiques collector who recognised it. Now, thanks to Vince, it would be my new reception desk when I opened my gallery.

Doing my maths, I'd worked out I'd have enough for two year's rent in advance for premises, and much more. I felt a trifle anxious about going into business for myself for the first time, but told myself it was cautious optimism, and would be backed up by my new confidence I made a final visit to Ruth Warner to bring her up to date. My visit sponsored more by friendship now, than anything.

#

There she sat in her usual chair. Her face as fresh and beautiful as ever. Her tone friendly.

"Why don't you join me and the rest of the hospital staff on the Christmas cruise? It's time you got out and mixed with people in practice for your business enterprise," she suggested. "You'll have a great night. They have entertainment planned, and Sydney Harbour is so lovely at night. Especially this time of year."

"Oh, I, I'm not quite ready for that!" I quickly retorted.

"Nonsense! You're practically part of the place here at the hospital. So many of the staff know you now. You'll be among friends. Come on. Besides, Davenport's done a great job on you. You look terrific. Really terrific!"

He had, too. I was no longer afraid to look at myself in the mirror.

"It's been a terrible ordeal for you, but you've come out the other side looking like a brand new person. He's made you look ten years younger!" We both laughed. "Come on, it's Christmas!"

# CHAPTER 58

With my disguising sunglasses now discarded in public, I headed out to enjoy myself among friends. The December air was warm and still, with only the hint of a breeze created by the motion of the chartered launch as it glided across the smooth harbour. The city of Sydney had on its celebratory face, with sparkling lights, and reflections of expensive waterfront homes dancing on the water.

The landmark Harbour Bridge and the Sydney Opera House dominated the scene. Gazing at them from the stern of the MV *Captain Bligh*, I thought of Georgie describing the scene, saying how easy it was to imagine the Sydney Opera House to be a great ocean liner ready to sail away. I smiled as I remembered my dear friend, and wondered how she was spending her English Christmas. She'd laugh when she opened my Christmas card to see Santa riding on a surfboard.

The overworked hospital staff had put together a floor show along the lines of a university revue, and sitting watching the performers with Ruth, it occurred to me that many of the medics had wasted thespian talents.

As midnight approached, the launch headed back toward Circular Quay to unload its very happy, but weary passengers, and a voice called out to me. Turning, I saw John Davenport making his way through the crowd toward me.

"I thought it was you, Lilly." His whole face lit up with his smile. "I didn't spot you earlier because I've been up in the wheelhouse, talking to the captain most of the night."

"Hi, Mr Davenport," I said.

"Oh, come on now, Lilly, call me John, I'm off duty." He gave me a kiss on the cheek.

I looked up into his eyes and gave him my best smile.

"Have you enjoyed tonight?" he asked.

"Great fun! The nurses did a great job. They're in the wrong business."

"I thought the same thing myself. So irreverent. Just letting off steam."

We continued chatting as the vessel berthed and the gangway slid down to the dock. We disembarked amid the boisterous crowd. Several chartered buses waited on the quay, and I was separated from my new playmate before I could say a proper 'good-night.'

Next morning the phone rang before nine.

"Hi, Lilly. John Davenport. We were interrupted during an interesting conversation last night. Could we perhaps have lunch?"

"Lunch?"

"Now don't hesitate, I'm not your doctor any more, Lilly. You're no longer my patient, and I know a great restaurant with a balcony that overlooks Elizabeth Bay. The food is out of this world. Just tell me where and when to pick you up."

"You mean today?"

"Of course I mean today! You haven't had any better offers, have you?" I could hear the mirth in his voice.

"Well, no…"

"And you do eat lunch?"

"Yeeeees, I do eat lunch," I returned with a smile.

"Then how about I pick you up at twelve. What's your address?"

My answer seemed to eject involuntarily from my lips.

"See you at noon."

I heard a click and he was gone. Holding the receiver away from my ear, I looked at it as if it had lied to me. I put it down slowly, not believing what had transpired. A pounding began in my chest. Did I have the confidence to go through with this? Ruth Warner's words sprang to mind. 'It's time to get back out there. You have to contribute to the world again.' I thought that if I were going to be brave, I'd better get a move on!

#

Showered and dressed I stood in front of the bathroom mirror and applied my make-up, silently thanking Mother Nature for her forgiveness. Contrary to what I'd been told, my eye-lashes had grown back as long and as thick as before. My eyebrows too, had grown back in much the same way, needing only a touch-up with a pencil. There was a time when I would never have believed it, but 'The Elephant Man' no longer stared back at me from the mirror. The skin of my brow was smooth, like sculpted butter. I said, "Thank you," out loud when I flicked my light fringe over a still visible, but fading scar above my left eye - a V-shaped scar I didn't mind too much - a constant reminder of my narrow escape – from both Mary Campbell, and death.

Davenport had been right when he'd said the physical healing would take a long time. But now, three years after the accident, I thought myself very fortunate indeed. Only on close scrutiny could anyone see the miniscule white lines which remained to tell the tale of five separate visits to the operating theatre, which with practice, I'd learned to camouflage with make-up. I really did look like a new woman!

As midday approached, I was ready. Just the same, when the doorbell rang, I nearly jumped out of my skin!

# CHAPTER 59

The smile he gave me nearly melted me. My God, he was a handsome brute. My mind was never on his good looks when he was plucking black stitches from my face.

"Ready?"

"Ready!" I answered, excited inside.

"You look terrific. Except that you look so young, I feel as if I'm cradle-snatching."

"That's why I like you, John Davenport. You say exactly the right thing!" I smiled as I looked again at my escort, hardly believing what was happening, then closed the front door behind me.

He ushered me the short distance to a sparkling brand new white Mercedes 350SL convertible which sat, top down, double parked, in front of number seventeen.

I wore new tan sharkskin slacks, a crisp white YSL blouse, tan wedge shoes, matched by a woven belt and handbag. And I took with me my new Ralph Lauren dark blue blazer over my arm. My only jewellery, a watch and pearl earrings.

"You look so different in civvies, John," I remarked cheerfully, as he held the passenger door open and I slid onto the black leather seat. As he closed the door, I complimented him on his dapper outfit – sea-green silk shirt, cream cotton pants, and brown loafers.

"Like the gear, huh? Italian. I'm Italian from top to toe today." He slipped in behind the wheel and pulled his door closed. "Don't get much time to shop," he went on, pushing the button that sent the engine purring into action. "But, when I do, I head straight for Pedro's here in Paddo, and voila!" He gave me a boyish grin, pleased that I'd noticed his stylish gear and his trendy look. His personality had also come out to play today.

With the wind in my hair and a smile on my face, we drove only a short distance to Elizabeth Bay, while he told me his plans to join a team of yachtsmen on the Sydney to Hobart yacht race. An annual event, the yachts would leave Sydney on Boxing Day, from Rushcutters's Bay, to sail down past Tassie's east coast, to Hobart the capital of Tasmania.

I was just becoming comfortable, when he pulled up outside the private garage door of a stately mansion. It slid open.

"It would have been a grand manor house once upon time," he said, coming around to help me out of the car as I sat a little stunned.

"But where's the restaurant?" I asked.

He gave me a mischievous look. "No more questions," he said, pretending to be stern, as he led me up the front steps to the entrance of this noble villa. Then inside, to a magnificent, glass-ceilinged foyer, and on to a grand baronial door to which he gave a push. It opened up to a more modern, bright and lovely space, full of art.

"Ah, you're an art connoisseur?" I said with delight, spotting a contemporary nude Brett Whiteley, an early Donald Friend, and a rather novel Sir Sidney Nolan, showing a backside view of Bushranger Neddy on his steed. "You collect?" I asked, rather pleased to see these lovely works by Australia's best. "And you have good taste!"

"Thank you. I have my favourites," he replied, as he led the way through the main room, a huge loungeroom, and into a spacious dining room with a kitchen to one side. It all led out to a balcony overlooking the harbour. "Lunch is nearly ready. Welcome to Davenports."

"You cook too?"

"Yes," he laughed. "Matter of having to learn. My wife died five years ago from breast cancer. My crazy hours made me learn to whip something up after work." He was already uncorking a vintage Bollinger. "I have to tell you, that tables here are not easy to come by."

"In that case," I said with a smile, "I consider myself privileged." We clinked glasses after he'd cleverly dislodged the cork without the vulgar 'pop.'

"What shall we drink to?" he asked.

"Surprises!"

We sipped, shared a smile, then headed out to the balcony under the umbrella.

"How absolutely marvellous!" I had quickly taken in his taste in furnishings. An eclectic blend of antiques, with a good touch of the Orient, and a sparkling, stainless steel kitchen with all the mod cons.

"Forgive my artifice, Lilly. But I didn't want to share you with an entire restaurant. Call me selfish, if you will. But I wanted you all to myself." He leaned close and gave me a peck on the cheek. "Besides, I'm a great cook."

"Modest, too!" said I, as he moved to play James Galway's magic flute on the Bang and Olufsen.

He gave me time to unwind, with Monsieur Bollinger's help, then delivered up a fish compote, prawns, snapper fillets, and scallops, all in a delicious white wine sauce. Served with a dry Riesling from Freycinet. Our conversation flowed without halting throughout, and he made me feel comfortable, relaxed, and very much welcome.

"That was delicious, John. How did you know I love seafood?" I asked, dabbing my moist lips with a napkin.

"I know a great deal about you, Lilly. More than you might imagine. I do my interviews when my patients are fast asleep," he joked, as he drank the last drop of his wine. I responded with a good-natured mock gasp with like-minded humour. Then he added sweetly, "I've been your doctor for a while, now. It's easy to read people, and differentiate between the deserving, the grateful, and the vain. I meet all kinds. You've been the one I've been rooting for the most. You're very easy to love."

Wow! If John Davenport thought that, then maybe life really was on the up for me!

We talked non-stop, covering everything from art, to television, books, psychology, family, and partners. As our lunch had lasted long into the afternoon, it was inevitable that it became personal.

"It took me a long time to adjust to losing my wife. You understand that, Lilly, I know. You lost your beloved children. You lost your lovely face. Now you have a beautiful new one, and I'm very proud of us both, achieving what we did, you and I. You stayed healthy, did all the right things, and I did the very best job I could."

I thanked him, then asked why he hadn't re-married.

"I've found no replacement for my wife, as yet. No-one who fills all the boxes." He looked over at a photograph of an elegant Oriental woman, whom I imagined to be his late wife. Then after the briefest silence, he spoke again. "I suppose I could say that I miss marriage. You'll agree it's not much fun coming home to an empty house, all the time!"

It was only when John found the need to put on a small table lamp that I realised it was time to go. As I rose from the sofa beside him I noticed a painting I hadn't spotted before, at the entrance to a small hallway leading to the bathroom suite. When I returned, I had a closer look. It was signed 'DRAKE'. "John!" I said excitedly. "This painting, where did you find it?"

"Oh, that one? A young artist came to the hospital selling them." Moving closer, he explained how he'd come by it. "He was in the hospital canteen one morning canvassing the staff with his work. I liked it because it was so bright and jolly. Like dancing. You do dance, don't you Lilly?"

"Yes, yes, of course! I mean, I hope I remember how. I don't suppose you have his telephone number?" When he shook his head, I dared to ask a favour. "I don't suppose you'd look on the back of it for me, to see if there's anything there? I'd love to find him."

"You like it that much? Of course I will, but you'll probably catch me out with my dusting - or lack of it."

It was way too large for me to lift from the wall, but between us it was easy. Sadly there was nothing written on it that I could chase up.

After our scrutiny, John spoke out again. "No, sorry, nothing there. Maybe one of the staff at St Vincents would have a contact, or know where to find him. Reception! Try the girls at the front desk of the hospital. Why the interest, Lilly? Want to buy one?"

"It's just that I recognised his work, John. He came into The Goldberg wanting exhibition space. Eva wouldn't show his work, but it's really good. I remember him well. I advised him to treble the size of his paintings, and to use all that gold leaf, and it's improved his work out of sight! It's stunning now. I think I could get him an exhibition immediately, if someone else hasn't already found him." I held the painting steady as John returned it to its spot, and together we straightened it, and stood back to admire it.

I looked at my watch. As much as I'd enjoyed our lingering lunch, my mind was now focussed on Nicholas Drake. "I should go, John."

"I'll drive you home then, dear Lilly!" He gathered up his keys, and off we went after a very pleasant day.

In the fast-moving, early evening traffic, he drove me back to Paddington, via New South Head Road. The road that had led me to disaster, now recovery, and the friendship of this marvellous man. With the red and gold sunset streaking the western sky, more wondrous than any painting, it was as grand a finale to the day as one could ever imagine.

"I've had a great day, thank you, John," I said, looking directly at him as I stood at my front door.

"Me too, Lilly. Thank you for spending the afternoon with me." He bent and kissed me tenderly on the lips.

I closed my eyes, and allowed myself to drift away.

Gently, he lifted my chin so that our eyes met again. "You're a very special lady, Lillian Lightwood. And you look so lovely. I'm very happy that I played a small part in making you whole again." Then the gallant gentleman took his leave.

Inside the terrace, alone again, I thought how safe the world would be without love. How tranquil. But how dull!

# CHAPTER 60

I began my search for Nicholas Drake at St Vincent's Hospital, having decided that I had to seriously start planning for my own gallery. A colourful exhibition by Drake would be an explosive debut, I thought. I'd start by becoming his agent, if he didn't already have one! The fact that he'd been hawking his beautiful work around the hospital suggested that he didn't! That young man needed me!

The reception girls at the hospital were unable to help me with an address or phone number. They suggested I visit the small galleries around the area to ask them. Well, I knew very well that they wouldn't give out his telephone number to anyone, in fear of losing their commission!

I asked the friendly reception girls if they knew of anyone other than John Davenport who'd bought a painting from Nicholas. They remembered the young artist when I described him from memory, and said they'd seen Nicholas talking to a patient who came in regularly for chemotherapy. Perhaps it wasn't quite the right thing to do, but, in knowing me well as Davenport's regular patient, the girls kindly provided me with the ladies' name. Hesitating, I thought it a bit insensitive, but then it occurred to me that if I explained my story to her, she, like me, might think some good could come of it for Nicholas. If he were still struggling, I genuinely wanted to help him get established. It would be a win/win situation.

The head nurse in Radiotherapy told me that the Mrs Piotrowski I was looking for had died. I felt sad for her, and uncomfortable about my mission.

This was not going to be easy. I began to wonder why Nicholas hadn't been spotted by an art dealer with a good eye. Had he been sick? Had he moved? Had he been on drugs? Then I remembered there was an art school near Selwyn Street. Nicholas was young. Maybe someone there would know of his whereabouts.

Running almost all the way from the hospital, across Oxford Street to Paddington and the College of Fine Arts, I went straight to the top. I asked to meet with the director.

"Not in, I'm afraid," said his PA. "Won't be back for a week. He's in Melbourne."

"Look, forgive me for taking your time," I said from the doorway of her busy office, "but I'm trying to find a young artist by the name of Nicholas Drake. He'd be around 22 or 23 by now. I'd like to help him. I'd like to give him an exhibition in my new gallery." Fully aware I was a bit ahead of myself, I was, nonetheless determined. "Trouble is, I don't really know where to start looking for him."

She looked at me as if I were crazy. It was probably the first time this sort of thing had happened. It would be like saying, 'He's won Lotto.'

"I don't suppose you could look into your records to see if you ever had a Nicholas Drake at the College?" She took a bit of coaxing, but gave in when we did a deal. "If I find him," I promised her, "I'll make sure he gives you a painting! I'll even have it framed for you at my own expense."

Again she gave me the 'crazy' look, but I knew that every deal in life is about negotiation. And most everyone had an attitude of, 'What's in it for me?' So, I took down her name and address in case she moved on. Her name was Gloria. And, thanks to my persistence, she found that yes, Nicholas Drake had been a student at the College! He'd completed his course only the year before. There was a good chance that some of the other students knew where he was.

Telling myself that I was a new, brave Lillian Lightwood now, I 'hung around' the college entrance at nine next morning as the student artists arrived for class. I held up a card with his name on it, the way they do at airports. I was there again at lunchtime, and at 5.00, when they flocked out. Next day,

I went into the College's cafeteria. "Anyone know Nicholas Drake?" I called out, only slightly embarrassed amidst the shabby-looking youngsters. But I was on a quest. I spoke to anyone who'd listen, but mostly they treated me as if I had leprosy.

I did this for five consecutive days. No luck. I was disappointed to say the least, but on day five, when I was just about to retreat and go home defeated, a pretty young girl approached me. She was dressed the way Japanese youngsters dress, with wildly mixed colours, gay outlandish patterns in layers and lengths, to stand out in a crowd.

"I'm Emily Woo," she said in a sweet voice, with head bent, and a perky black hat atop it. "I live with Nicholas. I've seen you every day for five days, and I came to the conclusion you must want to see him, real bad. And you look okay, so I told him last night you were looking for him, and he said to say hello."

"Say hello?"

"Yes. 'Say hello.' He thinks you worked at The Goldberg Gallery."

"YES!" I could feel myself want to give her an enormous hug, but I restrained myself, not wanting to frighten her. "YES! I'm Lillian Lightwood, and I did meet Nicholas at The Goldberg Gallery." I told her what my intentions were, and with each word, I could feel her response warming. "I don't suppose you would ask him to come and see me? I live nearby. Anytime. Anytime at all," I added, enthusiastically, while containing my real excitement.

"I can do better than that. I'm going home now. You can come with me!"

I wanted to yell out 'Yippee' after all my efforts, but I held it in. I'd found my potential star artist! From what I saw of John Davenport's painting, Nicholas had taken my advice. He'd stuck to that same style, and followed my suggestion of adding lots of gold leaf to make the 'dancing' work look unique and extraordinary. And, he'd trebled the size.

As we walked together, Emily told me of the couple's financial struggle, trying to make ends meet on their student allowances. She said that it was only when Nicholas sold a painting they had any small luxury. She remarked that I looked as if I 'had a bob or two,' and would maybe buy a painting, then asked me straight out if I would.

"Yes, Emily," I responded, "I think I might!"

Only two streets away, in a less salubrious area from where I lived, toward Albion Street, Emily climbed the two front steps of their rented accommodation, and took me in through the dark, claustrophobic hallway to the bright kitchen/dining area, where I found Nicholas, and a treasure trove of his work.

"Hello, Nicholas," I said, finding him at the sink, jiggling a tea-bag into a big mug, ready to have a cuppa. His back was to me, his shoulders still bony, his hair long. And I smiled inwardly when I recognised the long rainbow-coloured scarf that he'd worn at our very first meeting. "Remember me?"

He spun around with the tea-bag in hand, and his big hungry eyes opened wide at the sight of me. "You're Lillian Lightwood! Yes, of course I remember you! From The Goldberg!" He tried a smile, but the skin was still tight on his gaunt face as if he could do with a good feed. The tea-bag dripped freely onto the wooden floor-boards.

"Nicholas, this is your lucky day! I'm going to be your agent and make you a wealthy man!"

#

"Heidi, it's me, Lilly, I'm calling from…" Heidi was, of course the Brisbane friend who'd recommended that I apply for the PA position at The Goldberg in the first instance.

"Lillian! Oh, Lillian! Are you okay? I've worried about you." Heidi was a unique, original character. She'd been born in Germany to a mix of parents, one of whom, I'm sure, had Japanese or Hawaiian blood. She was exotic, colourful, great company, with a big and loving heart, and had become a very successful businesswoman, owning and running her own art gallery in Brisbane – the Paint Palace. It was in a fabulous location, bang slap in the centre of Brisbane's Queen Street shopping mall! I'd known Heidi now for a very long time, and I knew she had a good eye for vibrant, colourful contemporary art.

"No need to worry. I'm back on track. I'm healthy, and I have a special 'friend.'"

"You must be alright then. I wish I had one. A special friend, I mean. Don't suppose you could find one for me?"

I laughed. She hadn't changed. Many's the time, in the days of my television career, I'd told her to choose someone with the same interests. The art scene is a different realm. And I was blunt on one occasion, telling her to go for someone her own age, not ten years younger, as had been her habit. And, not to choose married men!

"Look, Heidi, I know you're busy on a Saturday morning, but, I've found this artist, Nicholas Drake, he's young, with a big future. He needs an exhibition. The work is already done. I'm willing to pay the cost of the advertising and the framing, if you'll give him a full exhibition. I'll even pay for a good wine!"

"Wow! Now that's the way to start the day! He must be good if you recommend him! And, if you're prepared to back him financially. What's his style, Lillian? Tell me more."

"You're style, Heidi. But he's got a girlfriend! Look, I won't take up your time now - I'll courier a painting to you overnight. If you like the work, and agree to an exhibition, I can send thirty."

"What? How many?"

"Thirty. And their big! But trust me, Heidi. He's good. You'll sell out, I swear. I'm going to act as his agent. I won't permit anyone else in Brisbane to sell his work. But I intend to have a gallery of my own, here in Sydney. Could you possibly hold an exhibition for him... the end of next month? That gives you seven weeks."

"Thirty paintings? If they're big, I'd have to clear out the back studio to make space. But if you say he's worth it?"

"Trust me, Heidi, he's worth it. As soon as you receive the work, will you contact me? The number's the same. I'll start the advertising as soon as you okay the exhibition."

Then I had a cheeky thought. Heidi was still single, and had always said she wanted a man who was fun, as well as being independent. I just happened to know someone the right age for her. And he happened to have his own business! To me this was a match made in heaven. I'd call him and entice him to get involved. I knew Heidi would be up for it. But business first. I had to call Stella.

#

"Stella, it's me, Lilly." In response to my voice, she screamed out my name in her usual, exuberant, excited way which was so endearing. It made me smile every time. I knew she would always be my friend.

"LILLY!"

"Yes, it's me, how are things? The programme? Everything? Can you ring me? How about tonight? I need a favour. I need help with promoting an artist. Morning Show, maybe? I'm going to be an artist's agent Stella. For starters! Then very possibly, have my own gallery."

"You're own gallery? That's great news! Oh, Lilly, how I love you."

"I'll tell you more when you call, Stella. Love you. Bye"

#

"Charlie! How would you like to go to Brisbane for a week or so, to do some work?"

"Who do I have to make love to?"

"Not me, Charlie. Not me!"

"Aaaaaah?" he said in mock disappointment. "What's the deal?"

"I have forty paintings, and I want you to frame them." I'd decided to keep ten for myself as the start of a Sydney exhibition for Nicholas. One of which would go to Gloria at Paddington's College of Fine Arts. "But I want thirty of them done at my girlfriend Heidi's Paint Palace, in Brisbane. Want some Brisbane sunshine? Heidi's gorgeous, and she's single, Charlie! It's her own successful gallery! Her house has a pool, and it's in St Lucia. Very classy! Swim. Have barbeques. Red Snapper. Coral Trout. Barramundi. Play naked tennis, maybe?"

# CHAPTER 61

John was excited for me. We'd become close. Were a 'couple,' intimate in every way. We shared a bed and happy times together. I'd given him my heart. He brought out the best in me, and I trusted him. He'd cook me a meal, then I would cook him one, and we'd endeavour to outdo each other with new recipes we thought would please. When I told him I'd signed a contract with Nicholas, he was thrilled, though cautious.

"I'm a little apprehensive about you investing so much of your money in the young fellow, but I trust your judgement," he said agreeably, standing in his sparkling modern kitchen. "You know I like his work."

"I will admit, I've gone to quite a bit of expense. But I see it as an investment."

John nodded his acceptance as he prepared a potato, pumpkin and walnut gratin.

"The thing that will always amaze me, is that these two youngsters have been sitting on a veritable gold mine taking no action. His work will command high prices, if the right clientele see it."

"What sort of prices?"

"Thirty thousand plus."

"I only paid $1,500 for mine!"

"Well, their worth thirty times that! Nicholas has worked like a sausage machine churning out paintings, and no-one's done any marketing for him. Emily's been too shy to approach galleries. Thank God I found him before someone else did."

John smiled across at me as he moved to the Bang and Olufsen to play a new classical recording. "Yes, but he is only one artist."

"I have to start somewhere, John. Nicholas Drake is by far the best thing that's happened to me. Apart from you!" I gave him a saucy grin.

"Now you're talking!" He came close and kissed me tenderly, as the soothingly mellow sounds of cello wafted over to me to enhance his embrace. I stayed there in his arms resting my head against his chest, as if to pass on my happiness through to his heart.

"He looked down at me, proudly. "You've put a lot of time and effort in for his benefit. I hope he realises just how lucky he is." He gave me a loving peck, then moved to the wine rack to find a suitable wine.

"Nicholas and Emily both appreciate my interest. They know what hunger is." I'd bought a beautiful bunch of bright Ranunculus and placed them centre table as I spoke.

John had a mischievous twinkle in his eye. "You do realize, that all the time you've been here today, you've done nothing but talk about another man?"

"I think Nicholas deserves me," I said cheekily. "He's already proved to be a hard worker. But after this first exhibition, he'll be treated like any other artist I find," I stated in my re-born business tone. My man just smiled at me and held up a French Cabernet Sauvignon-Syrah, Barons De Rothschild (Lafite), and a Tasmanian Chartley Estate Riesling 2014. I pointed to the Chartley Estate – World Class!

"Talking of finding new artists," I said enthusiastically, "Jean said that while she was in the Caribbean, she found a girl on St Barts that deserves a helping hand. She's sent a painting for me to look at."

"Anyone that lives on St Barts doesn't need a helping hand, believe me! I've been there. They're already in heaven!"

"You must take me there sometime." I looked over at him suggestively. "Oh, and when Jean does land on terra firma, I'm finally going to move in with the Picassos. The sale of the terrace is finalised. Next thing for me is to make a success of this exhibition, then concentrate on getting my funding together for a gallery of my own."

"You know I want you to stay with me," he said lovingly, moving close.

"And I might well do that! But not yet."

He gave me another kiss that seemed to say, 'Please don't stray. It took me a long time to find you.'

#

We liked to work together in the kitchen whilst we shared a glass of pinot, or the like. That way, we could learn from each other. John being more naturally precise than myself, while I was built for speed, not precision, having been raised in a boarding house

"How would you feel about coming to Scotland with me, John?"

"Scotland?"

"Look…" I picked up the envelope that had come in the mail that day – a surprise wedding invitation from Georgie, which was printed in gold, on the finest cream paper, with a stately Scottish castle on the front. "Georgie has invited us to Scotland! She wants us to stay for a week with the family in the Scottish Highlands before the wedding ceremony - they're going to have two, apparently. One grand ceremony in the Cathedral, in London, when royalty will attend. Then a more intimate affair with the family at the small church in Balmoral that the Queen attends when she's there."

"Oh my, that looks grand."

"You'll absolutely love Georgie!"

"I've always wanted to go to the wild and windy Highlands. I've been itching to buy a new camera, so now I can buy one Duty Free."

"Georgie means a great deal to me, John. I wouldn't miss her wedding for the world! This of course gives me the chance to visit my mother. I'll go visit her in Birmingham, when you head back home."

Surreptitiously, I thought I'd take advantage of being in the UK, and spend some time in London at the galleries, and window-shop in Chelsea, after John's departure.

#

The tiny Braemar church looked fairy tale picture-perfect decked out in garlands. Georgie was absolutely radiant in her Vera Wang when she arrived in a horse-drawn carriage. I had no right to be, but I was so proud of her! Just because she was my friend. She was stunningly beautiful, and took our breath away. The menfolk all wore kilts, which was enough to stir the heart-strings of any Scot. The bagpipes played the beautiful bride into the church, and the excitedly happy couple out, as they set off to a chateau in France - until the next wedding ceremony, the following month.

The whole affair was grand and extravagant. The sumptuous lunches, dinners, and dances went on for days. Amid gaiety and laughter I'd rarely known, John and I danced Scottish Reels, and watched the Highland Fling danced by experts. All in all, it turned out to be an experience not to be missed, or forgotten. Our gift to Georgie and Jeremy was a king-size Nicholas Drake painting, and identical, monogrammed umbrellas from Harrods – for a rainy day.

# CHAPTER 62

"We try to rehabilitate them," said the friendly nurse who stood in conversation with me in the large commercial kitchen at Broadlands aged care facility in Birmingham, England.

Betty, my mother, was shown how to plug in the electric kettle and set up the cups and saucers. She'd been told that her daughter was coming to visit, and had welcomed me warmly, but I knew there was no real recognition in her mind as to who I was. Betty – that's what I called her, acted as if I was an old school friend.

It had been the nurse's idea that I take her out for 'a pint' at the local, where she normally spent each Saturday lunch time. I could tell from Betty's smile that she loved the outing. Loved the local pub, was known well there, and devoured her fish and chips greedily, washed down with a huge pint of lager. Her speech, though lively and friendly, showing a happy disposition, was repetitive. No sooner had she made a comment, told me something of importance to her, she would repeat it. Over and over.

"This is lovely, this is." Again and again. "I love coming here." Again and again. "I'm enjoying this, I am." Again and again. Her short term memory was irreparably damaged. There could be no retraining.

I could see she'd been a beautiful woman. Her hair was thick, with just tiny streaks of grey. Her skin was naturally good. Her hands had done no hard work. There was a continual smile on her face. She kept repeating the words, "Best to be happy," like a stuck record. The person inside her was trying to keep her spirits up. Just as I had done all through my growing years; perhaps most of my life. She was trapped inside a diminishing state of wellbeing. I meanwhile, was free. It was one of the saddest days of my life.

Learning that I was about to depart, the matron of the home made an appearance, and halted me, just as I was about to exit at the front entrance.

"She needs clothes," the matron instructed tersely. "And she could do with some regular pocket-money!" She snapped. "I presume you're leaving her here?" Her tone was scolding as she eyeballed me.

I was quite taken aback by her aggression, but I was in a good place mentally and emotionally now, and handled it calmly, with control, like the mature woman I'd become. I knew there would always be judgemental people in the world - with their own axe to grind - but I must accept what I couldn't change. I found no need to share with any of the staff the fact that I'd just discovered my mother; or tell them that the Elizabeth they knew, had deserted me as a child, and, as a consequence, my own future had, until recently, been in grave doubt. How could I explain that not so very long ago, I myself was in danger - that I too had been on the road to self-destruction.

The frosty matron seemed to hold me responsible for Betty being institutionalised. She showed me utter contempt for not being willing to rescue her. "She gets no visitors you know!"

Another knife in my heart. There was no family locally that I knew of who could visit her. I held myself together, and handled the condemning confrontation in a calm, but assertive manner. I did not allow myself to be intimidated, informing the matron, that as soon as I returned to Australia, I'd make arrangements to provide my mother with clothes and any extras she needed. I wanted to ensure they would find their way to her, seeing no reason why she couldn't for example, take a friendly nurse with her to the movies, or do some shopping.

As for any guilt I had about leaving her there, I had to tell myself that visits from me would in no way benefit her, for she'd forget I'd been there as soon as I departed. And I knew that I myself had not the capacity to care for someone so damaged. This was a new burden I'd have to carry with me - the plight of my mother in this very basic facility, in this cold, bleak grey town, while my grandmother lived out her days in luxury in sunny Australia.

It was with a heavy heart that I left my mother behind in Birmingham. My only consolation, was that she was adequately cared for, with people who thought well of her, living in a place with which she was familiar. I would endeavour to send her treats from time to time.

I did not dally in London as I'd wanted to. I was way too sad to shop.

#

There seemed to me to be a kind of justice in the message I received, via William, as soon as I arrived back in Australia. Sydney's Palm Beach Retirement Home had phoned The Goldberg Gallery, and Randy had made contact with William to inform him that my grandmother was terminally ill. Going above and beyond the call of duty, William had found out my ETA, met me at the airport to deliver the news personally, drove me home, and wished me well. I went straight to Palm Beach.

There she lay wearing the cashmere wrap I'd given her. There were photographs all around the room of a seemingly happy family life. Joe, her 'fancy man,' was at her bedside, but retreated abruptly to allow me time alone with her.

Mary Campbell was in a coma. Her death imminent.

I had no need of words. I just sat, and thought. No-one, nor any memory could make me angry with her now. I was not her judge. The photographs around the room said it all, as I sat remembering the pride she had for her boys and Betty. Snapshots of her life. But there were none that included me. Remembering well her coarse laughter. The loud music throughout the boarding house. Ivy Bensen, Gloria Gaye - Betty's bands. The Tommy Dorsey and the Glenn Miller Big Bands. Dean Martin. The devine Rosemary Clooney. Nat King Cole, and the great Bing Crosby, with whom she sang duets as she scrubbed on the washboard, or stirred the porridge. And her favourite of all time Vera Lynn, who sang, "We'll Meet Again." I wanted it to remain that way. Remembering the music of her life.

# CHAPTER 63

Brisbane. Young Nicholas Drake was about to have his first exhibition! Heidi's Paint Palace in Brisbane looked splendid decked out in Drakes. Jean had ordered a giant sign which was to be hung on the facade of the gallery. So now, the name NICHOLAS DRAKE was seen in bold gold lettering above Heidi's Paint Palace - which, originally, in 1856, had been a hotel, a dance hall, then a cinema. Now, as a gallery, with a glass window either side the wide doorway, a giant-sized 'Drake' in each, with the sign above, it looked absolutely fabulous.

Heidi had cleverly made herself a 'Drake' outfit, throwing paint onto shiny, black silk/polyester, then splashing it with flecks of gold leaf; this had been fashioned into an elaborate dress, with an African turban to match.

The Paint Palace had a long existing invitation list, so we expected a full house for the 'Drake' opening. Imagine how thrilled I was to discover that fifteen paintings had already been sold following the invitation mail-out. With a dynamic 'Drake' on the cover, it was very enticing, despite the high prices. We were all excited.

Jean very kindly gifted young Emily Woo the most glorious little black dress she'd bought in Paris, and I had sent Nicholas to Pedro's the Italian menswear shop in Paddington before he flew to Brisbane. For the launch, Nicholas, with his hair trimmed, wore a French silk/cashmere jacket in a rich tobacco colour, smart black pants and shoes, and a white shirt. They both looked splendid, and I told Emily that I expected this standard at public exhibitions, saying there was no excuse for being a shabby-looking artist couple. After all, they were trading to an elite clientele.

With my new confidence, it would be my duty to make the speech in front of the thankfully, crowded gallery, introducing this remarkable young artist to his new audience, while standing on a platform that Charlie had made for the occasion. Noticing a generous smile from John across the room, I walked to the podium, and, taking a deep breath, I proudly began the introduction to my first artist/client, at his first public event.

"Nicholas Drake is well aware that art can cross barriers of time and culture." I was now centre stage, just as Eva Goldberg had always been. "His unique style, his integrity of purpose, tell us that his works will stand the test of time as they speak to us all. Great art is constant - his art is constant. He is an artist who comes to his canvas to make something beautiful. He has no interest in competing with contemporaries."

It was plain to see the appreciation of Nicholas' work on the receptive faces in the crowd. And I prided myself on still having the knack of 'holding an audience,' from my years of television experience. All it took was confidence.

"Nicholas Drake makes great art indeed with his commanding technique," I said boldly. "He is a cleverly disguised draughtsman. His gold and silver leaf are arranged in harmony with vivid hues, then held secure by balanced composition. He casts a spell on the canvas. Drake will live on to be known as one of Australia's greatest artists."

There was real joy in my heart for Nicholas, who declined to respond to my speech because he was 'way too shy.' I announced that his work would speak for him. There was great applause. It was a successful night, for, as I'd promised Heidi, it was a sell-out. All thirty paintings had sold by night's end. I couldn't help but notice, that Charlie was grinning like a Cheshire Cat, as was a very happy Heidi, who'd put her trust in my word.

# CHAPTER 64

My Terrace was sold. SOLD! I was all cashed up, and I was free of all encumbrances. My loneliness had evaporated. John was my love, Jean my friend, and I was living in Point Piper with the Picassos. Living in splendour. Now I had a grand view of Sydney Harbour, was living on the eighth floor with a sun terrace, and a luxurious indoor pool, which was truly romantic in the moonlight. The beauty of my surroundings was unsurpassable.

Jean had just returned from overseas, and was settling back in, and we were enjoying each other's company over morning coffee, when the phone rang. I heard her express her thanks, but didn't know to whom, until she put down the telephone. She turned to look at me with an impish, girlish grin on her face. "I've purchased the corner building, Lilly. All signed and sealed!"

"You did? You have?"

"I did! I have!" she giggled.

I felt my heart flutter. Then race. Was this a dream come true? Did Jean mean for me to make it into a gallery? My own gallery, to run as I saw fit? I would be the director?

"What are you going to name it, Lilly?" She stood looking over at me, enjoying my reaction.

"Oh, Jean, how wonderful. The corner?" Stunned, I refrained from embracing her, as if I dare not think of it as mine. It just seemed too good to be true.

"The corner!" She repeated. "It will be seen from both main streets. The buyers will get to you, first, Lilly." She made her way over to me, wrapped an arm around my shoulder and gave me a hug, her eyes alight with the pleasure of it all. "You'll get the overflow from the Treadmore, as well as The Goldberg!" said she, smiling, and looking directly into my eyes. "They've spent years building their reputations, and you'll get the benefit! I'm rather happy about it, Lilly! Even if I do say so myself, it's a fantastic property! It's twice the size of an ordinary terrace, and it will give me such pleasure to see you in it."

She sat back down with a very satisfied look on her face, while I sat trembling with excitement beside her, saying, "This seems so incredible!"

"What do you have in mind for your opening exhibition, Lilly?" Jean queried. "Before I make a suggestion, I want you to know, that I will never, ever, tell you how to run your gallery. But I'd love you to showcase Nicholas Drake as your first! Don't you think? Especially after the success in Brisbane. Put on huge prices, Lilly! They'll buy them!"

"Yes. I think they will!"

"Oh, yes. It will be so colourful! Have you ever thought of having a jewellery showcase? I see the most beautiful pieces on my travels, you know. You will too, once you take off to buy art around the world."

This was going to give us both so much pleasure, though I really did find it difficult to believe. Knowing it was Jean's building would give me extra confidence to 'settle in.' It would feel 'safe' to invest my time in it. Jean had become a loving mother figure to me. She genuinely cared about my welfare.

"There's plenty of space, you know, Lilly. You don't want it any bigger. Especially if you want to be an artist's agent, too. You'll travel quite a bit, I'd imagine, buying art for the gallery, and signing up artists." Her glee knew no bounds. "I think I'm the more excited of the two of us!" she said, patting my hand. "It'll be another interest for me, listening to all your tales of the art world." She had a dreamy look in her eye.

"And I'm so proud and grateful, to have your support, Jean."

"It really is a beautiful building as it stands, Lilly, but it must be custom-made to your specifications. You can draw up any changes you want. I have a reliable builder friend, and know a most talented interior designer." She kind of hugged herself with excitement. "I'll call them now, and we can all inspect it together. Then we'll celebrate with a bottle of Dom."

#

How marvellous it would be if my children could see me established in my own gallery. And be proud of me. That dream too, would come to be - I was sure of it. I would work toward it. That was the ultimate goal. The main event. I wanted my children returned to me. Legally. Or at least have them back in my life.

# CHAPTER 65

'Lightwood Rise.' Where the name came from, I'll never know. I just woke up with it one morning. When I stopped to think about it, I realised it had great meaning to me. Lightwood, after all, was my married surname. It was my children's name. I wanted to retain the same name as them. They had it on their birth certificates having been born into the Lightwood family, and were Christened Lightwood. It was my identity. I felt comfortable with it. I would never change it.

Then, there was 'Rise.' Was that not appropriate? After all, I was on the rise, and I was determined that the fortunes of the artists I chose to patronise, would also rise.

#

Such excitement! Opening day of Sydney's Lightwood Rise Art House. My first exhibition. My launch. The Sydney launch of Nicholas Drake. Jean's new toy. John's pride. My future. The gallery looked fabulous. I'd bought a new and expensive red Versace suit, and I felt glamorous. Many bouquets of flowers arrived.

Dearest Georgie wrote to wish me well, adding that 'Being married to Jeremy was simply a dream!' And she informed me, she'd just had a children's book accepted by a London publisher, and gave me the basis of the story. 'It's about the friendly ghost of William Wallace who haunts the chapel of a Scottish castle, and there's a collie dog that leaves no footprints in the snow.

I plan to do a whole series, Lilly.' Georgie sounded really happy in her letter to me, and I was as pleased for her, as I was for myself.

There were one or two old friends from Brisbane who made contact, with best wishes, and there were good wishes galore from Jean's friends. William had given me a special gift. He'd been personal overseer to the installation of my new gallery's security system, and had given the security company his personal telephone number to use if ever he was needed.

As for future exhibitions, I'd not a thing to worry about! Artists had come out of the woodwork once the word got out about Lightwood Rise. I would have my pick of the best. And amongst them, I found great potential. As for the building, the major structural change was to the very front, the protruding face of the corner that could be seen from the two main streets. I'd requested that some light be brought in. The builder complied, and made two identical glass floor-to-ceiling windows. For one thing, it would create a wonderful, natural light, and save on electricity.

But John had some concerns, "Won't watercolours fade in so much light?"

"Not if I sell them quickly," said I, with a grin. At last, I had people barracking for me. I was part of a team. It felt good. Really good.

I'd chosen to paint the walls in some of the rooms a dusky blue, warmer than grey, and certainly livelier than the flat black which some galleries used. This was to be a happy place. I also chose a complimentary, flat emerald green, and a Valentino red for the gallery's back room, which I'd use to exhibit new, upcoming artists. And of course I could change the colours at the drop of a hat. It only took as long as the paint to dry to create a whole new 'feel.' And yes, I would go to that trouble. Every day was important. Every exhibition was important, driving me closer and closer to my children.

We had an early, private ceremony, my darlings and I. That is, John, Jean, and Stella - who was accompanied by Roger, her new 'permanent' boyfriend. Emily and Nicholas who were excited and proud to see the new, framed and finished art works hung and on display. Heidi and Charlie, who'd teamed up, and were now a couple you couldn't pry apart if you tried, which was lovely to see. William was there of course, and declared himself to be in-attendance, in a 'public relations' role - being charming to everyone.

Then there was Louisa, my new assistant whom Jean had recommended, and whom I'd won from 'Sydney Rocks,' a gallery down at Sydney's famous Rocks tourist area. Louisa was a lovely, young and energetic French girl, whose only request when I offered her the job, was that she bring Fifi, her well-trained miniature poodle to work with her each day. Louisa, like Heidi, fashioned her clothes to give a stunning, original, Avant-Garde look, and she always wore a flower in her hair. Lightwood Rise was in a much more suitable location for her than her previous workplace. She'd been catching trains to the city, daily, back and forth, because she and husband Anton lived in nearby Woollahra.

The thought of the tiny pet worried me at first, until Louisa explained that her husband Anton would only drop Fifi off late afternoon, when he started work each day in his French restaurant in Woollahra. I was so taken with Louisa because of the 'class' she'd add to the gallery, that I simply had to agree. She, together with Fifi - equalled chic! Her accent alone was mesmerizing. I would have paid her just to be there. She was knowledgeable, smart, experienced, and easy on the eye, and capable of taking charge of all business when I was overseas.

We all toasted to Lightwood Rise with Jean's donation of Chrystal champagne. It was the first time I'd tried it. Delicious! And Jean was as excited about the birth of her new 'baby,' as I was about my re-birth. I nicknamed Jean my Fairy Godmother.

"TO LIGHTWOOD RISE!" We chanted. "TO LIGHTWOOD RISE!"

We had invited the VIP's of Sydney's social set. The VIP's of the art world. The VIP's of the medical fraternity. All of Jean's friends who happened to be in Sydney at the time. The gallery was overflowing with celebrities and friends. When I say overflowing, the crowd really did flow out onto the street. They were noisy, but not rowdy. My friend William was there to oversee the conduct, and re-direct the police-force that was called in by neighbours - who shall rename nameless - to cull the crowd. William was proud of me. He gave me the biggest hug, and a kiss on the lips I'm sure John would have been jealous of, had he seen it! I knew very well that William liked me. He took me aside at the first opportunity, to tell me his own good news story.

He held both my hands in his as we stole a moment from the crowd, and spoke privately together in my office. "I've had a promotion, Lilly," he said with his cheeky grin stretched across his boyish face.

"You have? Tell me, William, tell me."

Proudly, he looked into my eyes. "I'm to be the new Assistant Commissioner of Police."

"NO?" I tugged at his hands gleefully.

"Yes. I am, Lilly. Yes, I am!" We hugged with joy. "You know what this means, don't you?"

"No, William. I don't." I shook my head.

"I'll travel in a chauffeur-driven car!" he said with an impish grin, eyes alight.

"Oh, how grand!" We laughed together. "Congratulations!" I said, joyfully grabbing hold of my dear friend, and giving him another hug for good measure. It was obvious he was thrilled to share the news with me first. We headed back to join the others, but I intended to tell the whole team about William's good news over dinner, so they could all congratulate him.

The scene at the launch was familiar to me. As, one by one, two by two, the invited guests entered in a steady stream after six o'clock. Art patrons, celebrities and media thronged together in the hallowed halls of the prestigious Lightwood Rise Art House. I was still fascinated by the famous faces, but on this grand occasion, they were attending my gallery, and there was great joy in the air!

In came the peacocks, the aficionados, the critics, entering my foyer and having to pass Vince's antique table, which displayed the most magnificent bouquet of red roses given me by John. The guests, because that's what they were to me, merged into a patchwork of colour and style. Smiling, posturing for each other's benefit, and for the cameras. Society women still wore clothes that didn't fit, hats that didn't suit. They wore minks, long and short. Leather, chiffons. The weather playing no part in choice. A scattering of jean-clad males, several with flowing scarves. There were party frocks, business suits, formal attire - with many guests on their way to, and from other functions. It made for the most Pickwickian of gatherings.

I took great glee in watching posers holding champagne flutes, drinking delicately, glancing at, admiring paintings, all now sold. I took equal glee in seeing heads bobbing, ducking, nodding in agreement. Mouths wagged, pouted and sipped. The best of wine was all complimentary, and I smiled to myself at the thought. The practised stance, when spectacles went on, spectacles came off, and familiar little ceremonial dances were performed. Two steps forward, one step back, with much exchange of artistic thought, till artistic thirsts demanded further slaking.

A Gala event! I had put Nicholas Drake's name on everyone's lips, and his work in their homes, and Lightwood Rise on the social and artistic map. My team and I went out to Anton's for dinner together to celebrate. And William came too!

# CHAPTER 66

"It's Eva Goldberg, Lilly," Jean said, down the phone line. "She's had a stroke! The left side of her face and body are completely paralysed. They didn't get to her in time, it will be permanent. She and Henry have different bedrooms, and she lay on the floor unattended for fourteen hours till the housekeeper found her."

What could I say? It came as such a shock, I was speechless. Eva Goldberg, glamorous, vibrant she-devil, was not meant to be struck down like that! I knew what this would likely mean. If the condition was irreversible then Eva would not want to be seen by her public. She would hide herself away. I was sure of it. "Knowing her as I do, Jean, she won't be seeing anyone. Having visitors, I mean?"

"That's exactly what came to my mind, too, but she's asked me to visit immediately, which really surprised me. She told me she has something to ask of me, so I'm going to her home this morning. She has a personal round-the-clock nurse. Won't stay in hospital."

"Will you give her my regards? Tell her I'm sorry it happened." Although my relationship with Eva had been a love/hate relationship, I really was genuinely fond of her, despite the pain she'd caused me.

"I will. Talk to you soon, Lilly."

Later that morning, Jean popped into Lightwood Rise, telling me to grab my coat and go with her. She would explain on the way. She was sworn to secrecy.

We pulled up outside the Goldberg mansion and an attendant showed us the way in. We were to keep this visit private, and not let anyone know I was making a visit - especially Henry, who was already at his solicitor giving instructions that The Goldberg Gallery was to be sold for condominiums. The very last thing Eva wanted!

I'd been summoned to her bedside, but had no idea why.

When I entered the house, I did not feel the gaiety of the previous time I'd been there. I did not notice or appreciate the décor, or the luxury of her mansion. My feelings were melancholy, because misery seemed to hang in the air. 'The Queen of Arts' would no longer be queen.

"Come… closer, my angel," she said to me in a faltering whisper from her grand bed. "Come… closer."

The room was so dark that I had to follow the voice. I approached her bed very gingerly, because I'd no idea what was expected of me. Moving slowly toward the voice, I was nearly alongside the pillows on her right side, when suddenly she reached out to grasp my hand, startling me a little.

Her voice was weak. Her words slurred. Her speech halting. But I felt strength in her grip, nonetheless. There was urgency behind it, and she held on tight. "Hello, my… angel." She was using her maternal voice. "I want… to… say sorry… to you. You should… know… you were… the best." Almost out of breath, she halted momentarily.

I waited.

Releasing her grip, she slowly moved her hand to rest on an object on top of the bedclothes close by. Whatever it was, it rustled, just the way the plastic bags containing her groceries used to do. She thrust the small package into my hands. "For you… I'm sorry… what happened. My luck… my luck deserted me… when you left. I wish……" She couldn't go on. Her last words to me were, "Goodbye, my angel."

#

Later, in the car, Jean and I sat stunned, both feeling profound sadness in seeing the mighty Eva in such a frail state. We thought it such an inglorious end to her fabulous career. It was as if the brightest light had gone out of

Sydney society and its art arena. We knew the likes of Eva Goldberg would never be seen again. She'd appeared on her stage, just when the magnificent city of Sydney with its natural beauty, was about to blossom on the world stage. And no-one could be said to have contributed more than Eva had, to create an elite and sophisticated art community.

It could very well be said, that she was the one responsible for giving birth to the Australian art culture. She had nurtured it, and raised it to prominence. And, thanks to her many visits to Kakadu and the Outback, the whole world was aware of, and appreciated Australia's unique, Aboriginal art. Sadly now, Eva would fade from mind, and the famous Goldberg Gallery would go with her.

Jean went on to explain what Eva had wanted from this visit. "She wanted me to buy The Goldberg Gallery - for you - Lilly! Before Henry knocks it to the ground."

I looked over at Jean in a state of shock. "But I have Lightwood Rise now Jean. I don't want The Goldberg."

"Of course not Lilly!" She patted my hand lovingly. "Besides, Henry is determined to knock it down. He always wanted to make condominiums out of the space." Jean shook her head at his plan. "He'll make yet another fortune from the land!" Then kindly, Jean added, looking at me with affection, "You should feel proud of yourself, Lilly. Eva saw you as her protégé, the perfect replacement for herself." Then she had to look away, her eyes were moist, and she rummaged in her handbag for a handkerchief to wipe away a tear. She had known Eva for many, many years, after all. She tried a smile, but it was obvious to me that she was greatly affected by this distressing turn of events.

"It's all so sad, Jean. So very said," I said glumly.

"It's the way of the world, Lilly." she snuffled. "Everything must end," she said philosophically, in an effort to help us both come to terms with the events. We sat in silence for a moment or two, until Jean asked me about the gift. "Tell me, what did Eva give you?"

I'd forgotten about it until Jean reminded me. Looking down to my lap I saw one of Eva's plastic bags wound tightly around something. When I unwrapped the parcel, and looked at it in the light of day, I could see that Eva had given me the gift of her beloved Paspaley pearls.

# CHAPTER 67

"He wants me to go to New York with him," I blurted out, as soon as I sat opposite.

"New York?" Dr Warner exclaimed. "He's mentioned nothing to me!"

Was that a slip of the tongue? No, she was much too smart for that. Were they that close? I asked myself, in the split of a second. After all, they did work closely together. They were part of a close-knit fraternity!

"He's been offered a post with the Cornelius Vanderbilt Medical Foundation," I told her. A new corrective surgery unit has been set up in New York. He'll be leading a specialist research team in micro-surgery. He'll probably have to travel to all sorts of war-torn places to teach as well." I was a little on edge as I told my tale, and could feel my heart thumping in my chest.

"And what do you feel about that?" Warner asked.

"It would be absolutely wonderful for his career – he'd never look back." This unexpected turn of events had unsettled my newly stabilised world so much, that I could feel myself gush out my story like an exuberant child.

Not having seen me for quite some time, Warner was cautious with her language.

"Let's analyse this, Lilly. You've been intimate now with John for over a year? Yes?"

I nodded.

"You should know how you feel about him, then."

"I er, well… I'm not sure! I have to confess I'm a little overwhelmed by this!"

She looked me directly in the eye, and spoke very succinctly. "You've told me all the aspects of the story from John Davenport's point of view. But how do YOU feel about it? No doubt you've been asking yourself many questions. You must ask yourself what you want for your future, keeping in mind that there are no guarantees in life. That which transpires today, will not necessarily continue tomorrow."

She was sounding a bit like a schoolteacher, but then, I was feeling confused like a school-child. This new predicament I found myself in felt like a Mohammed Ali left hook to my jaw.

"You know I will only give you options, Lilly. Never advice! You seem to me to have many options. And each one will have a consequence. You know that, too."

"Yes. I do."

"Am I right in thinking that you're just getting yourself established here in Sydney?"

I nodded.

"Could your gallery be left to run itself, if you weren't here?"

I was just about to answer, but she kept talking and asking questions.

"It's all about spending time, Lilly. Do you want to spend your time in America? Or do you want to spend it here? Are you afraid of going? Are you afraid of not going? But the main question is, do you want to be with John? Do you want, or NEED to be with him enough, to leave behind what you're building here? Or… could you have both?"

I could only sit and listen, in my usual chair!

"Could you replace what you now have here - in New York? Would you be unhappy if you left it behind and couldn't replace it in New York? Would you be happy enough with what you have here - without him?" She paused before she delivered the next one. "Has there been any mention of marriage?"

It hit home like a sledgehammer! I couldn't speak. There'd been no mention of marriage!

"Do you really love him enough to leave behind the life you chose to have

- have been lucky enough to build for yourself?" She wouldn't seem to let me speak. "Do you feel secure enough in your own skin to let him go out of your life? Do you feel strong enough to be on your own?"

My head was full of yes's and no's. It was feeling decidedly murky in my head.

She paused, I thought, to give me time to reflect. But no, she was waiting for the 'right' moment to strike! She produced a blow to the gut from left field that I hadn't seen coming! "Do you see him as a saviour figure who made you whole?"

This pretty much stunned me! It was not a question I'd confronted before.

She gave me time to digest this one with a questioning look on her lovely face, then asked, "For all the questions that are running around in your head right now, what have I been teaching you to say if something weren't to work out?"

"So what! It's not the end of the world!" I stated, firmly.

She nodded. "You have to see your life as an adventure, Lilly. Which adventure do you want? Your own adventure, or someone else's? Can you make John's adventure - a shared adventure - despite operating from two completely different fields? Talking two distinctly different languages. Will you be equal partners? Or will his work eventually come between you, and you're left scrambling to build a new empire on the other side of the world, on your own?"

"I… don't know," I confessed.

Then she floored me with an uppercut! "Will he have the time, or the inclination to help you get your children back whilst he's helping the world's children?" She smiled that glorious smile that transformed her from a cool professional, into an angelic cherub. "Some decisions, my dear Lilly, are only for the brave."

# CHAPTER 68

Needless to say I had a restless night, but without vivid description, just let me say, I was back in the poo again. When I woke up, I just snuggled up in my bed, didn't move, just stayed curled up, trying to make sense of the murky mess in my head, compounded, if not created, by Ruth Warner vomiting out the facts at me.

My life had never been so good, till John threw in that hand grenade!

Then it hit me! Out of CHAOS comes CLARITY!

John had already made up his mind! He'd asked me to, 'come with him.' He'd already chosen his course! His mind was already made up. The decision was made for me! He wanted the job in New York! A new career. The leader of a team in ground-breaking scientific medicine.

I would be an 'ADD ON!'

I wanted freedom. Not glory! And I certainly didn't need reflected glory. I needed freedom, and I DESERVED it! Now I had the money to buy it! What I needed now, was to save myself! I owed myself this chance to grow on my own, although, I realised full well that freedom could mean loneliness. But, I rationalised, that I owed John the chance to find a new fraternity, a happy propinquity with someone who spoke his language, the language of science and medicine. I would set him free to find that person, and perhaps to win a Nobel Prize one day.

I would be able to pursue my own rewarding personal life, within the boundaries of my own new freedom. I had my own goal - to have my children returned to me.

#

John and I had arranged to have dinner together at his apartment. I drove there in Romeo, my new car - a previously-loved Alfa Romeo Spyder, a dynamic red convertible I'd become very fond of, now that Jeremy Jag was deceased. I hadn't wanted to be too extravagant, although the dashing little road runner did give me a sense of pride. It was just my size, and suited my bank balance. Any money I made was to be invested, carefully, not wasted on overly flashy cars.

Now that my mind was made up, I drove with calm confidence to arrive at John's apartment at dusk, the most tranquil time of day, to sit and look out from his balcony at the water and the yachts bobbing up and down at their moorings. He'd prepared a special meal, and I didn't want to put us through a feigned 'togetherness.' I told him my feelings as soon as he offered me champagne, and sat down beside me.

"I'm very happy for you, John," I began, and could see immediately he knew what was coming. "I'm so pleased that you asked me to join you in New York, because it's made me focus on the direction I want my life to take. Made me focus on my priorities. My every waking day from now on, has to be dedicated to try and reunite with my children."

He went to speak, but I asked him to let me finish first, because my decision had been so difficult for me, as was this speech I was making, which I delivered with love, and cool conviction. "You won't have any time in your life for me, John. I want to be special in someone's life, or I'll travel alone."

"I had a feeling this was coming," he said, sadly, squeezing my hand. "But please, please understand why I want to do this. I honestly feel that this teaching role is the best way I can make a lasting contribution to the world of medicine, given my experience."

I smiled warmly at him. He was a dear, dear human being.

He treated me with kind tenderness, not anger. He was genuinely happy that my life had turned around. We sat out the evening together, holding hands in loving camaraderie, watching the moon come up over the horizon and blaze its magnificence on Sydney Harbour. We kissed tenderly when we said goodbye, and I promised to keep in touch, by sending him the invitation for every month's exhibition at my new gallery. I also promised to visit him when I travelled to New York.

#

Having just made a life affirming decision, I wanted to wrap my arms around it, so I went to my gallery. I was so proud of it. I imagined that this was how Eva Goldberg must have felt when she launched her institution all those years ago.

On the way from my car to the front door, I spotted Barry Butler going into The Goldberg, which I found to be rather strange, at eleven at night. All was quiet there. And dark, only a single street light illuminated the area from further up the street. But I gave him no more thought. He belonged to yesterday.

I only turned my lights on enough to see my way upstairs, where I could 'feel' the space with the night lights from the other street shining in. I walked my halls, I walked my gallery rooms, then I sat at my desk for a while, and simply revelled in the wonder of it all. What a lucky girl I was! The thought of the gallery's future and the colour it would bring into my life made me happy, and, despite feeling bitter/sweet about my earlier decision that evening, I would sleep well tonight.

After locking up securely, I filled my lungs with the cool night air, ready to start anew, and headed out along the street to my racy red road-runner, when I heard a sharp sounding whistle from across the road. Looking around, I could see no-one in the quiet street. Then, in a car window almost opposite, I spotted a face I knew well. I hadn't recognised the car, but the face belonged to William! I made my way across the street toward him.

As I approached, he wound up the window again. That was odd! It meant, that in the dark, with only that solitary street light to guide me, I had to go around the car to the passenger side without a word passing between us. "What on earth are you up to, Assistant Commissioner?" I quipped, as I opened the passenger door.

He smiled as I slid onto the seat beside him and closed the door. "I'm on my last stake-out, Lilly. Before I take over the new job on Monday."

"A stake-out? You're joking! You're much too senior for that, now, William!"

"Bosses prerogative." He flashed me a cheeky look. "And no, I'm not joking. I told you, when it comes to work, I never joke." He paused, poker-faced now, then added, "It's not a game Lilly. This is Big Time! Ever since Eva's stroke, someone has been removing artworks from The Goldberg without permission! Christies are coming to the gallery again tomorrow, to take an inventory of the stock for the final auction, and it looks like our boy is making one final withdrawal while he's got the chance. We're about to catch him in the act." Then that wondrous smile of his lit up his face. "Wouldn't miss this for the world!"

"Oh, my Goodness. Is that why you don't have your own car?"

"Yep!"

"But who are you… watching?" Then I put two and two together. "You mean… you're suspicious… of Butler? I saw him when I went into the gallery, earlier."

"We sure are! We've been watching him for a week! We've counted twenty three paintings leaving the gallery – without permission." His head was turning now, from The Goldberg back door, to me, then away again, to look at The Goldberg doorway. The door I'd seen Butler enter.

"You may not know it, Lilly, but Justice Viers has been in love with Eva for the past thirty years." His head swivelled around to me again. "He phoned me. He lives right there." He turned a little more and pointed to the house next door to where we were sitting. "He can see everything that goes on from his window. He noticed Butler going in late one night last week, when he came home from a dinner party, so he went straight upstairs, and over to the window without switching on the light, and watched Butler taking paintings out. Viers phoned Eva, and was told that she hadn't sanctioned the removal of any paintings! He phoned me there and then."

Next thing I knew, I was given instructions in a serious tone. "Don't move, Lilly. There he is now!"

I felt my heart beat fast as I watched, too scared to move a muscle. Sure enough, Barry Butler was exiting The Goldberg Gallery, carrying a huge painting wrapped up in an old blanket. It reminded me of David, the one-time resident drunk wrapped up in his old carpet.

"That's it! Caught red handed! Sorry, Lilly. Have to go…." And William leaned over and gave me the briefest of kisses on the lips. "This will give me the greatest of pleasure, after what Butler put you through!"

William shot out of the car like a panther about to catch his prey. He had to apprehend Butler with the painting in his arms before he re-entered the gallery. That way, Butler would be caught in the act, with no chance of an excuse for being at the gallery - or for removing the stock. Simultaneously, four more detective types materialised from nowhere, and ran across the road after William.

I couldn't believe what I saw. Barry Butler was stealing from Eva Goldberg! Taking advantage of the old girl after God had incapacitated her. Spitting in her proverbial face, after all the love and kindness she'd bestowed on him. And I was witness to the crime, after he had tried to pin a similar one on me! The irony of it!

#

Collecting my mail from an always colourful Louisa, my French assistant with the flower in her hair, I was pleased again to find news from Georgie, who'd written to tell me that she'd had to cut short a skiing holiday in the Austrian Alps because of morning sickness. She'd included a happy snap.

"Georgie is pregnant, look, Louisa. This is my Georgie." Louisa came to look over my shoulder at the photograph of Georgie and Jeremy in the snow. "She wants me to send over two Nicholas Drakes for her friends who love his work, and she's given me a telephone number for 'The Royal Gallery by The Thames.' They want to give him an exhibition. Looks like I have a co-agent in Europe, Louisa."

She gave me her sweet, glistening smile. "How wonderful, Mademoiselle Lilly!"

Then I felt the earth move. Literally! I heard a roaring noise and the biggest bang the likes of which I'd never heard before. Louisa dashed for little Fifi, and we three scurried out into the street. Although I'd been made aware this was to happen, we were rooted to the spot when we saw a bulldozer, and wrecking ball begin to knock the historic Cook's Brewery building to the ground. The world renowned Goldberg Gallery was being demolished to make way for Henry's condominiums. I felt a tidal wave of sadness. For The Goldberg, and for Eva, as we three, Louisa, Fifi and I, stood and watched the end of an era together.

Now… for me, it was time to begin a new era. When we walked back inside, I went directly to my office to make a private call. I lifted the telephone, and called the number Jean had presented to me the night before, saying, "They'll look after your interests. Mark my words, Lilly."

I called my new team of smart American lawyers in New York, Bailey, Banks and Biddle.

I was now on my mission to get my children back.

## THE END

www.ingramcontent.com/pod-product-compliance
Lightning Source LLC
Chambersburg PA
CBHW071052250626
47159CB00002B/450